What others are saying about *A Cowboy's Destiny*:

"*A Cowboy's Destiny*, E. Joe Brown's debut novel doesn't just promise – it delivers – an absorbing family saga with drama and deep humanity, firmly rooted in the grand tradition of American Western literature. Saddle up and enjoy the ride!"

Robert D. Kidera, Tony Hillerman Award winning author of the Gabe McKenna Mysteries

-----

"*A Cowboy's Destiny* is an easy-to-read account of the Nineteen-Teens American Frontier – a period too often over-looked by novelists. E. Joe Brown is a promising new voice of the American West."

Johnny D. Boggs, nine-time winner of Western Writers of America's Spur Award

----

"From Oklahoma to Kansas City a most impressive debut by a western singer with great performance credentials who is now showing that he knows his way with a pen as well as he does with a guitar. Anxiously awaiting the next volume(s) in the saga."

Ralph Estes, author of *My Own Story: The Autobiography of Billy the Kid.*

"*A Cowboy's Destiny* is a big, sprawling tale of a young man's journey from a difficult childhood with an alcoholic father to be-coming a top hand on the legendary 101 Ranch in Oklahoma. Life and love present Charlie Kelly with almost insurmountable chal-lenges but if anyone can overcome them, Kelly Can."

Jim Jones, western singer and author of the Tommy Stallings and Jared Delaney series.

"Charlie Kelly, a young man of compassion and wisdom, crosses the West following his dream to be top hand at the 101 Ranch. Along the way he faces challenges head on and embraces each new opportunity with relish. There's something for every-one – stampeding cattle, oil strikes, and...love. I'm eager to find out what happens next!"

Bobbi Jean Bell, co-host *The Writer's Block Radio Show*, LA Talk Radio

----

"In *A Cowboy's Destiny*, author E. Joe Brown shows us an early 20th-century Southwest that still boils with bunkhouse brawls, saloon shootings and cattle rustling. And in Charlie Kelly, he gives us a character bold enough and tough enough to take it on and look for more."

Ollie Reed Jr., recipient of the Western Writers of America Stirrup and Branding Iron awards.

"Charlie's adventures as he journeys to Oklahoma, fulfills his dream of being a top hand, and achieves more than he ever hoped to accomplish is an engrossing tale of life in the American west as it transitions to a modern society. Charlie's intelligence, strength and integrity shine through the story as he learns who he is and what he can accomplish as he strives to make himself worthy of the woman he loves."

Carol March, author at Ellysian Press and Compass Rose Press

The Kelly Can Saga Book 1

By

E. Joe Brown

Artemesia
Publishing

ISBN: 978-1-951122-37-9 (paperback)
ISBN: 978-1-951122-51-5 (ebook)
LCCN: 2022937994
Copyright © 2022 by E. Joe Brown
Cover Illustration and Design © 2022 by Ian Bristow

Artemesia Publishing
9 Mockingbird Hill Rd
Tijeras, New Mexico 87059
www.apbooks.net
info@artemesiapublishing.com

First Edition

Acknowledgments

I want to acknowledge the support and wisdom I'm provided every month by my fellow members of the Corrales Writers Group—Chris Allen, Maureen Cooke, Peter Gooch, Sandi Hoover, and Pat Walkow. Thank you seems way too little.

Dedication

To Clarence Ashley Kelly, my granddaddy, and the finest man I've ever known. He inspired me to be a person of integrity and to dream big dreams.

And to my wonderful wife, Linda, who with her love, kindness, and patience inspires me daily to be the best man I can be.

Chapter One
July 1913

Sweat poured off Charlie Kelly's strapping six-foot frame as he performed his chores on the Cullum Ranch outside Loco in Stephens County, Oklahoma. Charlie was fourteen and he and his family had worked on the Cullum the last two years.

Charlie gazed across the blue stem grass pastures as he packed the tools he'd used to mend the barbwire fence near the corral, when he heard a pained scream coming from the direction of the barn. Charlie dropped the tools and ran a hundred yards to the barn.

He entered the big double doors to find his older brother thrashing on the ground. "Jess, what happened? Where are ya hurt?"

"Charlie... It's... my leg... aw shit... brother." Jess gathered himself, "It hurts somethin' terrible. Git someone... quick!"

Charlie knelt next to Jess and looked up as Bob Nash, the foreman, ran into the barn, "Charlie, what happened?"

"It's Jess... his leg. He's hurt bad."

Bob, knelt next to Jess and Charlie, "How'd you hurt yourself, Jess?"

Through gritted teeth, Jess said, "I was pitchin' hay bales down from the loft, and I... I lost my balance and fell. I landed funny on my leg—" He yelped and twisted as Bob touched the leg to assess the injury. The foreman leaned back on his heels and pulled off his hat, wiping sweat from his forehead.

Bob turned to Charlie, "Go find your father. I'll see to Jess."

Charlie nodded and ran out of the barn. His dad was supposed to have been working in the south pasture mending fences and Charlie hoped he was still there. He hoped today was not a day that his dad had decided to sneak some moonshine down by the creek. Charlie ran flat out to the pasture and was glad to see his dad was where he was supposed to be.

"Dad!" Charlie yelled. "Dad!"

His mom had always said that his dad, Joe, was the most handsome man in the entire county. He was tall, over six feet, and had a strong barrel chest that was good at setting fences or wrestling steers for branding. As Charlie ran and yelled his dad stood up, pulling off his hat and wiping his brow.

"What is it, Charlie?"

"Dad, come quick! It's Jess. He's hurt his leg bad."

His Dad said something Charlie couldn't hear and threw down his tools. In about five minutes, Charlie and his father ran into the barn, both out of breath.

Joe said, "Bob, how is he? Charlie said he's hurt his leg."

Jess hollered, "Dad, it hurts somethin' awful."

Bob said, "He has. He took a fall from the hayloft. We need to get him to a doctor. Let's get a wagon hitched and ready to go into Loco. Doc Patterson can fix him up."

Charlie jumped to help get the wagon ready. As they hitched the horses Charlie's mom, Elinor, arrived, having heard that Jess was hurt. News traveled fast, even on a ranch as big as the Cullum. They got the wagon ready in record time and they lifted Jess into the wagon as gently as they could, but he still let out a howl of pain. By now several other hands and the rest of Charlie's family, his sister Annabelle and his younger brother Dan, had arrived to watch. As they got ready to go Charlie's mom climbed into the wagon bed to hold Jess's hand, while his dad climbed up onto the bench seat with Bob.

Charlie and his brother and sister started to climb into the wagon but Elinor told them to get down. "I don't need one of you hurtin' your brother's leg more than it is. You can walk behind. It ain't like we'll be driving fast." She glared up at Bob and Joe.

"I'll do my best to make it as smooth as possible, ma'am," Bob said as he flicked the reins.

* * *

By that evening the doctor had done what he could. As he and the entire Kelly family sat in his parlor, Doc Patterson said, "I've got the leg immobilized now, and I think the bones will heal. But Jess's Achilles tendon is damaged. It may not heal back to normal. He'll walk, but he could have a limp for the rest of his life."

Rocking back and forth, Joe said, "Are ya sure, Doc?"

"No, Joe. I'm not sure, but it could turn out that way." Doc Patterson rubbed a hand across his weary face. "That tendon's ruptured and may never be the same. I wish I knew more about those things. We covered it in school, but I'm a general doctor, and it would take a specialist to know more. I don't have any idea short of getting Jess to Oklahoma City where we could send him for that kind of help."

"Oklahoma City!" Joe exclaimed. "That's at least three days by wagon."

Elinor put a hand on Joe's knee and asked, "Any idea what a specialist might cost?

Doc Patterson sighed and shook his head. "I'm sorry Mrs. Kelly, I have no idea what that might cost. Or even if it will work."

"I can't take over a week off from the ranch on something that might not even work!" Joe said, his face turning red.

"I can help cover at the ranch, Dad," Charlie offered, hoping to ease his dad's worry.

"You can't do the work of two grown men, boy," his dad said. Charlie could tell it was the anger talking, but he couldn't help but feel the sting of the rebuke. His mom gave Charlie a small nod of appreciation for offering to help, and she brought Joe's hand up to her lips and gave it a kiss to try and calm him.

"If you don't want to take Jess to Oklahoma City, then let me keep him here for a couple of more days," Doc Patterson offered. "Maybe keeping him off the leg for a few days will help." He gave a hopeful shrug.

They agreed that was the best they could do, and they gave their good-byes to Jess before returning to the Cullum Ranch. The family returned and took Jess home from Doc Patterson's in a few days, and by September, he, Charlie, and their siblings were back in school.

* * *

Charlie's mother, Elinor, was a slender, attractive woman of fifty, tall with silver-gray streaks in her hair. Charlie had always looked up to her and did everything he could to please her. In October, she became sick and had taken to her bed with a bad fever. Her mother, Sarah McDaniel, came over from Graham, Oklahoma, to take care of her and help with the chores and keep their house running. At that point, Jess's leg had healed but the Doc had been right, and he had a pronounced limp. Charlie had turned fifteen in the intervening three months.

One evening, as she prepared biscuits, Grandma McDaniel said, "Charlie, help me and your sister fix the meal for the family."

Charlie put down the schoolbook he'd been studying. "Grandma, why do I need to know about cookin'? I'm gonna be a top hand someday, not the cookie."

Grandma McDaniel gave a stern shake of her head. "You won't make a very good top hand if'n you don't know how to feed your men."

Annabelle laughed from where she was peeling potatoes. Grandma McDaniel gave her a stern look. "Just peel the skins, dear. We want to keep the potato."

"Yes, Grandma," Annabelle said, but Charlie could tell she was still happy that their Grandma was putting him to work as well.

"But I don't know nothin' about cookin'," Charlie said, wanting to get back to his studies. He didn't want to do them either, but they were better than learning to cook.

She smiled, "I can teach ya what to do, and it would mean a lot."

Charlie nodded. He put his book down and walked over to the kitchen table.

"Now I'm gonna show you how to make my special biscuits," she said, setting a bowl and a sack of flour next to him. "I learned how to make biscuits from a cowboy back after the War. And I'll tell you about him as I tell you how to make 'em."

Charlie was eager to learn how to make the biscuits then. That was the start of a close relationship between Charlie and his Grandma McDaniel that would affect his life for years to come.

* * *

In the early spring of 1914, Charlie was helping Grandma McDaniel clean up in the kitchen when a banging and shouting came from the front screen door, "Charlie, come quick, your dad is in a big fight over at the bunkhouse."

Charlie rushed out and Dan and Jess trailed behind him.

Charlie looked back and said, "You two can stay home."

Dan said, "Nope, we're comin'."

Charlie didn't have time to argue with his brothers and ran to the bunkhouse. As Charlie entered the building, he could see the fight was over and his father was sitting on a hay bale, blood dripping from his nose and looking up at the foreman with a dazed expression.

Charlie heard Bob Nash say, "Joe, this is four times in the last two months you've fought with someone on the ranch. On top of that, me and Charlie have had to go to Ringling to get you outta jail for fightin' at some bar. As much as I hate it for your family, it's time for you to pack up and leave the Cullum. I need you gone by this time tomorrow."

Bob turned and headed toward the door. As he passed him, he put his hand on Charlie's shoulder, "Son, I'm sorry, but this has gone on too long. Come see me in the mornin'; I need to chat with you."

Charlie and his brothers shared a look and then took their father back to the house. They practically carried Joe in the door as Elinor said, "Joe, what have you done now?"

Charlie said, "Bob fired Dad. We have to leave here by tomorrow."

Joe shouted, "That son-of-a-bitch Skinner was cheatin' me."

Ellie shook her head and said, "You're so drunk; I don't see how you would know if someone cheated. Why can't you stay home with the family? Let those single cowboys lose their money to each other."

Grandma McDaniel said, "Ellie, he ain't hearin' ya. Don't git yourself all worked up."

Charlie nodded, "Mom, we'll work things out. Bob wants me to see him in the mornin'; maybe I can change his mind."

"I doubt it but see him first thing."

* * *

At sunup the following day, Charlie found Bob Nash in the barn saddling his horse. "Mornin', you said ya wanted to talk to me?" Charlie said as he walked up.

"Yep, I need you to understand your father made it so bad that many of the men here won't work with him. I know this causes a hardship on Ellie and you kids, but Joe left me no choice." He shook his head in sympathy, though Charlie wasn't feeling it right now.

"Charlie, you've become a top hand after your brother's accident, and I'll miss you. I've a good friend who's the foreman down at the Four Sixes near Guthrie, Texas. I got a letter from him yesterday. He said there's a big ranch called the Cornerstone near Fort Sumner, New Mexico hirin' a lot of new people for the spring gather. You might go out there and see what happens. With a fresh start maybe Joe can do better out there."

Charlie had to keep his anger at his dad in check as he said, "I understand, Mr. Nash. Thanks for all you've done for my family. What ya did when Jess got hurt was sure appreciated."

"I wish it could have been more. I guess he's gonna have that limp from now on, right?"

"It's likely, but he'll do okay. I'll tell Dad about the Cornerstone."

The family was in a sullen mood as they packed their wagon. They saddled their horses and after saying their goodbyes to Grandma McDaniel who returned to Graham, they were on the trail to New Mexico by noon. Charlie was angry as they rode off the Cullum Ranch for the last time. His dad had ruined what had been turning into a good thing for him here. Now they were going to have to start over on a new ranch in a new state. He'd have to prove himself that he could do the work, and he'd have to make sure his dad stayed out of trouble.

Outside of Hollis, Oklahoma, they made camp. Joe said, "We've done good today. Let's have a meal and git some sleep. If the weather holds up, we'll git to the Cornerstone in a few days." Charlie and his siblings managed to hide their annoyance at their father. He was acting like this had been his decision all along.

Chapter Two
April 1914

As Charlie and his family crossed the plains of eastern New Mexico they felt the changes in elevation from western Oklahoma. Charlie turned to his dad and said, "The terrain sure is desert-like. I see this is short-grass country, with mostly blue grama and galleta on some of the gravelly slopes."

Joe said, "Yep, and there's some big bluestem in the heavier soils that seem to git some run-in water. I've seen some buffalo grass too."

Charlie nodded, "We may cross the old Goodnight-Loving trail before we git to Fort Sumner and the ranch. I look forward to experiencing that and seeing the same country the cowboys from fifty years ago saw."

Joe smiled, "We lived on the old Chisholm trail back on the Cullum, now we'll live on the Goodnight-Loving. Who'd a thought it?"

Charlie stood beside his father as the Cornerstone foreman, Fred Turpin, interviewed them. He now towered over his father by at least two inches and the foreman noticed it.

"You're a mighty big young man for fifteen. So, you a cowboy too?"

"Yes, sir," Charlie said with a nod.

"Fine, and Joe, you still cowboy some, but you said earlier you can do carpentry and leatherwork too, right?"

Joe said, "Yep." He pointed across the yard, "That's my other two boys there."

Dan, at thirteen, was already the size of many men, and Jess stood six feet tall himself.

Turpin said, "So, all of you want jobs?"

Joe said, "My boys go to school, but yes, we're available to work. I want full-time, year-round work, and the boys can work summers and when school is out. All three boys can do a man's work."

Turpin looked at Charlie and laughed, "I'm guessin' this one could do the work of three."

Charlie smiled and nodded.

"Kelly, you and your boys, are hired. We'll find work for ya, and I'm good with your sons stayin' in school. I got more schoolin' than most, and I know it has helped me." They shook hands and worked out the details, including a two-room dug-out house that the family could live in. It was small but would suffice for their needs.

Turpin put Joe to work in the tack room, mending saddles and bridles. Jess only needed to complete his last year of high school and in his spare time he was a handyman around the place, his bad leg didn't slow him down much. Dan worked the remuda, keeping the horses fed, watered, and groomed. Charlie was the only one who went out on the spring cattle gather and branding.

As the string of cowboys brought the herd back to the holding pens from the gather, a tall, beautiful stallion off in the distance caught Charlie's eye. He pointed as he said, "Mr. Turpin, I'd like to go check out that horse up on the mesa."

"Sure, Charlie, we're about done. I can see the barn and ranch house from here; go ahead. That horse has been around for a year or two now. No one's got up close to him. Good luck, 'cause you'll need it."

Charlie rode around behind the hill and climbed to the mesa behind the cow pony. The horse was nervous, always shying away from Charlie and his mount, but it never bolted or ran too far away. It was almost like he was teasing Charlie, testing his resolve and patience. *This big, wonderful horse must be only two or three years old, and I love that sorrel color and those intelligent eyes.*

It took more than an hour, but Charlie eventually got a rope on him. The horse reared on its hind legs and Charlie prepared to let it go if the horse tried to run. It wouldn't do to be dragged from his saddle. The horse dropped its front legs and shook its head, the long mane looking like a golden waterfall in the light.

He gave a gentle tug and tied the rope off onto his pommel, then slid down from the saddle. He walked slowly over to the horse, hand outstretched as Charlie talked to him, "Easy boy, we're gonna become friends for a lifetime."

The horse seemed comfortable and took to the rope easier than Charlie expected. He jerked his head a few times but didn't pull and strain against the rope. With a couple more tentative steps Charlie managed to reach out a gloved hand and rub the horse's muzzle. "That's a good horse. See, we're gonna be friends."

Charlie took him back to ranch headquarters. Turpin could see them coming and joined Charlie as he turned the big sorrel into the corral, "Charlie, that's a miracle. How'd you, do it?"

"I took my time and started talkin' to him as soon as I got in earshot. I suspect he'll not be happy when I try ridin' him, though."

It took most of the next day, to get a saddle on the stallion. And after several long hard days of Charlie's soft voice and the sorrel's wild bucking; Charlie broke him to ride. It was quite a show and the talk of the ranch for days. After the sorrel and Charlie came to their agreement, it was time to name him. Charlie picked Tony. When asked why he chose that name, Charlie said, "I've always liked that name. My favorite teacher in high school back in Oklahoma was Anthony Morelli. We became friendly, and now Tony will be my best friend."

* * *

Over the next few years, things for the Kelly family seemed to improve. Charlie's mom was doin' well in the hot, dry climate of eastern New Mexico, and the Charlie and his brothers and sister enjoyed school—Charlie was the top student in his class, even though he spent a lot of time daydreaming about working the ranch or riding the hills with Tony. Charlie's dad was also doin' better to Charlie's relief. He worked hard, stayed out of trouble, and had even managed to save money to put an extra room on the small dug-out they lived in. He got along well with the folks at the ranch and had stayed away from alcohol. At least he did until March of 1917 when he discovered the Pecos Bar in Fort Sumner. It was a new saloon in town, and the cowboys from all around Baca County went there on weekends to play poker and get drunk.

After one Friday at the Pecos, Joe came home late, and he and Ellie got into a big argument that woke up the house. Annabelle and Dan looked at Charlie with worry and concern in their eyes. Charlie looked to Jess, but his older brother motioned for Charlie to do something. They all knew that only Charlie could get their dad to settle down. Charlie sighed and ended the argument by stepping between his mom and dad. "This needs to stop." He turned to look at Joe, whose eyes were already red-rimmed from drink. "Dad, we don't want another situation like we had at the Cullum, do we?"

Joe staggered a little as he said, "Of course not, but a fella can go blow off some steam, can't he?"

Ellie said, "You ain't no kid anymore, Joe. Ya gotta family that needs a father, and that's gotta come first."

"Alright, woman, you've had yer say, let's get some sleep." Joe headed toward the bed.

Charlie started to return to the room he shared with Dan and Jess when Ellie said, "Charlie, let's step outside a minute."

"Sure, Mom."

Outside she said, "Son, thanks for steppin' up in there, but you're not the parent. Your dad's gotta straighten up and quit these trips to town."

"Mom, I know I'm not the parent, but I was afraid somethin' bad was about to happen."

She said, "He'll never hit me. He knows I'd never put up with that, and I don't think your dad would ever forgive himself. But I don't understand what's makin' him want to go into town."

"Well, I don't either, but I'm here for ya, Mom."

* * *

In May, Charlie and Dan were helping their mom get supplies

from Foster's Mercantile in Fort Sumner. As they loaded their wagon, Charlie spotted Marshal Sam Bernard riding down Main Street leading three horses tethered together with prisoners in the saddles. The prisoners had their hands tied behind their back, and their horses were linked together so the Marshal could easily guide them.

Charlie said, "Dan would ya look at that. I've never seen the like. The Marshal has three prisoners, and that rope there is tied such that he can control them by himself."

Dan said, "I'd like to have seen him in action as he got them tied up. I guess we'll never know how he made that happen."

Charlie and Dan speculated what the three men had done to get afoul of the Marshal until Ellie told them to stop lollygagging and finish loading the wagon. After the wagon was loaded, they took off toward home. About halfway, they met Joe headed to town.

Ellie tugged at her hair as she said, "Where ya goin', Joe?"

"I'm meetin' some fellas for a card game at the Pecos."

Charlie looked down as he rubbed his hands together, "Dad, is that a good idea?"

Joe stiffened in the saddle, "Who are you to question what I do?"

Ellie said, "Settle down, Joe. He's right, turn around and let's all go home."

"Naw, I'm playin' cards and havin' a beer. Don't wait up."

* * *

Charlie woke up early, as he usually did, and was heading outside to the outhouse when he spotted his mother sitting in the rocking chair in the front of the room that was a combination kitchen, dining area, and living space. She was slowly rocking with a quilt wrapped around her shoulders to keep out the morning chill. Charlie looked into his parent's room and saw that his father had not made it home that night.

Charlie held in the sour words he wanted to say about his dad. Instead, he walked over and knelt next to his mom. "Dad didn't make it home last night."

She shook her head and Charlie could see that she had been crying at some point.

"Mom, I'll go into town and get Dad."

Ellie shook her head as she wiped away a tear, "Thank you, son. It shouldn't fall to you to see after your father. I know he's not a happy man, but I don't know how we fix it. Be careful."

Charlie got Tony ready and headed into town at a quick pace. There was no need to push Tony as there were only two places his dad could be. He arrived and went straight to the Pecos Bar, the first place he'd look. The bartender stopped sweeping the floor when Charlie walked through the batwing doors, "Mornin', I'm Charlie Kelly, have ya seen my father, Joe?"

"Yeah, Marshal Bernard has him locked up. He and an old coot got into it over a card game last night, and they both ended up in jail."

"I see, well, thanks." That was the second place Charlie would have looked.

The jail was about a block from the bar, and Charlie recognized his father's horse tied up out front. He tried the door and found it unlocked. He stepped in and could see Joe asleep on a cot in one of the cells. There were three cells along the back wall, and the Marshal sat at a desk to the left of the front door.

Sam Bernard said, "Charlie, I guess you're here for Joe. This is twice this month, isn't it?"

"Yep, and no offense, but I'm tired of havin' to come to see you and this place."

"No offense taken, and I don't blame you. Let's wake your father. The old coot he tangled with is already gone. Too much beer mixed with hot tempers. I have Joe's horse tied up out front. I expected you." The Marshal woke Joe, and Charlie and his father headed home. Neither of them with much to say.

As the cottonwoods around their house came into view, Joe said, "Thanks, son. I'm sorry you had to do this again."

Charlie looked directly into his father's rheumy eyes, "Dad, you've gotta promise me that this is the last time."

His father nodded, but Charlie wasn't sure if it was a promise or the left-over shakes from last night's drink.

Chapter Three
June 1917

A few weeks had passed, and Charlie and his younger brother Dan had returned to Fort Sumner for another visit to Foster's general store. An early morning shower had given way to another hot, muggy afternoon. Sweat dripped down Charlie's back as he and Dan carried their supplies from Foster's to the family wagon. "Charlie, did ya see that?" Dan asked.

"Yep."

As he exited the store with his arms full, Charlie saw their friend, Little Deer, slapped and shoved to the ground. The man who stood over Little Deer looked ten years older than the boys' dad, short of stature he had silver-gray temples showing below his rumpled hat.

The Kelly boys and Little Deer, a Mescalero Apache, were friends from their school days. Little Deer had graduated high school last year with Charlie. They had often hunted and played baseball together. Little Deer was shorter than Charlie but had shown incredible strength when he'd carried a deer carcass over his shoulders a half-mile on their last hunt.

Charlie turned to Dan. "Little Deer wouldn't have started this."

"You're right. What are you goin' to do?"

"What I always do. Clean up another mess."

Charlie dropped his supplies into their wagon and entered the street to help his friend. He could see the old man's eyes narrow. The troublemaker's face filled with tension as he rocked back and forth. In a calm and confident voice, Charlie asked, "What's the problem?"

The man stepped away from Little Deer, looked up at Charlie, who was a head taller, and grumbled, "This here savage was uh goin' tuh steal my horse."

"He was goin' to steal your horse?" Charlie took another step forward, "Why do you say that?"

Charlie could smell the reek of liquor as the old man staggered then gathered himself, "Coz, he was uh standin' next to it when I come outta the Pecos."

Little Deer dusted himself off. "Are you good, my friend?" Charlie said.

"I'm fine. You be careful. This old coot is drunk, crazy, or both."

Charlie moved in on the old man, "Mister, Little Deer owns a beautiful buckskin pony. He doesn't need your horse."

The drunk staggered, his face a sneer, "So you're ah takin' his side, huh?" He pulled his knife, "I'm gonna cut you." He lunged, the blade almost catching Charlie's right shoulder.

"Whoa, old man. Take it easy." He grabbed the wrist of the hand that held the knife. Charlie's face burned red with the anger raging inside him and he could feel his limbs begin to shake. *Oh no, I'm reactin' like Dad would.*

The old drunk fell to his knees, and dropped the knife as he bellowed, "Ya, son-of-a-bitch, let me loose." Charlie kicked the knife away and released his grip.

Marshal Bernard walked quickly toward them. "Hold on, there." He stepped between Charlie and the old man. "Reuben, you can't stay out of trouble for two minutes. I just broke up a fight you started over cards, and now you're out here starting another one." He looked at Charlie, Dan, and Little Deer, "You boys git outta here!"

Charlie hesitated and said, "Marshal, I was defending my friend; are we in trouble?"

"No, I saw a lot of it from down the street. Reuben needs a couple of hours in a cell and a pot of coffee. You can head on home."

The three boys walked to the wagon and Charlie asked Little

Deer, "You okay?"

His friend nodded as he watched the Marshal lead the old man toward the jail. "Nothing hurt but my pride." He held out his arm and Charlie clasped it. "But thanks for being there."

Charlie nodded. "Glad I could help. I hope the Marshal keeps that old coot locked up for good."

* * *

Charlie and Dan sat in silence, riding east as they enjoyed a light breeze that had come up. Spring and the morning rain brought the smells of desert plants alive. The yellows, oranges, and reds of the flowering cactus lit up the trail. They both sensed the need to let their nerves settle down.

Dan eventually said, "Charlie, what would you have done if the Marshal hadn't arrived when he did?"

"Brother, I don't know for sure; I couldn't let him cut me." He gave a flick of the reins to urge Tony up a small ravine. "I was angry at that old man. I was shakin' inside and ready to beat 'em into the ground when the marshal came up. That scared me, and I'm not sure how to make it stop." With a deep sigh, he continued, "I'm also gettin' mighty tired of cleanin' up other people's messes."

"Whattaya mean?"

Charlie looked up at the clouds, "I'm ready to git out on my own." He looked at Dan and smiled, "Go back to Oklahoma, maybe find work on a good-sized ranch."

"What about Cornerstone?" Dan asked. "What's wrong with workin' here?

"The Cornerstone is okay, and Fred Turpin is a decent boss, but it's tiny compared to other ranches. I want to work on a big spread, someplace where I can prove what I can do." He tilted his hat back and looked off to the eastern horizon. "What I really want, what I'd love to do is to work on that big Miller's 101 Ranch, out in northern Oklahoma. Bein' a cowboy workin' that huge spread must be heaven. Everyone knows about the 101."

Dan nodded. "That sounds great, but why now?"

Charlie paused and rubbed the back of his neck, careful with his words, "That guy beatin' up Little Deer reminded me of Dad. For years Dad's been gettin' in scrapes. Fightin' over nothin'. Big brother Jess, or me... mostly me since Jess's accident... have had to keep him out of trouble or get him outta jail when that fails. Remember last week he spent the night in the Fort Sumner jail after punchin' some guy at the saloon? That wasn't the first time. Ain't likely to be the last time. Today I had to help Little Deer with some old geezer, and I'm tired of it. I'm also seein' myself react with the same kind of anger Dad does, and that's not the way I want it."

Dan gave a nod as the wagon crossed an arroyo, "I guess you gotta right to be upset about Dad. But Little Deer needed help."

Charlie sighed, "You're right, Dan."

Their silence returned, as did the cool breeze. Tony pulled the wagon around a hill and through a large stand of cottonwood trees. Charlie could see the small three-room dug-out house his family called home through the trees in a few minutes.

Charlie looked at Dan and smiled. This has been home now for several years. I've got some good memories here, but it's time to move on.

The house's front door faced the south with a window on either side as part of a wooden frame structure built out from the hillside. It was a short, shaded walk east from that front door to the bank of the Pecos River. The barn was south across the big yard from the front door. It was made of logs and adobe and was large enough to house four stalls on its corral side and hay storage with an area set aside for the care of the horses on the other. The corral bordered the barn and the river.

Charlie pulled on the reins, and Tony slowed to a stop. Dan let out a holler, "We're back."

Mom, Annabelle, and Jess came out of the cabin and met them in the front yard to help unload the wagon.

Mom asked, "Did everything go all right? Mr. Foster let you sign on our account, didn't he? Your Dad finally got us the account last month, and we haven't charged on it yet."

Charlie said, "We did fine; you didn't need to worry." Charlie looked at Dan, "We gotta tell Mom before she hears it from someone else. But let's not tell Dad." Dan nodded as Charlie told them what happened.

"We were comin' outta the store and saw Little Deer git knocked down and beaten by an old man. Little Deer was on the ground, and the old man was goin' to hit him again. I went into the street to defend our friend."

Hearing this, Jess, who had finished unhitching Tony from the half-empty wagon, limped as fast as he could toward Charlie, "Who was this guy?" He tilted his head back, looking directly into Charlie's eyes, his brow furrowed with concern. "Didja have to fight him? Ya, look okay."

Charlie said, "Careful, Jess, you practically fell there."

Jess said, "I'm okay, but how are you?"

Charlie said, "I'm..."

"Charlie did good," Dan said. "The old man shouldn't a pulled his knife on him."

Charlie gave Dan a hard look, "Why'd you say that. You knew that would upset Mom."

Her eyes got as big as Morgan silver dollars. "What? He did what? Oh, Jesus, are you alright, Charlie? Let me look at you!" She reached and grabbed his right arm and pulled him close, and started inspecting his chest, back, and arms for wounds.

Charlie said, "Mom, I'm fine, ya don't need to do all this."

Annabelle ran from the wagon as she yelled, "Charlie are ya hurt? Dan, why didn't ya help him? How could ya let this happen to Charlie?"

"Folks, I said I'm okay." He looked toward the barn and could see his dad on his horse as he dismounted and ran across the yard.

"What's going on here? What's all this commotion about?"

"Everythin' is okay, Dad," Charlie said.

Joe shook his head and raised his voice, "Somethin' sure has y'all worked up. What is it?"

Charlie reluctantly retold the story. His dad's eyes bugged out, and his nostrils flared. Every one recoiled from him as he became animated. "I know who yur talkin' 'bout. That rascal is a mean summabitch."

"Dad. Take it easy, like I said, I'm okay, the Marshal's got the old man. You don't need to git involved." Charlie assured him.

"Yeah, Dad. Charlie's right and everythin' is good," Dan added.

It was like he heard nothing they said. "Reuben needs to learn to stop messin' with me. It's about time I put a stop to this." Joe ran, jumped on his horse, and headed west at a gallop.

Charlie looked at his mom, "He's headin' for trouble."

Mom said, "Yes, he is. It seems I'm always askin' you to do this, but please go after him and try to keep him from makin' a fool of himself again."

Tony was standing next to the wagon with the bridle and bit still in his mouth, so Charlie grabbed the reins and jumped on him bareback.

"Be careful, don't get hurt," said Mom.

"I'll be fine." Charlie headed west, dust flying as he pushed Tony hard.

Charlie could see the town off in the distance, and he spotted his dad with his horse at a trot. He caught up with his dad as they neared town.

His dad turned to Charlie, "I've been mullin' over what ya said about this bein' takin' care of, and you're wrong. You don't know Reuben like I do. He's a skunk, and I know the Marshal has always had a soft spot for him. He won't do nothin' to put a stop to this." He urged his horse to go a bit faster. "You go on back home, you hear me. I've got this."

Charlie gave a squeeze of his legs and Tony kept pace with his dad's horse. "Dad, you don't need to do this. The Marshal can handle things."

"Nope, ya need to go back home. I said I'll take care of this."

Charlie said, "Damn it, Dad, okay, I'm outta here."

Charlie turned Tony east and headed back toward home.

Halfway back home Charlie's anger at his dad had cooled some and he started thinking clearer. *He's gonna end up in jail again, and I'll be back here in the mornin' gettin' him out and takin' him home. Good God a mighty, I hate this. Mom's gonna be real mad at me for lettin' that happen.*

With a sigh, Charlie turned Tony around again and headed

back to Fort Sumner at a gallop.

Charlie pulled up outside the Pecos bar. His dad's horse was tied to a post out front, and Joe stood next to the horse, putting something into his waistband.

"Dad," Charlie said as he jumped off Tony. "Let's go home. You know mom wants you to stay outta trouble."

His dad said, "Son, you're as hardheaded as me sometimes. I already went to the jail, and like I thought, Sam hadn't kept Reuben there for long. Just gave him some coffee and let him go. Didn't even make him sleep it off like he does with me."

"Dad, he's not worth it. Nothin' bad happened earlier. Let's just git home before Mom gits worried."

But his dad ignored Charlie. He stepped up onto the boardwalk in front of the Pecos and called out to a man sitting on a bench. "Ya know Reuben Johnson?"

The man nodded.

"You seen him come in recently?"

"Yep. He's inside drinkin' and braggin' how he run off some kids this afternoon."

Charlie's dad stepped forward and peered over the Pecos's batwing doors, and turned to Charlie, "It's a full house."

Charlie sighed and decided that if Dad wasn't going to come home, he'd have to go with him. That was the best way to keep him out of trouble. "Is he in there?"

"I don't see him, but he's here." His dad pushed the doors open and stepped inside. Charlie climbed the steps and took his place at the batwings. By the look on his dad's face, the musty smell of stale beer, sweat, and vomit was a lot harder on him cold sober.

They both recognized a loud voice to the left. Looking across the bar, a man sat menacingly in the dark at a table in the corner. Charlie licked his lips as his dad walked across the room to the table. Charlie followed. He could see Reuben Johnson sitting at the table, a bottle of whiskey by his side.

His dad stepped closer, "You tried to cut my boy."

Reuben looked up with a derisive snort and said, "Joe Kelly, that was your kid I run off, was it?"

Charlie stepped up and put a hand on his dad's arm. "Dad, let the Marshal handle this. Reuben's as drunk now as he was earlier."

His dad shrugged off Charlie's hand and said, "Get back, Charlie. And Reuben; you shouldn't a tried to hurt my boy."

"He was uh sayin' that injun was not stealin' my pony. That the injun had uh better horse than mine."

"He probably does. That don't matter. I ever hear that you pull a weapon on my boy or anyone else in my family, you'll pay."

Reuben stood and pulled his knife. "You're a sorry son-of-a-bitch. You don't have the guts, an nobody tells me wha' I can and can't do." He lunged at Joe's gut.

Someone hollered, "Go get the Marshal, quick."

Joe jumped back, "Back off, Reuben."

The bar crowd scattered, pushed, shoved, and shouted. The tables tumbled, and chairs flew. Everyone scrambled to get outside.

Charlie shouted as he dodged chairs and bottles, "Dad, stop before someone gits hurt."

Reuben tipped over his table and lunged again at Joe.

Joe picked up a chair, and threw it, "Reuben, back off!"

Reuben staggered and stumbled toward Joe, slashing the air as they moved across the room.

Joe pulled out his .44 Smith and Wesson from his waistband and yelled, "Back off, you bastard. Put the knife down, or I'll shoot ya!"

Reuben didn't stop.

Joe shouted again, "Stop, put that knife down."

Reuben came at Joe again.

The blast echoed down the street as the bar filled with smoke. Reuben lay motionless, his head against the bar footrail and a spittoon.

Chapter Four
June 1917

The smoke and stench from the gun that remained in Joe's right hand filled the Pecos Bar as he stood motionless and stared at Reuben. His chin trembled.

Charlie called out, "Dad... Dad!"

With fear and anxiety written on his face, Joe looked at Charlie and barked, "What?"

"We need to talk to the Marshal."

"He looks dead, shit, oh shit... I had to do it. He was tryin' to kill me."

"Talk to the Marshal. The bartender saw it all."

"There's no need to talk to the Marshal. He knows we've been at each other for weeks."

Joe broke and ran.

Charlie hesitated, looked over at the bartender, and then ran to the batwings, "Stop, Dad, let's talk."

Joe jumped on his horse, spurred him to a run, and headed home. Charlie swore to himself. *Damnit. Don't do this, Dad, runnin' ain't the answer.*

Charlie turned to the bartender who stood at the door and said, "This ain't good."

"No, it's not, son. Joe was defendin' himself, but it's not good that he's run."

Do I stick around here and wait for the marshal or go after Dad? Looking back at the bartender, "I'm going after Dad."

Charlie leaped on Tony, grabbed the reins, and like a jockey and his horse in a stakes race, they headed toward home.

As Charlie rode Tony hard he thought, *How can I git Dad to listen to me? I'm not sure, but Sam Bernard may come after us. I gotta try once more when I git to the house. I'm so frickin' tired of this.*

* * *

His horse at full gallop, Charlie pulled on the reins hard as he approached their home. His dad's horse was hitched to the wagon, and Annabelle, Dan, and Jess were loading their belongings into it. Charlie jumped off Tony and asked Jess, "What's he done now?"

Jess said, "He came back and said we had to git outta here now. Made us start loadin' the wagon."

"Charlie, what happened?" Annabelle asked tears on her cheeks. "Dad was yelling at mom, and she was yelling back. Is dad in trouble again?"

Charlie ignored his sister's question and headed into the house. His mom was busy loading an old crate with their meager kitchen supplies. She had a weary, resigned expression that told Charlie that she'd already given up. She might have, but Charlie hadn't. He headed into his parent's room where his dad was filling a chest with clothes. "Dad, runnin' like this ain't right. We need to go back to town."

"Charlie, hush up, we ain't goin' back. Help us finish loadin' our stuff in the wagon, and let's git goin'."

"No, Dad, you were defendin' yourself, and the bartender will speak up for ya. We can settle this today. There's no need to act like you're a criminal or somethin'."

"I said hush up; we're movin' on. I've been thinkin' about goin' back home to Oklahoma for a while now. This happenin' makes my decision easy."

Charlie glared at his dad's back, turned, and walked outside. He stood next to Tony as his dad dragged the chest out to the wagon. He'd made up his mind too, riding back from town. If his dad wouldn't listen to reason, then it was time for him to move on. He'd help get his mom, brothers, and sister settled, but he wasn't going to stay to keep getting pulled into his dad's troubles.

With a resigned sigh that matched his mom's mood, Charlie got Tony's saddle and tack. Jess, Dan, and Annabelle each gave him questioning looks, wanting to know what they should do, but Charlie was tired of being the one they looked to when things got messy. When he didn't respond, and prodded by their dad, they went back to loading the wagon. It took a while to load everything they'd take with them from what had been accumulated over the years, but they were on their way before dark.

* * *

Charlie rode Tony beside the wagon and listened to his dad tell what had happened back at the Pecos. Having stood nearby when his dad shot Reuben, he looked off in the distance and shook his head. Now he wondered whether he would need to be on the run from now on. He didn't want that life. It was time to make some changes.

On the evening of their second day out a few miles south and west of Clovis, New Mexico, the Kellys found a small lake, abundant grass, and a good stand of trees. They stopped for the evening. Charlie helped make camp, then walked off by himself. He needed time alone to think everything through.

Charlie began to feel intense pangs of anxiety about what had happened back in Fort Sumner. *I've had this hankerin' for months about leavin' and chasin' my dream of workin' on a big ranch and becomin' a top hand. I should have acted on them feelin's before all this. Now I'm gonna leave Mom and everyone, and they ain't gonna understand that this is because of what I wanna do, not because of what dad done.*

Charlie sat on a big rock when Dan called to him, "What ya doin' out here?"

"I needed some time to myself."

"What's wrong, brother?"

"I'm not happy with things the way they are. I'm always cleanin' up messes other people are causin'. It's not the life I want."

"Things'll be better when we git to Oklahoma."

"Maybe, but I'm ready to go find my own way. I need outta

here, Dan."

"But we need ya right now."

Charlie looked around. They were still close to camp, and he didn't want the others to overhear. Dan was two years younger than Charlie, and they had always been each other's closest friends. He owed it to his brother to tell him first what he'd decided. "Let's go somewhere and talk."

They walked along a path that followed the bank of the lake for about ten minutes and got out of sight of the camp. They found downed trees for benches and sat.

Dan picked up a stick and poked it in the mud. "What's goin' on, brother?"

Charlie didn't respond at first, trying to get his words in order. He picked up a stone and skipped it across the surface of the lake. As it sank into the water, he said, "Dan, since we were kids, people shared stories about the big, beautiful Miller's 101 ranch up in the northern part of Oklahoma." He skipped another stone. "I want to see and experience that hundred an' ten-thousand-acre ranch. I want to see the home of the 101 Wild West Show that goes around the world with Tom Mix, William S. Hart, and all those stars. We talked about it on our way back home from Fort Sumner the other day. Remember?"

"Sure, Charlie, you talk about it all the time. So what?"

Charlie turned and looked at his brother. "I've made my decision. I wanna be a top hand there. With the family movin' again, this is the right time to make my exit and go chase my dream."

"Now? Is this because of what Dad did in Fort Sumner?"

"A bit. I'll be honest I'm tired of always savin' Dad, and what he did was the last straw in that regard, but I should have left earlier. I just never had the right time to tell Mom or Dad."

"And when we're movin' at the spur of the moment is the right time?" Charlie could hear the bitter accusation from his younger brother, and it gave him pause.

"No, it probably ain't, but if I don't do it now, I'm afraid I'll be forever tied to keepin' Dad out of trouble. I'll never be able to make a name for myself."

Dan considered this, and after a moment he nodded his head.

"So, you're sure? When ya gonna tell Dad?"

"I'd like to tonight, but I think I need to give it a day or two more. He's still yammerin' about Reuben and Fort Sumner."

* * *

By late afternoon the next day, they'd made it to the edge of South Plains, Texas. They camped east of the post office along a stream and the Fort Worth and Denver railroad tracks.

Charlie said, "Mom, can I give ya a hand preparin' dinner?"

"Sure, honey. What's on your mind? You must need somethin', cause ya haven't offered to help with this in a moon."

"Mom, I plannin' to head out on my own. I need to find my own way. My concern is for you, Jess, Dan, and Annabelle."

"Honey, I know you're of age, but you're still young, and I would like to see ya stay a while longer."

"I need to be my own man and see if I can become the person I want. I want to be a dependable top hand at a big spread, and someone people respect for how he treats people."

"Is that all, dear," his mom asked like she knew there was more.

"An' I'm tired of always havin' to save people," he lowered his voice, "especially Dad. I'm scared too that I'm sometimes reactin' to things like Dad does. Losin' my temper and settlin' everything with a fight. I need to get away from his influence."

"I can't say I'll be happy to see ya go, but I understand."

"Mom, I want your blessin' and assurance ya think everythin' will be okay, with me leavin'."

"We'll be fine. Dad is always good to us, but he hasn't been happy in New Mexico, and maybe gittin' back to Oklahoma's what he needs."

* * *

Over the next two days, the family saw lots of agave and yucca growing wild. They spotted a few deer off at a distance, and even a bobcat crossed in front of them as they worked their way across the rolling desert of west Texas. They saw few other travelers. They stopped for the day south of Turkey, Texas, along the North Pease River.

That evening while everyone ate, Charlie poked at his food as the others laughed and described what they wanted to do once they got to their new home in Oklahoma. Finally, he gathered up his nerve, turned, and spoke directly to his dad.

"I'm outta here at first light. I'm gonna miss all of you, but it's time I go out on my own."

"Why, Charlie? We need you with us in Oklahoma," Jess pleaded.

Charlie said, "Jess, you're the oldest, and you and Dan can be there for mom and Annabelle."

Annabelle whimpered through her tears, "I don't want you to go, big brother."

Mom settled them down and turned to Charlie. "Charlie, honey, like I said before, you're just barely of age."

Charlie's face showed his determination and his voice his intensity, "I'm nineteen, I can fend for myself."

"I'm sure of that, honey. But what are you going to do for food and a home?"

"I'll find ranch work," Charlie reassured her. "There's still plenty of ranches looking to hire on a good cowboy."

Annabelle and Jess said their piece, but Charlie didn't change his mind.

Joe had remained quiet, but now he stood and moved to the campfire to get a cup of coffee. He cleared his throat, ran his hands through his hair, and pondered Charlie's words for a minute. Concern showed on his face. He raised his right-hand palm out to gain control of the moment and said, "Son, I hope we ain't bein' chased by the law, 'cause what I did was self-defense the way I see it. But it may be best..."

Charlie stood and interrupted, "Damn it all, Dad. It was self-defense. I was there when it happened, and I've been sayin' that from the start. We should have stayed there at the bar and dealt with the Marshal. But no, as you've done so many times before, you uproot the family and take off for someplace new. I'm tired of it. I'm done here."

Joe took a step toward Charlie then stopped before getting

within reach, "Well, God damn it, we'll go our separate ways then."

Charlie turned and walked away from the fire and stared up at the darkening sky.

Mom followed him after a minute and put her hand on his shoulder, "In the morning, you take some food and supplies with ya. Nuff to last 'til you can get hired on somewhere. I'll let you have my old coffee pot, and you can take the utensils you've been usin'. Like we were sayin' earlier over the meal, the rest of us'll be settlin' back in southern Seminole County. Dad and I have been thinkin' maybe around Maud, Wolf, or Vamoosa if ya need to come home."

* * *

The following day, Charlie struck out southeast for Childress, Texas. The rest of the Kellys headed north and east toward Oklahoma, hoping to get across the Red River and maybe as far as Hollis by nightfall.

Charlie started the day filled with concern about his family. A feeling of emptiness that he hadn't expected filled his stomach as he realized that he didn't know when he might see Mom, Jess, Annabelle, or Dan again. He was happy to be leaving his dad, that felt like a weight had been lifted from his shoulders. But he was surprised that he was feeling lonely for the others after only a couple of hours.

As he and Tony rode across the land, the feeling changed. As he took in the splendor of Mother Nature's beauty—remnants of the tallgrass prairie, steep hills, pronghorn, and the occasional jackrabbit—Charlie's mind began to fill with the possibilities that were ahead of him. As he took in the wide horizon from the top of one hill, he imagined himself ranging across the land driving a herd of cattle. He knew that someday he'd be doing that.

As evening approached, Charlie came to the North Pease River. *This should be good. There's a nice stand of cottonwoods over there.* He rode over and saw there was good grass as well and decided to stay with the water and made camp for the night. He had everything set up at dusk.

"Hello, the camp."

Charlie thought, *Whoa, who's that?* He looked toward the voice and there was a horse and rider silhouetted against the setting sun.

The rider rode in slowly and a friendly voice called out, "Good evenin' to ya, mind if I join ya?"

Charlie stood, smiled, and said, "Sure, git down and stay a spell."

The stranger appeared to be in his late twenties, six feet tall and lean.

"Happy to. I see you're makin' supper. Can I add some beans and taters as thanks for your welcome? I go by Slim Talbott. Who might ya be?"

"Charlie Kelly and I appreciate your offer."

Slim tied off his horse, pulled the saddle and bags off, rubbed his horse down, and made sure his pony could easily get to water and grass for the evening. Then he dug into the bags for his part of their meal.

Charlie had already started the fire, so he put the coffee on.

As he prepped to cook, Slim said, "The coffee and bacon sure smell good."

Charlie chuckled as he said, "It sure does. I always like havin' a little at the end of the day because it puts me in a good mood."

They were enjoying their second cup of coffee when Slim said, "Where ya headin', Charlie?"

"To find ranch work; thought I might try the OX south of Childress. It's a big place. I hear it stretches across three counties."

"Good idea. Yeah, it covers a lot of Childress, Cottle, and Hardeman counties. If there's no work there, you might find work at the Four Sixes. I spent a night in Guthrie near the ranch last week."

"Thanks, I'll keep it in mind; where you headin'?"

"I hear some guy found gold out at a place called Magdalena, New Mexico. Thought I might see what I can find."

"Well, good luck to ya. I hope I hear a story someday about you findin' gold too. But I'm a cowboy at heart and I'm following my dream."

They parted at daybreak. Charlie worked his way toward the

OX. He thought as the day wore on, *Slim seemed a nice enough fella. I hope I don't need his advice about the Four Sixes.* By midday, he arrived at the main gate of the OX. A sign said, "No Help Needed."

"This may be a little tougher than I hoped," he said to Tony as he patted the horse's neck. "Don't you worry none, I'll find somethin' soon. Guthrie is only a few days away. The Four Sixes is a big ranch with a top reputation for some of the best quarter horses and Hereford cattle anywhere. Next to ridin' for the 101 brand, the Four Sixes brand would be a real privilege to ride for." Tony snorted and nodded his head, which Charlie took as an agreement.

It took two hot and dusty days to get to the Four Sixes' headquarters outside Guthrie, Texas. He found Slim's story was true, but Charlie got there a little late. The foreman Boots O'Shay, a leather-skinned cowboy with a friendly smile, said, "I just hired the last hand I needed two days ago. My new hire moved back to the Four Sixes from Oklahoma, where he worked for an old friend of mine, Bob Nash. I'm sure Bob never expected to lose him, so he might need help. His place is the Cullum Ranch in southwest Oklahoma near the town of Loco in Stephens County."

Charlie didn't let on that he knew the ranch and Bob Nash. *I was born within a fifteen-minute ride from there. Dad's temper cost us good jobs at the Cullum, though. But Bob Nash liked me well enough; we became friends, as much as a ranch foreman was friends with anybody. I sure hope that could mean something good.* He thanked Boots O'Shay and headed north toward Oklahoma.

Over five hard days, Charlie marveled at the beautiful landscape he traveled through. The brilliant yellows of the prairie zinnias, silvers of the beard grasses, and the occasional elk and deer off at a distance. And as he left the rattlers and cactus of Texas behind, he got reacquainted with the animals and plants of his youth.

So it was with high hopes that Charlie approached the gates of the Cullum, as more pleasant memories of working this ranch filled his head. He walked Tony confidently toward the ranch house like he was returning home. But his hopes were soon dashed as he talked with Bob Nash, who said, "It's good to see ya, Charlie." He scratched at the back of his neck as Charlie told him he was looking for work and heard that the Cullum was hiring. "I'd love to hire you, but to do it, I'd have to fire someone."

There was a silence between the two men as Charlie tried to keep a hold of his temper at missing another opportunity. It seemed like nothing was going his way. Eventually, Bob asked, "How's your mom and the other kids?"

"They were fine a couple a weeks ago, sir. Dan is better than six feet tall now. Jess is doing well, though I guess he'll always have his limp from when he fell out of the barn loft here. Annabelle is sixteen years old now, and she's a tall blond, blue-eyed, beautiful young woman. She's been a real help for mom for some time now. I expect she'll be startin' her own household when the right fella comes along."

"How's Ellie doin'?"

"She's better now. It seems like the desert air out there in New Mexico helped her breathin' a lot."

Bob tilted his hat back, and gazed off toward the horizon as he asked, "And what about your dad?"

I knew he'd ask about Dad. He's cost himself and the family a lot because of his temper, but Charlie wasn't going to voice that concern with Bob.

Charlie sighed, "He's okay. He and the family are headin' back to Seminole County. New Mexico wasn't home." He looked at the ground, and kicked the dirt, then met Bob's eyes. "Thanks for your time, sir."

Charlie nodded and turned to leave.

"Hey Charlie, wait a minute, I could use you for a day or two and pay you with some supplies. We gotta corral busted up yesterday. Could ya' repair it?"

"Yep, I sure can, and happy to get the supplies."

"Good, then the hand I had planned on usin' for that can stay out repairin' a fence." Bob pointed in the direction of the corral. "Let's go over and look at what I need your help with."

As they approached the corral, Charlie stopped and burst

into laughter, "Bob, this corral doesn't need repair; it's gotta be rebuilt. What in the hell happened here?"

Bob chuckled, "I guess it was kinda funny at the time, but I'm still a little hot about it. The fellas had themselves a bull ridin' contest here over the weekend. A couple of Brahma bulls got outta control and destroyed this corral and part of the wall in the barn. I guess you're right. We need to rip out that last piece of fence that's still sorta standin' and build a new corral. Are you willin' to take this on?"

"Yep, but ya know that'll take me more'n a couple of days."

"I figured that. We'll give ya a cot in the bunkhouse and feed ya while you're here. Go ahead and figure out what's needed to rebuild it, and I'll send someone with ya to Ringling for supplies."

"What about my horse?"

Bob pointed across the yard, "There's an empty stall next to my horse in the stables. I'll show ya. He can stay there. Of course, we'll feed him too. What's his name?"

"Tony, and I'm sure he'll enjoy the company of your horse."

Charlie was able to use a little lumber from the old corral, but what he created over the next four days with a lot of his imagination was mostly new and showed he had some solid skills with carpentry tools.

At the end of the fourth day, Bob walked up, "Charlie, you did a fine job. I'm glad you could use some of the old corral. But that trip to Ringling for wood has sure paid off. These corrals are nicer than what we had. Let's walk over to the chow hall and I'll get you paid."

Bob had the cook load Charlie's saddlebags to the brim.

"Charlie, thanks for your help. You came along at just the right time."

"Thanks, Bob, for the work and the supplies,"

"I wish you well in your search for permanent work. I'd keep ya on at the Cullum if I could."

Charlie shook Bob's hand, then mounted Tony and together they rode away from the Cullum.

Chapter Five
July 1917

Charlie rode north out of Stephens County deeper into Oklahoma. At the end of his second day away from the Cullum, he camped along Rock Creek on the outskirts of Elmore City in Garvin County. The next morning, Charlie awoke to the crowing of a nearby rooster. He enjoyed the songbirds up in the cottonwoods as he warmed up the last of his coffee and fried his bacon. "This is pretty country here along this creek." He realized he had been talking to Tony again and smiled. After he finished breakfast and saddled Tony, he rode into town. Elmore City didn't feel like it deserved the moniker "city", though Charlie had to admit it was bigger than Fort Sumner. There were several buildings along a wide, dusty Main Street, including a bank, a small hotel, and a few other businesses. He found Blackaby's General Store on the west side of the Main Street in the middle of the town. He needed to buy some coffee and a few other things. He wasn't broke yet, but the money he had from his last pay back in New Mexico was about gone. A tall man, slim with gray hair, struggled to control some of the contents of a wagon parked in front of the store on this windy morning.

Charlie got down off Tony and tried to help the man, "Good day to ya mister, anybody in the store to help me?"

As he continued to move his goods to the rear of the wagon, the man said, "No, there's just me today. This shipment of supplies arrived last night from Pauls Valley. What do you need, young man?"

Charlie took a couple of sacks of flour from the bed of the wagon and put them on a cart the man had on the sidewalk, "Did you get some coffee in this shipment?"

"Yes, I was able to get a fifty-pound bag. I'm concerned we're involved in that awful war overseas, and so I ordered some extra. It's not certain we'll still be able to get our basic supplies in the coming months."

"That's somethin' to be concerned about for sure. How much for two pounds?"

"That's ten cents a pound."

Charlie pondered that amount for a minute. That's about all I have left. "Have you unloaded the coffee already?"

"No, I've just started. I may not be able to get to it for several hours. As you can see, I have my hands full."

"If that's the case, can I make you an offer, sir?"

"Sure, what's on your mind?"

"I unload your wagon as you check things off your list. I'll put them where you like, and you give me the two pounds of coffee in payment."

The man smiled, pulled out a handkerchief, and wiped the sweat from his brow. He adjusted his glasses and said, "Young man, you have yourself a deal. My name is Jasper Blackaby, I own this store, and I want to welcome you to Elmore City."

"I'm Charlie Kelly, sir. I'm originally from Stephens County, but I recently lived in New Mexico. Happy to help ya with the supplies."

It was already hot, so Charlie took off his shirt, hoping to stay a little cooler and avoid sweating in his best shirt. His muscles rippled when he carried the fifty-pound bags of flour inside and stacked them where Mr. Blackaby indicated along the north wall. A little later, as he walked out the store's front door, he noticed several women in front of the next building watching him, all smiles and pointing his way.

Charlie nodded, "Morning ladies, it's sure a hot one today."

One answered with a lilt in her voice, "Morning." They laughed as they rushed into what he could see was a dress shop.

Charlie chuckled, "Foolishness."

He continued unloading the wagon and marveled at how organized and neat the store was. He enjoyed the smells inside the building of leather, grains, sugar, and the coffee brewing. It took Charlie a few hours to finish as Mr. Blackaby was meticulous with recording what was in the wagon against his invoice and made sure that Charlie rotated the stock inside so that the older material was where people would buy it first. It took time because Charlie kept asking questions and Mr. Blackaby was always willing to answer. When they were done, he pulled the wagon around the back of the store for Blackaby and came in the back door. He had walked back in front of the store to rinse off at the water trough and pull his shirt back on when Blackaby walked out the door. "I've got your two-pound sack of coffee here. But let me ask, "Where're you heading?"

As he climbed up to the sidewalk he said, "I'm workin' my way north to the Miller's 101 Ranch. It's been my dream to get hired on there."

Mr. Blackaby handed Charlie his coffee, "Have you worked ranches before?"

"Yes, I've been a hand for all my high school years."

Blackaby's eyes widened, and the pitch of his voice raised, "So, you finished high school?"

"Yes, sir, I graduated a year ago May from Fort Sumner High back in New Mexico."

Mr. Blackaby leaned in as his head tilted, "Are you in a hurry to leave town?"

Charlie smiled, "The 101 isn't gettin' any closer with me standin' here, but I could stay a spell."

Blackaby offered his right hand, "How does a home-cooked meal sound to you?"

Charlie hesitated for a moment, then gave a light squeeze to the handshake, "That always sounds good."

"Wonderful, come home with me tonight." He paused, scratched the back of his neck, and smiled, "I have a subject I want to discuss with you."

He has a subject he wants to discuss with me? "Uh... sure, Mr. Blackaby."

Mr. Blackaby turned to go into the store but paused and looked back at Charlie, "I'll be closing the shop soon. Why don't you see the sights and come back here in an hour or so and we can walk over to my house. It's just a short distance from here."

Charlie walked around the main street to pass the time and was surprised to see what the town offered. He found a bank located in a substantial brick building and a new-looking two-story hotel. It surprised him to see more churches within Main Street's view than saloons. Besides the dress shop, there was a tailor, a barber, and a livery stable. He found everything here in Elmore City that Fort Sumner had and then some. Charlie returned to the store and smiled as Tony drank at the trough. He patted him and gave him some attention before he went inside and found Blackaby prepared to close for the day.

Blackaby looked up and said, "I'm about finished here. Why don't you get your horse and meet me around back?"

Charlie and Tony walked around the building, and as they came into view of the back door, Blackaby was locking up. He turned and said, "Follow me and watch your step." He led Charlie down a path that followed Rock Creek. The trail turned north and led to a house hidden back in the oak trees. It had two stories and looked like one of the fancy Victorian houses Charlie had seen in pictures. These folks must be rich.

"Charlie, welcome to the Blackaby House. I built this nearly thirty years ago. I settled here along the bank of Rock Creek and started my general store. More people began to settle around here, and now we have Elmore City."

A beautiful young woman, nearly Charlie's height, met them as they entered the house. She had big blue eyes and raven black hair that flowed down past her shoulders. Her dress showed off a slim body that was curvy in all the right places. Charlie had never seen a beauty like her, especially one with her hair not up in a bun. Sensations stirred in his loins stronger than he had ever experienced before as he took in her beauty. Blackaby turned, smiled, and said, "Charlie Kelly, this is my wife, Susan."

Charlie nodded, "Please to meet you, ma'am, and thanks for your hospitality." He nodded in greeting. He didn't dare offer his right hand and tucked it behind his back to hide the way it trembled.

"Please to meet you too, Charlie. We love it that you could join us. Dinner will be ready soon."

To Charlie, her voice seemed angelic, and her eyes seemed to focus only on him. He was becoming concerned he might do or say something foolish. Please don't ask me to say anything right now. Charlie's mind was full of questions. She's practically my age, and they're married? Susan pointed toward the chairs in the parlor and said, "Welcome to our home. Please find a seat and be comfortable."

Jasper sat in his favorite chair as Susan went back to the kitchen. He reached over and picked up his pipe and packed it with tobacco, "Charlie, what do you think about our little town?"

"You have a nice place here. It's bigger than Fort Sumner, New Mexico. I lived on a ranch outside of that town, and of course, that's where I went to school."

"We're proud of the progress we've made over the last few years. Our farmers are doing well, and a few ranches are beginning to pop up out west of here."

Blackaby went on, describing the history of the town, and telling Charlie about the town's founders. Charlie was only half-listening, his mind still focused on Susan. After several minutes, Susan reappeared and said, "Jasper, you and Charlie come to the table; dinner is ready."

Blackaby said, "I guess my pipe will wait until after our meal."

They sat around a table more massive than any Charlie had ever seen. The detail and carvings made it like a work of art. It looked to him large enough to hold his whole family plus his hosts. Susan had prepared fried chicken and mashed potatoes with buttered corn on the cob.

"Mrs. Blackaby, how did you know this is my favorite meal?"

"Why Charlie, it's Susan, and we ladies can't tell you gentlemen all our secrets." They all laughed and after Mr. Blackaby said grace, they began eating.

After a few bites, Susan asked, "Charlie, what brings you to Elmore City?"

"I'm passing through on my way north to a ranch called the Miller's 101. It's up near Ponca City."

Susan's smile wavered as she asked, "Is there something about this 101 that makes it important that you only go there?"

"To a cowboy like me, it's probably the most respected and successful ranch in the country. They also have the world-famous Wild West Show with people like Tom Mix performing in it."

"Oh, yes, now that you mention it. While I was in college back in New York, that show was at Madison Square Garden. I didn't attend, but I had friends who saw it, and they were amazed by the cowboys and Indians."

Charlie couldn't tell if she was being nice, but he was mesmerized by her beauty, and a bit dumbstruck that she'd gone to college.

Charlie turned to Blackaby and said, "You mentioned earlier you had something you wanted to discuss with me. Can we have that talk now?"

"We haven't had our dessert yet, my man. We'll get to that, don't you worry."

They enjoyed each other's company, and even with the new and unexpected emotions, Charlie eventually became comfortable at the Blackaby's dinner table.

After warm cherry pie with homemade ice cream for dessert, the gentlemen took their iced sweet tea out to the veranda that overlooked the creek.

Their conversation transitioned to fishing and hunting around Rock Creek and Garvin County and what life was like in Elmore City.

Susan came out with a pitcher of tea to refill their glasses, "You gentlemen ready for more tea, and how about another piece of pie?"

Jasper said, "I believe I'll decline, you Charlie?"

"I'd like to have both, and thanks for the offer," Charlie said.

Susan looked pleased; her eyes glistened as she slowly bent down to pick up Charlie's glass from the side table. The low cut of her dress gave Charlie a view that aroused those feelings again. My gosh, I hope I'm not blushing. "I'll bring your pie in a few minutes," Susan said.

Jasper Blackaby had gone to the parlor on his way out and retrieved his pipe and makings. After lighting and enjoying a few more puffs, he turned to Charlie and began asking Charlie questions.

"Charlie, I take it you must be about eighteen or nineteen since you're a high school graduate, is that so?"

"Yes, sir, I'll be twenty in October."

"What were your best classes?"

"Well, I enjoyed school and learnin' all the different subjects. My grades were good, especially in math."

"So, working with numbers comes easy to you?"

"It always seemed that way, and I did well in my English, too. They asked me to read my senior essay at my graduation ceremony."

"You mentioned you want to find work at the Miller's 101 up near Ponca City. What do you want to do for them?"

"I worked ranches south of here in Stephens County and out in De Baca County in New Mexico. At both, I worked cattle and repaired things as needed. I hope to do the same up at the 101."

Susan returned with Charlie's pie. As she laid it on the table next to him, she smiled and said, "Here you go, I'm glad you enjoyed it." She then took a seat behind Jasper and in clear view of Charlie.

Jasper continued, "It would seem that you haven't used your education in any of these jobs; is that right?"

"I guess you could say that. It has been helpful that I read and write and can use math, but the work typically didn't require it. Many of the ranch hands I've worked with had little more than a third-grade education; if that. But, they were respected, and some were top hands."

Blackaby said, "Is your family still in New Mexico, and what do they do for a living?

How am I gonna answer this without getting into why they are no longer in New Mexico? "No, they've moved back to Oklahoma, too. They're settled over in Seminole County. Dad is a rancher with considerable mechanical skills as well. For years, he's hired out to someone rather than own his place. The last place he owned was over at Wanette in southern Pottawatomie County. That's north and east of here about two days' ride."

"I'm acquainted with Wanette, and yes, it's sixty miles or so from here. Are you the first in your family to graduate high school?"

"Yes, I have an older brother, Jess, but he fell from the loft of a barn some years back, and it took him two years to recover. He still has a limp but is back in school. He should graduate next year if he can get into school this September."

"That tells me your folks value education, and it certainly speaks well of them. I had a reason to invite you here tonight. This afternoon you were very well-spoken. You handled yourself well, and you showed an ability to barter. I often don't see those abilities, and I need someone like you at my store. Do you have any interest in a discussion about you staying here in Elmore City?"

Behind Blackaby, Susan leaned forward, her lips parting, and looked directly at Charlie.

Charlie couldn't miss the view she offered, and he easily read the expression on her face. After a moment of hesitation, he said, "I'd be foolish if I didn't listen to what you have in mind."

A big smile filled Susan's face along with a crisp nod as she leaned back in her chair.

Jasper said, "That's what I wanted to hear. It's July, and I need help in the store now, but it will be even busier for me in a few months as harvest time starts. September and October are very busy here in Garvin County. Apples, blackberries, peaches, pears, and pumpkins are huge crops around here. My store becomes the center of commerce. We stay busy through the holidays, and it's more than I can handle alone. A few weeks back, my clerk had to return to Oklahoma City to be near his mother as she turned very ill."

"Mr. Blackaby, I've never worked in a store before. Are you sure you want me for your clerk? I appreciate your interest, but my dream is to become a top hand at the Miller's 101."

"I've gathered that, but I believe most ranchers would have

their string of hands already in place for this year's gather, and I need a bright person like yourself to help me through the coming months."

"You could be right about what's ahead for me up north at this point, but why would you want me instead of someone else? I would have to learn everything from scratch."

"I'm not concerned with you learning what will be needed. I'm sure you could learn all you need over the next month, and we'd be ready for the busy times that are ahead. I do have one final question because of the war in Europe. You're the prime age for the military draft and some young men have volunteered. What is your status?"

"I was called into the post office at Fort Sumner to meet with some recruiters for the military the week after graduation. They asked a bunch of questions, and the Army seemed interested in me. That changed when their doctor said I had flat feet. He said, especially at my size, I'd struggle to hold up on long marches and anytime I had to run a long distance. My feet have never been a problem for me as a cowboy or anything else I've tried, but the Army decided it didn't want me."

Jasper perked up, "That makes me even more interested in you as a potential employer. Please think about this tonight. We can discuss your pay and anything else important to your decision in the morning. I want your answer then." He looked Charlie in the eye and said, "The job is yours if you'll take it."

Susan stood and said, "Charlie, I've never seen Jasper so sure of anything. Would you please make him a happy man with a yes in the morning?" She smiled and Charlie had a hard time not reading into that smile that she'd be a happy woman if he said yes. "Do you two need anything else from me, Jasper?"

Jasper looked at Charlie, who shook his head no, "I guess not Susan, thank you."

* * *

Charlie camped back at the same place along Rock Creek. He didn't get as much sleep as the night before because his head spun with possibilities. He couldn't get Susan Blackaby off his mind. The man who'd offered him a job last night was her husband. But she filled his thoughts more than the job. Could he take the position because of her, or should he pass on the job for the same reason? He had his share of girlfriends back in high school. So, he had experience—he thought—with women, but those relationships couldn't have prepared him for this.

Chapter Six
July 1917

Charlie rolled out at daybreak after a restless night of little sleep. A beautiful grove of trees along Rock Creek had given him and Tony a place to bed down for two nights. After a quick dip in the creek to freshen up and get rid of the smell of the trail, he started a fire to brew some of the coffee from yesterday's deal with Jasper Blackaby. He would cook some bacon and beans to go with it. Nothing smelled better to Charlie than freshly brewed coffee, except maybe bacon frying. Everything seemed alive there on the creek bank. He enjoyed the sounds of the water flowing over and through the rocks and the songbirds chirping high in the trees.

As Charlie ate his breakfast, he mulled over what he would do today when meeting with Mr. Blackaby.

What do I do? I'm not excited to become a store clerk. But I'm about out of money. And being around Susan Blackaby would be pure pleasure in many ways—and possible trouble for me too. She's the prettiest thing I've ever laid eyes on. And she's a married woman and should not be my concern. I know I shouldn't take this job just to be around her, but I shouldn't pass on it because of her. If I take it, that sure doesn't mean I've given up on my dream up at the 101. It means I can make some money over the next few months and get there in the spring when they should be hiring.

Charlie looked over at Tony, "Yep, I think that's what I'll do, buddy. I guess I'll stay and make some money to set us up for the rest of our trip north. Whattaya think, Tony?"

Tony neighed softly and nodded his head.

"Yeah, me too."

* * *

He arrived in town before the businesses other than the café were open and decided to take another walk on Main Street. This time he paid closer attention to what businesses were there and how many. He had completed only half his trip through town, yet he found there were three good-sized protestant churches and one catholic church. He saw two bars, both a block off Main Street on what appeared to be E Street. He remembered the Pecos was one of six bars on Main Street in Fort Sumner. This community is different. But how much?

He was across the street from Blackaby's and he could see the front doors were open. He finished his tour of the town by crossing over onto E Street and going east one block to Missouri Street, and there he found the Post Office and a small produce market. He hadn't wanted to give the impression he was too eager to hear the rest of what Jasper Blackaby had for him, so he took his time visiting the owner of the market.

It was about a half-hour later when Charlie walked through the front door of the store and said, "Good mornin', Mr. Blackaby."

"And good morning to you, Charlie. Did you sleep well?"

"I got plenty of rest last night, and you, sir?" He wasn't about to tell him he hardly slept.

"I did. But I do admit I was more restless than usual. I was thinking about the conversation we were to have this morning."

"I admit, too, that although I got my rest, I thought a lot about the same thing."

"I'm ready for another cup of coffee; how about you, Charlie?"

"Sounds good to me."

Blackaby said, "Let's sit around this table I put here to allow the town folks to relax and visit when they come into the store."

Charlie took a seat and said, "There was a similar table in Foster's store in Fort Sumner. Some regulars, mostly men, would arrive to spit 'n whittle and enjoy their first cup of coffee."

Blackaby smiled as he said, "Yeah, that's what happens here

too. Now, Charlie, I want to hire you. Why don't you give this a try? I'm ready to commit, but I sense you have some doubts, am I right?"

"Yes, I do. Workin' in a store is different than anythin' I've ever done. It's somethin' I never considered as a way I would make my livin'. I still dream of bein' a top ranch hand on a big spread like the Miller's 101. I know I shared that with you last night and that desire hasn't changed one bit. But I could use the job you're offerin' to put some money in my pocket, and you're right, I have no assurance the 101 is hirin' right now."

Blackaby interrupted and said, "How about this; you commit to trying the job for a month and if it isn't working for you, feel free to go on to the 101, no questions asked. I'll start you at a dollar a day for the thirty days. If you stay, it goes to a dollar and a quarter."

"Well, sir, that's a mighty fine offer. I wouldn't make any more as a hand at a ranch, but they would be offerin' room and board as well. Here I'd have to get a room at a hotel or somethin' because I couldn't keep campin' along the Rock Creek as the weather changes."

"You know that's a good point, young man. Susan and I have recently converted a storage room off our barn to a bedroom. It has a good bed, a washbasin and a chest of drawers and it's yours to use free of charge if you like. We had thought we would rent it out, but this works even better. If you want it."

Charlie took a sip of coffee. *He seems to have an answer to everythin', but what about his wife? I can't bring that up to him. I guess that'll have to work itself out.*

"That room sure sounds like it would work out fine. But again, I have no experience workin' in a store. You'll teach me what to do?"

"Over time, I'll teach you everything I know."

"Okay then, I still have some concerns, but it's a deal, sir. When do I start?"

"You just did, son, and maybe it's time for you to call me Jasper when it's just us."

They shook on it, as Blackaby said, "Charlie, I want to teach you the best business practices I can, so we'll go down to the bank after a while and draw up an agreement between us and have Ben Childers, the banker, notarize it for us. It would be best if you met him anyway because I want him to know you work for me. You might want to open a bank account with him too."

"That sounds important and must be something I need to know more about."

Just then, Susan walked in the front door, wearing a bright yellow summer dress with a plunging neckline that showed off her figure. It was as if a ray of sunlight had walked into the room. She waved and said, "Good morning, gentlemen."

"Honey, Charlie, has agreed to become our new clerk."

Susan's face lit up, "Well then, it's my pleasure to welcome you to the Blackaby Mercantile family." Susan and Charlie's eyes met and lingered. Warmth pulsed throughout Charlie's body. He hoped no one noticed a change in him on the outside because of the change inside.

"Th-Th-Thank you, ma'am."

"Charlie, it's still Susan." She smiled as she reached over and squeezed his right bicep. The spot tingled with anticipation.

They laughed and sat around the table to tell Charlie about the business. Jasper stepped over to the counter, picked up a cup for Susan, and poured her coffee.

"What brings you to town this morning, Susan?" Jasper asked.

She looked over at Charlie, smiled, and said, "Why Jasper, I couldn't wait to hear if Charlie had decided to join us or not."

Blackaby beamed, "Charlie starts today. We'll go to the bank and draw up papers to make everything official. Charlie has agreed to move into the room out at the barn for now."

Susan beamed as she said, "That sounds wonderful." She reached her right hand over and placed it on Charlie's, "You can join us for some meals from time to time. I know you'll want some alone time, but breakfast and dinner can be times to talk about business and be social too."

"Thank you, but I don't want to intrude." His face flushed as he gently pulled his hand away.

Jasper said, "You won't be, and Susan's right, we can use

those times for business, and we may invite others over to make it an evening party. We can use the parties to help you meet the folks of Elmore City. They'll need to see you as part of Blackaby's and someone with whom they want to do business."

Charlie began to feel some mixed emotions about his decision. Had she been too much of an influence on his decision to stay? He was sure of two things. This new world was exciting, and Susan seemed happy he had decided to stay. She couldn't have made that clearer. As a relatively inexperienced man of nineteen, even he could read her. He hoped that Jasper had missed that, but he doubted it.

"Susan, can you watch the store for a while? I need to take Charlie to meet Ben and get our agreement formalized."

"Of course, Jasper, you go take care of everything. I'll be right here."

Jasper pointed out several businesses along Main Street and told Charlie who owned them, and how long they'd been in Elmore City as they walked toward the First State Bank a few blocks south on Main Street. The bank was the only brick building in town, on the corner of Fourth and Main. As they walked inside, Charlie could see two teller windows with steel bars atop oak counters. The receptionist, a young, round-faced brunette, was seated at an oak desk and cheerfully greeted them, "Mr. Blackaby, how can I help you?"

"Hello Molly, I need to see Ben if he's available."

"He's here, but with a client, why don't you and your friend wait in the conference room."

"Oh, let me introduce you two. Molly, this is Charlie Kelly. Charlie, this is Molly Weatherby, Ben's right hand here at the bank."

"My pleasure, Miss Weatherby." Charlie looked Molly up and down. She was about his age and was professionally dressed, with a pleasant smile. He found her attractive, but nothing compared to Susan Blackaby.

"Glad to meet you, Mr. Kelly. You folks find a seat in the conference room, and I'll let Mr. Childers know you're waiting. Can I get you anything to drink? Coffee? Water?"

"No, we're fine, thank you," Jasper replied.

A distinguished-looking man in a three-piece, blue pinstriped suit walked into the conference room. He appeared to be about fifty with a full head of gray hair matching his beard. Blackaby stood, and Charlie joined him as Jasper introduced him. "Charlie, this is Ben Childers, our bank president, and my friend. Ben, this is Charlie Kelly; he's my new clerk at the shop."

Charlie sensed Ben giving him the once over as they took their seats.

They immediately got down to business. "We need you to help us create and then notarize our signed agreement for Charlie's employment. We have agreed on his compensation, which will include his monetary pay and living quarters. Can you do that for us?"

"Of course, Jasper. This sounds a little more serious than your arrangement with your last clerk."

"It is. I discussed this with Susan last night, and we feel this could be more than a temporary relationship. We want Charlie to see us not only as employers but business mentors and hopefully close friends."

"I see, and this document would serve as a business contract?"

"Yes, and although I think Charlie's handshake is as good as a contract in all the important ways relating to his character, this notarized document shows him how we do business with people we want long-term relations with."

Ben turned to Charlie, "You're comfortable with this and understand all we've discussed?"

"Yes, sir. I'm happy to sign and agree to what Mr. Blackaby and I have discussed. I want to do this right."

Ben asked, "I mean no disrespect, Charlie, but do you read and write?"

"None taken, sir. Yes, I'm a high school graduate. I had the highest scores in my class."

Blackaby showed his pleasure when he said, "I knew you graduated, but I didn't know that last part, congratulations."

Ben smiled and nodded, "We don't see enough young folks finish high school. I can see why you and Susan are excited. Let's get this paperwork done. I'll have Molly type the paperwork for us, and you two can come back tomorrow and sign it and have it notarized."

Jasper and Charlie laughed at Ben's concern and how easy he made the paperwork sound. They enjoyed their short walk back to the store.

"Why don't you take your gear and horse to the house and get settled in, then come back, and I'll use the rest of the day to get you acquainted with the store."

"Okay, I'll be quick about it. I won't waste any time."

"Take the time you need; Susan will show you your room and where your horse's stall will be. We're going to take care of your horse too. Susan can also show you where to find his feed and anything else you'll need."

Jasper entered the store first. "Susan, we have the documentation in work. I would like you to take Charlie and show him his new home and where he can bed down his horse."

Susan said, "You want us to go now?"

"Yes, unless you have something else you need to do. After you're done, Charlie will be coming back to the store."

Susan said, "Okay." She gave Jasper a quick peck on his cheek and turned to Charlie, with her excited eyes focused and sparkling, "Are you ready?"

Charlie gulped, "I have Tony tethered out front. I'll get him and meet you out back?"

"That'll be fine." The lilt in Susan's voice could not be missed.

Chapter Seven
July 1917

Charlie met Susan behind the store, and Susan stepped up and stroked Tony's muzzle. "And who's this handsome fellow?"

"This is Tony," Charlie said, patting his neck. "I found him on the Cornerstone ranch back in '14 and broke him."

"You broke him?" From the look Susan gave him he couldn't tell if she was serious or teasing him.

"It means I got him tame enough to accept a rider," Charlie said. "He's been with me since then."

She scratched Tony's muzzle again, then smiled at Charlie and started walking. As they followed the path to the house, they continually looked over at each other as they walked side by side.

Susan said, "Let's take Tony and get him settled in his stall first."

"That's a good idea. I didn't notice a barn last night."

"It's around behind the house and sits a little farther from the creek. There are corrals to let him stretch his legs a little and a tack room. You'll find plenty of feed, for him too."

"Tony won't know what to make of all that."

Susan giggled, "I bet he'll get used to it real fast."

As they walked around to the back of the house, a large red barn with a loft for hay and storage came into view. It had a corral on the creek side and huge double doors facing the house. A side building was opposite the creek that housed a buggy and a motor car.

"That's a fine-lookin' barn, ma'am. That looks like fresh paint, and it's a big barn for a place in town."

"Charlie, you better start calling me Susan, or you're going to have me mad at you. I'm not old enough to be your mother. I'm not much older than you."

"Okay, Susan it is. How many stalls does the barn have?"

Susan sighed, a little exasperated, "Six for horses, and we have another one set aside for a cow. We don't have one right now, but Jasper plans to get another one soon."

"I see you have four of the six stalls full. Is that two Suffolk Punches back there?"

"Good eye, Charlie. Jasper uses them to pull the supply wagon. That one's Polly and the other one is Anna. I know together that's Pollyanna, but that's Jasper's humor for you."

They had a good laugh at Jasper's expense, then Susan turned toward Charlie and took a step and stumbled. He reached out and caught her, stopping her fall well short of the ground. He then pulled her up to her feet. She collapsed into his arms, her face and breast pressed against his chest. She made no effort to back away and seemed to cling to him.

Charlie, his arms around her, looked down, stunned and confused, "Are... are you hurt?"

"No, I'm a little dizzy, or maybe a little clumsy."

Charlie enjoyed the smell of her hair until she placed her hands on his chest and slowly pushed herself away from him.

Charlie stammered, "Is...is it... hot in here to you? I feel flushed all over."

Susan purred, "I'm feeling hot myself. You're certainly strong and quick on your feet. Thanks, Charlie."

"Glad I was here to catch you," he said with a smile.

"Me too." The message in her voice said it all, and she didn't try to hide it. Charlie didn't mind.

They put Tony in his new home and left him with water, a bundle of hay, and a small ration of oats.

"I'll be back this evenin' to care for you, buddy. You enjoy an easy day."

Susan reached out and took Charlie's hand, "Come with me.

I'll show you your room."

They went back out the barn's double doors, which faced the back of the house, and walked around to what would be Charlie's new home. It was near the rear of the barn behind the side building that housed the motor car and could not be seen from the house. Susan unlocked and went through the door and into the room. She walked over and opened a window for more light. As Jasper had described, there was a bed, washbasin, and a three-drawer chest. There were also a table with an oil lamp on it and two chairs. The room was much bigger than Charlie had expected. It measured roughly fifteen by thirty feet, and it did not seem cramped even with the furniture.

Susan looked up into Charlie's eyes, batted hers, and almost whispered, "Will this do?"

Charlie wasn't sure at first if she was talking about the room or her.

"This room will be great, Susan. I'll have all I ever need here."

"I want to make sure you do." As she turned and headed to the door, her breasts had brushed firmly against his arm. She stopped in the doorway, looked back, and said, "Tell Jasper I'll have dinner ready at 5:30. You join us, okay?"

"I'll see ya then."

He walked to the door, looked out, and was mesmerized as Susan walked away, headed to the back door of their Victorian house.

Charlie's head spun from all that had happened in the last few minutes. This beautiful woman, about his age, who was married to his boss, was openly flirting with him. He had to admit he enjoyed the attention but was a little guilty about how she made him feel. Had he read her wrong? Could he misunderstand what just happened? Maybe, but not likely. But he would be careful until he figured everything out.

As Charlie walked back to the store, he looked at the Blackaby's house, thinking about Susan inside, and wondered what he could expect next. He cleared his mind as he walked through the back door of the store. As the door closed behind him, Jasper called out, "Come over here, let's get you started by giving you a tour of the floor and our storage room. In a well-run store, there is a place for everything. There is a reason for where we place things."

"You mean merchandise location matters in a store?"

"Oh, yes, it matters a lot. There are basic things every customer will need. Everyone needs flour, salt, sugar, and maybe some dairy items. Those we place at or near the back of the store. You want the customer to walk past other products they may want but not require. The customer will see them and often buy them. Chances are they did not think of them before they left home, but upon seeing them displayed in the store, they buy them."

Charlie thought back to all the times he'd gone to Foster's mercantile in Fort Sumner but didn't remember that store being laid out in a special way. "That happens?"

"Every day, and that's how a store makes its profit. You understand what profit means, don't you?"

"I think so; let me see if I can describe it. You buy something for a dime and sell it for twenty-five cents. The fifteen cents difference is profit."

"Charlie, there are other costs and issues involved, but that's basically true, and that tells me we aren't starting your business education from scratch."

Somebody walked in the front door.

"Anybody here?"

Jasper laughed and said, "Just us big business people. How are you, Bill?"

"Oh, I'm fine. I came in for some tobacco and papers."

"Well, we can fix you up. By the way, Bill, this is Charlie Kelly, my new clerk. Charlie, Sheriff Bill Connors."

Charlie offered his hand, "Pleased to meet ya, sir."

"Back at you, Charlie. And no reason for sir."

Jasper let the sale to the sheriff be a teaching opportunity, and then they went back to where they were.

Jasper continued telling Charlie more about how he ran the store and introduced him to more customers that came in until it was time to close for the day. They knew Susan would have dinner ready soon. As they walked to the house, Jasper said, "It's been a hot one here today. Must be over ninety-five. You did a good job on your first day, Charlie. I know I made the right decision in hiring you."

"Thank you, sir," Charlie replied as they headed up the path.

Jasper pulled out a handkerchief and mopped his forehead. "Yes, it's been a hot one today, that's for sure. A cold glass of sweet tea sure sounds good."

Charlie nodded and pointed at the creek. "I bet that'd feel real good on a hot day like today."

"It might. It's been years since I did anything like that. But the cool water does sound refreshing."

"Jasper, I think I may go for a swim later."

Susan had finished setting the table when the men walked in. They could smell the food from the front door, and it brought a smile to their faces.

"I hope you two are hungry because I have a big roast ready with all the fixings waiting for you."

Jasper replied, "That sounds great, Susan."

"It sure does, ma'am."

"Charlie, I've told you before to please call me Susan."

"Oh, right ma'am, I mean, Susan." Charlie looked at Jasper and smiled as if to say, I'm trying.

They sat at the table and began their feast. Charlie could see strained looks on the faces of Jasper and Susan. For some reason, tension filled the air. I hope it has nothing to do with me. Susan never misses a chance to smile and show attention my way.

After supper, Charlie went to his room. He put away his things and sat on the bed, thinking of what had happened earlier. He sat for a while thinking about how Susan openly flirted with him and then how later he enjoyed learning about Jasper's store. Charlie wondered, *why does life have to be so full of conflicting feelings?* He got up and went and checked on Tony, refilled his water, and put a little more in the feed bin. It was late, and Charlie knew he wouldn't get to sleep in his hot room and decided to take a walk down to the creek.

He walked behind the barn and headed directly down to the creek bank. The moon was full, and the moonlight filtering through the trees allowed him to see a path to follow. As he approached the creek, there was a splash and a giggle. He stopped and remained still, only partially hidden by the bushes along the path.

Charlie stood in a trance on the trail with no place to hide and unable to look away as Susan stepped out of the water. She wore a pair of bloomers over her legs but was nude from the waist up, and she unabashedly looked directly at Charlie. The light of the full moon highlighted the curves of her ample breasts and glistened off drops of water on her skin. Her waist was so tiny compared to her hips that Charlie thought he could wrap his hands around it with ease. The vision took his breath away.

Susan said, "I knew it had to be you. I could see you coming in the moonlight."

"Susan, should you be out here alone? You're naked."

"I've got my drawers on, and nobody ever comes out here, well, now except you."

She stepped closer to Charlie. "I can't believe you're here, but I'm so glad you are. I have things I need to say, and you might too."

"Huh, what?" His attention was focused entirely on her breasts. They were the most tantalizing things he had ever seen.

Laughing, she took a finger and gently raised his chin as she said, "Charlie, look up here, we have some things we need to talk about, don't we?"

He mumbled, "I guess… maybe… like what?"

With no hesitation, she said, "I think you're charming, handsome, and I find myself drawn to you like nothing or no one ever before."

Charlie sighed, "Well… uh… I'd be lying if I didn't admit the same thing is happening with me, towards you, but you're married to Jasper."

"Yes, but what you don't know is that the marriage has become more of a business partnership than a warm, loving, intimate relationship. I think any woman wants to be loved and to be the focus of her man. Jasper's mind is somewhere else. I'm never fulfilled as his wife or as a woman."

Charlie was more astonished by her forthrightness than at

her beauty and trembled with the desire to take her in his arms, but he stepped back and said, "Let's be straight with each other. Does that mean I'm a man for you tonight? I'm not interested in that with any woman."

She started to slap him, stopped, and said, "Maybe I deserved that, or at least something like that. But I haven't tried to hide the passion you stir in me, especially when we've been alone. I'm truthful with you when I say you're the first man to ever affect me like this."

Charlie thought for a moment, then said, "A part of me wants to hear you say that, but you're another man's wife. He's a man I respect and one who has offered me a job opportunity I want to keep. Susan, I'm drawn to you as well. I've never had feelings this strong stir inside me before."

She stepped forward and embraced him tightly. He could feel her shake with emotion. He hesitated at first, then almost involuntarily, he hugged her back, loving the touch of her soft skin against his rough ranch hands. She stepped back slightly and guided his right hand to her left breast. As big as his hand was, he could not cover half of her breast and could not stop himself from caressing it ever so gently.

She whispered, "I want you and will accept whatever we can have. We'll come to understand, in time, what all this means to us. Okay, Charlie?"

He looked down into her dark eyes, smiled, and said, "I'll be selfish and say I can live with this. Are you going to get dressed now?"

She smiled wickedly, "Maybe later."

Chapter Eight
September 1917

As Charlie walked in the back door of the store, Jasper said, "Charlie, get over here."

Charlie teased a little and put his hands up as he said, "What's up?"

Jasper laughed and waved Charlie over. "I want you to start doing some of our articles and ads for the local paper. People see you as part of the store and the community, and I think you need to use some of that high school education."

"You want me to write for the paper?" Charlie asked.

"You won't be writing newspaper articles, we will leave that to the editor and his journalists," Jasper chuckled. "But you know that I put in ads about our products, and sometimes include tips about using new products."

Charlie nodded. He'd seen Jasper doing that plenty of times and had read a few of them at Jasper's urging. "I may have gotten good grades, but I was never what you'd call an author."

Jasper waved that concern away. "You'll do fine. This isn't the New York Times. It's not even the Oklahoma City Times." He chuckled at his joke. "I'll give you some of my old articles and you can use them as an example.

"Well, if this is what you want me to do, I'm game," Charlie said.

"Good. It should be quiet this morning, so you can get started. I'm gonna go take an inventory in the back."

Charlie was writing some notes for his first article when the bell on the front screen door alerted him to a customer's arrival. He looked up and saw Susan walking toward him, "Good morning, Sweetheart, where's Jasper?"

"He's in the storeroom. Are ya out shoppin'?"

"I ordered a new dress at the shop next door, and I'm gonna check and see if it has come in. See ya later, I hope?" She leaned down and kissed Charlie on the lips.

Charlie leaned back in shock and looked toward the back. "Aren't you worried he'll see?"

"You know how cute you are when you're nervous, Sweetheart?" She gave him another kiss. She turned and headed out of the store, leaving Charlie to sit there, amazed at her boldness, and liking the secret thrill it gave him.

* * *

Charlie and Susan had been frequently meeting in the evening at the creek bank, or in the barn, or wherever they could. They shared intimate details about their lives with each other as freely as they shared their bodies. Charlie told Susan about his family, growing up in Oklahoma, living in New Mexico, and about his father and what had brought him back to Oklahoma. Susan shared that she was the only child of a businessman in Kansas City. He learned that Jasper had been married before and that Susan was only twenty-three, and this was her first marriage. As summer passed into fall, they fell deeply in love with each other.

One evening in September as they sat along the creek bank, Charlie sensed a problem within Susan. She continually rocked back and forth and was tugging at her hair. She turned and looked at Charlie and said, "Charlie, I love you deeply, but you need to understand that I love Jasper too, for the good life he has given me. But I need more. Because of you, I know what intimacy and passion are. I can't wait to see you when we are apart. I feel your passion for me with each embrace."

She grasped Charlie's hands and pulled them to her chest. "Jasper's never intimate with me, and that tells me that while he may care about me, there is no true love and passion. There is seldom a day that he does not mention his first wife. Now more than ever, I'm convinced he is not over the loss of her."

"Did she leave him?"

Susan released his hands and brought her knees up to her chin as she answered, "In the worst way possible. She died from consumption after a long illness."

Charlie's eyes widened, "Oh my, that is terrible. I didn't know anythin' about that."

As she stared at the water, she said, "He may never share that with you, and it is a wall he has created between us. It may be something he never intended, but it's there."

Charlie leaned in and put his arm around her shoulder, smiled, and said, "I want to be here for you. I hope I can always put a smile on your face. When you need a shoulder, mine will always be here."

"I know, my sweetheart. Your smile and embrace are what I need." She continued to look at the creek and then grinned at Charlie.

Charlie smiled and said, "Let's go for a swim." He stood, and took off his shirt, pants, and drawers.

Susan looked up and sighed, "Okay, but first, you need to know, your love fills that void." She smiled and stood up. "And your body looks like a six-foot-four-inch Greek statue with those huge shoulders and rippling chest muscles." She ran a hand across his chest. "It doesn't hurt that I get lost in your strong arms." She let her hands rove over his strong biceps and tilted her head back. "Yes, I think I'm ready to wash this sadness away with a swim."

Charlie grinned, "I guess you like my looks almost as much as I like yours. Can we swim now?"

"Uh, huh." She gave him a firm kiss and let her hands drift lower on his body.

* * *

The next day at the store, Jasper asked Charlie to take the wagon and pick up an order in Pauls Valley. Susan walked in as Charlie was about to leave to get the wagon, and Jasper said, "I would like to go with Charlie. Can you stay and watch the store, Susan?"

Susan smiled and said, "I can, and you guys enjoy your time together."

Charlie went to the barn and hitched the horses to the wagon. He drove it around to the front of the store.

As he waited for Jasper, he thought, *I wonder what's on Jasper's mind. Does he suspect something? Maybe, he only wants out of the store for an afternoon.*

A few miles out of town, Jasper asked, "Are you glad you stayed with us?"

Shifting in his seat and looking straight ahead at the horses' rise and fall, Charlie said, "I am, Jasper; you have been a wonderful friend and mentor, and I doubt I can ever repay you for that."

Patting his palms on his knees, Jasper said, "I want you to feel like you can stay with us as long as you want. I know Susan has grown as close to you as I have. I'm grateful for that. She does not get as much of my time and attention as she deserves. Has she given you our backgrounds?"

Charlie hesitated, then said, "What do ya mean? She has shared some things. Is there anything you want me to know she may not have said?"

Jasper's face grew soft as he began to speak, "I was a widower when we met. My first wife died in 1911 from a long bout with consumption. I was devastated."

Charlie sighed, "I can't imagine that kind of loss."

Composing himself, Jasper continued, "We had been married for over twenty years. She came west with me from Charleston back in 1889." He paused and brushed a tear from his right cheek.

Charlie asked, "Are ya okay?"

"I'm fine." He took a deep breath before continuing, "I met Susan on a business trip to Kansas City in 1913, and we were married a year later. She was nineteen years old, and I was forty-eight. I know that age difference raised a lot of eyebrows when I brought her home with me. After all, I was a former Mayor and I'm still considered a leader around town. But Charlie, my feelings of loss for my first wife and the pressures of this growing business are all-consuming. I'm not able to give Susan the time, attention, and closeness she needs. I can't give her the friendship and intimacy of a husband and wife. Do you understand what I'm saying, Charlie?"

"I... uh... I believe I do, sir. May I ask, have you shared this with Susan?"

Jasper lowered his head as he said, "I have probably discussed this subject better with you now than I ever have with her. That's a terrible shame, isn't it?"

Charlie leaned over and placed his hand on Jasper's shoulder, "She deserves to hear it from you. The little I know; I think that would answer some questions for her."

Looking into Charlie's eyes, "Has she said anything?"

"Enough that I know she is lonely sometimes."

With tears showing, he reached over and squeezed Charlie's arm and said, "Thanks, and please be there for her in whatever way she needs. I may never be able to give her that. How can a young man be so full of compassion and wisdom?"

Charlie smiled at Jasper in response to the kind comment. Then for the next few minutes, all he could think about was what Jasper had said. *Is he giving his blessing for Susan and me to be lovers? Is it that he already knows that we are?*

For a while, they continued to talk about business, fishing, and hunting until Pauls Valley came into view.

* * *

Susan continued to watch the store after they returned while Jasper and Charlie inventoried and unloaded the wagon. As he was working, Charlie tried more than once to talk with Susan. It never worked out that they could be alone. Jasper finally told Susan she could go home when they got far enough that Charlie could finish with the wagon while Jasper counted out the register and closed for the night. As they approached the house, Jasper said, "I bet tonight is leftovers. Susan was at the store almost all day."

"Sounds good to me, boss, and if it's more pork roast, you won't git any argument from me. I want to check on Tony and wash up. I'll be in shortly."

Jasper smiled and said, "Okay, see you soon."

Charlie put out some feed in Tony's stall and checked the trough for water. "Tony. It's been days since we went for a ride. Tomorrow's Sunday, let's go somewhere tomorrow whatcha say, buddy?"

Charlie stopped off at the pump, washed up, and then went in the back door to the house. Susan was standing in the kitchen. She reached over and patted Charlie's shoulder and said, "Ready for some more pork roast?"

With no hesitation, "Yep, are there carrots and taters leftover, too?"

"Absolutely, go sit down, and I'll have it on the table in no time."

* * *

Later that night, Charlie wandered out to the creek. Susan wasn't there, but he sat for a while to think about his conversation with Jasper. He was deep in thought and was startled when a soft voice said, "Hey, where are you?"

"Over here," he called out.

Susan appeared and sat down next to him, "What are you doing out here, all alone?"

He hesitated and then said, "I... uh... was thinkin' about today. I wanted to tell you about my conversation with Jasper since we got back but didn't have a chance earlier."

She leaned against him and said, "I could tell that you had something on your mind. Does it have to do with me and Jasper and where our relationship is? What he's prepared to give me? What does he want or need of you?"

Charlie's eyes widened, and his jaw went slack as he said, "Yes, to all of that. He talked with you?"

"Yes, we talked."

"It's like he knows we care about each other."

Susan nodded, "He knows, but I don't know if he understands how deeply I feel for you. He does appreciate I get a lot of my loneliness and needs satisfied by our time together."

Charlie looked out across the water and said, "I figured he must know we spend time together some evenings. He must know we are together now."

Susan joined Charlie's stare at the creek and said, "Charlie, I think at this point, he needs our relationship as much as we want it. Like I've said before, he and I have been existing for some time more as business partners. Much longer than you've been in the picture. Now, he needs it so long as I don't leave him for you. He is, after all, a past Mayor of Elmore City and a pillar of the community. He'll expect us to be discreet so he can keep up appearances with a wife and a successful business." With tears in her eyes, she said, "He has used me to host his business parties and create a certain image, and maybe I'm using him in some ways too. This marriage doesn't work for Jasper or me without you, Charlie. Now he's admitted his desires to us, and we certainly have ours."

They turned and looked intently into each other's eyes and smiled broadly. Charlie put his arms around Susan and pulled her close. He lost himself for a moment in the fragrance of her hair and the warmth of her body. He sighed, "Sweetheart, we've been given the freedom to love each other and to express it."

"You're right, within reason, and if there is anything I'm sure about, it's us."

Charlie said, "It's hot, ready for a dip?"

Off came her clothes, and she went into the creek without answering.

Chapter Nine
October 1917

With a big smile and a wave, Jasper said, "Charlie, I'm going to the bank, and then meeting Ben and Dr. Noble at Flo's for lunch. You've got the store for the next several hours."

"That's fine, Jasper, have a good lunch."

Charlie had been in Elmore City for three months. Jasper now treated him more like family, and the relationship was beginning to feel like father and son. They both seemed comfortable with that arrangement. They had worked hard and prepared for what looked like a big Fall harvest for Garvin County and the store.

There was a knock at the back door.

"Hey, somebody, open the door."

Charlie unlocked the door, "Sorry, I didn't know Jasper had locked it."

Susan whispered, "I thought I would surprise you with lunch."

"Jasper is having lunch at Flo's with Ben and Sam."

Susan grinned, "I know, so, it's just us; that's okay, isn't it?"

"Of course."

The store was quiet, as many Tuesdays were. So, they sat down at a table near the back, partially hidden from the front door. There was a bell on the front screen door to alert them to a customer's arrival.

Susan reached up, took hold of his collar, and pulled his face down to hers. She kissed him long and passionately.

"Good afternoon, big guy, and how is your day going?"

"Better now, and yours?"

"I'd say it's improving."

Susan sat with her back to the front of the store, smiled, and began unbuttoning her blouse. She pulled the blouse open to reveal she was not wearing anything under it.

Charlie asked, "Ain't we bein' a little risky, darlin'?"

"Oh, I can button it back up!"

"No, this is fine, thank ya."

With a wink, she said, "I know you need to watch the store too, but I figured you might be able to do two things at once."

She opened the bag of sandwiches she had brought with her, and they enjoyed each other's company for a while.

* * *

That night after dinner, Charlie went down to the creek as had become his habit. It wasn't long before Susan arrived.

"Hey, Sweetheart, want some company?" she said.

"Love it."

"Jasper went back to the store for a few hours. He needed to prepare an order to send to Oklahoma City. He said for me not to expect him until bedtime."

He looked up at her, "Good; then we'll have a few hours together.

"Charlie, does it seem like he is finding ways to give us more time together?"

"You know, it sure does."

"I'm glad because I love you, and the more time he gives us to express it, the better."

She sat next to him, he pulled her close, and they enjoyed the quiet.

Susan's face became ashen, and her lips trembled as she said, "Charlie, do you smell something burning?"

"Yes, I do, Honey, whattaya suppose?"

Charlie stood up and ran toward the path that ran between the house and Jasper's store. He looked toward the house and didn't see anything, then looked toward the town. He could see flames dancing between the trunks of the trees in the direction of Main Street.

Charlie looked back, "Susan, it's the store!"

Susan jumped up and joined Charlie. She cried, "Jasper!"

He ran up the path, turned toward the store, and saw that it had become engulfed by the fire. He ran around toward the front and when he got to the street, he saw that the volunteer fire department had arrived. They were laying out a hose from the fire truck, as two men worked the pump jack. The wind swirled and carried sparks and ash up into the air, threatening other buildings.

Charlie hollered, "How kin I help?"

Fire Chief Andrews said, "Have ya seen Jasper?"

"No, ain't he the one who sent for you?"

Susan caught up with them and looked around frantically. "Where's Jasper!"

Andrews said, "We don't know, Mrs. Blackaby."

"He's inside, Jasper!" She darted toward the store heedless of the fire. "Oh, Jasper!"

Charlie chased her down and pulled her away from the flames that were white-hot now.

Ben and his wife arrived, and they took charge of Susan. Charlie said, "I'm gonna try and get in through the back door." Chief Andrews nodded as they started to finally get water from the hose to spray on the fire. It was like a pitiful trickle when they needed a flood.

Charlie ran around the back, ignoring the heat that was already searing his skin. Charlie was within ten feet of the door when an explosion ripped the door off its hinges. The fire had reached the firearms, gunpowder, and ammunition that Jasper had stocked up within the store in anticipation of the fall hunting season.

Charlie was knocked to the ground by the force of the explosion, and two firemen assisted him to his feet and brought him back to Main Street.

The fire crew was eventually able to knock down the fire before it spread to other businesses, beyond the dress shop that shared a wall with the Blackaby store. But the store itself was full of the perfect fuel for a fire and was in ashes before anything could be done to save it.

After everything was controlled, a fireman came over to the Chief and said, "We've found what appears to be Jasper's body amid the ashes with a broken lantern near his body. It may be a tragic accident."

Charlie shook his head as he stood next to the Chief. He turned and saw Susan in the street visibly shaken. He walked over to comfort and console her.

He said, "Let's get you back to the house. There's nothing for you to do here."

Susan melted into his arms, "Was Jasper in there?"

"The Fire Chief said they found a body in there."

She leaned on Charlie as they walked back to the house. Dr. Noble arrived at the house immediately thereafter. He found Susan in the parlor in Charlie's arms, trying to hold back tears. He opened his bag and took out a small bottle. He poured out a tablet and knelt on one knee and offered it to Susan. "Susan, take this. It'll help you relax and get some sleep."

Susan said, "I'm not taking anything. I need a clear head for what's coming. Charlie, can you..."

She fell into Charlie's lap and wept.

Charlie squeezed her shoulder, looked at Dr. Noble, and said, "I'll stay here with her all night. You might stop back by in the morning."

* * *

The following day Susan had slept all night in Charlie's lap, and now he gently moved her enough to get off the sofa. It was shortly after dawn, and he could still smell the remnants of the fire. Looking out over the veranda and Rock Creek, he pondered, *What next? Jasper is gone. Susan seems devastated, and I know I'm sad about all this. There's no business to support Susan or me now, so what do we do? We love each other, but what will this turmoil do to our future together?* So many questions.

Charlie went into the kitchen and made some coffee for them.

The coffee was ready as Susan walked into the kitchen, "You've made coffee already?"

"Yes, here's yours. I'll try and dish up some eggs and biscuits."

Susan sat at the table and took a sip of the coffee, but her gaze was staring far off into the distance.

Before Charlie could get the oven started for the biscuits, there was a knock at the front door.

Charlie said, "I'll git it, just sit still."

Susan broke her far-off stare and looked at her disheveled and soot-stained clothes. "I look awful. I don't want anyone to see me like this."

"Ya look fine, but okay."

A few minutes later, Charlie returned to the kitchen. "The County Sheriff wants to talk to ya. He is willin' to meet ya in an hour at Flo's. I said we'd be there."

Her face reddened, and her nostrils flared as she said, "Damn it, everyone needs to leave me alone."

Patting her shoulder, "Susan, we'll git through this. I'll be with ya all the way."

Susan sniffed and wiped her nose. She said, "I know you will, Sweetheart. But Jasper's gone, and I didn't get to say goodbye."

* * *

Susan and Charlie arrived at Flo's twenty minutes early, but the Sheriff was already there, as were Sam and Ben. Other than Flo, the rest of the place was empty. When they entered, Flo immediately came up to Susan, and the two women hugged for nearly a minute, Flo whispering her condolences and rubbing Susan's back the whole time. The Sheriff sat at a table with Sam and Ben. Susan and Charlie joined them, and Flo provided them all with coffee. She locked the front door and put up the "Closed" sign.

Sheriff Connors began, "Susan, we want to say how sorry we are. We considered Jasper a friend and are here to support you in any way. I have been over to the store and started my investigation with the help of the Fire Chief. I have a preliminary opinion and report to share with you."

Susan replied, "Thank you for your kind words. Jasper considered each of you a close and dear friend. I'm sure he is comforted that I have you to help me. Charlie and you folks will be my rock to lean on. I assume you want to share the information you have gathered?"

"Yes, and it means I have a good amount of work ahead of me. I found the cash register open." He looked at both Susan and Charlie and asked, "Would it have been normal for Jasper to leave it open overnight?"

Susan answered, "No, he was a businessman who always closed the register before closing up. I know some disagree with that philosophy, saying to leave it open at night so a thief would know it's empty. But not Jasper. There would have been money in it until he closed it out and come home for the night."

Charlie added, "I agree. When he was teaching his methods of running the store, he emphasized that point. Although he had already been home for dinner when he went back, he might have opened it again for some reason, or someone may have forced him to open it."

"The cash register, as I said, was open, and it was empty. It appeared to the doctor and me that someone hit Jasper over the head. That person stole money and possibly other things and set fire to cover up any evidence of a crime."

Charlie said, "We're talkin' murder?"

The Sheriff said, "The evidence I see tells me it was not an accident."

Susan cried as she said, "This is horrible. I can't believe there's violence like this here in this small town. I'm struggling to grasp how this could happen."

Charlie said, "How can I help ya with this, Sheriff?"

Connors said, "I appreciate that, but we'll do a thorough investigation, and I promise we'll not leave any stone unturned, Susan. Whoever did this will be brought to justice. Charlie, you stay focused on Susan and give her all the support you can."

Ben said, "I know you aren't prepared now to think about the business and the issues that will need addressing. I'll start working those for you, so when you are ready, something can be ready for you."

She said, "Ben, work with Charlie to get those things settled. I'm willing to sign what I need to, but I need you two working them for me, please."

Sam said, "Gentlemen, she needs your help, and I'm glad she understands that. Susan, I'll come to check on you later today. I recommend you go home and rest."

* * *

The day after meeting with the Sheriff and the other men Charlie moved out of the room next to the barn and into the house. Susan had insisted, saying she wanted him close by in case she needed anything, and because she needed someone to lean on in her sorrow. Charlie moved into the guest room, and Susan spent her nights there. For several days after the fire, they were less intimate than they had been before the tragic events, Susan telling Charlie that she only needed his strong presence. She would lay on the bed and would cry herself asleep folded within Charlie's comforting embrace.

Two days after the fire, as Charlie was cleaning up the ruins of Jasper's store, the Sheriff and Doctor Noble came by to discuss their findings so far, and to talk about the funeral arrangements. The Sheriff gave a list of items they'd found on Jasper's body, which hadn't been much.

"Anything missing there that you can tell?" he asked Charlie. "I'm hoping you can help us out, so we don't have to bother Susan with this terrible duty.

Charlie reviewed the list and said, "I think that's everything, but I don't see his pocket watch listed. He carried it with him all that time, and he'd always pull it out and wind it at noon each day when the clock at city hall chimed. I know it had an inscription on it as Jasper said that Susan had given it to him as a present."

Sheriff Connors thanked him, and then Doctor Noble discussed the funeral for Jasper. Again, Charlie worked out the details, and on a cool, overcast afternoon four days after the fire the entire town came out to pay their last respects. Charlie stood nearby Susan all day as people came up in a steady stream to give their respects and tell her how much Jasper had meant to Elmore City. Charlie was taken again not only by her beauty but by her grace and charm as she endured what was a painful time for her.

They walked home from the cemetery and paused at the

creek. Susan took Charlie's hand in hers. "Charlie, Sweetheart, you have been such a dear friend and companion to me these past few days."

"I'm only doin' what's right," Charlie replied as he squeezed her hand.

They continued up to the house, and once inside Susan turned and gave Charlie a long kiss. He was a bit taken aback after the lack of interest Susan had shone in being intimate since the fire.

He pulled away and put his hands on her shoulders. "Is this what you want? If you need more time to mourn—"

"Charlie, I've mourned enough. I loved Jasper, and he loved me, in his own way, but I've told you before we hadn't been intimate in a long time. I am ready to get on with my life, and that means that I want you." She gave him another kiss, then pulled him along to the guest room.

* * *

Three days later Charlie entered the parlor and found Susan reading. He said, "Can we talk a minute?"

"Of course, Sweetheart."

"Sheriff Connors just told me they caught a man in Pauls Valley, trying to pawn a pocket watch with "Love, Susan" on the back. The pawnshop owner was on the lookout for it because of the bulletin listing the missing items from the shop that the Sheriff spread across the county. Sheriff Connors arrested the guy, and he has already admitted his guilt. Honey, you can have a little closure now."

Susan said, "I guess that does help with that part of all this, but we still have so much other stuff to deal with."

"Ben and I have worked some every day on all the store's accounts, settled the debts owed, and we're ready to provide ya with a clear picture of where ya stand financially. Ben asked me to arrange a meetin' when you're ready."

"I'm ready, so let's meet tomorrow."

Susan, Charlie, and Ben met the following morning at the bank conference room. Ben had Molly there to take notes on the discussion.

Charlie took charge, "Ben, I believe ya have everythin' ready, so please provide Susan with what she needs to know."

Ben nodded, then stated, "Susan, you're financially in an excellent place. Charlie and I have gone over every document multiple times, and Jasper has left you an estate worth over a million dollars. As his banker, I knew your assets went beyond what you had here in Elmore City. Jasper had some stocks I was unfamiliar with stored in the safety deposit box here at the bank. He owned a substantial amount of stock in Standard Oil, which transferred to you after his death."

Susan said, "I had no idea. I'm sure Jasper purchased that stock before we married. Charlie, you've known about all of this for several days but didn't tell me about it? I know Jasper required me to let him handle all the business regarding the store and any other financial things as well. But you could have said something."

Charlie looked down at the table, took a deep breath, looked up, and smiled, "Because of the magnitude of the value of the stock, I thought it best you hear that from Ben. He could and did verify everything as your banker before sharing it with you."

She quietly nodded that she understood, but he could see questions written all over her face.

* * *

That evening Charlie was in the barn brushing Tony when Susan walked in. She sat on a hay bale nearby and said, "We need to talk. Is this a good time?"

"Of course, what's on your mind?" He scratched Tony behind the ears. He'd been thinking a lot since they had left the bank that morning.

"You know that I'm over the shock of Jasper's death," she said with a coquettish smile, "and that I did love Jasper, but never in the way that a woman should love a man. Certainly not the love a person should have for your life's partner. I also know that's the kind of love I have for you."

Charlie looked at Susan's beautiful eyes that she had fixed on him. He cared deeply for her, but at that moment, as he had all day, he was trying to come to grips that Susan was now one of the wealthiest people in Oklahoma. *How can I fit into her world as a $30 a month cowboy? And without Jasper here what's her reason for living there in Elmore City?* Everything seemed more confusing to him now than it had after they'd left the bank. He needed some space to think. He wanted to live his dream, to get on Tony and ride north to the 101, but he didn't see how Susan would fit into that dream.

He wasn't sure about anything right now, or what he should say, so he said, "I love you, too."

Susan stood up from the hay bale and pulled Charlie to her, giving him a passionate kiss. As they rolled in the hay, Charlie's mind continued to be confused about what he should do.

* * *

Several nights later, Charlie sat on the creek bank at about midnight. It was still hot, even though the calendar showed it was October 11th. He sat there in his drawers, feeling quite comfortable. He had considered taking a swim before going to bed.

Susan arrived and sat beside him, "What's on your mind?'

He looked out over the water, "Not much of anythin', and yet lately my mind spins in confusion."

She put her hand on his shoulder, "I could feel that. We haven't talked or even been together for days. Sweetheart, that's not right."

He looked up at the stars, "I've missed ya; that's a fact. I needed some space."

"Is that why you've been taking long rides with Tony? I was worried you were avoiding me."

"No, but I think better when I'm in the saddle."

"And what have you been thinking about?"

Charlie shrugged. "You. Me. Us. And what comes next." He was afraid to tell her what he'd been thinking about on his long rides with Tony. How he'd found himself each day riding a bit farther north like the Miller 101 had a rope tied around him and was pulling him there. He'd returned each day to the house, but his mind was still thinking about the 101. And he didn't know how to tell Susan what he felt.

Touching his arm and laying her head on his shoulder, she said, "I guess you have had a lot on your mind. But Sweetheart, I know you're my everything."

He looked down into her eyes and said, "And you're mine." He put his arm around her, "Did you know I would be here?"

"I didn't know, but I hoped you would be. I wanted to swim and be in our place tonight. She had worn her favorite robe and brought a blanket. She stood, laid the blanket across the grass, and dropped her robe. In the moonlight, her nakedness glistened.

"You look beautiful."

"Lay with me, darlin'. I truly need you tonight."

Chapter Ten
October 1917

Several mornings later, Charlie was up before dawn and prepared breakfast. Standing at the stove, Charlie looked over and saw Susan in the doorway. She said, "Sweetheart, you spoil me. Breakfast again and with my favorite biscuits."

"Can't a fella treat his lady special sometimes?"

"Oh yes, and this lady sure appreciates it."

"Well, have a seat at the table, and I'll dish everything up for us." He poured coffee into her cup, bent down, and kissed her.

As she enjoyed her last piece of bacon, Susan smiled at Charlie and said, "I've been thinking over the last few days. We should sell out here in Elmore City and move to Kansas City. My father is there, and he wants me to return and work in his company. I'm sure he'll value what you learned here with Jasper and find you a good position with a future."

Charlie's mouth fell open, and he stuttered, "Wh… wh… what? You've never mentioned anything about going to Kansas City."

"You know that's where I was living when I married Jasper, and that's home for me. We can have everything we want there."

Charlie leaned back in his chair, folded his arms across his chest, his head cocked to the side as he looked at Susan, "Maybe, but remember when I arrived here in Elmore City, I was following a dream of becoming a top ranch hand up at the Miller's 101. I haven't stopped considering that as my future yet."

"But Sweetheart, even Jasper saw that you're capable of so much more than that. I'm not saying that a cowboy can't be special, but over the last few months, I know you were beginning to see there can be so much more to your future than what a cowboy's life offers you."

"Yeah, well, ya've been through college, and it appears the family that raised ya had a lot more to start with than I've ever experienced. I'm not in a position to give ya that life, and maybe this sounds stupid, but I believe a man needs to provide for his wife and kids. Can ya see that?"

Susan pulled at her robe and rubbed the back of her neck as she said, "I don't see why that should be a concern for us. I love you for the man I've come to know, although you surprise me here. I have no reason to stay here in Elmore City. Kansas City makes more sense to me right now than a bunkhouse on some ranch, so we need to decide what our future holds for us, don't we?"

Charlie leaned forward, "I can see you're frustrated with me and maybe a little angry. I'll admit, I'm not the man that arrived here three months ago. I do see the world differently now, and a lot of that I owe to you. I'm curious about things I never thought about before, but I still have this fascination with becoming part of this world at the 101 Ranch. I can see that you should go to Kansas City and be with your father and return to that world and chase your dreams. But I need to stay true to my dreams as well."

Susan's face turns red with anger, "So you're saying that being with me isn't part of your future now. That these last few months have been a lie, and you don't love me and never did?"

"That's not it at all. I can see that I'm not making any sense to ya. Susan, I think we both need to git away from each other for a while. I think we should live apart for a while, say at least six months to a year. Ya can tell me how to reach ya in Kansas City, and ya can reach me at the 101 if'n I git on there. I promise to let ya know how to reach me if I don't."

Susan began to sob, "Don't you want me? I thought you loved me. Has all this been a lie?"

Charlie took her in his arms and held her tight against his chest, "I do love and want ya, but Susan, I'm a cowboy. I'm a $30 a month kind of guy. I learned a lot from Jasper in these three months, but I've no idea if that'll make a difference down the road in Kansas City or anywhere but here in Elmore City. We've had Jasper and the store provide all we needed. We could be together on our creek bank and enjoy each other. But I need to know that we want and need each other for all the right reasons."

Susan pushed away and then slapped Charlie. He wasn't prepared for that and stumbled back as he said, "Holy shit, Susan. I'm not meaning to hurt ya. I'm tryin' to be reasonable."

She struggled to hold back tears as she said, "How can you be so stupid to think I would want you to join me and meet my father in Kansas City if you couldn't be successful and make us both have a happy life there. Together."

Looking down into her eyes red from crying, he stumbled for his thoughts "I git it that this may not be smart and for sure leavin' ya is the hardest thing I've ever done, but I want to chase my dream and understand this; we must keep in touch because I'm not prepared for ya to be outta my life."

With her chin high and nostrils flaring, Susan said, "Well, cowboy, I guess you need to hit the trail, don't you?"

After some convincing, Charlie got her address in Kansas City. They gave each other a final hug, her grip imploring him to change his mind and stay, his trying to tell her to wait, that he'd be back. Charlie climbed onto Tony then looked back over his shoulder and saw Susan on the steps with her head between her knees. He could see her shoulders move as she was racked by sobs.

With a heart filled with mixed emotions, Charlie gave Tony a squeeze of his legs and together they rode to the north.

* * *

Charlie had saved almost all the pay he'd received from Jasper, and now that he was leaving as Fall was turning toward Winter, it was a good thing because he had no job assured at the 101.

On his third day away from Elmore City, he rode into Shawnee at dusk. He was impressed at the size of the town. It was much bigger than Fort Sumner, and Elmore City combined. He decided to stay the night. He found a livery stable for Tony one block off

Main Street and two blocks from the Norwood Hotel, where he could enjoy dinner and a regular bed. Charlie and Tony would live it up a little tonight. He was given a room on the second floor where he cleaned up with running water from a tap. He marveled; this is one fancy place with running water, electricity, and a big feather bed. He opened up his bedroll and found his best shirt to put on and went down to the restaurant off the hotel lobby.

"Good evening, sir, and welcome to The Cattlemen's, right this way."

"Thanks."

"Will you be dining alone?"

"Yes, and can I have a table near the front windows?"

Charlie looked around the room at the splendor thinking, I guess this could have been my everyday life in Kansas City with Susan. White tablecloths, elegant, cushioned chairs, and the well-dressed people all made him question his jeans and boots. He wished he had wiped the dust off his boots back in his room. He self-consciously ran his hand along his jeans and realized how out of place he suddenly felt here. How out of place he'd have felt in Susan's world in Kansas City.

A well-dressed gentleman seated at the next table met his eyes. He asked, "First time at the Norwood, young man?"

"Yes, sir, this is grand."

"It is even to me, and I've been coming here since it opened. "I'm Claybourne Stephens. My friends call me Clay."

"Charles Kelly, my friends call me Charlie."

"What brings you to Shawnee?"

"I'm on my way to Miller's 101."

"That's quite a spread. Do you know the brothers, Joe, George, and Zack?"

"No, sir, I have never been to the ranch or met anyone associated with it."

"That's a mighty fine outfit. I knew their dad and the boys are keeping everything first-rate up there. What's your business with them if you don't mind my asking?"

"I want to find work there. I have always wanted to be a top hand at the 101. If you make it there, you'll know the cattle business about as well as anyone."

"I agree, although I'm pretty proud of my ranch hands and what they know. Have you ranching experience? You gotta be no more than your late teens."

"I've worked about five years part-time and a year or so full-time at the Cornerstone Ranch in eastern New Mexico. Four of those part-time years, I was in high school at Fort Sumner."

"You finished high school?"

"Yes, sir."

"Charlie, you can call me Clay, that is if we are to become friends."

Charlie's waiter arrived to take his order. "What can we prepare for you?"

"A T-bone, medium rare, baked potato, beans, and coffee."

Clay had finished his meal and was rising from his chair when he said, "Charlie, I have enjoyed this. I must send a wire to a business associate. Can we meet later in the lobby and continue our conversation over another cup of coffee?"

"It'd be an honor, Clay."

"Well then, I'll see you after you've finished your meal."

Charlie continued to enjoy the surroundings. Someone played piano in the corner of the room. It didn't sound anything like the one at the Pecos. He stood long enough to see that it must be one of those big fancy ones called a grand piano. It was a guess because Charlie had never seen one before. He shook his head. *This place is how the rich folks live, and I could get used to this. Was I as stupid as Susan said for not going with her?*

Charlie's steak dinner arrived soon and looked like a meal fit for a king. He finished eating and paid his bill. Charlie walked back into the lobby, where he found Clay Stephens seated near the massive glowing fireplace as he enjoyed a cigar.

"Sit down, Charlie. How was your steak?"

"One of the finest cuts of beef I think I've ever had."

With a chuckle, Clay said, "Glad to hear it; they get all their beef from me."

"They do? You mentioned ranch hands working for you earlier. Is your ranch nearby?"

"I own the Double Bar S. It's about sixteen miles east of Shawnee. I've got about five thousand acres there and run a thousand head on it."

"That's a sizeable ranch, Clay. You must have a lot of help to keep that place going."

"I do, and I have another ten thousand acres down near Wanette. Do you know where that is?"

"Yes, my dad grew up down around there."

"Does he still live down there?"

"No, he, mom, and the rest of my family have recently moved to Seminole County."

"Charlie, would you like a cigar?"

"No, I've never taken up smokin'. I do appreciate your offer."

"Let's talk some more about your plans. It sounded like you wanted to become more than just a wrangler. You want to learn the cattle business, is that right?"

"When I left home, my goal was to become a cowboy at the 101. I did have a dream to become one of their best hands. I also started readin' books in high school by big thinkers like Ralph Waldo Emerson and Orison Swett Marden about success and what it takes. After some time in Elmore City working for a businessman, I've changed some these last several months. I no longer want to limit myself to the cowboy life. It's okay, that—"

"Pardon my interruption, but who did you work for in Garvin County?"

"Jasper Blackaby; he owned a mercantile and was teaching me how to run it."

"I know Jasper, he was the mayor there for some time, and we met at the Capitol working together on some committees supporting the Governor. You were unhappy there with Jasper?"

Charlie hesitated a moment to gather his emotions. "Oh, no! He was a great man and mentor. I had a lot of respect for him. There was a fire that destroyed his store. The fire was set to cover up his murder."

"Damn it, when did this happen?"

"Back in September. I stayed until a few days ago to help his widow, Susan, get things settled. She is returnin' to Kansas City, where she's from, and I'm continuin' to go after what I want by headin' to the 101. Do you know Susan?"

"No, he mentioned her, of course, but I never had the pleasure. Jasper was one of the best business minds in the state, and if he was teaching you the business and you were paying attention, he gave you a real gift. I'm leaving on the train in a few hours. I wanted to get to know you better. It's nice to meet someone young chasing his dream."

"I'm happy to have met you. Where are you goin', if you don't mind me askin'?"

Clay gave a smile at the turnabout on the questioning. "Chicago, I have a meeting at the Chicago Mercantile Exchange next week. I'm meeting with the Armour Company there. We could do some of our business by wire or telephone, but this will be a huge deal, and I want to look those folks in the eye on this one. We can walk over and see the cattle futures market's status and agree on a price, then close the deal."

"I've no experience in any of that, but it sounds excitin'. I hope ya get what ya want to make the trip worth your time and effort."

"I will, and your words and questions this evening tell me you may understand things better than you think. I want to stay in touch with you. Can you give me how I can get ahold of you before we go our separate ways?"

Charlie said, "I don't know where I'll be, but if you can give me your information after I'm settled, I'll write ya."

"Happy to Charlie."

Back in his room, Charlie's mind retraced the events of the evening. He couldn't believe his luck meeting Jasper several months ago and now Clay tonight. Maybe this isn't a coincidence.

Chapter Eleven
October 1917

After a breakfast of three eggs, fried potatoes, bread, and chicken-fried steak, Charlie went to the livery and got Tony. They were out of town heading north right after sunrise.

"Tony, I sure hope your night was as good for you as mine was for me. I may have met a man who could be mighty important to me somewhere out in the future." He patted Tony's neck and looked at the landscape. "Will ya look at those colors, Tony. The trees are sure beautiful here, and those may be hackberries and redbuds there." He pointed for Tony's benefit, and the horse turned his head in that direction. "Ya know Tony; these hills would sure make for great cattle country here along the river."

By late afternoon the weather turned from a typical chilly fall day into early winter. The temperature dropped, and the light rain turned to snow.

I can't stop shivering. I'm so cold. "Tony, we better come to a town soon, or I'm in trouble."

In another hour, Charlie could see a town along the horizon and knew this needed to be where they would spend the night. At the south edge of town, he rode past a sign welcoming him to Perkins, Oklahoma: population 603. Charlie continued along the Main Street trail until Mathias Mercantile came upon his right. He tied Tony off to a post and went inside.

A tall, skinny, grizzled old man of a least sixty stood behind a massive wooden counter as he said, "Good afternoon, can I help you?"

Charlie sneezed, then said, "I'm lookin' for a hot cup of coffee and an idea where my horse and I might be able to git outta the weather for the night."

His German heritage showing in his accent, the clerk replied, "Gesundheit! Coffee, I have, but I don't have a room for ya. I did hear that Hank Cottrell, the foreman out at the Meehan Ranch, needed to hire a hand. Are ya lookin' for work?"

Through a cough and another sneeze, "I am, but my plan is for that to be up north at the Miller's 101. But for tonight, where can I find this Meehan ranch?"

"It's about four miles east of town and two north. Ya need to take the road you're on a block further north from the store, then head east. You'll come across Meehan Road. There's a sign out there, and that's where ya go north."

Charlie tipped his hat in thanks and headed back outside. As he and Tony rode away from the store, the weather got worse. The sun was nowhere in sight.

"Well, Tony, I'll git ya outta the weather as soon as I can."

I wasn't plannin' on takin' any work until I got to the 101, but if this Hank needs a hand, I think I might take it if offered. Another few months of experience and its bein' here in Oklahoma couldn't hurt. I don't know; right now, a warm bed and gittin' rid of these shivers come first.

Charlie found the Meehan sign and rode north. The weather was miserable. The sun was still nowhere in sight when the fancy main gate to the ranch appeared over the crest of one of the rolling hills. As Charlie rode past the gate, a sign swung in the wind, "Help Wanted," and his hopes rose as he spurred Tony to trot. "Yep, we might have found ourselves a place to stay awhile."

Charlie rode up to the house and climbed off Tony. He walked up to the door, took off his hat, and knocked. The door opened, and there stood a tall beautiful young woman about Charlie's age. Her long blonde hair flowed over her shoulders. She had curves that reminded him of Susan. Her partially buttoned shirt showed cleavage, and her blue trousers were snug fitting. She looked Charlie over from his boots to his tousled hair with eyes as big as saucers. Charlie looked down at her, smiled, stifled a sneeze, and said, "I'm Charlie Kelly. I understand ya have a need here for a ranch hand."

"I... I'm Tess, uh, Tess Meehan, and I think you're right; let me get my dad. Uh... please step in here and get outta the cold."

She went to the back of the house. A few minutes later, a man who stood less than six feet tall, in his mid-forties with thick dark brown hair, walked into the foyer with his hand out.

"I'm Bill Meehan, and my daughter says you're Charlie Kelly."

Charlie coughed as he said, "That's right, sir. Pardon the cough." He sneezed, then said, "I'm here to apply for a job. I understand you're hirin'."

"We are. Are you okay?"

Charlie tried to smile, "A little south of town, I started to chill."

Meehan said, "I want to have my foreman join us when we talk. Let's go back to the kitchen. Hank is back there, enjoying a cup of coffee, and we need to get something hot inside you too."

Charlie followed him through the dining room into a large kitchen with a table set up for eight. A handsome woman stood at the sink smiling.

Meehan said, "Charlie, this is my wife, Claudia. Claudia, Charlie Kelly."

She toweled off her hands, smiled, and offered a warm two-handed shake, and Charlie grinned as he said, "My pleasure, ma'am."

A big man with a handlebar mustache was seated near the end of the table. He rose as the owner and Charlie entered the room.

"Charlie Kelly, this is Hank Cottrell, my foreman. Hank, Charlie is here to discuss our need for a hand."

Hank's eyes looked him up and down as he offered his hand, "Good to meet ya, and we need someone with a fair amount of experience. Have you worked at ranches in the past?"

Charlie apologized as he coughed again, and he then described his Cornerstone and the Cullum years. He shared his schooling and the past few months in Elmore City.

Cottrell looked Charlie in the eye and said, "I'm likin' your story and the experiences you bring to us. I can put you on ridin' fences, feedin' cattle, and helpin' git us through the winter. You've come along at a good time."

Meehan said, "Hank, I agree with ya. Take Charlie and show him where he can bed down and board his horse. Have ya had supper, Charlie?"

"No, sir, I haven't. And it's only right that ya understand now that I'm hopin' to git on at the Miller's 101 as soon as I can. That has been a dream of mine for years."

"I get that, Charlie; we know the Millers, and their ranch is a real showplace. We do business with them from time to time, and their foreman and Hank go way back to when they were your age. Hank, bring him back up to the kitchen after you get him acquainted with the barn and bunkhouse. We need to get him fed. Tess, go tell the cookie about our new hand."

Charlie started coughing again, and Hank looked at Meehan and said, "I think we're gonna need to git him fed and in bed with a toddy of whiskey, lemon, and hot tea."

Meehan took Charlie by the arm, and looked at his eyes, "You're feelin' pretty rough, aren't you?"

Charlie nodded, "Yes, but I need to see to my horse, and some food sounds mighty good."

Hank and Charlie went around front and got Tony. They took him to the horse barn and put him in a stall. Hank said, "Looks like a fine piece of horseflesh ya have there. I'll get some feed."

Charlie asked, "Where do I store my saddle and tack?"

"Put them away in the tack room." He pointed across the barn past the stalls, "See the door over there?"

"Yep, I see it." As he carried his saddle and tack, Charlie chuckled then coughed as he looked back over his shoulder, "Tony, you best thank the man for your feed, now."

As they walked back toward the house, Charlie asked, "How big is this place? How big is the herd we'll be working?"

"The ranch has about 1000 acres, all in Payne County, and we work about 250 head of adult beef cattle. We have maybe another fifty head of new calves. We expect more to drop over the winter."

After eating, drinking the toddy prepared by Claudia, and before he and Hank went to the bunkhouse, Charlie found Tess in the front room, reading. He asked, "Could I bother you for some writing paper and a pencil? I need to write a letter to someone."

"Sure, and will you need an envelope and stamp?"

"Yes, if you have some. The stamps are three cents, and how much for the envelope?"

"I think we can afford to give them to ya, Charlie."

"Oh, thanks, and I meant no offense by that."

She grinned, "None taken; I'll be back in a minute."

Well, I handled that great. Tess probably thinks I'm an ignorant hayseed.

* * *

By lantern light in his bunkhouse bed, he wrote Susan.

Susan,

I'm writing from the Meehan Ranch outside of Perkins, Oklahoma. I got caught in an early snowstorm, and it appears I've come down sick with something. I'm sneezing and coughing, and these folks are giving me a warm place to stay. This evening ended up with me agreeing to stay on as a hand for the winter. The 101 will wait till at least Spring. I hope this finds you safe and doing well.

Sweetheart, I miss you very much, even though it hasn't been that long since we left each other. I wanted to let you know where I will be for the next few months. I know this letter may arrive in Kansas City before you do. Write and let me know you are safe and sound.

Warmly,
Charlie

* * *

Charlie's first night at the Meehan ranch was almost sleepless. When the rooster crowed, he wasn't ready to get out of bed. He tried to roll over and go back to sleep, but the noise created by the other hands wouldn't allow it.

After the place quieted down, he sat on the edge of his bed, allowing his aching head to clear when the door opened, and in walked Hank. He said, "Charlie, are ya gonna make it to breakfast?"

"I think so, but I'm feelin' kinda weak. I don't think I got two hours of sleep last night. The coughin' has stopped, but I'm still not any good."

Hank walked over a put his right hand on Charlie's shoulder, "Come up to the house as soon as ya can, and we'll chat a while over coffee and biscuits and gravy."

"Will do, Boss."

"Boss is my old friend; you call me Hank."

"Got it. I'll be up there shortly."

Tess greeted Charlie as he walked into the main house's kitchen, "Good morning, Charlie. How do you want your eggs cooked?"

"Over easy, Miss Meehan."

"Whoa, now. It's gonna be Tess or we're not gonna get along at all. And we've got bacon, sausage, or ham. What'll it be?"

He gave her a sheepish grin, "Tess, I'll have a little of all three if that's okay?"

"You bet it's okay."

She brushed against Charlie as she carried a platter of meats and a carafe of coffee to the table, "Help yourself, cowboy."

Charlie grinned at her, then took a seat across from Hank and poured coffee in a cup already waiting on the table.

Hank said, "Good to see that grin. I guess you'll make it through the day."

Charlie said, "I hope so, but I don't like missin' a day of work."

"You won't, this first day was gonna be gittin' ya settled, and I wanted some time to talk to ya about what Bill and I have planned for the winter months."

Tess brought Charlie's plate over and placed it in front of him. As she reached across from the other side of the table, her blouse opened enough to give Charlie another lovely view of Tess's assets.

Wow! Tess has curves that remind me of Susan, and she doesn't seem to mind lettin' me have a look. I like lookin', but I'm not....

Charlie gathered his thoughts and said, "Hank, I'd like ya to tell me about the ranch and your plans for the winter."

Hank said, "What I had in mind for you was to use those skills you mentioned last night about what you did for Bob Nash at the Cullum. I called him last night, and he said you did some excellent work on a corral. He said it's better than it was before the damage the bulls did."

Charlie hadn't known that the Cullum's had gotten a telephone installed, or that the Meehan's had one too. It certainly made checking up on a fellow easier. "I'd be happy to do whatever ya need. Will ya want me horseback some too?"

"Of course, but we planned to redo our corrals and add some storage buildings around the ranch. Bob said he would trust you to do that work, so will I."

Charlie started sneezing again, and Tess grabbed a towel and offered it to Charlie to cover his face.

She said, "Charlie, are you okay?"

"I thought I was, but I'm feelin' hot. Is anyone else warm?"

Hank said, "Maybe we need you to go back to bed."

Tess looked at her mom, "We've got that extra room upstairs we never use. There's a bed there. Can Charlie use it?" She put her hand on his forehead, "Mom, he's got a fever, come feel."

Claudia walked over and checked, "It sure feels like it."

Hank said, "If that's an option, Claudia, it would be better if our hands weren't around Charlie until his fever passes."

Charlie said, "I don't want to cause ya any trouble, folks."

Tess said, "It's no trouble." She walked to the door and looked back, "Come, Charlie, let me show you the room."

Charlie followed her out the kitchen door. The planning would have to wait.

* * *

It took several days, but Charlie's fever broke. Tess was at his bedside, seeing to his every need.

Charlie roused when the fever had broken; he got up and began to dress to go downstairs for breakfast. Tess walked into the room and found him facing the door wearing only his drawers.

Charlie looked up, smiled, and said, "Good mornin'." Her eyes were as big as saucers and worked their way up from below his waist to focus on his chest and shoulders. A grin filled her face. Tess put a hand over her eyes, "Oh my, Charlie, I'm sorry. I thought you would still be in bed."

Charlie chuckled, "Well, as ya can see... I'm up and around. But I do need to get some clothes on.'

"Charlie, I'm sorry..."

"It's okay, Tess. No harm done. I'll be down in a few minutes."

"I'll go start you some breakfast." She turned and ran down the stairs.

When Charlie arrived in the kitchen, Claudia greeted him, "Good to see you feelin' better."

Tess didn't look his way and continued building Charlie's breakfast plate. As she placed it in front of him, he looked up at her, "Good mornin'... again, Tess. How are you doin'?"

Her chin quivered as she said, "I'm fine, Charlie. Uh... you must be a lot better this mornin'."

"Yep, I feel like a new man, compared to the last few days. I guess I need to find Hank and git to work."

Claudia walked over with his coffee, "He and Bill went out to the barn to do some measuring. I think they're starting to plan for the new corrals, storage, and maybe a few other things. I'm sure you'll find them still there."

As Charlie rose from the table after finishing, "Well, I need to go find those two at the barn."

Tess stood wiping her hands on a towel, "Are you sure you're up to startin' to work. You were mighty sick even yesterday."

"I'll take it easy today, but I gotta git outta bed and move around. A man could go nuts stayin' in bed like that. Tess, I appreciated you checkin' on me the way ya did. I owe ya for that."

Tess walked over and squeezed his right bicep, looked up at him, and said, "You don't owe me nothin', big guy."

Claudia giggled and said, "We better let him go. He wants to find out more about his new job."

Charlie found Bill and Hank measuring for the new corrals, and by the end of the day, he understood the work that would keep him and a helper busy starting tomorrow.

* * *

A week had gone by, and Charlie was nearing completion of the first corral when Tess walked toward him.

"Afternoon Tess, what do ya have there?"

"It's a letter. I wouldn't normally interrupt your work, but this is for you, and it's from Kansas City. You know someone from there?"

"I do." I know Tess is dyin' to know more, but not now. Not yet, maybe never. She is somethin' special for sure, but... "Thanks for bringin' it out to me."

Charlie put the letter inside his shirt, "I do appreciate ya. I need to git back to work."

Tess said, "Can we talk after dinner?"

"Sure, maybe we can take a walk. It's been a nice warm day."

She beamed, "That would be wonderful."

Charlie went back to work, and his helper, Sam Chavez, said, "I think she's sweet on you, Kelly."

"Maybe Sam, but I've not intended to give her a reason to be."

"Oh sure, 'maybe we can take a walk' that's pushin' her away."

"Okay, I guess I did create a situation there, but I've already got someone I care for, and that letter; it's from her. Let's take a break now, and I'm gonna read it."

Charlie went inside the barn, sat on a hay bale, and opened the letter.

Dear Charlie,

It was wonderful to receive your letter. I'm here in Kansas City, safe and sound. I hope you are feeling better. Please write me soon and let me know you're well. I think you made a wise decision to stay for the winter at this ranch in Perkins. Perkins is a new town for me. I need to get an Oklahoma map and see where you are.

I miss you too. I'm still dealing with losing you after losing Jasper. You not joining me here in Kansas City hurt me, Charlie. I hope you feel the loss too, and then maybe you'll realize we can be together again.

I went into the offices at my father's company, and it looks like I'm going to work in the bank he owns here in Kansas City. He wants to groom me to take over his business someday. I'll know more in a few weeks about what he has in store for me.

Write me soon if you still want to see where all this leads us.

With continued deep affection,
Susan

If I want to see where this is leading us? It's leading me into confusion. I miss Susan more than I could ever have imagined. But I do enjoy being here on the Meehan ranch, even though Tess is also adding some confusion. On top of that, I still have this dream of working at the 101. I'll keep writing because I still hope that Susan and I can be together somehow. But it does seem like a long way from working at the Meehan ranch in Perkins, Oklahoma to helping run a bank in Kansas City.

That evening after dinner, Charlie and Tess took their walk. They ended up out at a pond sitting on the grassy bank closer to each other than Charlie had planned.

Tess looked over at Charlie, "Did you know it when I kissed you?"

"Wha... What?"

"Yesterday afternoon, you were sleepin', when I came in and checked on you. I touched your forehead, and it seemed like the fever was gone. I bent down and kissed you on your lips."

"Why?"

Tess turned to face Charlie, "Why does any woman kiss a man. Because I care for you, I hoped you might care that way for me."

She opened her blouse and took Charlie's hand and placed it inside on her naked breast, "I'm not sorry I saw your beautiful body this mornin' Charlie, and I'm ready for you to enjoy mine and I hope you will."

"Tess, this is movin' a little fast for me. I've gotta admit you've had my attention from the night I arrived. But... I have a lady I care deeply for that sent me that letter you gave me earlier."

Tess gently squeezed his hand into her breast and said, "If you care that much for her, why aren't you in Kansas City with her?"

Charlie slowly pulled his hand away and looked at the ground, "I wish I could answer that question. It's a fair one, and I don't have a good answer."

Tess got to her knees in front of Charlie, took both his arms, and pulled him to her, "Then that tells me you aren't taken. You need to give us a chance before you make any decision about her, don't you think?" She kissed his lips, and he didn't back away.

What is happening here? Tess is so tempting, but not in the same way I immediately experienced with Susan. I shouldn't let this continue. Should I? His only answer right now was to kiss Tess back.

* * *

Over the next few months, Charlie and Susan continued to write letters. They became more about their sincere feelings for each other but never addressed the big question of how and when they might get together. As it happened, Tess also continued her pursuit of Charlie.

The new corrals and structures project around the ranch

ended in January. Bill and Hank were more than pleased, and Charlie was happy to get back to working more from the saddle on Tony. Charlie had become a valuable hand in many ways. He showed more skills and talents than they expected when they offered him a job. Charlie enjoyed working with Hank and was glad he had stayed at the Meehan, but as time passed, he knew he would continue going after his dream.

* * *

As February of 1918 arrived, Charlie had turned twenty and stood a husky six feet five inches. His size alone had made older men step aside as he walked down the street in Perkins, yet sweet little Tess had learned how to get Charlie to do most anything she wanted.

On Valentine's Day, she made Charlie his favorite meal and created a romantic evening for them. Instead, it became the night Charlie had to be honest with himself and Tess.

She had a special setting with a table, chairs, and candles in the room Charlie had occupied months ago when he was sick. As they finished their meal, Charlie said, "Tess, this was wonderful, but I need you to understand that someday soon I'll be leavin' the ranch. I've enjoyed our time together, and I hope you have too. But this can only be a friendship. It's a deep and caring friendship, but my heart still belongs to the lady, Susan, in Kansas City. I plan to move on to the Miller's 101 Ranch this Spring as I told your father and Hank back when I signed on."

Tess said, "This breaks my heart, but I could tell you were not developing the feelings for me I had for you. You're a special man, and I hope I can find someone like you someday."

"That's nice of you to say. You'll find your special someone, and he'll be great, and you shouldn't settle for less. You deserve the best."

A few weeks later, Charlie sat at the kitchen table enjoying a cup of coffee when Hank said, "Charlie, you sure seem quiet this evening."

"Hank, I gotta lot on my mind."

"Can I help?"

"It's been a while since we discussed it, but I told you when I signed on here and again right before Christmas about my plans of workin' at the 101. Someone in town yesterday said that the 101 is hirin'."

"I remember, and I told ya, I wouldn't stand in the way of ya chasin' that dream."

"I know that, but..."

"No, buts, is it time for ya to move on?"

"Yep."

"Well then, before ya go, let me write ya a letter of recommendation. As I said before, the foreman up there is a dear old friend. Boss Bellamy is a fair man, and I think he'll take a liken to ya after he gits to know ya."

"Hank, I don't know how I can thank you."

"You did many times over by the fine work ya did for me. And I expect ya to come to visit here when ya can."

Charlie rode out the gate of the Meehan Ranch for the final time the next morning.

Two and a half days later, he rode up to the main gate at a place that took his breath away. Across the road from the main house, was a large arena, corrals, barns, and a sign that said something about a wild west show. Inside the gate, he stared at the largest house he had ever seen, and there were buildings of all kinds spread over acres of rolling hills. And to his surprise, there were at least six oil derricks he could see from the gate. He rode in and picketed Tony at a hitching post nearby. A few minutes later, he stood in line with dozens of other guys and waited his turn to try and get on as a hand for the world-famous 101. Most of the other men trying to get on were turned away for one reason or another. By the time he got near the front, Charlie wondered, *Holy shit, have I given up a good job with Hank and the Meehans to come up here to be turned away?*

He arrived at the head of the line and was now the focus of the man who sat behind the table. He appeared to be the foreman. He was a big man. A grizzled old cowboy who likely had many years at the 101 and maybe other ranches. All Charlie knew for sure was people there had called him, Boss.

Boss said, without looking up, "Name?"

"Charles Kelly, sir." Boss look up at his response, and Charlie gave him a big friendly smile.

Bosses' frown broke into a grin, "Do ya have experience workin' cattle or doin' anythin' supportin' a ranch?"

"Sure, have, sir. I cowboyed in New Mexico at the Cornerstone outfit while finishing high school. I also worked the Cullum ranch down in Stephens County here in Oklahoma. I just rode in from Perkins. I have a letter here from Hank Cottrell, Foreman, down at the Meehan Ranch."

Boss looked up again, nodded, took the letter, and read it. He smiled big and said, "Okay, you'll do fine. We pay thirty a month plus room and board."

Boss hollered across the yard to a man standing under a tree, "Pete, come over here and take young Mr. Kelly to the bunkhouse and get him settled in."

Charlie stood silently as a slender man about his age gave him the once over as he strolled over to the table and then reached out his hand to shake, "I'm Pete, damn, you are a biggun', and we can sure use a guy like you at brandin' time."

Charlie nodded and offered his hand, "Thanks, Pete, I'm Charlie. I picketed my horse just inside the main gate. Can we go fetch him first?"

"Sure, Charlie, let's go git him."

Pete led them as they headed toward the gate. "Done much ranch work, Charlie? What's your story?"

"Sure have, Pete; I've worked ranches for the past seven years. My dad always worked on ranches, so cowboyin' is what I know best. I was born in Stephens County. It's right on the old Chisholm Trail. Ever hear of it?"

"Yeah, that's down almost to Texas, isn't it?"

"That's right. When I was thirteen, we moved to New Mexico, livin' on a ranch near Fort Sumner. I've worked horseback for the last several years. When dad decided to move the family back to Oklahoma, I was just short of nineteen. I told him I'm headin' to the 101 and gettin' me a job. I needed to get out on my own."

"How did he handle that?"

Charlie twisted up his face and said, "Well, he wasn't altogether happy about it. I was a big help when bosses made hirin' decisions." He chuckled, "A foreman seein' me standin' with him usually gave us jobs."

It had been nine months since Charlie left his folks at a campsite outside of Turkey, Texas. Although Pete had been full of questions, Charlie wasn't ready to talk about his dad shooting a man, forcing them to leave New Mexico in a hurry. *I hope everything is alright with my family.*

Pete said, "We've still got about a quarter-mile to the bunkhouse."

"There's more buildin's here than in some towns, and I didn't expect all these oil wells. That house over there is the biggest I've ever seen." Charlie said.

"Yeah, this place has a lot goin' on. Around the Miller ranch, we call that big thang "The White House". We've our own general store, a cafe, hotel, blacksmith's shop, a filling station, a meatpacking plant, a dairy barn, and the post office. There's every convenience you could want. As for the oil wells, that's all come about over the last five years or so. I hear the 101 is one of the biggest oil producers around."

They headed to a large wooden framed building, "What's this big place we're headin' to, a warehouse? I thought we were goin' to the bunkhouse."

"This is the bunkhouse."

"This is larger than some barns I've seen. Speakin' of barns, let's git Tony put away first."

Pete pointed, "Right, that's our barn over there. I'm sure Tony could use some water, feed, and a rub down."

It didn't take long to see to Tony's needs, and they were back at the bunkhouse. As they stepped inside, Pete said, "You bunk there, that cabinet in the corner's where you can stow your things."

"This bunkhouse is a palace compared to the back of the family wagon and most places I've lived, although I did have my own room when I lived in Elmore City," Charlie said.

A couple of fellas walked over, and Pete said, "Charlie, these two guys are brothers. This is Matt and Ephraim Koch. Guys, this is Charlie Kelly. Boss hired him on less than an hour ago."

They shook hands, and Charlie said, "Glad to meet ya."

Matt smiled and pointed, "Our bunks are these next two, so I guess we'll be neighbors."

Pete said, "My bunk is over near the fireplace. We'll be havin' evenin' chow in about thirty minutes. I'll be back to get you, Charlie. You Kochs help him git acquainted with some others and his new rack." He looked at Charlie, "Get some rest, tomorrow we're goin' to work you hard." Pete grinned from ear to ear as he went out the bunkhouse door.

Charlie laid back on his bunk and stretched out. The bed fit him, bringing a smile as he looked up at the ceiling. It all seemed right, and he seemed settled for the first time. *I have a chance at everything I ever dreamed of, and now I need Boss to see me as a top hand as soon as I can make it happen. I need to write Susan and let her know I got on here. I sure wish I could hold her right now.*

Ephraim said, "I wouldn't get too comfortable. There's still plenty to learn about this place. We'll show you around."

Charlie and the Kochs had returned from a get-acquainted tour of the facilities when Pete returned and called from the doorway, "It's supper time. Let's get some food in our bellies."

Inside the chow hall, dozens of men sat at tables with food stacked high, "Look at all that food. I guess we won't go hungry here." Charlie said to Pete.

"It takes a lot o' men with full bellies to keep everythin' fixed and workin' at a ranch that's one hundred ten thousand acres of prime Oklahoma soil."

"I guess you're right. I'm lookin' forward to seein' some of it tomorrow." He sat next to a man who looked to be in his thirties. Charlie said, "Evenin', I'm Charlie Kelly."

Burt Kilburn said, "Pleased to meet ya, Charlie. I'm sure everyone ya meet says somethin' 'bout your size. I'll leave it alone."

Charlie laughed then ate his share and someone else's. He slept like a baby that night.

Chapter Twelve
March 1918

The roosters did their job, letting everyone know it was time to get up and about the next morning. Charlie was already awake and excited with anticipation. Today would be his first as a hand on the ranch of his dreams. He dressed quickly and headed out the bunkhouse door when Pete stopped him, "Come with me. After we put some breakfast in us, I'll show you around the ranch and maybe to some folks you need to know."

"You bet, thanks."

As they ate, Pete explained more about the ranch and some of the other operations. He then told Charlie that he needed to locate cattle in the east pastures in preparation for the Spring gather. The gather was still a ways away, but they had to get prepared now to make sure it went smoothly.

After breakfast, they went to the barn and saddled their horses. As they entered the double barn doors, Charlie said, "Who's that guy over there? What's he doin'?"

"That's Fuzzy. Hey, old-timer, come meet one of our new hires, Charlie Kelly."

The old guy was bent over and walked with a limp as he ambled toward them. Fuzzy said, "Hey young feller, Fuzzy Newsome, which of these new ponies is yours?"

Charlie walked over to his stall and stroked Tony's nose as he said, "This 'un here. He's my best buddy and my pride 'n joy."

Fuzzy moved over and patted Tony's cheek, "He's a mighty fine horse and a pleasure to care for."

Pete said, "Fuzzy runs the horse barn for us. He'll feed and water our horses. Shoe 'em when they need it and all that. He has a few helpers, but he's the man in charge."

Charlie looked at Tony, "You're gonna get spoiled rotten, aren't ya?" He rubbed Tony's muzzle and then turned back to the others. "Fuzzy, it's good to meet ya, and let me know if you need anythin' from me."

They saddled up and headed toward the rising sun, enjoying the birds chirping in the trees and the smell of the moisture from last night's drizzle. Most of the trees were still bare and that made it a bit easier for Pete to point out landmarks as they rode.

Charlie looked over at Pete, "Is this heaven?"

"If it ain't, I guess I don't need to go there."

"I'm still tryin' to git used to the size of this place."

Pete said, "The 101 covers much of northern Oklahoma in Noble, Osage, Pawnee, and Kay counties. Yeah, it's big."

They found the first cattle grazing in a valley along the Salt Fork of the Arkansas River. Pete said, "Are ya ready to go to work?"

"Sure, what do ya have in mind?"

"Let's move these cattle back toward headquarters. We'll keep 'em near water, but we won't have ta come out this far to get to 'em next time."

Charlie moved Tony around the group of cattle and proceeded to move them out of the valley. He had to do some cutting as a couple of cows tried to turn back, and at one point had to rope a cow that tried to walk off a small ravine. Pete wasn't much help, letting Charlie do most of the work and Charlie realized that Pete was testing him, seeing how well he worked. Charlie was glad that he and Tony were a fine-tuned team, and that the time at Meehan's ranch had worked out the rustiness from the time in Elmore City.

When the herd was milling in its new location Pete rode up next to Charlie, "You're pretty good. Everything seemed natural to ya. And that horse is a good one. Did ya train him yourself?"

"Yep, my dad's a fine horse trainer. He started teachin' me as soon as I could get on a horse. I owe him a lot for that. Thanks for sayin' that, Pete."

"No problem, it's the truth. Let's head back to the barn."

The day's work had given Charlie a feeling for the size of the 101. It took close to half a day to get out to the closest herd, work it back closer, and then get back to headquarters.

As they got within view of the White House Charlie asked, "Pete, I didn't see many oil wells out the way you took me. Didn't you say that oil was big business here too?"

"It is, but we don't run cattle around the oil derricks or the pumps if we can avoid it."

As they rode up to the gate, Charlie again saw the large set of stock pens, corrals, and arena. "Pete, is that area there for the Wild West Show? I saw a sign for it yesterday."

"I guess it'd be okay if I took you over across the road to see where the show folks practiced during the day and bunked at night."

"Ya know, I grew up with stories about this fantastic Wild West Show from the 101. Now I'm goin' to see where it all started?"

"If you'll keep your pants on."

Charlie said, "Tom Mix and Hoot Gibson are now in Hollywood making movies and had been here at this ranch only a few years ago. Right?"

"You bet."

Charlie noticed how the corrals and other buildings looked tired like they hadn't had a show in a while. "What happened to the show?"

"The show shut down because of the War," Pete said. "Bill Pickett stayed along with others who were in the show. They're now workin' as ranch hands. Burt Kilburn is one; you met him at supper last night. You'll soon meet them all." Pete pointed to his right, "That arena holds more than 10,000, and we held bronc ridin', steer wrestlin' and bulldoggin' events as well as the wild west show there. We built those buildings, corrals, and pens to support the show, and they are still used some for daily operations around here."

As they toured the practice grounds, Charlie saw one of the chuck wagons used in the show. He stopped, looked closely, and said, "This wagon appears ready to go out on a gather or a cattle drive. Do the hands still use it?"

"I don't know, but Boss has always required the show folks to keep any equipment they use ready for ranch work. Why? Do you cook?"

"Well, I can. My grandma taught me everything she knew and because of her I became the best cook in my family as I grew up."

"Good to know."

Shit, did I say too much? I hired on as a hand, not a cook.

"Pete, a cookie is a very respected man out on a drive, here, right? Everywhere I've worked, the foreman or his trail boss wanted a cookie who could keep the drovers well-fed and happy."

"Right, sometimes the cookie does the doctorin' and often takes charge if the trail boss is away from camp."

As they wandered back to the barn to put up their horses, Charlie was uneasy. "Pete, you know I was hired as a hand, not to cook, so I'd just as soon you didn't mention anythin' about my cookin'."

"Sure, Charlie, although it could be to your good if Boss needed ya."

Charlie let it go. It was about time for evening chow, so they went to the pump and washed up.

* * *

Boss saw them and walked over, "Well, did Pete get you settled in and oriented to what we're about here at the 101?"

"He sure did. This is one first-rate place. It'll be an honor ridin' for this brand."

Boss nodded and turned toward the main house.

After he was out of earshot, Pete said, "Boss is headin' to his evenin' meetin' with the Millers at the White House. Do you know the history of this place?"

"Some. I know Colonel George Washington Miller, the founder, died back in '03. I guess the three brothers are runnin' the ranch?"

"Right, after their pa's death, Joe stepped in to run the overall operation, while Zack, the trader amongst 'em handles the livestock, young George is the money man, and he keeps the books in order. They make one tough outfit."

Later, Boss walked by Charlie's table during the meal and said, "Son, you'll be workin' for Tom Grimes ridin' fence lines along the southern part of the ranch down beyond Marland, Oklahoma.

"Yes, sir, I look forward to it."

Pete looked over at Charlie, "It's Friday night. Let's go to the Salt Creek bar down in Bliss and git a beer. Ya need to know about Mabel's place."

"I rode through Bliss on my way up from Perkins. It sits out in the middle of the tall grass. I guess I missed this bar ya mentioned. Sure, I'm game."

Bliss was a small prairie community, and the Salt Fork bar had been a favorite hangout for the hands at the ranch for years. It was a wooden frame building on the edge of the town, large enough for an eight-station bar and a dozen tables scattered around the hardwood floor.

When they arrived, Pete introduced Charlie, "Mabel, ya need to meet a new cowboy, this is Charlie Kelly."

"Evening Charlie, I'm Mabel Little Feather. I'm the bartender and I own this place." She was stout, and maybe thirty-five-year-old. Charlie knew from his friendship with Little Deer that most Indians didn't usually get the chance to own a business, especially a bar. Little Deer always said the whites were making sure the Indians couldn't gain any power that might let them get their land back. So, Charlie knew it was unusual for an Indian to own a bar, but Charlie wasn't asking any questions.

Charlie said, "It's my pleasure."

"We'll take two beers," Pete said. "Charlie git us that table over there."

After Pete sat down, Charlie said, "A woman owns a bar, and an Indian at that?"

"Yep, and you don't want to git on her wrong side. She always has her pistol and a loaded sawed-off shotgun ready behind the bar. She knows how to use them and won't hesitate."

* * *

At the Monday morning breakfast, a young, tall, and slender

cowboy came over to Charlie's table. "I'm Tom Grimes, and you'll be goin' out with me today. I'll put you workin' near me once we get out along the fence line. Boss says you have some experience at this; I want to see how you do."

"Good to meet ya. When are we leavin'?"

"In about a half-hour, finish your breakfast."

Shortly after daybreak, Tom, Charlie, and about a dozen more hands headed south to start work. A large wagon carrying dozens of fence posts and rolls of barbed wire followed along. As they rode Charlie noticed there were more oil derricks as they passed Marland, reminding him that this wasn't just a cattle ranch.

A menacing voice said, "So, you're the new guy, huh?"

Charlie turned to his right to see a big, bearded man straddle a pretty appaloosa who had a most unlikeable, even nasty voice.

"Yep, that would be me. Charlie's the name, and you?"

"Thad Spencer, we gotta lot o' ground to cover, so keep up, ya hear me."

"I git your message, but I take the lead from Tom Grimes, not you, mister."

"Don't give me no lip, kid."

"Fine, you don't give me no orders."

Spencer spat out a stream of tobacco juice and spurred his horse forward. Charlie was getting the same feeling in his stomach that he'd had back in Fort Sumner when Reuben tried to knife him. His insides were on fire, and all he wanted was to pound this asshole in the ground. He found that he was gripping the reins tighter, and that Tony was starting to shy to the right from the squeeze Charlie's legs were applying to the saddle.

I will not be my dad, Charlie told himself. He loosened his grip on the reins and tried to relax.

Tom rode up next to Charlie and said, "Come with me. I want to ask you a few things." He nudged his horse off to the left and rode up a small hill. Charlie followed him.

"Sure, boss, whatever you need."

"I'm Tom. Boss is back at headquarters. You got your fence kit before we left, didn'cha?"

"Sure, you said we'd be on the fence-line." It seemed like a dumb question to Charlie, but he figured that it wouldn't be a good idea to say that.

Tom stopped and stood up in the saddle. He pointed off to the south and Charlie turned to look down the hill. Below them he could see a long, battered section of fence, the wire was broken and scattered in several places and dozens of fence posts had been knocked down, a few had been snapped as if they were matchsticks.

Charlie gave a low whistle. "Wha' happened here?"

"A few days back, we had a thunderstorm come through here, and the cattle got scared and ran through and destroyed about a half-mile of the fence. I'm going to put us as a team, so I can see what you know. I need to know if your last boss taught you the same way we do things here."

Charlie said, "If I don't, then I'll learn your way fast enough." He pulled off his hat and scratched his head. "It don't look like there's a lot that can be salvaged."

"Yep, and we need to get it done today if we can."

Charlie replaced his hat and said, "Then let's git started," as he spurred Tony forward.

The crew settled into work. They split into teams, some heading east, and some west, so they could work and meet up in the middle somewhere. Charlie showed he was a skilled hand as he quickly dug out the damaged posts and set new ones. He thought he showed good judgment too when he found a post that wasn't damaged and could still be used.

After they'd done about a hundred yards of fence Charlie said, "Tom, if it's okay, I'll keep setting posts, and I'll come back and help with the wire."

Tom said, "That'll be fine. I've already seen enough to know you have done this before, and you're doing it right."

Charlie set posts ahead of Tom, and when he had about ten set he'd come back and help string the wire, then repeat the process. They made good time that way. At one point, as Charlie worked the wire alongside Tom, he said, "How long have you been here at the 101?"

"I've been here about seven years. I was on the show team

until it folded because of the War."

"What did ya do in the show?"

"I was a trick rider, and I also was the lead horse wrangler responsible for their care and feeding. I had a five-man crew helping me."

Charlie was glad he had worked with Tom. By the day's end, they were a good match as workers, and Charlie felt that a friendship had begun as they were able to talk as they worked. The wagon dumped the last of the posts and the wire and headed back to the ranch late in the afternoon. As the sun approached the western horizon the crews met up and drove in the final posts and strung the last of the wire.

"Good job, men," Tom said. "I figured we'd get done at sunset and we beat that by maybe an hour. Let's head back and get some grub."

It was an hour's ride to the barn. During that time, Spencer came alongside Charlie and growled, "Well kid, are those lips o' yours chapped from all your ass kissin'?"

"Look, you don't know me, an' I don't know you, so I don't know why you got a burr up under your saddle about me. But I ain't gonna take no shit from you. I've only ever done a fair days work, an' if you think that means I'm kissin' ass, then you can kiss mine, asshole. You git on outta here, and I'll consider this matter over between us."

Spencer laughed and said as he moved on, "This ain't over by no means."

Charlie shook his head as Spencer rode ahead and tried to strike up a conversation with Tom. He leaned down and patted Tony's neck. "I guess there's one asshole in every outfit."

At mealtime, Boss again walked by Charlie's table, "I hear you had a top first day, Charlie. I'm glad we brought you on. I'll be moving you around quite a bit here at the beginning, so's to find where you fit best."

Charlie put his fork down and looked up, "I'm happy to help wherever I'm needed, sir.

* * *

That evening Charlie was tired and worn out after the long day, but before he hit the sack he wrote another letter to Susan.

Sweetheart,

Today was my first day as a member of a string of cowboys working out on the ranch. We were mending fences, and it seemed right and good. I'm still amazed at how big this ranch is. There are more people here than live in Elmore City and Perkins combined. At the end of my day today, Tom Grimes, my leadman said he was pleased with my work. Then the ranch foreman, Boss Bellamy, stopped by my table and praised me at dinner. I don't think my day could have been better, except there is one fella who seems to have it in for me. I haven't figured him out yet, but he won't get the best of me.

How are things in Kansas City? I think about you often and wish we could see each other. I'm sure you're happy working at the bank as I am here at the 101, but I still have an empty feeling in my life that I'm sure only you can fill.

Write soon; I love reading your letters.

Always,
Charlie

Chapter Thirteen
August 1918

The sun was high overhead, and the day was hot and humid as Charlie walked toward the bunkhouse after lunch. He had a few minutes before he needed to head over to complete his afternoon task of mending fence along one of the corrals.

"Charlie, can we talk?"

Charlie looked toward the voice. It was Boss, walking toward him from the direction of the White House. He stopped and waited for Boss to join him. "Sure, Boss, what can I do for you?"

"I wanted to let ya know what I've been thinkin'. Over the last few months, I've moved ya to different jobs around the ranch. It gave ya a chance to learn from the old cowboys, and you've quickly proved out a top-hand, workin' cattle and horses. You've also shown solid skills mending fences, corrals, and even tack. I didn't miss this, Charlie, you're provin' worth your salt around here, dadgummit, and that's good on ya."

"Thank you, Boss," Charlie said, letting pride swell his chest.

Boss clapped him on the shoulder. "I've let Mr. Miller know how well you've been doin' too." Charlie nodded, wondering which of the three Miller sons Boss was referring to.

"I'll keep up the work. You won't have to worry about me."

"I expect as much." Boss turned and headed toward the mess hall. Charlie smiled and walked a bit taller as he continued to the bunkhouse.

Charlie was about to enter the bunkhouse when he spotted Thad Spencer standing under the shade tree that stood right outside the bunkhouse. Spencer's buddies, Roy Taggert and Ben Somers, both good-sized men, were standing with him. As soon as Spencer spotted Charlie he spat and walked in front of Charlie and stood nose-to-nose, "Who in the hell do you think you're becomin' here?"

"Wha'd'ya mean?" Charlie retorted, his shoulders back and chest out with his chin up.

"I think you're becomin' an uppity kid who don't know his place. I think it's time to teach you a lesson."

Charlie's nostrils flared and his hands turned into tight fists as anger swelled inside him. I'm not going to be like dad and settle everything with a fight. That was one of the reasons I went out on my own. He forced himself to get a hold of his anger. With a calm, measured voice, he said, "Look, what's it gonna prove if we fight?"

"You afraid o' me, Charlie?" He raised his arms to the sky and laughed. Roy and Ben laughed along with him.

Charlie took a step forward, surprising Spencer and forcing him to take a step back toward the tree. "Of you? No."

Spencer swung his right fist. Charlie ducked and grabbed Spencer under his arms and shoved him hard into the tree. "I don't think this is what we need, Thad."

Spencer stood up and rounded on Charlie, but already several other hands were starting to gather around to see what was going on. Spencer stammered, "M... M... Maybe this isn't the best time or place, but we'll meet again."

Charlie nodded, turned, and walked into the bunkhouse.

"I meant it, Charlie, we ain't done yet."

You're right. We ain't.

Charlie found a letter on his pillow back at his bunk postmarked Avoca, Oklahoma. He said to himself, Oh wow, it must be from the family. He quickly forgot the altercation with Spencer as he tore open the letter.

Charles,
I'm writing to let you know we're doing well.
We have some good news. I had written Mrs.

Henderson back on the Cornerstone that we're settled here in Oklahoma. It had been months, and she had not replied, so I was surprised to get a letter. She said that Reuben Johnson didn't die from the gunshot. Everyone in the Pecos Bar that day agreed Reuben had it coming. We were relieved to hear that. Since coming back to Oklahoma, Dad has been a new man, especially after we got that news. We hope you can come to visit, and by the way, there is a mighty cute young thing down the road from us named Jenny Farley. You might find her interesting.

Love Always,
Mom

Charlie was happy with the news. But, shook his head and whispered to an almost empty room, "What's this about a girl? I don't need another female." Charlie put the letter into his things and headed out to finish mending the corral.

* * *

That night at dinner it seemed to Charlie that the mess hall was fuller than usual. He leaned over to Pete and said, "Is it me, or are there more people than usual here tonight?"

Pete laughed. "It's gettin' close to the gather. Boss will be makin' an announcement tonight after dinner."

Charlie ate his food quickly and then had to wait impatiently for Boss to finish. Finally, he stood up and walked to the front of the large room. Conversations all stopped almost at once and Boss called out, "I'll be takin' fifteen of y'all out on the gather, plus the Cookie. The cattle'll be scattered, and it could take us several weeks to find and brand them. But, I'm hopin' the cattle won't be too far from water, and that'll help. Those picked will get an extra ten dollars in their monthly pay, and of course, you git braggin' rights as our best hands until next Spring." There were some hollers and whistles at that.

Brown

"Gentlemen, I'll post the list of who'll work this gather on the main bunkhouse door tomorrow evenin'. Y'all git out of here, git some shut-eye. We've still got work to do in the mornin'."

Charlie and Pete walked together back to the bunkhouse, "Pete, Boss'll pick us, right?"

"I think we gotta chance, but there's a lot of fellas who've been here a long time and who know their stuff. In my six years, I've got to know most of 'em, and I've never been picked for a gather."

Charlie tried not to let the odds of him not getting picked get him down. He knew he was one of the ranch's top hands, Boss had said so to him just that day. But Pete was right, there were a lot of good cowboys on the Miller 101, many of them with more experience.

Charlie settled into bed, still thinking about the gather and how much he wished to share his excitement with Susan.

* * *

As promised, Boss posted the list the next afternoon so all could see it when they arrived back in at the end of the day. Charlie, Pete, and Tom were standing next to each other, along with the other hands, trying to read the list. The three of them had for several months done most everything on and off the job together and had become good friends. Several others were standing in the way, so Charlie couldn't see the list at first. He heard quiet curses and saw men walk away with their heads low. Pete managed to get around someone and looked at the list.

"We made it!" Pete said as he slapped Charlie on the back. Charlie finally got up to look at the list. He saw his name clearly on the list.

"Yep." Shoving his fist in the air, Charlie shouted, "Tom, you're there, too!"

Making the gather was a feather in their hats, and they whooped it up a bit. Charlie noticed a name missing. Spencer's name isn't there. Even though it was Boss's decision, I'm sure he'll be mad at me. He shook his head, he wasn't going to let one man's inability to work spoil his excitement.

Pete said, "Let's go over to Bliss to git a beer at the Salt Fork tonight."

"Good idea, Pete," said Tom. "Are you in, Charlie?"

"Sure, guys, when do we leave?"

The trio got to the bar at sundown, and they knew it couldn't be a late night as daybreak would bring another hard day in the saddle. But a beer to celebrate sounded good, and then they would head back.

They noticed a few hands had beat them there and sat at a table in the corner. Charlie recognized one as Thad Spencer and he was sitting with Roy Taggert and Ben Somers. It looked like Spencer was drowning his sorrows instead of celebrating, so Charlie did his best to ignore Spencer. He ordered a beer from the bar and then joined Pete and Tom at a table near the door.

Charlie shook his head and sighed, "Did you see Spencer over in the corner, Tom?"

"Yep, and he doesn't look happy, does he?"

Pete said, "He's probably pissed because he wasn't on the list."

Tom rubbed the back of his neck as he said, "Yeah, maybe that's it."

The three of them lifted their beers and clinked them together to celebrate the moment. Charlie wiped the foam from his lips. "I tell ya, I'm excited to be on the gather."

"It's quite a recognition by Boss," Tom said. "A greenhorn like you," he smiled to show that he didn't mean the slight was personal, "almost never gets on a gather."

They heard a crash and turned to see Spencer standing up, his chair on the floor. Roy and Ben looked stunned at how Spencer was acting. He didn't seem to care and crossed the room to loom over their table. He spoke in a voice that allowed everyone in the bar to hear, "Well, if it ain't the Three Musketeers. Out for a celebration, are we?"

"Take it easy, Spencer, you've been drinkin', and we ain't lookin' for trouble," said Tom. He looked over to Roy and Ben and motioned with his head that they needed to come corral their friend before he did something stupid.

"Grimes, you are a back-bitin' two-faced son-of-a-bitch. You cost me the extra pay for the gather by puttin' this kid ahead o' me, and now you're gonna git the shit beat outta ya."

Tom rose from his chair in time to get the full impact of Spencer's fist, and he fell back onto the table, knocking over their beers.

Pete said, "Holy shit, Spencer, you're in for it now!" He pushed back from the table and stood up; hands ready to swing. Roy and Ben got up and headed across the bar.

"Shut the fuck up, Pete. I don't give a shit what ya think." He turned his back on Pete and pointed at Charlie. "I told you, runt, that I'd get you."

Charlie stood as Spencer swung a right hook at Charlie and caught him with a glancing blow across the top of his head that caused him to fall back into his chair. Charlie stood up quickly, like he was rolling away from a bronc that had just thrown him in the rodeo arena, and gathered himself. He ignored the yells and calls coming from the others in the bar. He was surprised that he wasn't filled with anger, as he expected, but with a determination to protect his friends. He took a step forward, favoring a bit to his left to lure Spencer into taking another swing. Spencer obliged him and Charlie leaned back to the right like he was directing Tony to cut a heifer from the herd. Spencer missed and was off-balance, and Charlie swung hard, connecting his right fist to Spencer's jaw. The big ranch hand's eyes rolled up until Charlie could see only white and he was out cold as he crumpled to the floor.

Silence filled the room for a moment, then it was broken by a loud voice yelling, "That's enough!".

Mabel stood at the bar with her shotgun aimed at the ceiling. With a loud, steady voice, she said, "Fellas, let's call it a night." She pointed at Roy and Ben, "Take him with you. He's been an asshole since he got here."

Pete countered with, "Mabel, we didn't even finish our beers."

"Next time, Pete. Right now, I need ya gone."

Roy and Ben took Spencer out with them, and they were followed by Charlie, Pete, and Tom. Roy stuck Spencer's head into the horse trough and brought him to. There wasn't any fight left in him.

"Ready to go home, Thad?" said Tom.

"Sure, boss."

"I'm not Boss, but let's go."

Pete said, "So much for celebratin', and Tom, you remind me to never ever git Charlie mad."

They all laughed, even Roy and Ben. Everybody except for Spencer.

Chapter Fourteen
August 1918

After their trip to Bliss, the trio was grateful for the roost-er's crow the following day. As much as they needed to sleep, they couldn't be late on the first day of the gather. Charlie scrambled into his shirt, Levis, and boots. He grabbed his coat and hat off their pegs as he stepped into the warm morning air. The smell of freshly brewed coffee and crackling bacon welcomed all the hands to the morning table.

"Eat up, boys; be saddled and ready to ride in fifteen min-utes," Boss shouted as he headed out the chow hall door.

The sun was not quite above the horizon as they rode out. Pete rode up close enough to ask, "Charlie, doesn't it seem cool for August to ya?"

He shook his head as he replied, "I'd call it perfect since the sun ain't already baking my neck, but I suppose we could get some rain later today. My saddle's cool, and Tony's likin' this a lot."

Pete grinned as he said, "I doubt that Boss asked your horse for permission to start the day's work." They laughed as they headed south toward Marland.

About an hour later, as they passed the spot where Charlie had helped repair the first of many fences on the Miller, he asked, "Pete, how long do ya think we'll be out on this gather?"

"I'm not sure, but..."

Tom rode up and overheard Charlie's question, "Boss said a few minutes ago he thought this would take at least two weeks, hopefully not more."

Charlie asked, "Tom, can ya give me a rundown on what we'll be doin' with the cattle? How big is the herd? After brandin' will we bring them back to headquarters, or take them to the railhead at Marland or maybe somethin' else?"

"Sure, we'll round up the cattle into a herd of about three thousand head, then bring them back north to headquarters for shipment. We have a railhead over east from headquarters, as you know. We don't know right now how long that'll take us, but we expect at least two weeks. The 101 has a contract with the Army for this beef to support the war effort. We need to get this done in less than three weeks. There's a ton of money involved here."

A while later the skies darkened, and rain began to fall. Charlie broke out his rain slicker which seemed to only funnel the rain to get him even wetter. The rain continued as they made camp, and the cookie did his best, but the best tonight was soggy beans that were cold. Cookie apologized to the men, coughing and shivering in the rain.

Charlie looked forlornly at his spoon and said, "The weather sure has turned on us today. We could have some long miserable days with this rainy weather. I hope the wind blows the rain outta here."

There were agreements from the other men until Boss told them all to quit their griping. They were cowpokes, not candy-ass clerks or office workers. The crew agreed with that, and they made the most of the evening, with somebody pulling out a harmonica and another man pulling out a mouth harp. They sang a few songs and Charlie realized that the first day of the gather hadn't been that bad, even if they were wet.

The wind did take the rain away overnight, but the clouds stayed with them, and it was windier and wetter than Charlie expected. The next two days passed in a blur for Charlie and the others as they rode out each day to gather the cattle and bring them closer to their base camp.

Boss walked over to where the drovers were sleeping on the morning of the fourth day, "Hey, wake up, men, we have us a real pickle here. Theo, the cookie is awful sick."

There were grumbles from some of the men, and concern

from others. Boss let them get the shock out of their system before he said, "We still have a lot of cattle to gather, and I can't spare the time to send someone back to headquarters to get a replacement. Now, who of ya can step in?"

Boss looked from man to man, meeting each of their eyes. Nobody volunteered to step in to help Cookie. Charlie knew he could do it, but he'd signed on to be a cowboy, to drive cattle, not to keep a bunch of men's bellies full. He met Boss's eyes but didn't say anything.

Then Pete hollered, "Charlie Kelly can!"

Stunned, Charlie blurted, "What'd you say?"

Boss looked back at Charlie, "You can cook?"

He looked down at his boots, "Yep, I can cook. I guess I can fill in."

"Come with me."

They walked over to the chuckwagon. "Git with Cookie. He'll tell ya where he's stowed the pots, pans, and supplies. Thanks for helpin' out."

Charlie nodded, but he didn't feel like he was helping. It felt like he was being punished. Charlie found Theo still in his bedroll. He bent down to ask him for the needed information. "Theo, it's Charlie. Can we talk a bit?"

"I was able to hear you and Boss, I 'preciate you helpin' out."

Theo rolled out of his bedroll. Charlie was shocked at how pale Theo looked. Despite the cool morning air, he was sweating like the sun was beating down on him. Theo coughed and said, "Follow me, and I'll show you where everything is." After a short talk, interrupted by powerful coughing fits, Theo asked, "Do ya have any questions?"

Charlie shook his head, "No, I think I got it."

Theo coughed again. "Jus' be careful with those new pots of mine. I got them last month and I don't want to find them all banged up." He didn't wait for a reply and went back to his bedroll.

Charlie got to work making biscuits for breakfast. Today, he would feed the men and hope Theo would be better tomorrow. He would prepare the meals the same way his grandma had taught him if the supplies allowed it.

116

Boss and Tom walked over to the chuckwagon to check on Cookie and Charlie was able to overhear their conversation as he got breakfast ready.

"Theo, you feelin' any better?" Boss asked.

Charlie couldn't hear the reply, but after seeing Theo this morning Charlie didn't know how he could look any worse.

"I think he's got a fever real bad," Tom said.

"I was afraid of that. It might be nothin', but fevers can spread, and I can't have any more men gettin' sick on me. This gather is too important."

The men were silent, and Charlie kept getting the breakfast ready but straining to hear what Boss was going to do.

"Git a horse outta the remuda for Theo and take him back to the bunkhouse. Tell Doc Combs to look in on him."

"Should I bring back one of the other cooks?" Tom asked.

"No, they'll be busy with everything else. If Charlie's a decent enough cook, it'll be better if we add a hand, so, as much as I hate it, bring Spencer back."

Charlie felt his mouth go dry and almost dropped the batter. *Spencer is gonna be ridin' on the gather while I'm stuck as the cook?*

He must have missed some of the conversation because he now heard Boss saying rather forcefully, "—is the most experienced and prepared to step in. Until that fracas a while back with Charlie, he was on my list for the gather. Bring him back with ya."

There was a pause, then Charlie heard Tom say, "I thought ya were firin' him."

"I considered it. Thad's a good hand most of the time, but he has a real problem getting along with some people for some reason. We've talked, and he knows this is his last chance with me."

"Okay, Boss, I'll git right on it."

Charlie finished the breakfast and got the men fed, but he was already wondering how he could change Boss's mind.

* * *

Later that day, Boss walked over to the wagon and found Charlie peeling potatoes. He lifted his hat and rubbed his hair.

"Charlie, Tom's back, and we're facing some problems, and we need to talk about Theo."

"Okay, Boss. Is he gonna be able to come back tomorrow?"

"I'm afraid not. Theo may have that new flu and the doc has put him to bed away from everyone else."

Charlie hadn't heard much about a new flu, and he felt some sympathy for Theo.

"Doc also said we need to clean all the cookin' gear in boilin' water before usin' 'em. The plates and utensils too before we eat."

Charlie kicked the dirt as he said, "I'll git to work on it. That'll take me a while. The guys'll be back and hungry before long."

Boss met Charlie's eyes and said, "Talk to me. Somethin' botherin' you?"

"I'd hoped Theo would be back in the mornin' so that I could go back to workin' from horseback or brandin'. Something besides cookin'."

"That's not going to happen now, son. But I'll think about bringin' another cook out."

The prospect that Boss might bring a proper cook out lifted Charlie's spirit some. He got the pots, pans, and everything else cleaned and scrubbed with boiling water. And that evening, Charlie cooked beef steak to medium-rare, crispy fried potatoes, and melt in your mouth biscuits covered in sausage gravy made the way his grandma McDaniel taught him to make it.

After the meal, Charlie overheard Pete talking to Boss, "Charlie's great, can we keep him cookin'?"

Boss leaned against the chuckwagon as he said, "He's good, I agree with that, but he's also a top hand. I know I had Tom bring Spencer out, but can we afford to lose him as a wrangler? I was thinkin' about bringin' one o' the other cooks out tomorrow."

"They's okay," Pete said, "But I ain't never had biscuits and gravy like Charlie made for us. We'll all work extra hard to make up the slack if we can keep him feedin' us. We don't need to waste time bringin' another cook out here."

Charlie groaned quietly. *Maybe I shoulda burned them biscuits.* He headed back to the wagon to clean up.

Boss came up to the wagon as Charlie was putting a kettle

for coffee on over the fire. "You're one fine cook. Where'd ya learn it?"

"From my grandma McDaniel. Mom, for a long time, was sickly and she helped out."

"Well, the guys are wantin' you to stay on as the cookie. How do you feel about that?"

Charlie poked at the fire, stirring up the coals. "My grandma told me one time that if I wanted to be a top hand someday, I needed to learn how to cook to keep my men fed proper."

Boss smiled and chuckled. "Sounds like I'd get along real well with your grandma."

Charlie managed a smile too at the memory. "I enjoy cookin', that's no lie, but I'd also be lying if I didn't say that I'd be happiest earnin' my keep from the back of Tony."

"You're plenty good being a cowboy, but for the next couple o' weeks, you're worth more to me keepin' my wranglers happy and well-fed." Boss knelt by the fire and added a log to the coals. "Tell ya what I'll do; I'll give ya an extra twenty dollars in this month's pay if ya finish the gather cookin'. That's what old Theo would have made. Don't think for one second you've lost your spot as a hand 'cause you're one of the best I've seen in the saddle." He looked up at Charlie. "But I need you cookin' for now. And I'll keep this in mind for later, too."

Charlie heard the implication and realized his grandma had been wiser than he'd given her credit for. He smiled, "I'll do what ya need."

Before everyone bedded down that night, Boss broke the news, "I think y'all will be glad to hear, Charlie will finish the gather cookin'."

The group whooped it up a bit until Boss said, "Settle down and git to bed. We gotta tough day ahead of us."

Over the next two days, the gather was impacted when a few more wranglers got sick. Boss sent them back to the doctor and asked Tom, "Pick out the best available hands. I trust your judgment. I know we're down to the guys who have limited time with cattle."

The crew continued the roundup by spreading out over 100

square miles to find the cattle and bring them to a central location within a workable distance from camp. The wranglers knew the territory, but trees, shrubs, and ravines made finding the cattle hard work. That made for long days.

Charlie used the time to practice his skills by baking cobbler in Theo's Dutch oven and some recipes he hadn't used for years his grandmother had given him.

One evening when he gave the crew some cobbler, Spencer said, "Yeah well, this is good pie, I gotta admit that to ya."

Charlie didn't look at him, "'Preciate it. There'll be some left if ya want more."

I guess he's not going to start anythin' out here. That's smart. Of course, I've seen Tom and Pete everywhere I've noticed Spencer.

At the end of the first week, Boss took time one night after supper to give his ideas on their progress, "We've had a good week. The sickness hurt us, but we've covered most of the country we planned to work in. Startin' tomorrow, I'll divide you up into crews. Some will still do the gatherin', and some will start the brandin'. If we're lucky over the next few days, we may wrap this up in another week."

Boss put the Kochs and Spencer on nightguard, and a storm rolled in after midnight. A loud clap of thunder spooked the herd starting a stampede. The cattle headed away from camp toward some of the roughest terrain on the ranch.

Charlie and the other hands stirred as they became aware of the cattle. Boss hollered, "Get saddled. We've got a stampede."

Charlie on Tony was among the first to head out. He yelled as he passed Boss, "I'm headin' for the ravine."

Tony worked through the cloud of dust in the darkness and quickly caught the back of the herd. Charlie could see a rider up ahead on the right. Charlie let Tony find his way through the maze of cattle and eventually could see the rider was Spencer.

As Tony got them closer, Charlie gave out a holler and a whistle, "Thad Spencer, it's Charlie Kelly!"

Spencer looked around, "We need to get 'em turned."

As he caught up to Spencer, "Yeah, let's see if we can turn 'em left. There's a deep ravine a mile or so ahead on the right, isn't there?"

"Yep, let's do it."

They spurred their mounts and took off as fast as the horses could run. The night was pitch black with the clouds hiding the moon and stars. Bushes and trees seemed to appear as if by magic from out of the darkness, and Charlie and Spencer had to do some fancy riding to keep from being knocked off their mounts.

Please don't take a fall Tony, I know we're running hard in the dark.

Charlie and Spencer soon met the Kochs as they neared the lead bunch of cattle. Charlie hollered, "We're steering 'em left Matt, can you and your brother help us get 'em turned?"

"You bet, Charlie."

The cattle began to slow down in another quarter mile, and Charlie, Spencer, and the Kochs had the herd pointed back toward camp. The rest of the hands fell into their typical roles. In less than an hour, the herd was milling around where they were before the storm.

Boss gathered everyone at the herd and counted heads. "Well, we cowboys all made it through that disaster, but we're missin' some of our beeves. Let's git some sleep and find 'em in the mornin'. We all need to git back to our bedrolls. But first, Charlie, you were a top hand out there turnin' the herd. Fine job."

The crowd started yelling; "Kelly Can! Kelly Can! Kelly Can!"

Charlie raised his hands high above his head and said, "Hey guys, thanks. But Spencer was out there before me, and he did everything I did. So, give him his due too."

Before anything could be said or done, Boss said, "Okay then, fine job, both of ya."

Charlie looked at Spencer, "Ya done good, Thad."

He hesitated, "Yeah, you too, Kelly."

Boss moved his pony over next to Charlie, "I hate it, but..."

Charlie grunted, "I know. I'll git back to the chuck when the sun comes up."

Boss smiled, "Thanks."

* * *

The hands completed their work out on the prairie in the next week and drove the herd to the Santa Fe railroad spur east of the White House. They stayed there overnight. Tom and several of the hands came up to the chuckwagon that last evening of the gather, "Charlie, ya' done a fine job cookin'. Now, you gotta promise to teach the cooks back at headquarters how to make your biscuits. We won't hear to nothin' else."

Charlie smiled, "I promise I will. I'm glad you've enjoyed my food, but I still would have rather been out workin' horseback with y'all. Now ya need to let me pack up this wagon tonight before I can git some shuteye?"

The next morning, they loaded the rail cars with almost 3,000 head of prime Oklahoma beef and then headed back to headquarters. As they got to the main gate, the hands began chanting, "Kelly Can! Kelly Can! Kelly Can!"

A crowd met the drovers as they rode in the gate, and they joined the chant. Charlie nodded to the crowd, put up his hands, palms out, and hollered, "Okay, okay, I appreciate it. I didn't do nothin' special folks."

Tom said, "Oh, he sure did!"

* * *

A week later, Boss, a man of his word, made sure that Charlie got the extra money in his paycheck. He also caught Charlie during evening chow and pulled him outside. "I'm gonna soon be puttin' you temporarily in charge of five hands who'll ride fences and handle repair jobs around the ranch. You've done all I asked of ya, and you've become one of my top hands. Good on ya, young man!

From then on, around the 101, you often heard these words. "Kelly Can."

Chapter Fifteen
September 1918

Charlie, smiled, as he lay on his bunk and daydreamed about where this new adventure as a temporary Lead Hand would take him when Thad Spencer and his two buddies Roy and Ben walked in. The trio appeared to have returned from another trip to visit Mabel Little Feather.

Spencer growled, "Charlie, how is it as a damn bigshot now that you've got Boss to give you a team?"

"Whattaya gittin' at?"

"I ain't gotta tell ya nothin' 'cause ya know what I mean, ya brown nosin' son-of-a-bitch."

He's drunk. I thought maybe we were past this after the gather.

Charlie rolled out of his bed and headed directly for Spencer.

"How many times are we gonna have this conversation, Thad?"

Spencer staggered some as he ducked his head and ran at Charlie.

"Git him, boys," Spencer hollered as he dove.

With his massive right hand, Charlie easily drove Spencer to the floor.

Charlie eyed Taggart and Somers as he hollered, "You two better stay back. I'm in no mood to put up with anythin' more than kickin' this drunk's ass tonight."

Taggert spoke first, "Ya think ya can handle all three of us?"

"Whattaya think? Are ya wantin' to find out?"

Ben said, "This is Spencer's fight. We got no skin in this game."

Spencer got to his feet, and swung a roundhouse right landing a glancing blow to Charlie's left temple, followed by a left hook that missed its mark.

"Ya went first, now I'm gonna make short work of ya," Charlie spat out as he slammed Spencer hard against the wall and landed a quick left to the gut followed by a crunching right to his jaw. Spencer dropped to the floor.

"Git him outta here and keep him as far away from me as ya can. I'm done with this asshole and don't want to be 'round him any more than I have to."

They dragged Spencer feet first out the door. Charlie flexed his sore hands, looked them over, and saw there was no damage, so he flopped back on his bunk.

"What happened here?" Pete asked as he ran in from the yard.

"I don't want to talk Pete, can ya leave me alone?"

"Maybe I can, but everybody, 'cludin' Boss, will be in here askin' the same question in no time."

"What?"

"A bunch of us were out in the yard throwin' horseshoes and messin' 'round when Taggert and Somers drug Spencer out that door a minute ago."

"Damn it all to hell. What was I supposed to do?"

"What happened?"

"Spencer come in here drunk callin' me all kinda shit and wantin' to fight."

Pete shook his head, "Didn't he git enough over at Mabel's?"

"I guess not. Spencer hates it that Boss gave me a team that he must think should be his."

Tom hollered from the door, "We got Spencer up and out of sight. You are two wild mustangs, always fightin'."

"That's not what I want, but he sure wants me outta here. He thinks I have it in for him, and the jobs Boss gives me he would git if I weren't here."

"He's a talented cowboy sober, but Boss has no plans for Spencer other than what he has him doin'. He told me that himself."

Charlie said, "Well, Tom, Boss needs to tell that to Spencer."

Pete and Tom left Charlie to his thoughts, mostly about how

he found himself settling things with a fight, much as his dad did when he still lived at home. That did not make him happy.

That evening at supper, Boss told Charlie, "You'll finish this week with Tom's crew. Next Monday, I'll have you take your crew out. There's fencin' near White Eagle I want checked and repaired. I'll have a map to help you find it. The fence is still up, but some hands saw places today that needed fixin'. They didn't have the tools to do the job, and it can wait 'til Monday. Also, the loadin' chutes we used during the last gather need some repair. I've selected four of the men for your crew. Burt Kilburn, Jodie Elkins, and the Koch brothers Matt and Ephraim. I plan to give ya one more hand. I'll make my mind up and have him with me Monday morning.

"That's fine Boss, I've worked with the Kochs and Burt, but Elkins is new to me."

"They're all good workers; Burt has been here a long time and will be a good right hand for ya."

* * *

Charlie rolled out of his bunk early Monday. He wanted to get to breakfast and have Tony ready before the crowd of cowboys hit the barn.

Boss found Charlie eating, "I see your horse is already saddled and waiting outside. You must have climbed out early."

"Yep, I guess I wanted to git goin' with the crew."

"Well, ya can't leave without your fifth member."

Boss smiled as he turned and pointed to Thad Spencer, "Here he is, Thad; you've met Charlie here?"

"Oh, I think everyone knows Charlie. He can ride, rope, and cook with the best of 'em, right?"

Boss said, "Good. Charlie, I look forward to you and your crew havin' an outstandin' first day."

Charlie looked away; *You gotta be shittin' me. He gives me THIS asshole?*

Charlie turned back and looked Boss directly in the eye, "Boss, can we go outside and talk a minute?"

"Sure, Charlie, walk with me as I head over to the White

House."

Outside Charlie said, "Why Spencer? You've gotta know we've had our differences."

Boss chuckled, "You've had your fights. I would say they've been more than differences. Charlie, you both are fine cowboys. Thad has a drinkin' problem and a short fuse. You've been the only man who has stood his ground with him as far as I know."

"That's all well and good, but why don't ya fire his ass?"

"Because when he's right, he can do the work of two good hands. And he does it well. I just had my last talk with him. He knows this is his last chance. His good work on the gather earned him that. You treat him fair, but don't put up with any bullshit from him, okay?"

Charlie nodded, "Okay. We'll see how it goes. Thanks for your confidence in me."

Boss offered his right hand, "We'll talk again in a few days. I gotta go."

Charlie pulled himself together and walked back into the chow hall.

Spencer was still standing in the same place. Charlie looked at him and asked, "Ya eat yet, Spencer?"

"Nope."

"Sit here, join the rest of us. I'm sure ya know everyone."

Charlie tried to remove the obvious tension by saying, "We all were part of the last gather, and we'll make a solid team. I'm lookin' forward to workin' with ya."

Charlie got nods from everyone, and Spencer said, "Yep, that 'bout covers it." His face said he wasn't buying it.

Spencer lived up to Charlie's expectations, which hadn't been high, to begin with. He was lazy whenever he could be and did his best to ignore Charlie's orders at every opportunity. It usually took Burt to also get on Spencer to get him to do even the simplest of tasks. But Charlie wasn't going to back down or give in to Spencer's pettiness. At times it reminded Charlie of trying to get his dad to stay sober and focused on helping the family. In the crew's second week together, Boss came to Charlie with a request. "I need you to take your guys and go out south below Bliss.

I got word we have some stray cattle down that way. Maybe fifty head out there, and we need to get them back to the herd."

"Sure, Boss, we'll pack for overnight just in case we need more than today to find them and get them back to the southern herd."

"That's a good plan. There are plenty of places out that way for cattle to hide and make it hard on ya."

Chapter Sixteen
September 1918

Charlie found his guys and gave them the news on what Boss needed. In no time, they were packed and down the trail toward Bliss.

Charlie rode up next to Spencer, "Durin' the gather we worked down in this area south of Bliss, and I remember there were some rough areas, but since I was tied to the chuck most of the time, I didn't see them up close. Did ya?"

Spencer grudgingly replied, "Yep, we'll have our work cut out for us if those beeves have gone into some of those gullies."

"I'm thinkin' you, Jodie, and I will work those areas, and Burt can take the Kochs and work other areas on over east. You good with that?"

"That'll work for me."

They were past Bliss and several miles south of the Salt Fork Bar when Charlie had them stop to have lunch in the shade of some blackjack oaks and let their horses graze along the river. At their meal, he said, "We didn't see anything yet, so let's talk about a plan for the rest of the day. Burt, you take the Kochs and work your way south and east from here. I'm sure the cattle won't be too far from the river, but they may have crossed over to the eastern side. Jodie, Thad, and I'll work south and west. We saw a lot of this area durin' the gather and should have some ideas about where to look. Let's get back to this spot around four o'clock. If you have found, cattle bring 'em back here, and if ya haven't found anythin', we can discuss what we'll do next."

They'd rode out that morning hoping for an easy day and have found the strays and had them back to the herd by afternoon and that the crew would be back to headquarters by nightfall.

Charlie knew from the gather and some fence-mending he had done weeks before that the area Burt and the Kochs would work was mostly rolling hills with stands of blackjacks. That could make their search tough. Charlie, Jodie, and Spencer found their territory as they remembered, with lots of trees and gullies, which meant they would have to work slow.

Jodie meandered out on his own but stayed in view.

"Charlie, I don't recall this bein' as rocky and sandy, do you?" Spencer asked.

"No, I don't, and I've come across tracks showin' me cattle have come through here."

"That's good, but I don't favor the idea of tryin' to drive them back through this stuff."

"Me, either."

Because of the terrain, Spencer and Charlie drifted apart as they searched but could see each other. Charlie was following some cattle tracks when there was a scream to his right. He looked that way just as Spencer's horse reared up and came down in a fall. The horse and Spencer disappeared. He turned and spurred Tony to a gallop over to where he last saw them. He found Spencer and his horse at the bottom of a twenty-foot-deep ravine. Charlie jumped off Tony, laid back, and skidded down the gully wall to Spencer.

"You hurt?"

"Yep, my horse landed on my leg."

"Your horse seems okay." Charlie pointed, "he's over there. Is your leg broke?"

"All I know is that it hurts like a son-of-a-bitch. It's on fire."

Charlie glanced to the right and said, "Didja hear that?"

Spencer's horse bolted and ran up the ravine.

Charlie could hear the distinctive sound of an angry rattle-snake. He looked around frantically, knowing it must be close. Both horses' must-have, too, as now Tony ran away.

"Where is it?" Spencer asked, the fear clear in his voice.

"I see it, Spencer." The snake was about five feet in front of them, and the buzz of its rattle grew loud and angry. "It must have been what spooked your horse."

Spencer was racked with pain and fear, "Charlie, I can't move. What are ya gonna do?"

Charlie worked hard to remain calm as he looked around for something. Charlie's rifle was on Tony and he didn't carry a pistol, and Charlie didn't want to try and take on a rattlesnake with his small knife. Then he saw something that might work. "I'll git to that rock over there and use it to kill the bastard." He pointed at a rock that was to his left, outside of the reach of the snake. Charlie leaned over, and even though he was leaning away from the snake it still struck out toward him angrily.

"He's really mad," Spencer said.

"Well, so am I," Charlie said. He picked up the rock, which was about the size of his palm, and aimed at the snake. He threw it and hit the snake.

Excited, he hollered, "I hit him, Spencer!"

"Is he dead?"

Charlie could see that the snake wasn't dead. "No, he's dazed... but he ain't dead."

Spencer looked around and leaned to his right with a grunt of pain but managed to reach a broken limb. Through his pain, he tossed it toward Charlie, "Here... see if you can... use this."

Charlie grabbed it, "This is perfect." The stick was about four feet long and had a fork at one end. He stabbed the snake near its head. He had him pinned, writhing and twisting, trying to get away.

"Got him."

Charlie took out his knife, stepped on the snake's body, and then cut the head off.

"Good job, Charlie; I couldn't have done that from here the way I'm hurtin'."

"I'm the one that didn't kill it with a rock. We made a good team. Now, we need to get you outta here and to a doctor."

"I know you're right, just thinkin' 'bout that hurts."

"We need to protect that leg," Charlie said. He started to look around. "See if you can git your belt off while I look for another stick to go with this one," he lifted the one he'd used to trap the snake, "to make a splint." Charlie walked around the gully, an eye peeled for any more snakes and a good, stout stick. He found what he needed and headed back. Spencer looked pale, and sweat beaded his face, but he had managed to get his belt off. Charlie pulled off his belt and knelt.

"This is gonna hurt."

"I know," Spencer grimaced and gritted his teeth, then nodded.

Charlie gingerly straightened Spencer's leg, eliciting a small cry of pain. He laid out the sticks and then dug in the sand under Spencer's leg so he could thread the belts through without having to lift his leg.

Charlie said, "I'll be as gentle as I can." He threaded the belts through holes and tightened them to hold the leg as straight as possible.

After he finished the splint, he said, "I'll get my canteen for us. I'm dry as a bone, and ya must be, too. I gotta git to work makin' a travois so we can git ya outta here and back to headquarters."

"You ain't just leavin' me here for the critters?"

"Why'd I do that?"

"Charlie Kelly, I owe ya a lot, cowboy."

"You're sweatin' a bunch and look a little pale, hang in there. We've gotta ways to go."

Charlie climbed up the ridge and whistled for Tony, who trotted out of the brush. He tethered him to a blackjack sapling and brought the canteen and some jerky down to Spencer. Charlie had seen a way to get Tony down to Spencer safely from the ridgetop, and he also could see that Spencer's horse wasn't too far away.

"Thad, I'm goin' to git Blackie and bring him and Tony down in the ravine with us. I think with your saddle and some branches, I can rig up a travois to your horse, and you can ride back on it."

Charlie had no trouble with Blackie. He came to him, bringing both horses down into the gully. Charlie got to work on the travois. He found two long thick branches and a few sticks to build the travois. Charlie used twine he carried in his tool kit to hold it together. He took out the bit and bridle from Blackie and used it and the reins to tie the travois to Blackie's back. Kelly placed Spencer's saddle on the device to lay back into to keep his head steady.

"It looks like it should work, so let's git you on it and see."

"Careful now, Charlie, that leg's killin' me."

Charlie lifted Spencer onto the travois. Spencer's face told the story, but he handled the pain quietly.

Charlie said, "Ya did good, Thad, we need to get movin'. Do ya agree this setup with Blackie pullin' can hold ya?"

"Yeah, it seems strong enough but take it easy."

Charlie wrapped Spencer in his saddle blanket, and they started up and out of the gully. Once out, Charlie pointed them toward Bliss.

"Spencer, I want to get us to Bliss. We can use Rachel Little Feather's phone and call the ranch."

"That makes good sense. Can you hurry up? My leg wants this over."

They both found some humor in that but settled into silence. Both knew it'd take a good long while to make it to Bliss.

* * *

Several hours later, Charlie cried, "Hey, there's Burt and the others up ahead." Charlie whistled and waved, and Burt waved back and rode hard to get to Charlie's side.

Burt said, "What happened to Spencer?"

"A rattler spooked his horse as Spencer rode near the edge of a gully. He and his horse ended up at the bottom of the ravine."

Spencer said, "I think my leg is broke."

"Burt, ride into Bliss and call the ranch from the bar. Tell Boss what's happened. We'll keep movin' toward Rachel's. Ephraim, you and Matt help me by ridin' where ya can watch Spencer. We will take it slow, so Spencer's ride won't be so rough on him. Burt, we need a wagon and a doc' out here as soon as possible."

"I'll git there as fast as I can."

"Wait at Rachel's and bring the Doc to meet us if we ain't made it by the time he gits there. Hurry, Burt."

Burt yelled, "Yah!" and he took off in a cloud of dust as he spurred his pony into a gallop.

"Jodie, you ride ahead of us. Watch for holes, snakes, and anything else that could ruin our trip back to Bliss."

"You bet, boss."

"Let's check our riggin' one more time, then let's git a move on."

Charlie figured it was a good two hours from Rachel's at the pace they could safely carry Spencer. It wasn't likely they'd make it there before dark. The conversation was sparse. Spencer had settled into some level of quiet agony that walled him off from the rest of the world. The guys knew to let him rest, though his clenched fist on the travois said he wasn't comfortable. Shortly after dusk, the crew arrived at Bliss, and they used the travois as a stretcher and carried Spencer into the bar. Burt had given Rachel a rundown on the situation, so she had moved some tables together to allow them to lay the travois across them.

"Burt, did you reach Boss?"

"Yep, it's been about an hour since we talked. Boss said they'd git here as fast as the wagon could git 'em here."

"Well, that should be any time now."

Rachel walked over to the group with a tray full of beers and said, "Y'all must be spittin' dust, so here's somethin' to wet your whistles."

As tired and dry as they were, the crew managed a shout of approval, and even Spencer took one from the tray. Before they could finish their beers, Jodie, who had taken his beer out front with him, ran into the bar and said, "Boss is comin' hard this way with dust a-flyin'."

Boss and the ranch doctor arrived and went immediately to Spencer.

Doc Combs said, "Son, tell me where you hurt and what happened out there."

"It's my right leg, and it hurts awful below my knee. Me and my horse fell into a deep gully after a rattler spooked us."

"Okay, then that'll help me get started. You lay back and let me have a look."

Doc Combs began his examination by cutting the right pants leg to the knee. He then said, "I'm sorry to destroy a good pair of trousers, but I need…"

Spencer surprised the room as he interrupted with, "Yeah, Doc, these were my Sunday go to meetin' pants."

Everyone enjoyed the humor. It seemed to provide a moment for all to exhale and lower the tension.

Boss tapped Charlie on the arm and said, "Bring your beer and come over here."

Charlie walked over and joined Boss with Spencer as Doc continued his work.

Boss looked at Spencer, "What happened and what did Charlie do as you remember it?"

"First, let me say that Charlie really 'Cowboyed Up' out there. After I fell, my horse landed on my leg, and although my horse was able to git up and run off, the fall also made me kinda fuzzy. But the snake had come down the hill with us and was mad as hell. Charlie came slidin' down the hill after me and saw the snake a few feet from me, rattlin' his tail to beat the band. He was about to strike when Charlie hit him with a rock and stunned him. Then he took a stick, caught the snake, and cut off his head. I couldn't move, and I'd have been helpless to fight off that critter."

"Charlie, where were you when he fell?"

"I was maybe a hundred yards away and had found some cattle tracks. Suddenly, I hear a scream and look over and see Spencer and his horse fall out of sight. After I got down into the ravine, Spencer, even with his injury, grabbed a stick and tossed it to me to help me kill the snake. But Boss, we both were more concerned about gittin' Thad outta that ravine and here to a doctor than about that snake."

"Charlie, you handled this situation of gittin' Spencer safely to the help he needed like a top hand. As we on the 101 have said for years, sometimes ya gotta 'Cowboy Up,' and I agree with Spencer, ya did, son."

Boss stepped back and looked over at Doc, "Whattaya think?"

Doc wiped some dried blood from Spencer's leg as he said, "Whoever immobilized this leg did a fine job, and because of that, this fella can expect a full recovery if he follows my advice."

Spencer heard this and blurted out, "It was Charlie. He saved me from that snake, and you say Doc that he saved me the use of my leg too?"

"Yes, young man, he did a fine job of preparin' you and your leg for transport, and I'll take it from here, but you must follow my advice over the next weeks and months."

Boss nodded, "Thanks Doc, and now can we git this guy back to headquarters?"

"Yes, we can, and the sooner, the better. I'll put some additional wrap on this, and we can go."

Charlie and three other hands lifted the travois and carried Spencer outside and gently slid him into the back of the wagon, and all rode back to ranch headquarters. Despite the late hour, Boss had asked the cook to keep dinner warm for them, and after they got Spencer settled in Doc's office, they all went to the chow hall for a late supper.

Over supper, Boss said to Charlie, "You and your men handled a tough situation, and ya did yourselves proud." His smile showed his pleasure with them as he said, "But we still got some missin' cattle out there. I need ya to git back out in the mornin' and finish up what you started. Did ya see anythin' that'll help ya find the cattle?"

"I was startin' to follow some tracks when Spencer took his fall. Did anyone else see anythin'?"

Burt said, "Nothin' fresh, and we covered several miles along the east side of the river,"

Boss said, "Thanks, men. That sounds like the beeves are somewhere west of the river and knowin' that will help ya in the mornin'. You won't have Spencer tomorrow and probably not for several months. So, Charlie, do ya need me to give another hand?"

"Now that we know where the fresh tracks are, the five of us can handle it. We can talk about another hand after we get this done."

"That's some of the roughest country around here. It'll probably take you a full day to find 'em, maybe more. It'll be 'nother day gittin' them back to the herd. Make sure the cookie gives ya plenty o' vittles. And if you need it, take a packhorse with ya."

"Will do." After Boss walked away, Charlie turned to the crew and said, "Gents, we better finish up here and git some shuteye. Mornin'll git here before we know it."

Charlie stopped in the kitchen to let the cooks know they needed food for five to last two days ready in the morning. Then he headed to the bunkhouse.

Chapter Seventeen
September 1918

Charlie was the first one up and out to the barn to get Tony saddled and ready for the day as had become his habit. While he was there, he found Blackie and gave him some attention, too. One of the barn hands arrived and approached him, "Hey Fuzzy, Spencer got hurt bad last night. Can ya keep a special eye on Blackie 'til he's up to helpin' take care of him?"

"Happy to do it. Blackie's one of my favorites; course, I'd do that for any of 'em. Thanks for lettin' me know. Spencer will be alright, won't he?"

"Yep, but he's gotta broken leg, and it'll be a while before he's up and around. Gotta git to breakfast, thanks for doin' that."

"No problem."

Charlie got his meal at the chow hall and found a seat where his guys could join him when they arrived. He was deep in his thoughts about the day ahead of him when Boss walked up with a tall, well-dressed man beside him.

"Mr. Miller, this is the young gentleman I was talkin' about. Charlie Kelly, this is George L. Miller, one of the owners of the 101."

"Please to meet you, Charlie."

Charlie stood, "Yes, sir, it's an honor to meet you, sir."

"No need for sirs, and it's my honor as well to meet a young man with your maturity and quick thinkin' when the chips are down. I genuinely appreciate your actions in a tough situation yesterday."

"Thank you, and I'm certain others would have done the same."

"You would hope so, but my experience says not everyone is capable. You showed fine leadership." With a chuckle, he continued, "You also made Boss look smart havin' recently promoted you to Lead Wrangler. I'll let you get back to your food, but I wanted to meet you and share my appreciation for how you handled the events of yesterday."

"It was my pleasure, Mr. Miller, and thank you for your thoughts."

Boss walked away in a conversation with George L., and Charlie sat and returned to his thoughts and the food on his plate.

Burt walked up, "Who was that with Boss?"

"Mr. George Miller, one of the owners."

"You're joshin' me, Charlie."

"No, I wouldn't mess around about that."

"Why were they talkin' to you?"

"Mr. Miller asked Boss to introduce me to him and wanted to talk about what went on yesterday." Charlie smiled. "I guess we done real good, Burt."

"I've been here maybe five years, and that's the first time I've seen a Miller anywhere other than from way off at a big shindig, and certainly not in the chow hall."

Charlie hadn't realized that having one of the Miller's come by was such a big deal. "I sure hope I handled it okay and didn't embarrass myself."

"I doubt it," Burt said, "Boss was smilin'."

Jodie and the Kochs showed up with their plates full, and Charlie began discussing the plan for the day, "Let's git back out ta where Spencer fell and start working from there."

Burt finished a bite of bacon and said, "Didn't ya say ya saw some tracks?"

"Yep, I had seen some fresh tracks, so we can find them and start from there."

They all nodded.

"Let's finish these plates and all meet outside in fifteen minutes, Jodie; you go git our chuck from the Cookie. He should have it ready. We'll give our horses one more drink before we go."

The crew enjoyed the brisk morning air as the sun peaked over the blackjacks along the Salt Fork. They rode along the river south and west of Bliss and ate lunch where they had stopped yesterday.

Over their meal, Charlie gave his ideas for the afternoon, "Gents, it shouldn't take us long to git back to where Spencer fell. As I said, I was startin' to follow some fresh tracks when all hell broke loose. We can fan out and work our way across that series of ravines from there. We gotta stay within view of each other. Because the land, as our buddy found out, is dangerous."

Burt asked, "You were already comin' this way with Spencer. How far is it down to where he fell?"

"It's about two miles, so let's finish up and ride."

When they got to the accident site, Charlie allowed a quick look and discussed what had happened. "Here's the spot where Spencer fell; y'all have a look."

Jodie looked at Charlie, "Damn, that's a ways down there. Spencer's lucky to be alive."

Charlie nodded, "Burt, you stay here and continue the search. Me and the rest'll head up the ravine and spread out to start our search." Everybody nodded and spurred their horses. When Charlie reached the spot where he and Tony had been yesterday, he could still see the tracks from the cattle. They worked south and west from that point.

After a couple of minutes, Burt called out, "Hey, I'm seein' tracks here, and there're some goin' down in the gully."

Charlie hollered, "I'll come to have a look with you." He said to the rest, "Keep workin' where you are, but don't get out of sight."

Charlie and Burt rode down into the gully. They followed the tracks for about a quarter of a mile and found about a dozen head of cattle at a small water hole that must a collected during the recent rains.

Charlie said, "Let's leave them here for now and go back to the boys and see if they've picked up any more tracks."

They found Jodie and the Kochs off their horses, gathered heads-down, focused on the ground.

"What's up?" Charlie asked as they rode up.

Ephraim said, "I found these tracks of cattle here, but look, there are some of several horses too."

Burt got off his horse and looked closer, "I'll be damned. He's right, Charlie. What do ya make of that?"

"That's not what we expected, and I don't like what that could mean for us. Do the tracks appear put down at the same time?"

Burt replied, "Yep, and there's enough here to say the cattle were driven south by whoever was on horseback."

Jodie said, "It looks to be at least a few dozen head bein' moved across here because the tracks spread across east thirty yards or more."

"Gents, it appears we may have rustlers. Let's leave the cattle with the waterhole in the ravine and see where these tracks lead us. Let's spread out a bit to make sure we don't miss anything."

As Burt remounted Charlie added, "And let's keep alert. We don't want to be surprised by these rustlers." The others nodded in agreement, and they spread out to follow the tracks.

The tracks didn't alter their course, and it was late afternoon when Jodie pointed to the southwest. "Charlie, do you see what I see over there?"

Charlie looked and there was a low cloud of dust that hung on the horizon. "Yep, and we better go check it out."

"Burt, you take the Kochs and go out to the left and approach the dust cloud from that direction. I'll take Jodie and come in from the right. If what we find is just the beeves, that's good, but if we find rustlers with' em it'll be better for us to come in from two directions. Everyone have his rifle loaded and at the ready?"

Burt pulled his Winchester from its saddle holster and said, "Yep, that's a good idea." The others nodded their agreement as they pulled their weapons.

They split up, and Charlie and Jodie worked around carefully not to create dust themselves. They used stands of blackjack oaks and the terrain to hide their moves. They reached a spot where Charlie could finally see the cattle.

"Jodie, can you see the cattle? There must be close to forty head down there."

"I see them, and I also see some fellas on horseback down there too. Whattaya want to do about that?"

Charlie looked at the cattle and the rustlers. "Not quite sure yet. But my mother and the Lord taught me that it ain't right to steal."

Jodie patted his rifle. "I'm ready if need be."

"I hope it don't come to that, but these guys are up to no good and probably don't want to be bothered."

"Well, I hope we aim to bother them."

"Yep," Charlie smiled.

Jodie smiled, then frowned. "Oh shit, I hope Burt and the Kochs see what's happenin'."

"Let's follow the tree line and git as close as we can to them before they git wind of us."

They tethered their horses and began moving as quietly as bobcats from tree to tree and boulder to boulder. They were still well hidden and within twenty-five yards of the cattle when Charlie saw they were setting up a branding operation with obvious plans to steal the cattle. He could see four men, and they were all occupied at the time.

Charlie turned to Jodie, "I can see the 101 brand on the cattle nearest me. I'm going back to git Tony and ride in as if I just happened upon these guys. As I arrive and their lookin' at me, get as close in as ya can with yur rifle ready."

Jodie nodded and Charlie slipped quietly back to the horses. He put his rifle back into its holster and then jumped into Tony's saddle. He rode Tony into camp, catching the rustlers off guard, "Hello, is the coffee hot?"

The four men wore dirty brown dusters over blue jeans and ranch shirts. Charlie couldn't be sure but thought he'd seen at least one of the men around the bar in Bliss. All four turned to face Charlie, alert but shocked by him riding into their camp. Several stones had been gathered to make a fire pit and they had a fire burning, with irons resting in the coals.

Charlie rested his hands on the pommel of his saddle and whistled as he looked around. "My that's some handsome beeves ya got there."

One of the rustlers, the one that Charlie thought he'd seen in Bliss, stepped away from the others and said, "He's from the 101." His right hand flipped his duster back and he started to pull out his gun.

A rifle shot echoed around the hollow and the bullet struck the ground right at the rustler's feet, the puff of dust causing the man to hesitate. He pulled his hand away from his weapon.

Charlie had pulled his rifle at the moment after Jodie had fired and said, "The next one hits your heart, asshole. I am with the 101, and these are the Miller's cattle, despite your sorry attempt to rebrand 'em. Hands up, gents, and stand where you are." He leveled his rifle on them and the men all put their hands up.

"Jodie, come on in with your rifle at the ready."

"Okay, Charlie, I'm here."

Charlie dismounted, "All of you come to the fire and keep your hands up where I can see 'em."

One of the rustlers growled, "What do you mean these are 101 cattle? We ain't stealin'. We're movin' 'em from the Bar L to Ponca to ship 'em to Wichita."

Charlie looked at the rustlers and smiled, "So, that's why they have 101 brands on 'em? I can see your runnin' iron from here. Which one of ya is the brandin' artist? It's no doubt you planned to use it to change the brands." Charlie nodded his head slowly, "Turn the 101 brand to the Bar L, move 'em to Ponca, right, makes a lotta sense to me."

The familiar-looking rustler said, "Why you somnabitch, I ain't gonna let a runt like you ruin this for me." He went for his gun.

Charlie fired his rifle from the hip, hitting the man in his right shoulder. He fell backward, his gun still in his holster.

Charlie looked at the rest of them and said, "Anyone else?" The other three men shook their heads and made sure their hands were up even higher than before. "Then git your rustlin' asses to the fire."

The three others all moved carefully, while Charlie covered them. Charlie said to Jodie and pointed at the guy on the ground, "Git his gun, and help him to the fire."

While Jodie disarmed the wounded rustler Charlie met the others one by one and removed their guns. Once they were disarmed Charlie let out a holler, "Burt, can ya hear me?"

"Sure can. Do ya need us?"

"Come on in."

After they were all in the camp and had confirmed the wound was just a flesh wound, they tied the rustler's hands behind their backs. Jodie checked enough of the cattle to prove they were part of the 101 herds. It was close to dusk by this time, and ranch headquarters was a good hard ride away.

Charlie said, "Matt, you and Ephraim stay here with the cattle. Jodie and I'll take these guys to headquarters. We'll come back out in the mornin' to finish gettin' these and the cattle we found in the ravine back to the herd."

"Will do, and be careful, and you might go by the Salt Fork and use Mabel's phone to call and let Boss know you're comin'."

"Good idea, that's what we'll do."

Charlie pointed at the rustlers, "Burt check 'em over for anythin' they could use for weapons and then take their boots off. They won't git too far barefoot."

Charlie used a rope to loop all the rustlers mounted on their horses together. With their hands tied behind them and their horses looped together, they were easy to lead back to the ranch.

Down the trail a few miles, Jodie asked, "I have never seen anybody tie riders together like that. How did you think of that?"

"The Marshal in Fort Sumner did that once to three varmints he brought in by himself. I thought we could use that here with these four."

Jodie nodded and they led the four rustlers toward Bliss.

Chapter Eighteen
September 1918

Charlie and Jodie rode up to Mabel's bar with the rustlers in tow. He dismounted and said, "Watch 'em while I go call Boss."

As Charlie entered the bar, he saw several 101 hands and said, "Jodie is outside watchin' a string of rustlers. Can ya go give 'em a hand?"

Mabel shouted, "What'd you say, Charlie? Rustlers?"

"Yep, we caught 'em red-handed with 101 branded cattle south and west of here. Can I use the phone to call Boss?"

"Oh, of course." She grabbed her shotgun and headed to the porch.

Charlie got the operator to place a call to the phone at the Ranch. It took several minutes before one of the hands was able to get Boss on the other end.

"Boss, this is Charlie. Jodie and I are bringin' in four rustlers we found with a good amount of the herd."

"What! Did you say, rustlers? Where are you?"

"We're at Mabel's. We should be back with you in an hour."

"No, no, you stay there, and I'll git a few men and come to you. You be careful."

"Yes, sir, there's a couple of 101 fellas that were here havin' a beer and they're helpin' too. And I see Mabel's got her shotgun. We'll be fine."

Boss chuckled and said, "Don't let her shoot anybody. We'll be there soon."

* * *

In less than thirty minutes Charlie saw Boss and a couple of other hands riding hard toward the bar. They pulled up, their horses skidding a bit on the dirt outside the bar.

"Glad to see ya, Boss," Charlie said with a smile as Boss and the others dismounted.

"It's dad-gummed amazin' how you seem to find a problem and solve it. No one expected the cattle that were missin' from the herd were bein' rustled."

"We found tracks south of where Spencer fell and followed 'em till we found these guys holed up with our cattle. We surprised 'em and got the upper hand."

"Let's get 'em back to headquarters. I called Mr. Miller and told him. The Sheriff should be meetin' us when we arrive."

The rustlers were quiet and trying to shrink down in their saddles as all the 101 hands glared at them. None of them said anything, just gave a hard stare that would have unnerved anybody. Charlie gave his thanks to Mabel for letting him use the phone.

"Come back soon Charlie and I'll let you have a couple of beers on the house. First savin' Spencer, and now catchin' rustlers. You're all right."

Charlie blushed. That was high praise from Mabel, and it felt better to him than any praise he'd gotten from Boss or Tom.

He got back on Tony and together the entire group rode out, forming a circle around the four rustlers. As Charlie, Boss, and the hands approached the main gate with their prisoners, Charlie said, "Boss, whattaya suppose that crowds doin' out in front of the White House?"

"I'm not sure, Charlie. But I'd say they're expectin' us."

A roar began and got louder as they rode through the gate.

Jodie hollered, "This must be every hand on the place."

Boss looked at Charlie and chuckled, "I think this is all about you, young man."

Out in front stood Spencer on his crutches, giving his meanest glare at the prisoners, then turning to Charlie, smiling and tipping his hat.

The crowd parted to show the Miller brothers at the bottom of the stairs to the White House. George stepped forward and pointed as he said, "Charlie, I want you to meet my brothers Joe and Zack. Gentlemen, this is Charlie Kelly, who headed the crew that captured these varmints with our cattle."

Charlie and Boss dismounted. The brothers walked to Charlie, and they shook hands.

Joe said, "We appreciate what you and your men have done."

Zack added, "We owe ya Kelly, and you've made your mark here at the 101."

Boss said, "Where's the Sheriff? We need to hand these varmints off to him."

"He was out on another incident when I talked to a deputy, but he should be here soon," said George.

Charlie turned to Jodie, "Take a few men and go tie the prisoners off to a hitching post nearby. Don't let 'em out of your sight until we can hand them off to the sheriff."

Jodie nodded and said, "You bet Charlie. He looked at some hands and said, "Let's go."

With the crowd still gathered around them, George said, "Okay, Charlie, what happened?"

Charlie told the story and ended with, "And that's about it. Me and Jodie will head out in the morning to bring the cattle back."

Boss laughed and slapped Charlie on the back. "'That's about it.' Charlie, you're too modest for your own good." Boss looked up to the Millers. "Charlie did it again. He and his men come upon a tough situation and made good things happen."

The crowd began to chant, "Kelly Can! Kelly Can! Kelly Can!"

Zack Miller smiled, raised his hands to quieten the crowd, and said, "Charlie, you are a quick thinker."

"Thank you, sir."

Boss interjected, "We should be damn proud we have Charlie here at the 101, don't ya think Mr. Miller?"

George Miller didn't hesitate, "I'm not sure which one of us you're asking," the three brothers laughed, "but the answer is yes, and I want to get to know Charlie better."

At that moment the crowd parted again, and the Sheriff and his men finally arrived. Sheriff Verne Anderson said, "What do we have here?"

George turned to the Sheriff and said, "Cattle rustling, and Charlie Kelly, standing here, with four of his men, captured them for you."

"Where are these men you're accusin'?"

"I had Jodie tie 'em to the hitchin' post over there." Charlie pointed toward the barn.

The Sheriff had two deputies with him and instructed them to get the prisoners and take them to the Ponca City jail. He then turned back to Charlie. "Are you the one I need to talk to for my report, and can we go over here under the trees?"

George said, "Sheriff, let me offer you two my office. That'll give you some privacy."

"Sure, Mr. Miller."

"Okay then, follow me." George led them up the stairs and inside. Charlie marveled at the grandeur of the lobby and George's office. Beautiful woods and leather everywhere. Electric lights hung from the ceiling, not kerosene lanterns.

Charlie gave the Sheriff a complete description of the day's events and answered the few questions the Sheriff asked. In the end, Charlie offered, "I brought the runnin' iron they were using to change to brands. It's out in my saddlebags."

George, sitting as a witness to the proceedings, used the opportunity to add, "Of course, we have complete records of our herds, so we can certainly answer any questions that might come up about the ownership of the cattle."

The Sheriff smiled, "I think this is an open and shut case, Mr. Miller. To be thorough, I should go out to the where Charlie left his men with the cattle in question."

Charlie said, "Of course, Sheriff. I intend to leave in the mornin' at first light to go collect Mr. Miller's cattle."

"That's fine, and I'll be here and ready to ride with you." They all walked outside, and Charlie took the running iron from his saddlebags and gave it to the Sheriff.

"Thanks, young man. Again, I'll be here and ready to go with you." He and his deputies left with the prisoners.

George put his right hand on Charlie's shoulder and said, "My brothers and I want you to join us for supper. We planned to eat at the café."

"I'd be happy to join ya."

"Good, are you ready now?"

"Yes, but I need to take care of my horse first. Can I have time to take him to the barn?"

"Of course, then come join us."

At the café, as they finished their meal, George said, "Charlie, it seems this is the week where you are proving yourself a cut above the regular ranch hand. We think we have the cream of the crop working for us. But we don't expect to see anyone handle two emergencies in the same week. And you did it without loss of life or property."

"I appreciate the kind words, sir, but I was just doin' what you pay me for."

"Yes, that is what we pay our foremen and managers for, and we hope to see this from time to time in others. I need you to come to the White House after you return from your trip south tomorrow to gather those strays. I want to ask you a few questions."

"Mr. Miller, I'm not in trouble, am I?"

"No, anything but that. You be safe out there tomorrow."

Zack stood to go as he said, "Good job Charlie, see you down the trail."

Joe reached over to shake Charlie's hand and said, "You made us proud," and he laughed as he added, "And, you saved the 101 a lot of money too."

After they all left, Charlie had a minute alone to think; I don't think I've felt this good about a job since Jasper allowed me to run his store by myself when he would go to Pauls Valley for supplies.

He stood up and walked back to the bunkhouse. As Charlie got there, he saw a letter waiting on his pillow. He saw a Kansas City postmark and felt a thrill of excitement as it had been almost a month since Susan's last letter. But Tom and Pete came over to Charlie's bunk so Charlie couldn't open it right away.

Pete sat down next to him and eagerly asked, "How did it feel to spend time with the owners?"

"They seemed nice enough; George Miller wants me to come to the White House tomorrow night when I get back from movin' the cattle we found back into the main herd."

Tom said, "Why, did he say?"

"He said he has some things he wants to ask me. I have no idea as to what that might be."

They talked a while longer, Tom and Pete wanting to hear about what had happened again. Charlie wasn't tired of retelling the story and he provided more details with his friends, but his mind kept returning to Susan's letter.

Eventually, Tom and Pete left and Charlie opened the letter.

My Dearest Charlie,

I remain safe and sound in Kansas City, and lonely. I miss you terribly. We have been apart for a year now, and I miss your embrace, your strong arms around my body. I miss your kiss and the time we spent together. I know I want you, to spend my time with you

It has been a few weeks since your last letter, and I'm unsure if you feel the same way about me. Do you think about me when you are alone on the ranch?

I think you should know that a man who works here at the bank is pursuing me, and to this point, I've rebuffed his advances. I need to feel confident there is a future for us either here in Kansas City or in Oklahoma. I continue to enjoy working with my father in the family businesses, and he was happy when I returned home, as I previously mentioned, but I am worried, Charlie. He has acquired a persistent cough and a week ago, he finally went to his doctor. The doctor is not sure what is causing his cough. I hope it's not this awful flu. Being an only child and with my mother having died ten years ago, Father is all the family I have here except Uncle Curt. If I lose my father, I could end up owning these businesses with all the responsibilities involved. Father has had some wise men working for him for years but has only allowed me and Uncle Curt to see and understand his entire business empire. Oh, Charlie, I desperately wish you were here. Not only because I want to be with you, to be held in your strong arms, but because I know Father would see your talents and trustworthiness as I do. Maybe he would let you see it all, and it could be ours.

Please write me soon and let me know your thoughts about us.

Yours in love,
Susan

Charlie laid back and let this settle into his mind. They had written to each other several times over the year. This letter was the first time either of them had been so clear about their feelings for the other. He was feeling excited at the thought of Susan as his forever, but he wasn't as excited about running businesses in Kansas City. He knew he would need a few days to mull this over before writing his response.

In the morning, Charlie was up and had Tony saddled, and was at breakfast when Sheriff Anderson walked into the chow hall door.

Charlie stood and said, "Mornin' Sheriff, you must have missed a fair amount of sleep to be here already."

Anderson replied, "It was a short night, but we'll do fine."

"I expect Jodie here anytime, so let's have the cookie make you a plate, and after we get some food in us, we can head south."

Charlie took his seat and returned to his plate. His mind wandered again as it had been all morning. *How am I going to answer Susan? I want to be with her, to hold her in my arms. But I love being here at the 101. Could I ever be a businessman? Does being a ranch hand, even a top hand, give me everything I want?*

Charlie wasn't able to answer that question by the time the Sheriff had finished his breakfast.

Chapter Nineteen
September 1918

Charlie and his crew wrapped everything up, got the rustled cattle back with the herd, and returned to the barn by mid-afternoon. Charlie took care of Tony and then went to the bunkhouse to clean himself up. As he headed to the White House, Boss walked across the yard.

Charlie went over to Boss and as he tilted his head to the side and scratched the back of his neck, "Boss, you know I'm supposed to go see Mr. George Miller right now, don't you?"

Boss put his hand on Charlie's left shoulder, squeezed it, and said, "Yep, he mentioned it to me last night. I think you have made a good impression on him. Before ya ask, I have no idea what he wants to talk about."

"Okay... then I'll see ya later."

Charlie went around to the main entrance and entered the house. He didn't remember the sign that said "Welcome, Come In" hanging on the screen door from last night, but there were so many people around, and he was so disoriented by all the attention, he was sure there was a lot that he'd missed. A distinguished, middle-aged lady sat behind a desk in the middle of the big lobby and said, "May I help you?"

"I'm Charlie Kelly, and I'm supposed to meet with..."

"Mr. George L. Miller is expecting you. Please follow me."

She led him down the same hallway Charlie had taken last night when he'd met with the Sheriff. They stopped in front of the open door that led to Mr. Miller's office. He was on the phone.

She cleared her throat and whispered, "Mr. Miller, Mr. Kelly is here to see you." She turned and walked back to her desk.

Charlie remembered George's office was on the front of the building, and now in the daylight, he could see the tall, rolling grasslands of the 101 for miles out his windows. Charlie remembered being impressed yesterday, but now without the Sheriff there and the excitement of having captured the rustlers he was taking everything in: the smells of leather, the sheen of the polished mahogany, and the size of the room was almost overwhelming.

George smiled and motioned for Charlie to sit at the table they used yesterday.

He completed the call, stood, and came around his big desk and joined Charlie at the table.

George offered his hand, "I see you're back from down south. You get all the strays rounded up and back with the main herd?"

Charlie returned the handshake, "All done, sir."

"Good, good, glad to hear it. That was Sheriff Anderson on the phone with me when you arrived, and everything is in place for those varmints' conviction for rustling our cattle."

Charlie smiled, "That's great news."

"Now, Charlie, I asked you here because in the months you've been here, you've impressed every person you have worked for or alongside. And now, over the past week, you caught my attention, so I began asking Boss about you."

Charlie rubbed his palms on his jeans. "I'm glad he and the other people have been pleased; I take my work seriously. I'll always want to give you a solid day's effort for my pay."

"I appreciate that, but I get that from all our hands, or they don't make it here. We don't abide good-for-nothing loafers at the 101."

"Yes, sir. Boss said as much to me when I hired on."

"I suspect he did. I guess the first thing I'd want to know is, are you happy here? Does what you do now give you everything you want in life?"

Charlie was a bit surprised at how close George Miller's question was to what he'd been mulling over since reading Susan's letter. "Well, those aren't yes or no questions. I'm happy here at the 101. I've wanted to become a top hand here for as long as I can remember." He paused for a moment, unsure if he should go on. He didn't want to disappoint Mr. Miller and he hadn't answered this question for himself yet. "But, sir, over the past year, my dream has become bigger."

George smiled as if he knew exactly what Charlie was struggling with. "Tell me about that bigger dream."

"I can't say that it is clear to me, but the thing I know is I want more, a lot more than I can ever have as a $30 room-and-board cowboy. And I mean no disrespect for a cowboy or any of your hands."

"It's great that you have a bigger goal. I hear you finished high school somewhere back in New Mexico, that true?"

"Yes, and as I worked my way here, I spent several months learning to run a mercantile."

"Where did you do that?"

"I worked for Jasper Blackaby in Elmore City. He taught me a lot in a short time."

"I don't know Jasper personally, but through a close friend down by Shawnee, I heard he was a smart businessman. That should have given you a good chance at much more than what the job you have here could ever do. Why did you leave?"

"Jasper was murdered in the store, and a fire was started to cover up the crime. The store burnt to the ground."

George's eyes went wide. "I hope they caught the murderer."

Charlie nodded. "They did. He was trying to sell Jasper's pocket watch." George gave a nod confident that justice had been done.

"I may have met the man you mentioned. Is he Clay Stephens?"

"Absolutely, and how do you know Clay?"

"I don't know if I have a right to say I know him, but we met one night at the Norwood Hotel in Shawnee. We spent some time together talking. Clay asked me to look him up the next time I was in town. He wanted to show me the Double Bar S. I told him I was headin' here and asked me to say hello to you if I ever got a chance."

George smiled and said, "That tells me something about you too. Clay can pick a winner in a flash. If he spent time with you, he saw something special. Inviting you to his pride and joy says a lot as well. I want to go back to what Blackaby taught you. Give me some ideas about what he showed you."

Charlie smiled, took a deep breath, and said, "I had to learn the merchandise he sold. In quiet times at the store or in the evening after supper, we talked about profit and loss, credit, and advertising. One night all we talked about was how to pick employees. We spent the most time talking about how important it is to build relationships across the town, the county, the state, and even the country. Especially in your field of business, but in other areas as well. Jasper said you could never reach the top by yourself. You must find a partner with the same or similar goals and work hard together."

"That covers a lot of ground. You must have spent a great deal of time together?"

"Every day and sometimes at night for at least an hour as we ate supper. He knew I was good at math and English, so he gave me problems to solve, and he had me do articles for the local paper about what we had at the store."

George said, "I know Boss will not be happy if I take you away from our cattle business. But, I have a need in another fast-growing industry here at the 101. So, are you ready to discuss a new job I have in mind for you here at the 101?"

"As I said to Jasper Blackaby, I'd be a fool not to listen."

"I need someone I can groom as my right hand in running the 101 Oil Company. He must be someone who can think on his feet, make good decisions, and be someone I can trust with a lot of 101 resources. I think that could be you, Charlie. Does that sound interesting at all to you?"

Oh shit. He's offerin' me the chance of a lifetime. How is this happenin'?

Charlie gathered himself and said, "It does. But, again, I'll tell you what I told Jasper. I don't know anything about the oil business. But, I do hope—as Jasper did—you'll learn you can trust me with your business."

George grinned as he stood and said, "Let's start tomorrow with you following me as I go through my business day. We'll do this for a month or two, and at that point, we both will make a final decision."

Charlie stood, and with a furrowed brow, reached to shake George's hand and said, "That sounds good. That way both of us know what we want. We both need to make solid decisions that will be good for each other and the 101."

"You're already thinking the way I need you to, Charlie. I don't know that I need to, but I'll pay you two-fifty a month for these two months. That's almost ten times what you make as a cowhand, but that's the confidence I have that we both are going to enjoy this arrangement."

I can't wait to call Susan. I think she'll be as excited about this as I am.

"That's very generous of you."

"If you become my right hand, you'll be making more than that. I'll let Boss know what we're doing tonight at my meeting with him. We have plenty of time to talk about it. You come to my office in the morning after breakfast, and we'll get started."

As Charlie walked out of the White House his mind was in a jumble. He knew nothing about the oil business, and now George L. Miller wanted to make him his right-hand man in running the ranch's oil business. But he hadn't known anything about being a merchant either until he met Jasper. *I never wanted to be an oilman, all I ever wanted was to be the best cowboy I could be. And what about Susan? Is this an opportunity to get Susan to move here instead of me going to Kansas City? Could this be the chance for me to ask her to marry me?*

Chapter Twenty
September 1918

Charlie arrived at the chow hall to eat with his old buddies. He grabbed his food and then saw Thad Spencer struggling to carry his food and his crutches. Charlie went over and said, "Let me help you."

"Thanks."

Charlie took Spencer's tray and together they went over to join Pete and Tom.

"Did ya hear, the rustlers are goin' to trial next week," Spencer said as he sat down. "I wish I coulda been part of all that." He gave Charlie a friendly punch on the shoulder. "I hear ya got asked to meet with George Miller in his office. Is that true, too?"

"Yep, last night, and I'm to meet him this mornin' and start followin' him around. He may give me a shot at workin' directly for him. I wouldn't be workin' cattle anymore." Charlie looked down and sighed, "I'll be workin' over in their oil business."

"Oil business? Whattaya know 'bout the oil business?" Pete asked.

"Nothin'! And I told him that. All I know is that Mr. Miller was askin' Boss about me, then asked me a bunch of questions. He decided to give me a chance, and I'm takin' it."

"I don't blame you for taking an opportunity when it comes along," Tom said. "I hope you make the most of it."

"Well, I'm blamin' ya," Pete said. "Now I got to do more work to make up for you being gone!"

They all laughed, and some of the tension eased in Charlie.

He and the others finished their breakfasts and said their good-byes. As Charlie was about out of the chow hall, Spencer hollered, "Good luck, if it's what ya want, I hope ya git it."

Charlie started toward the White House, his mind filled with questions, Why am I so nervous about this. It's not like this was my idea. He looked up and enjoyed the fall colors and the birds chirping in the cottonwoods. He walked up the steps, entered the front door, and took a seat in the lobby. George came down the stairs in a few minutes and said, "Good morning, Charlie, you're earlier than I expected. Join me for breakfast. Have you eaten?"

As they went out the front door, Charlie said, "Yes, I started my day at the chow hall with the hands."

"If you're full, how about another cup of coffee while I eat?"

"Glad to. Where are we goin'?"

"I eat breakfast at the Ranch Cafe every day unless we have a bunch of guests, and we put on a spread at the house.

"I didn't know that, by this time of the day, I'm usually out on the ranch with Tony doin' one job or 'nother."

"I don't believe I know any hands by the name of Tony," George said.

Charlie laughed. "Tony's the name of my horse."

"Good for you, and I bet he's better company for you than most of us."

"Now, Mr. Miller, you said that not me."

They both laughed.

This seems to be goin' okay. I guess I didn't need to be so nervous.

"After breakfast, we'll head back to my office, and I'll show you the financial system I use to keep track of the 101 businesses. How are you with numbers?" George asked as he sat down at a table.

"In high school, that was my best subject," Charlie said as he took a seat. "I graduated at the top of my class. Jasper Blackaby was impressed with how quickly I picked up the bookkeepin' part of his business."

"I'm glad to hear that. Were you overall top of your class or just in the math part?"

"Overall, sir, I gave the speech at the graduation ceremony. I'm proud of that, but I don't want to brag."

"That's no brag; it's stating a fact. If you can pick up my unique accounting process quickly, that will make you even more valuable to me. Along the way, you'll become familiar with all the 101 industries. We may have started in 1893 as a cattle ranch, but here in 1918, we are a lot more."

George placed his order, and Charlie decided to have a plate of biscuits and gravy along with his coffee.

The waiter placed their food in front of them as George said, "Charlie, a few weeks back, the cook changed the way he makes his biscuits, and it sure makes them a lot better. I have some every day now, what do you think?"

Charlie laughed and said, "Oh, they're mighty fine, sir. And I know what changed."

George looked at him, a look of mild astonishment on his face. "How is it you know what the cooks did to change the biscuits?"

"You had no way of knowin' this, sir, but I taught the cooks how to make biscuits my way. Cookie took sick with the flu on the last gather and Boss had me fill in. And the hands loved my biscuits so much I showed the main cooks here at the ranch how to make 'em my way."

George laughed and said, "My goodness, you're already making improvements to the ranch. I need to thank you then, but I have no plans to put you back in that kitchen."

They enjoyed the meal, and George asked Charlie about growing up and New Mexico. After each had finished their meal, they left the cafe and went directly back to George's office.

George told Charlie to have a seat at the table and went over to a file behind his desk. He pulled a large ledger from a file drawer and took it to the table, then said, "Let's start by showing you the top-level financials. I know I've indicated I need you to focus initially on the oil business, but I want you to know and understand the entire 101 Ranch. This volume covers all our businesses, and I'll use it to acquaint you with every aspect of what we do here at the 101."

"I'm curious about everythin' here. But allow me to make

sure. You did mention last night that you wanted me to help in the oil business, right?"

"Absolutely, but as you assist me with the oil business, I need you to know how the decisions made there can affect the whole enterprise. Do you see how that could happen?"

Charlie nodded as he saw what George was doing, "Now, I do. Jasper Blackaby did this on a smaller scale in the general mercantile business back in Elmore City."

"Good, then we can move forward into more details."

Ledgers and conversations about dollars per barrel of crude oil, refining, gas stations, and drilling operations filled the day. They stopped only to return to the cafe for lunch. At the end of the day, he was impressed but not entirely convinced this was what he wanted to do. *This is all-new, and I still love working from the back of Tony.*

George stood and walked to his desk, "Charlie, I must say you have impressed me with the questions you asked during this first day. You're an intelligent young man, and I'm grateful to Jasper Blackaby for the business groundwork he gave you."

"Thank you, sir, and I'm excited to learn all I can. I want to give ya all the support you need."

"I'm sure you will be. Tomorrow let's go out to the oil fields and some of the other business locations here on the ranch, and I'll show you what I keep track of."

* * *

Charlie shadowed George for the next several days, and one evening as they rode back toward the barn, he said, "I'm seein' more land bein' used for oil than cattle, is that right?"

"It has become that way over the past few years. Less and less land is exclusive for cattle. I'm glad you recognize that. "By your questions and your answers to my questions, it's obvious, Charlie, you're the right guy for what I want."

It was at the end of the day later that week as they were still out near Bliss when George said, "If you're as excited about this as I am, then we have a good thing here. I don't think I need more time to make up my mind. How about you?"

"Well, I don't either because I feel good about this opportunity."

"That's what I wanted to hear. But I also needed to know that you see this opportunity the way I do. I needed someone I could trust who would work beside me, seeing this world as I do. I believe it's you."

Charlie said, "I'm glad you feel that way. I see my new role as you do. That's why I'm excited. I've some folks I need to share this news with. Can I have a little time when we git back to the house today to write letters?"

"Absolutely, and if they have phones, call them. Don't worry about the costs. Your life is part of doing business just as it is for my brothers and me."

They rode back to headquarters, gave their horses to the stable boy, and went directly to the cafe for dinner. They found Joe and Zack there and sat down with them.

With a grin on his face, George said, "Joe, Zack, you remember Charles Kelly. He's agreed to be my new assistant."

Joe said, "Happy to see you again. George has been talkin' about you for several days."

Zack said, "Yes, good to see you again and happy George has found a way to use you up at the White House."

"Good to see you both again, and Charlie is what my friends call me."

Charlie and the two brothers spent the next hour getting to know each other. Joe and Zack shared what was going on in the 101 industries they managed before everyone parted and went their separate ways to do their afternoon tasks.

Charlie and George finished at the cafe and returned to the White House. As they headed down the hallway to his office, George stopped at the door right before his and opened it. He led Charlie through the door and said, "Here is your new home. What do you think?"

Charlie's eyes were saucers. The office was smaller than George's, but it also had big windows overlooking the Salt Fork Valley. He thought, *I'm gonna love seeing the tall grasses bend in the wind, the cowboys as they ride out in the mornings, and return each evening.* Beautiful wooden wainscoting lined the walls, and his desk was as big as most dinner tables. He was stunned at how expensive everything looked.

"George, this is more than fine. I'm honored to have this and will work hard to deserve it."

Charlie decided his first task in his new office would be to call Susan. He walked down the hall, asked Beatrice (Miss Bea) if his phone worked, and confirmed how to get a long-distance operator.

"Yes, operator, I need the number in Kansas City, Missouri, for a Susan Blackaby." Charlie hoped she had a phone in her name.

"Yes, that number is Country Club 548. Do you want me to connect you?"

"Yes, please."

Charlie sensed the excitement build inside him as the phone rang once, twice, and then...

"Hello." Susan's voice filled his ear and a longing he'd forgotten, or ignored, for a long time swelled within Charlie. That one simple word made him realize how much he'd missed Susan.

"Susan, this is Charlie."

"Charlie Kelly, is that you?"

Laughing, he said, "It better be the only Charlie who calls you."

"Sweetheart, I can't believe this is happening. Where are you calling from?"

Charlie leaned back in his chair and looked out the window. "My office at Millers 101."

"Your office?"

"I now work directly for one of the owners, George Miller, as his assistant."

"You have your own private office?"

"Yep, and it's beautiful. I can look out of my window and see the ranch extend to the horizon."

"What do you do for him?"

"He wants me to work in the oil business. I don't have the exact details yet, but I spent the last week learning as much as I could about what an oilman does."

"Oh my goodness." He could hear Susan laugh and he again

felt a longing to be in the same room with her. "Father has become interested in the oil business. He knows several men who have done well in oil."

"Well, I guess, I'm in the oil business, now."

Susan said, "I wish you were here with me, but I guess that can't be right now."

"Susan, I got your letter. I was goin' to respond earlier, but the interview for this new job came up. I decided to wait. I need you to know that I love you and want you." He paused for a moment, shame digging out a hollow in his stomach. "I should have told you that in my letters."

Her voice became soft, almost childlike, as she declared, "Charlie, we must be together. I love you with all my heart and need you in my life."

"I want that too, Sweetheart. But we have a lotta personal business we need to take care of before plannin' how we'll make that happen. Ya need to understand that I want ya for my wife. I know I've kept that to myself, but all my plannin' for some time has had ya right in the middle of it."

"You're in my plans too, and we need to make them happen. Does your new job have a good future? Are they giving you a chance to show them how smart and talented you are?'

"Yep, this new job will give me everythin' I need to create a big future. Between what we shared in Elmore City and what I've learned since I know I want to build an empire of businesses with ya beside me. I'll be paid $500 a month with a furnished house and all the food I can eat as my basic compensation. George Miller is goin' to teach me the finances behind the 101 Empire. They have cattle, agriculture, oil, a hotel, a cafe, and I could go on. It is much bigger than Elmore City, and I will learn how to run it and be paid well while I'm doin' it."

"That's a great opportunity. You can't pass it up. By the way, we never talked about my family, have we?"

"Not really. In your letters, you told me you work in your father's bank, so I assumed he was a banker. And I know you are an only child and that your mom died. But, Sweetheart, I don't even know your maiden name. You were always Mrs. Blackaby in

Elmore City."

"I'm still Mrs. Blackaby, silly. But my maiden name is Kramer. And my father, Walter, is not just a banker. He created the Kramer Group." Charlie had never heard of the Kramer Group, but Susan went on, "The Kramer Group has made my father the richest man west of the Mississippi. In addition to owning several banks, Father owns a railroad, several dry goods stores, and a construction company that builds commercial and residential areas."

Charlie was shocked. Susan's father wasn't just a businessman like Jasper, or even like the Millers. He was like the moguls who'd built this country, like Rockefeller or Carnegie. "You're serious, Susan?"

"Yes, my darling. You have fallen in love with a wealthy widow and someone who will inherit a fortune, and you didn't know it. Jasper had created a successful business in that small town and did well with his investments, and I received over one million dollars in cash and stock from that estate settlement. My father gave me a small portion of his estate when I graduated from Vassar College. It's now worth over three million. I haven't learned, yet, what I'd be worth as the sole owner of the Kramer Group."

"I had no idea, Susan, but I still love you anyway." He said with a small laugh.

"You better, you rascal."

"The way it sounds, we have options."

"Yes, we certainly do, and I'm excited that you have big dreams, and I want to support them beside you. There are two things I should share. One is that I have a man who's about thirty and works in the bank with me who has blatantly shown his interest in me. I have done nothing to encourage this, but he is persistent."

"That concerns me, Susan. Have you talked to your father about us lately?

"I told him I cared a great deal for you, and his response was something to the effect, 'What kind of future can a common cowboy offer you?'"

Charlie said, "Your father was thinkin' the same thing I was when I left Elmore City."

Charlie could hear Susan sigh like she was having to swallow a bitter pill. "And he—and you—were right. I wasn't thinking about any of that a year ago, right after Jasper's death. I was in shock, and I only wanted to be with you. I didn't care about anything else. I was being selfish."

"I didn't think that, Sweetheart," Charlie was quick to say. "I was being selfish too because I knew that I needed to be able to provide for you."

"Charlie, I was rich back then, and I'm richer now."

"It's not about money, and your father understands that too, I think. I love you, and I want to be your husband, but I don't want to be dependent on you. I want to show that I can make something of myself. Maybe your father will then change his mind about us."

Susan said, "If you make good progress in the oil business, that would make a difference. And Charlie, the second thing is, my father has focused a lot of his time on grooming me to take over his company someday. I'm in the important meetings, and he includes me in more decisions than before."

"That's wonderful. I love you, Susan Kramer Blackaby, and are you willin' to become Susan Kramer Kelly?"

"I'll marry you, Charlie. Hurry up and get here, so we can make it happen."

"Okay, then I need to get to work so I can make that happen. I'll call you soon."

Chapter Twenty-One
October 1918

October 1st dawned with a crispness that suggested the summer was over. A change in the seasons was here and Charlie reflected how there was now a change in his life. He ate breakfast at the cafe early and arrived at the White House as George walked down the front steps.

"Morning, Charlie. You're up early, ready for breakfast?"

"I've already had my breakfast, Boss, but I could do with another cup of coffee."

"Come on. We can discuss our plans for today."

They headed to the café and sat at George's favorite table; the waitress poured their coffee.

George smiled and said, "Okay, let's get one thing straight between us. Boss is a cantankerous, crusty old cowboy for whom you once worked. Got it? If it's just us, call me George and Mr. Miller when we are around others."

Charlie nodded and said, "Got it.

"I've been calling you Charlie because you said that's what you prefer. But I'll introduce you as Charles Kelly to our fellow businessmen. You can offer the use of Charlie with them when you wish to create a more informal relationship."

"That's good advice. I know there'll be things that I'll need to learn in this new job. I'll let people in when it works best for the 101 and my ability to perform my duties. You agree?"

That brought another big smile to George's face. "You catch on fast. I couldn't have taught you that business technique any better than what you described. There'll be times you'll want to be Mr. Kelly, not even Charles."

They finished at the cafe and returned to the White House. As Charlie and George walked to their offices, a distinguished gray-haired man in a three-piece suit stood on the White House steps.

Charlie said, "Who do you suppose that is?"

George chuckled, "Oh, I don't know, let's go see."

George waved for the man to wait for them on the steps. As they got to the bottom step, He turned to Charlie, smiled, and said, "Charles Kelly, I want you to meet E. W. Marland. He runs our 101 Oil Company. You'll spend a lot of your time with E. W. for the next few months."

E. W. leaned forward and offered his hand as he said, "Good to meet you, Charles."

I see some doubt in his eyes. I suspect I'll need to prove myself.

Charlie smiled at Marland and looked at George, "Workin' with Mr. Marland sounds mighty fine to me. I've been wantin' to get a better understandin' of the oil business. When will I start?"

E. W. said, "How about tomorrow?" He looked at George, "Is that okay with you?"

George nodded, "Perfect; I want Charles to know and understand the oil business as well as the back of his hand. I also want him to have time in the office with me so I can keep him up on the rest of our businesses, so that means I'll need him with me every Friday afternoon."

E. W. offered his hand to shake with George as he said, "That works for me. He looked at Charlie, "You good with that, young man?"

"I'm good. Where and when do we meet?"

"I'll come to the cafe in the morning at 7:30 and pick you up. We'll use my motor car."

E. W. shook each of their hands and left. George and Charlie went inside the White House. George said, "Come to my office." They sat in some overstuffed chairs in front of the fireplace. George scooted to the front edge of the chair cushion, excited. His eyes sparkled. "Let's sit here for a minute and discuss what just happened. As I've told you, Charlie, the oil business is snowballing, and it's the most profitable of our 101 businesses. That's why I've needed and wanted someone to help me. I've functioned as E. W.'s main contact with the Miller family. The growth in oil demands more focus, and I can't give him more of my time and stay on top of everything else here at the ranch."

Charlie's eyes grew large, and his jaw dropped, "Do you want me... to become his main contact?"

"That's my plan. Marland has agreed to give you a try. If you work out, he'll teach you the oil business, and I'll have a lot of my time back."

Charlie said, "This is a great opportunity for me. As I've said before, I'll live and breathe the oil business if that's what it takes."

George said, "Good, but keep in mind, I don't want you to forget about the rest of the 101. I have you Friday afternoons, remember. And it would be best for you to keep a balance in your life."

I couldn't agree more. I'm sure Susan would agree if I could convince her to come to the 101. Charlie nodded at George. "I'm excited about this opportunity. I see the oil business as where a lot of money will be made, and I want to understand it."

George had a crooked grin as he winked, "You've got your chance, and I think the timing couldn't be better for you and the 101. Let's spend the rest of the day on horseback. I want to show you a few things around the ranch."

The previous night, Charlie had moved Tony to the barn with George's horse, so they walked together to the barn. Boss hollered at them from a distance. He walked over and paused; his eyebrows began to raise as a smile slowly crept across his face. He finally said, "Mr. Miller, you stole one of my best men, and I think you should go to jail for it."

George threw up his hands and said, "Don't call the Sheriff on me. I never meant you any harm, sir." They all laughed, and Boss then turned to Charlie and said with a sincere tone, "Congratulations, Charlie Kelly, ya deserve this chance, and I know you'll do a job we'll all be proud of."

After he saddled Tony, Charlie and George spent the morning on a nice ride around the ranch as George showed Charlie several buildings, corrals, and some land as he described the money made from each of them. The tour opened a whole new world to Charlie, and it brought him a sense of excitement and wonder. I hope I can live up to George's expectations.

* * *

Charlie arrived at the cafe early and comfortably finished his breakfast before 7:30. That was smart because Marland drove up on time. He looked smart in his light brown suit. His straw boater had a matching ribbon. The windows were down, so he didn't need to open the door as he greeted Charlie, "Good morning, young man. Hop in, we're headed to Cushing, and we may stop at the town of Yale, too. Have you ever been to Cushing?"

"No, can't say I have. Where is it?"

"Down in Payne County about sixty miles from here. We'll be there in a couple of hours, and that'll give us a chance to get acquainted. Cushing has been one of the biggest oil fields here in Oklahoma for several years, and now it's a huge refining location. People have started to pipe oil to Cushing to be stored and refined into gasoline, kerosene, and lubricants. You need to see this operation because we've started this on a smaller scale at the 101, and we may want to get bigger."

"I'm excited to see all this. I may be full of questions as we go through today. Hope that's okay?"

"Charles, that makes me happy. Questions mean you're interested. If I can't give you the right answer to a question, we'll find someone who can."

After a half-hour of small talk about things such as the size of the 101, Charlie wanted to sound business-like and said, "Where are you from, E. W., and how did you end up at the 101 Ranch?"

Marland looked over at Charlie, amused at his directness, "You may not know anything about oil, but you know how to get to the point with your questions. I was born and raised in Pittsburgh, Pennsylvania. After I graduated from University of Michigan law school in '93, I made and lost a fortune in the oil business back there."

Charlie interrupted, "Hold on, you're an attorney too?"

Marland nodded, "Well, yes, but the oil business fascinated me. I grew up hearing about the Drake well up in Titusville. I knew I had to try my luck in oil. I've been a landman in the business ever since. In 1908 my wife Virginia and I moved to Ponca City, and I found a location on the 101 that looked ideal to have oil underground. We did find oil, and that started what has become the 101 Oil Company. I had learned about and visited the 101 through a friend a little more than ten years earlier. Since the start of the 101's oil business, we've had joint ventures with the Watchorn, Magnolia, and Comar companies, to name a few. We've produced oil on several plats across the ranch for some time." Then Marland looked over at Charlie, "Tell me about yourself; what have you done? Yesterday it sounded as if you have no experience in the oil business?"

Charlie said, "That's right, this will be new to me. I've been workin' ranches as a cowboy, and I worked at a mercantile down in Elmore City, where the owner taught me a lot about how a profitable business works. He gave me a lot of responsibility and trusted me to run his place when he was gone. That was before I arrived at the 101."

Marland turned his head to the side as he raised his eyebrows, "Charles, you didn't mention anything about a young lady. I was already engaged by your age. George mentioned you had a lady you'd known for quite some time. If you don't mind my asking, how did you meet, and what is her background?"

"Her name is Susan. We met during my time in Elmore City. She was the wife of Jasper Blackaby. Jasper and Susan owned the mercantile where I worked. Susan and I became friends, and when Jasper was murdered, I stayed and helped her settle the estate. We've continued to correspond over the last year or so. Oh, hell, I might as well tell all of it. Susan and I have discussed marriage, but she wants me in Kansas City with her, but I'm not ready to leave this opportunity at the 101."

With an understanding look, Marland said, "I admire your ambition, and we'll see what we can do to help you make a little money in oil."

Charlie nodded, "That's the plan, and I've shared that desire with George."

"So, he knows all about Susan and your plans, such as they are?"

"He knows about her, but I haven't given him our complete picture because it continues to change. He knows my focus is here and that I'll work my butt off for the man."

Marland said, "We're about to turn here at Perkins and go east about fifteen or twenty miles, and we'll be in Cushing."

"I didn't mention it before, but the last stop before I got to the 101 was about four miles east here when I worked about six months on the Meehan Ranch. They were great people, and Hank, their foreman, is the salt of the earth. I was this close to Cushing back then and didn't know it."

They fell into a period of quiet. Charlie reflected on what they had shared. I know Marland has impressed George enough to be partners in the oil business with him, and he has the experience and knowledge I'll need. Now I've got to work hard to impress him enough, so he's willing to share his knowledge and expertise.

As the pair drove past the Cushing City Lake about five miles west of town, Marland said, "As I mentioned before, Charlie, this town is a key location in the oil business for refining. There are already about fifty refineries here, and the industry is building pipelines and storage tanks as fast as possible. Anytime now, we'll begin to smell those refineries. Consider it the aroma of big money."

E. W. Marland and Charlie Kelly would soon learn how vital Cushing would become for them.

Chapter Twenty-Two
October 1918

As Charlie and E. W. Marland entered Cushing from the west on Highway 33, they passed several oil refineries and crossed the railroad tracks for the Katy Railroad. The highway became Moses Street. Marland said, "We're about two blocks north of the business district, located on Broadway. We're to meet a gentleman named Hank Thomas at the hotel over on Broadway."

Charlie said, "You haven't said what we'll discuss with him. Is this about refining our oil at the 101?"

"That's part of it. There has been a lot of oil produced from the Cushing-Drumright oil field over the last six or seven years. I've recently purchased the mineral rights to land up around Yale, and I want to have Hank help me develop it. He's worked with Tom Slick and his buddy C. B. Schaffer. Do ya know of them?"

"No, can't say I do."

"The well those two drilled back in '12 out north of Drumright is what started this boom, and Hank went to work for them about four years ago. He's now out on his own with a crew drilling wells for others. I intend to find out what Hank knows about production in this area."

A few minutes later, they parked in front of a seven-story brick building with a magnificent, electrified sign on its roof stating it was the Hotel Cushing. They went inside and found the cafe on their left as they entered the lobby.

Marland pointed across the room as he said, "There he is at the table by the front window."

Hank stood, "I saw you park your motor car. It's good to see ya again, Mr. Marland; welcome to Cushing."

"Thanks, Hank, this is Charles Kelly. You'll see a lot of Charles if we agree to do business together."

"Oh, I think we'll arrange somethin'; it's good to meet ya, Charles."

Charlie offered his hand, "And you too, Hank."

Hank said, "Sit yourself and let's find the waitress. Oh, there she is, hey Cindy." He waved and got her attention.

A tall, slender, young blue-eyed blonde walked over to their table and said, "Good mornin', Hank." She looked around the table, smiled, and said, "What are we havin', boys? Coffee? Do you want breakfast or lunch menus?"

They all agreed on coffee and breakfast menus.

Charlie leaned back and chuckled as he said, "I don't know about you fellas, but I'd eat breakfast three meals a day."

Hank said, "I'm just like ya. I love my eggs and bacon. Let's talk some oil business while we wait for our food."

Marland looked Hank squarely in the eye, "Yes, let's talk oil. I've purchased mineral rights to about a thousand acres in the Yale area. What can you tell me about the luck people are having around there?"

"There've been good strikes east of Yale, but I think the best geology is west of Yale straight north of Cushing. But no oilman has been able to get any of those farmers or ranchers to deal with 'em."

Marland smiled, leaned forward, elbows on the table, "Well, I did. That's the location of my lease. To me, I have found the best anticline I've seen in a long time. Are you interested?"

"I'm interested enough to go have a look after we finish our meal."

"That's my plan, and I want Charles to see this and be part of our discussion. His focus will be on the 101. But I don't plan on limiting him to that piece of ground."

Charlie had been trying to keep up with the focus but so much of what Hank and Marland discussed went over his head. What's an anticline? I got some learnin' to do. He was relieved to see the waitress coming their way and said, "Here comes the food. I can't wait to see what you're talkin' about, so let's eat."

* * *

Hank drove separately to allow Marland and Charlie to drive directly back to the 101. They traveled north about eight miles over rolling hills through a heavy stand of trees along the Cimarron River and turned east and climbed a hill toward Yale. They drove about two miles and Marland turned south on little more than a well-worn livestock trail. After a quarter mile of ruts and dodging holes, he stopped.

Marland turned to Charlie, "Let's get out and open up this fence line."

Charlie said, "I see you have this barbwire section set up to work as a gate. I'll hold it open if you want to drive in."

"It's not far, let's leave the motorcar parked here. It won't hurt us to get a little dust and mud on our shoes."

Hank joined them, and they walked up a slope and were at the potential drill site in a few minutes.

Hank smiled as he stood next to Marland, "We're standing on the dome of an anticline, and it looks good for oil. You may hit gas first, but my guess is you won't need to drill deep for this one to pay off."

Charlie said, "I know a lot about cattle and ranches, but not much about oil. What's an anticline?"

Hank looked at Marland then at Charlie. "How long have you been in the oil business?"

Charlie smiled. "Well, about three weeks ago I was riding my horse, gatherin' cattle, and stoppin' rustlers for Mr. Miller."

"Charles here stopped four rustlers from trying to steal a bunch of George's cattle."

"That was you?" Hank asked. "I read about that in the paper. Sounds like you think quick on your feet."

"That's one of the reasons that Mr. Miller asked me to start workin' for him directly and learn the oil business."

Hank put a hand to his chin for a moment, then nodded. "That's good enough for me. We all had to learn the oil business at some point." He pointed to the hill they were standing on. "You see the hill here?"

Charlie nodded.

"Well, under us, the rocks have been folded," he held his hand out, palm down, and then curled his fingers, so it formed an up-side-down cup. "Like this."

"Folded? What did that?"

"Well, the geologists aren't quite sure. It doesn't matter to us. But the folded rocks form a trap for the oil."

Charlie nodded his head, catching on quick. He mimicked Hank's hand with his own, then pointed at the center of his palm. "It gets trapped here. The rocks around it must be something like shale so the oil can't escape."

Hank nodded. "Exactly. You catch on quick."

"I had a good science teacher in high school, and this makes sense."

Marland said, "I can see why George took you on." He turned and looked Hank in the eye. "I'll fund it. Will you run the drilling operation?"

"Depends; when do you want to start?"

"How about yesterday?"

Hank's face lit up, "That's what I would normally want to hear, but I have my crews workin' over in Drumright now settin' up on a site where we've agreed to drill three wells. I've got to honor that contract. You and I haven't finalized the details for this project, but what we discussed on the phone yesterday should cover everything based on what I see here." Hank offered his right hand and said, "So I'll agree to do this job for you under those terms."

"Good, then I'll send you a contract by courier tomorrow. How long will it take to get your crew and equipment here and start to drill?"

"I'd say it'll be at least two weeks. I'm sure that's not what you wanted to hear, but as I said, we have a contract for three wells to complete over in the Drumright field."

Charlie's eyes grew big as he said, "Hank, you seem more excited about this site than I expected for someone who's drilled as many wells as you have."

"I am. You drill five wells and maybe hit on one or two, but this site looks good, mighty good. I've gotta feelin' this may be a big one."

Marland said, "Hank, I'll live with your timeline. Charles, you recognize Hank's excitement, which verifies why I want you on this one. You need to see what it's like to bring in a gusher. I agree with Hank. This site looks and feels right."

They all shook hands and said their goodbyes. Marland and Charlie went straight west through Stillwater to the main road and headed north toward Ponca City and the 101.

* * *

As the White House appeared off in the distance, Charlie said, "I learned a lot today. The oil business is risky, but there's a big payoff when you hit one, right?"

"That's right when it's as big as I think this one will be at the Yale site."

"How many barrels a day do you want and expect to see from the Yale site?"

"One hundred a day would be profitable, but I think we might see ten times that."

Marland drove in at the main gate, stopped in front of the White House, and looked over at Charlie, "I'll see you at the cafe in the morning at 8:00. We'll explore some on horseback tomorrow."

* * *

Charlie checked to see if George was still around and found his office dark. He then went into his office and called Susan.

"Hello, this is Susan."

"Good evenin', Sweetheart."

"Oh, Charlie, it's so nice to hear your voice. How was your day?"

"It was great. I spent it with E. W. Marland. He runs the 101 Oil Company as a partner with the Millers. I'll spend a lot of time over the next few months with him. We were in Cushing, down in Payne County today."

"Tell me about Cushing?"

"It was impressive. It's a good-sized town. It's much bigger than Elmore City, and trucks, motor cars, and wagons filled the streets all the time."

"That must have been exciting to see. Now, tell me about Mr. Marland."

"He was friendly enough and all business, too. I liked that about him. Gray-haired, he comes to about my shoulders in height and probably weighs 180 pounds, and he's originally from back around Pittsburgh."

"Will you be with Mr. Marland again tomorrow?"

"Yep, we're going out on horseback. Marland has something he wants me to see that I guess is close by. What are you doing?"

Susan said, "Just reading weekly updates from my father's businesses. Nothing special. It's about 5:00; you must be hungry?"

"Yep, I could eat a side of beef by myself. Have you had supper?"

"No, Father has some people over tonight, so I'll wait and eat with them. Charlie, I hope your work in oil will create some interest from my father. No pressure, but..."

"I know, and I hope so too. We're adults, but it would be best for him to approve of our marriage."

"Yes, I agree. Yesterday Father seemed not to feel well, and he still had that cough. I hope he isn't sick."

"I'll let ya go so that you can be ready for your visitors, and I can get some supper. Let me know about your father."

"Okay, I will. I love you, Charlie."

"Love ya, goodbye."

Chapter Twenty-Three
October 1918

Charlie was up early and still getting used to living in his own place. The first few nights he'd had a hard time falling asleep without the sounds of dozens of other men snoring and making a racket. He got dressed quickly and headed over to the barn to check on Tony. The barn was quiet too, the horses in their stalls making almost no noise. He walked up to Tony's stall and the big horse's ears perked up and he made a soft whiny like he was trying to be quiet for the other horses.

Charlie rubbed Tony's nose and muzzle, "You doin' good, boy? Them fancy Miller horses are treatin' ya right?"

"Oh, they're playin' nice," a voice said, startling Charlie. He looked over and saw Fuzzy walking down the aisle carrying a bucket of water.

Charlie patted Tony's neck. "He's lookin' pretty good. Thank ya for takin' care of Tony. I'm afraid he's gonna be spoiled by all the attention."

Fuzzy said, "Charlie, he's a pleasure to spoil." He rubbed the side of Tony's head. "Eh, Tony, old boy, are ya gittin' spoiled by all my attention." Tony seemed to shake and nod his head at the same time, and Charlie and Fuzzy both laughed.

Fuzzy looked at Charlie, "You're a mighty lucky cowboy to own 'em."

"Thanks." He gave Tony another pat. "But you won't be spoiled today. We're goin' out with Mr. Marland to look at some wells here."

"Don't worry, Charlie," Fuzzy said. "I'll have Tony fed, watered, and ready to go, along with the horse Marland will be ridin', when you get done with breakfast."

Charlie gave his thanks and walked toward the café, feeling a little guilty at not takin' care of Tony himself. As Charlie arrived in front of the café, George was on his way over from the house, so he waited for him to catch up. "Good mornin', George, I see we're gettin' our breakfast times closer."

George smiled and said, "Somehow, I think you'll always be a little ahead of me. My wife sometimes says it takes two sticks of dynamite and a crowbar to get me out of bed."

Laughing, Charlie said, "Well, I guess she would know."

As the waitress poured their coffee, Charlie said, "I called my sweetheart yesterday with the news about my trip to Cushing with Marland. She's as excited as me for what the future may bring."

"That's great to hear. I knew about a lady in Kansas City and that she was special, but you called her your sweetheart. You two must be serious?"

"Yep, and I hope someday that she'll be my wife."

Charlie went on to explain to George what he and Marland did yesterday as they ate. George let him do most of the talking, only adding in a bit of insight into how beneficial it would be for Charlie to be working with Hank as well as Marland.

As they finished their breakfast, the door to the café opened, and in walked Marland.

George grinned, "Good morning, E. W., I bet you're here for Charles."

"Yes, that would be the case. There's still interest from other companies in the Bar L land. I want to take Charles to visit the Bar L property."

Charlie and George finished up and as George went to his office Marland and Charlie walked to the barn. True to his word Fuzzy had both horses ready to go. They rode out to explore the Bar L portion of the ranch.

Marland said, "We haven't drilled out on the Bar L yet, but we continue to receive inquiries from companies wanting to sublet from us and drill a discovery well."

Charlie asked, "If we sublet, then that would mean we couldn't drill unless we were able to void that contract or renegotiate it, right?"

Marland gave Charlie an appraising look. "Exactly right, but keep in mind, we don't have the resources to drill everywhere we think we might find oil. We have secured the rights to do it, but we don't plan to drill on all the land immediately."

"If we aren't drilling there, why go out to look it over?"

"That's a fair question, and the reason is, we may lease it to a company, and I want to see and walk it one more time before settling on a lease price I'll take."

"Okay, that does make sense."

They reached the Bar L property and Marland used the time to teach Charlie what an oilman looked for in terrain and rock formations. Charlie asked several questions and Marland made sure Charlie understood the answers. As they rode back to the headquarters in the afternoon, Marland would point to an outcrop of rock and ask Charlie what kind of rock it was, and whether it was good for oil or not. Charlie's head was swimming with so many new terms and he didn't think he'd be able to look at a simple pasture the same way again.

As they neared the headquarters, Marland said, "I was skeptical about you at first, Charles. I know George said you were smart as a whip and all, but you had no background in oil. I was worried that George was going to saddle me with a dead weight," he looked over at Charlie. "No offense."

Charlie smiled, "None taken. If it'd been the other way around and George had asked you to come help gather cattle, I might have felt the same way."

Marland laughed, "I think you'll work out fine. I won't need you in Cushing for a couple of weeks. Hank will be ready then to start at the Yale site."

"What do you want me to do in the meantime?"

"Do you drive cars and trucks yet?"

"I learned after George took me on. I'm good, and I've a license to prove it."

"Good, then I don't need to teach how to drive a truck instead of cattle." They both laughed at Marland's joke. "In the meantime, get with George and see what he wants you to do. And I'll send over some books that have been written about the oil business and the geology here in Oklahoma. You'll need to have a good understanding of all of that to be a successful oil man."

* * *

The trip down to the Yale site went smoothly. He'd gotten some more lessons on the 101's finances from George and had read about oil drilling and geology till he couldn't see straight. But he could take Tony out in the afternoons and the gentle breeze and wide-open spaces let his mind settle until he understood everything pretty well. He was excited to get started.

Charlie arrived at the Yale drill site and found Hank on the east edge of the property. He parked the truck and walked out to where Hank stood.

Charlie said, "I hope you haven't waited long."

Hank said, "No, I just got here. How's your morning?"

"Good."

"We don't have good news here. It may take two or three days before we can get our equipment across this field. It's rained here last week, and the mud is still too wet. The trucks and rigs would get stuck near the entrance, and it's not much better here where I want to drill. Let's hold off for a few days, and I'll check here again Friday. We'll either move in on the weekend or, do it Monday. If we can get our equipment in place and ready to start by noon Wednesday, I'll be happy."

Charlie said, "Let's hope the weather cooperates. I hear we're startin' a dry spell. Hopefully, that's true. Is there anythin' I can help you with at your office?"

"No, we're caught up, and we're waitin' to get goin' here. I guess we might as well go home."

When Charlie arrived back at the ranch, he called Susan.

"Good afternoon, Sweetheart."

"Are you in Cushing?"

"I was, and I've been to the Yale site. But we found a lot of mud out at the site. It was bad enough that Hank knew we couldn't hope to get the equipment in place. He's going back out there on Friday to see if it's dried up any. Hank's goal is to have everythin' in place and ready to start by next Wednesday."

"Well, at least you have a plan. What will you do for the next few days?"

"I'll do some work here for George, or some more studying. I figure I'll join Hank on Friday to check the mud situation."

"I told father you work in the oil business for the 101 with an E. W. Marland. He knows of Marland and said he's a top oilman. I think he was a little impressed but didn't want to show it."

"Good. Is that guy still hangin' around you?"

"He is, but don't you worry about that."

"Well, I do worry about it. I miss ya and would love it if ya were here in my arms."

"I want that more than I can describe, my love. My father is calling for me; I better go. Write or call me soon, okay? Love you."

"You bet. Love ya."

* * *

A few days later, Charlie met Hank back at the Yale site. Together they walked the ground and Hank pronounced it dry enough for him to get the equipment out to the site.

"Yep, this will be good," Hank said. "I'll bring the rig and trucks in over the weekend. We can get started Monday morning."

Charlie was feeling excited at the prospect of starting his first well. "Do you need me here tomorrow?"

"No, there won't be much to do other than moving the trucks."

Charlie wasn't sure if he was being brushed off or not but decided that Hank was probably right. The real work wouldn't start until Monday. "So, what time do you want me here on Monday?"

"I'll be there at 7:00 am, but we won't start until after the sun comes up, maybe around 8:00 am." He paused and put a hand on Charlie's shoulder. "Charles, this will be your first time at a drill site. I don't want you to get hurt. So, wait till about noon to show up. It'll take a few hours to get things going the way it needs to. The main crew has worked together before, but the equipment is new. They'll need to get acquainted with it."

Charlie nodded, but he was disappointed. He wanted to be doing more. "Hank, I understand about needin' to be safe, and I appreciate that. I'd feel the same way if I was teachin' ya to brand cattle. But Mr. Marland and Mr. Miller want me to be a part of this operation so I can understand everything that goes on. I think that means even the setup of the equipment. And the only way I will learn what you do is if'n I see ya doin' it. If I was a new rough-neck, you wouldn't coddle me, would ya?"

Hank nodded, "You're right, Charles. I'd put you to work, though I'd expect a roughneck to know something about what he was doing even on his first day."

"I get that. Why don't I show up at seven, and I can watch what you're doing from a distance. That way I'll be safe and can learn the ropes."

"Deal."

* * *

Charlie drove down to Cushing on Sunday and got a room at the hotel. He woke up early and left the hotel before breakfast and headed to the well site. He arrived around 7:30 and there was already a lot of activity at the site when he parked the truck.

Charlie hollered, "Hey Hank, good morning to ya."

Hank said, "Good morning." He pointed to the trucks carrying the drilling equipment. "They'll be getting everything into place here in a bit. I hope we'll be able to start drilling before noon."

Charlie nodded and watched the men get to work. A few hours into the job Hank came over and asked, "Any questions?"

"Well, it's more complicated than brandin' cattle, I'll give ya that." They shared a laugh. "Is this all the men you'll have here?" Charlie had only seen six men working to get the derrick erected to get the drilling started.

"Yeah, this is my day crew; there'll be more who show up around sundown. I've got six men on each crew. I'll have four men show up at about four o'clock to work until midnight. They give breaks to the crews. Once we're up and running, we will go twenty-four hours a day till she blows."

Charlie looked around slack-jawed in amazement. The workers were loud and dirty, but they moved like dancers. Each one seemed to know and anticipate his partner's every move.

Charlie said, "These guys are great. How do they work so in tune with each other?"

Hank smiled and said, "Probably the same way you cowboys don't end up getting a hot branding iron up your ass, a lot of practice." Charlie nodded, seeing the similarity. "This crew I've had with me for several years," Hank continued. "They are among the best around. It takes a long time to get as good as they are, and they take pride in being the best. So, they work at it."

Charlie said with excitement in his voice, "What do you need me to do?"

Hank's face turned serious as he said, "Nothing, please don't get too close to the action. You could easily get yourself or one of my men hurt."

"Okay, then how am I supposed to learn the oil business?" Charlie had hoped that by being on-site that Hank would see that he could be useful. The frustration was clear in his voice.

"I promised Marland you would become knowledgeable, and fast. Not by doing but by observing. George Miller made Marland promise that you would not be hurt out here in the field. I promised to keep Marland's promise. Get it?"

"I get it, so we'll just stand or sit here, and you'll tell me the what's and why's as the crew works?"

"That's my plan." Hank paused for a moment, watching the crew, then said, "Look, Charles, I don't get involved anymore. Now, I know every job because I've done them. If they need a tool and the tool pusher can't get it, I know what they need, and I can get it for them. That seldom happens."

"So, you find the location to drill, acquire the rights, and then hire the crew and step back and let them drill."

"Yep, you just described my life. I get paid to find and drill for oil. I'm no longer a roughneck. I haven't been since I quit my dad's crew."

Charlie realized that the same was true on a ranch. Sure, the foreman could do every job that the cowboys could do, but he seldom had to do the work unless there was a need for it. The foreman had his own work to do, and the best thing he could do was to stay out of his cowboy's way. He said as much to Hank.

Hank smiled. "I knew you were smart. Don't worry, I won't keep any secrets from you. And don't hesitate to ask any questions."

"How long until we hit oil or know that we won't find oil at this site?"

Hank laughed. "You do like to ask the hard ones. There's no one answer to that question. It depends, but I think we will hit something sooner than at most drill sites. I love what I see here. We should know before Thanksgiving." Hank smiled and said, "I also think you'll be knowledgeable about the oil business by Christmas."

Chapter Twenty-Four
October 1918

After the day with Hank and the drilling crew at the Yale site, Charlie was surprised at how tired he felt despite not having done any of the work. He walked into his room at the Cushing Hotel and lay on the bed for a few minutes. He finally decided to call Susan and headed back down to the lobby and had the hotel switchboard place the call to Susan.

She answered after a couple of rings. "Hello, this is Susan."

"It's me, Sweetheart."

Susan said, "How did your first day go at the drill site?"

"Good, Hank's great. I learned that I won't have dirty hands at the end of the day if everything goes the way Hank wants."

"Does that mean you won't be out there every day?"

"No, it means Hank and I watch the crew do all the work. After a while, I understood why it would be that way. We'll never be on a crew. Our job is to get the work done, not to do the work. Does that make sense?"

"I think so. Sounds like Hank doesn't want you to be in the way of the crew."

"Yep. They work as a team, and everyone knows what to do. I sure didn't. Hank said he would teach me the drilling operation as I watched the crew. I'm okay with that."

"So, you'll still go out there, right?"

"Yes, but as a new guy, I won't be doing any work. I feel guilty since I'm used to workin' with my hands every day when I was doin' ranch work. But I know that one of Hank's crew, or me, could easily git hurt if I was in the way."

"Well then, new guy, do be careful, so you can come to see me soon. I, too, continue to learn a lot from my father and Gordon Brayton, the bank president. I hear Beverly, the cook, call me to dinner."

"I love ya, go eat."

* * *

Charlie parked on the road and walked into the site. Hank had used some crates to create a work area. Charlie turned up a box for himself and joined him.

Hank said, "How's your day been?"

"It's been a good one so far. How's it been here?"

"I know I keep saying it, but this new equipment is great, and the crews are drilling deeper and faster than I've ever seen. I do have one bit of news that you need to hear." Hank put his foot up on one of the crates. "There's a driller by the name of Roland Willard. I've had to deal with him before. He's a crook and a bully. Last night I stopped at a diner for supper. Some drillers there said that Willard is pissed that we beat him to this site. He tried to get the lease, but Marland beat him to it. The men at the diner gave me the heads up that he's asked around on the sly and found someone who'll help him run us off."

"Hank, do you mean he plans to force us off this drill site?"

"That's the sound of it. He won't do it himself, but I could see him hire thugs to do it."

"We won't be intimidated. Should we let Marland know?"

"No, I don't know what to expect. This could all be a rumor and not true at all. I don't want to bother Marland just yet. I thought you should know what I know."

"Hank, we're a team. Always tell me anything and everything that's on your mind or givin' you concern about the project. I'll have your back. I'm a cowboy who happens to work in the oil business. A cowboy has his buddy's back, always."

Chapter Twenty-Five
October 1918

O n Thursday morning, Charlie went down to breakfast early as had been his habit since the drilling had started. He ordered breakfast and coffee and waved "good morning" to a well-dressed man talking to another fellow at a far table. He'd seen the man in the suit at breakfast since Tuesday morning, but the other fellow was new. He didn't give it much thought as his food arrived. He ate quickly so he could get out to the drill site.

Charlie arrived and parked his truck at the road that led to the site. He spotted Hank and said, "Hank, this is the fourth day we've drilled, are ya happy with the progress?"

"You bet, so don't jinx it, Charlie."

Charlie laughed then changed the subject. "You still hearin' rumors about this Willard fella?"

"It seems to have quieted down over the last few days. That may not be good, though."

"Are ya afraid they may have a plan that includes trying to lull us into a false sense of security?"

"It's possible. I'm set up to stay out here with the night crew tonight. If Willard's guys do show up, it'll be at night."

"Maybe, I should stay too. What kind of trouble would you expect?"

"People say he has vandalized equipment and used physical intimidation at several sites around the county. I hear he wants this site so bad he would do anything to get it. I don't know what that means, but I don't care for the sound of it."

"Should we be armed or hire some security guards to protect the site and our workers?"

"I've never had to do that before," Hank said. "I'm not gonna start now."

The day was quiet, except for the sounds of drilling, and Hank and Charlie discussed more about the well, with Hank showing Charlie the rock that was coming up from the drill hole, and how they could use that to tell where they were at in the rocks under them. Suddenly Charlie heard something above the sounds of the drilling and saw a puff of dust erupt from the ground near the crates.

Charlie grabbed Hank and dove behind some wooden boxes of equipment and shouted, "That was a gunshot! I know this place is noisy, but I'm positive that was a gunshot!"

Charlie looked around the crate and then pulled back as he heard another loud crack of a gunshot. "Hank, it came from the direction of the road. I can see someone down near my truck."

"Keep your head down," Hank said. He pointed toward the derrick and said, "The crew must not have heard them. They're still working."

"Hank, I recognized that guy. I saw him at the hotel this morning. He ate breakfast a few tables over with a man in a business suit this morning."

Several more shots rang out, and they hit the derrick close to the crew this time.

Charlie shouted, "Hey, you asshole, what's this about?"

The man with the gun responded, "This is a warning. Shut down, or my aim will improve."

He turned and ran to a Model T waiting with a driver and left, dust rising behind them as they drove away.

"Hank, I promise I saw that guy and the man he met with."

"So, what are you gonna do?"

"First, I'm gonna let Marland and Miller know about this. Then I'm gonna have a one-way conversation with the man I saw at breakfast. We need to protect our crew and our investment."

* * *

Charlie had done more than just call Marland and Miller when he'd returned to the hotel. He'd also stopped at the Cushing police department and filed a report with the police. After dinner, Marland called back and told Charlie that he'd gotten hold of some detectives from the Pinkerton Detective Agency, and they'd have men at the drill site starting in the morning.

At breakfast that morning, Charlie recognized the well-dressed man sitting at the same table he used all week. A few minutes later in walked the guy Charlie had seen shooting at them yesterday. They didn't recognize Charlie.

Charlie waited until his breakfast and coffee had been delivered then he stood up and walked directly to the table where the men sat.

"Roland Willard?"

"Yes, who are you?"

"Charles Kelly," Charlie stuck out his hand, and Willard tentative shook it. "I'm sure glad I got a chance to meet you this mornin'. I was afraid you might have skedaddled after this fella," Charlie turned to look at the other man, "failed to scare Hank's crew off the Yale site." He looked back at Willard. "I didn't appreciate bein' shot at one bit."

The shooter started to get up, and Charlie placed his hand on the man's shoulder and pushed him firmly back into his seat.

"Stay put, asshole, or I'll hurt ya."

Willard said, "I don't know what you're talking about, mister. I will have the police here and charge you with assault and disturbing the peace."

"Yes, you do," Charlie said, ignoring the man's bluster. He'd already told the Cushing police chief that he was going to confront Willard this morning. "Let me make myself clear. I work for the 101 Oil Company. Do you know who we are?"

Willard was trying to look tough and nodded like the 101 Oil Company didn't matter to him.

"You've been makin' threats that you were gonna drive us off the Yale site, no matter what. Then you sent this man," Charlie glared at the shooter, "out there yesterday and he took several shots at Hank, me, and our crew."

"You can't prove any of that," Willard said.

"No? Seeing as I saw you here every morning all week, and I saw this fella here gettin' his orders from you yesterday, I think that would be pretty convincin' to a jury. At least, the police chief was really interested in that fact when I told him about it yesterday."

Charlie had told the chief that information, but he'd not been that interested in some squabble between a bunch of rough-necks. But Willard didn't know that, and Charlie could see he was sweating.

"We're not leavin' the drillin' site. You," he pointed to Willard, "on the other hand, will be leavin' today. We've called in the Pinkertons. If we don't see you leaving the hotel and heading to the county line, they have orders to make sure that happens."

"You can't order me around like this," Willard said.

"Your right, but I'm just the messenger. Misters George Miller and E.W. Marland do have the strength to do that, though. And who do you think the police, or the sheriff, or a judge is more likely to believe?"

Charlie could see the resignation begin to set in for Willard. He turned to look at the shooter. "And in case you get any funny ideas, there'll be Pinkertons at the drill site from now until we bring that well in. And I'll be there too, with my Winchester. I didn't hesitate to shoot a rustler; I won't hesitate to shoot a rat like you." He stared hard at the man, who tried to look unafraid, but Charlie's unfaltering gaze finally made him look away.

"And don't think you can scurry away to Drumright or Ponca City or Stillwater or anyplace else in this part of Oklahoma. We've already put out the word to the authorities about you, and I heard Marland sayin' that he'll make sure you never find another drillin' job in the state again." Charlie wasn't sure if that was true or not, but it had the desired effect. Willard threw his napkin down on the table and got up. His hired goon glared at Charlie as he got up as well, but his fangs had been pulled.

Charlie picked up his coffee and drank it as he watched the two men head upstairs. A few minutes later they came down and left the hotel. He continued to watch as they got into the Model T and drove out of town. He returned to the restaurant. His break-fast was cold, but he didn't mind.

* * *

Charlie parked at the road and walked past the Pinkerton de-tective that was watching the road up to where Hank sat. Charlie turned up another box for a place to sit. He laughed, "It's not the lobby of the Norwood, but it'll do."

Hank said, "It's been quiet today. How did it go?"

"I took care of Willard and his goon. That's what you called him, goon, right?"

"Any problems with them?"

"Nope." Charlie described in detail what happened at the hotel.

"That's great news. Of course, we didn't plan for those costs."

Charlie said, "Until we are sure that Willard is out of the pic-ture, it's best to be safe. I scared him off today, but once he has a chance to calm down, he might be back. If we get a good well out of this, the costs'll be worth it, right?"

Hank smiled, "Yeah, if this well is as good as I keep saying it is, it will." He turned to watch his crew working on the derrick, lifting another pipe into place to continue the drilling operation. "I didn't thank you for saving my life yesterday," he finally said.

"Willard's goon was just trying to scare us off."

"Well, I'm still glad that you were here."

"Me too, who'd have taught me about being an oil man if you weren't here?"

Hank laughed and they went back to watching the drilling.

* * *

About a week after the confrontation with Willard, Charlie arrived at the well site in the late morning, and as he parked the truck on the road Hank ran to meet him, "Hey, we hear rum-bles through the drill hole. My men have got a feelin' we may hit anytime."

"This soon? I thought you said it might take 'til Thanksgiving to hit the oil."

"Well, drilling for oil isn't an exact science."

"What do we need to do?"

"We need to make some space around the derrick. I should have already moved everything back. Let's move our stuff back a good fifty feet from where they are now."

Charlie and Hank worked quickly to move everything away from the derrick. As they stacked the last of the boxes the ground rumbled, and a sound burst from the hole that was louder than a railroad engine.

Hank shouted, "It's about to blow!"

The drill crew ran from the derrick floor. Black gold boiled out of the hole. Debris flew in every direction and oil rained down on all the men, including Charlie, Hank, and the Pinkerton. The pressure from the hole continued the heavy flow for about twenty minutes. When it subsided, the crew went back on the derrick floor and attached a cap to the pipe to close off the flow.

Hank, Charlie, and their men shouted and danced to celebrate a true gusher on what was soon known as the Marland - Payne #1.

* * *

Two days after they struck oil Marland arrived in Cushing. Charlie had secured a banquet room for them to celebrate the event. After they all took their seats, Marland stood at the end of the table. He raised his champagne flute and said, "Everyone stand with me and raise your glass. I want to salute what has become the great team of Hank Thomas and Charles Kelly."

Everyone raised their glasses and gave a cheer.

Charlie said, "Thanks, E. W., and let's all agree that Hank sure knows how to find oil!"

The room resounded with another cheer.

Hank stood and said, "Mr. Marland, I know we told you about the threat that Roland Willard made. But I can't say it strong enough how impressive it was to me how Charlie handled that situation. I have seen and dealt with Willard and his types before. But never seen anyone handled so quickly and so decisively in my twenty-plus years in this industry."

Marland nodded in agreement. "Charlie, it seems that George Miller didn't exaggerate when he described you as a young man with focus, determination, and more than enough backbone to get a tough job done."

The crowd roared their approval.

Charlie raised his hands and said, "Thank you both for your kind words. I always have in my mind what I want to happen. I strive with everythin' I have to achieve that. Hank and I came here to get a job done. I can't imagine you could ever find a better oilman. I believed my role was to enable him and his crew to succeed. Willard was in the way. I was doin' my part by eliminatin' him from the picture."

Marland laughed and said, "I guess the word will likely get around that you don't want to cross Charles Kelly. You'll want to find a way to have him on your side."

The celebration continued for a few hours, then Charlie pulled Hank aside and said, "Let's go up to my room so we can talk in private."

Up in the room, Charlie said, "Hank, we got to know each other pretty well out at the well site. You know my original ambition was to become a top hand at the 101 Ranch. But since I started out from New Mexico a lot has changed and my ambition has gotten too big for its britches. I want to own an oil company someday. I was thinkin' maybe we could do somethin' together. I want you to be part of that company."

Hank said, "I don't have, and probably won't ever have, enough money to go in with you. But it's somethin' I'd be interested in."

"I didn't say anythin' about money. What you would bring to the company are your experiences and talent. I feel it would be up to me to create the money to start us."

"Charlie, it takes well over one-hundred thousand dollars to start an oil company. You're young and don't know this business as I do. That's why I do what I do for Marland and other men with money."

Charlie smiled and put his hand on Hank's shoulder and said, "Hank, I've some ideas about gettin' the funds, but I'm not prepared to say anythin' about it now."

"You gotta be shittin' me!"

Charlie laughed and said, "No, I'm not. Would you be interested in becoming one of the largest oil companies in Oklahoma?"

"Yes, I would; where do I sign."

Charlie said, "Not yet, buddy. But I've already seen enough to know there's a lot of money to be made in the oil business, and I know we're good together. I want you to run the operation, and I'll provide the startup capital and have funds ready to acquire the leases and drillin' rights. I need to find a way to create the startup funds."

Hank offered his right hand and said, "I'm in, and I sure hope you find the money." They shook hands.

Chapter Twenty-Six
November 1918

It was the morning after the celebration and Charlie rose early, packed his bags, and was out of the hotel by 7:00 a.m. *I can't wait to get back to the 101 and start the next chapter of this adventure. I'll call Susan from my office and share the last few days' happenings.*

As Charlie drove north he spotted the oil derrick at the Yale site poking above a few trees. He knew that Hank's men would soon be out there to take the derrick down and put in the equipment they'd need to pump the oil. Charlie reflected that the last two months had been good to him. He really couldn't imagine how it might have been better. *Well, maybe if I hadn't been shot at by Willard's goon,* he thought with a laugh. But all-in-all it was certainly a far cry from where he thought he wanted to be. He was right when he told Hank last night that his ambition had gotten too big for its britches. Charlie knew now that he would never be satisfied if he'd stayed a ranch hand. Even had he become foreman, he didn't think he'd have the same feeling he had now.

It was late afternoon when Charlie arrived at the 101. The light was on in George's office as he drove past the White House, so he dumped his bags and took them into his little house before heading up to the White House. Charlie knocked on the door jamb and said, "Good afternoon, George."

"Charlie! My, it's good to see you. When did you get in?"

"Less than five minutes ago."

"Come sit down, tell me about the gusher."

Charlie had already spoken to George about Willard and the goon, but he described his experiences at the drill site and how it felt to be drenched in oil.

"Marland called me right after he learned about the gusher. He and I were most impressed with how you handled everything on this job."

"I was doin' my job. Hank found the oil, and I gave him the freedom to do his job."

"I need to get you up to speed on what's happening here. The Fall gather and sale wasn't as good as we hoped. The price of beef is down, and we didn't have as many to sell. We made a profit, but just barely."

"Isn't that because we're givin' up grazin' land to drill for oil and gas?"

"That's true, and it won't likely change over the next few years, if ever. I'll need to let a lot of the hands go. I already did that after the gather, but in January, I'll have Boss let some more go."

"How did the produce crops do this last harvest?"

"Much better than the cattle. But nothing tops our oil business. Joe wants to get back into show business, both with the Wild West Show and the movies. I'm worried we'll lose money, but I guess we may try it next Spring."

"George, if you don't mind, I need to call Susan and go eat supper. I want to get down early after that drive, so I'll see you tomorrow."

"You bet, Charlie, good to have you back. By the way, you're in love with her, aren't you?"

"Yes, I'll admit I'm completely in love with her. I learned a while back that there's a fella in Kansas City who's after her. That bothers me some."

"Go call her and make sure she knows how ya feel about that."

Charlie nodded, immediately went to his office, and placed his call to Susan.

"Hello, this is Susan."

"Sweetheart, it's been too long since we talked."

"Yes, Charlie, but this has been better than when we were only writing. Tell me what's happened since we talked?"

"I'm back at the ranch. We brought in a gusher at the well site!"

"A gusher! Charlie, that's great... Hold on, Sweetheart, yes, Father, Charlie and his crew brought in a gusher down near Cushing, Oklahoma." There was a pause and Charlie heard mumbled voices. "Charlie, my father, wants to talk to you."

Charlie suddenly realized that his palms were sweating. He'd wanted to meet Susan's father, but he didn't expect the first time would be over a telephone.

"This is Walter Kramer, son. What's this Susan's all excited about?"

Charlie sat up straighter and realized he was gripping the earpiece too tight. Relax, he told himself. "Mr. Kramer, it's a pleasure to talk to ya. I'm workin' with E.W. Marland, who runs the 101 Oil Company for the Millers. We drilled a new well north of Cushing, and a few days ago, it flowed in as a gusher. Marland expects it to produce a lot of oil for the company."

"Charlie, right?"

"Yes, sir."

"I know of Marland. My friend Harry Sinclair speaks highly of him. So, you're involved in the oil business. I've developed an interest in it myself. I'll let Susan have the phone back, but I'll say congratulations, young man."

There was a pause and then Susan said, "Sweetheart, I've seldom seen him that excited. He's been pretty insistent that I've wasted my time caring the way I do for you. His views have been that I have no business with a ranch hand regardless of the size of the ranch where he works. And he's pushed me toward this fella at the bank. He's the number two man there and has a solid future, but I could see my father's eyes sparkle as he was talking with you."

"So, have you been seein' this banker fella?"

"He's come to the house a time or two, but we've never been alone together. Charlie, I'm not interested in him. Please come to Kansas City."

"What do ya want me to do if I come there?"

"Show my father that you want me as much as you say you

do. I think he'll see you for the smart, strong leader you are. He now knows you can be more than a cowboy."

"What's wrong with a cowboy?"

"Nothing, to me. But it's my father..."

"Susan, are ya sayin' we'll never be together if your father doesn't approve of me?"

"No, but I do think he'll want us together when he gets to know you. That would mean a lot to me. I don't need his approval, but I want it. I want to marry you."

"Well, I want that too. I don't want this banker sniffin' around all the time. I'll see what I can do about comin' there to visit before I take on another project here. Susan, I'm beginnin' to question whether I need to stay here at the 101 much longer. When I talked with George earlier, he said Joe is wantin' to start up the show again and spend money filmin' movies. Both of those businesses lose money. George and Zack won't stop him. That bothers me. I've seen enough already to know George does a marvelous job borrowin' from one business that's doin' well to pay for one that is not. You and I wouldn't do that for as long as he has had to. I know your father would get out of a business that loses money. I guess what I'm sayin' is that there may not be much for me to learn anymore."

Susan said, "What about the oil business? You could stay and learn more from Marland."

"I guess, but I think he uses Hank to find oil for him. Although Marland knows the oil business, he's the money guy, and Hank runs the business. Hank is willin' to leave Marland to create a business with me if we can find the money needed to start our own oil company. We would be equal partners, and that would give Hank more incentive to do his job well."

"Oh Charlie, I love you, and I need you with me. I've said it before, and I'll say it again, I'll marry you. Let's talk about you coming here soon."

"I call ya tomorrow. Give my regards to your father."

"Oh, I will, my darlin', I will."

* * *

Charlie sipped on his second cup of coffee at the café when George walked in.

George laughed, "I thought sure I would beat you today."

"I woke up ahead of the roosters today. George, I need to talk to you about a very important subject to me."

"What? Are you okay?"

Charlie nodded, "You know I've often written and called Susan in Kansas City. I even told you we've discussed marriage." Charlie paused and took a deep breath, "Well, it's time for me to go to Kansas City and take the next step. My sweetheart is Susan Kramer Blackaby, and you should and need to know she is the daughter and only child of Walter Kramer."

"Good God Charlie! My father knew Walter Kramer very well. Her father helped get the spur from the Santa Fe railroad extended out to the ranch for us."

Charlie leaned back in his chair, "I know he's a businessman of some means, but he must have quite a bit of influence to pull that off." Charlie paused and played with his coffee cup. "George, she asked me if there was any way you could allow me some time to go to Kansas City to get to know her father better. Now that I'm working with you in the oil business, he's showing some interest in me as her possible future husband."

George didn't hesitate, "Marland hasn't got you on any new projects yet so the impact will be small. It could benefit not only you as a possible son-in-law but the 101 too."

Charlie nodded, "I hadn't thought of that, but yes, it sure could. She said that my being in Kansas City is important to her becoming my future wife. We discussed it again last night; I believe we'll want to marry as soon as possible."

"Charlie, I realize now that she must be wealthy, as in probably millions of dollars. Why do you need to work here with me?"

Charlie put his elbows on the table and smiled, "I guess that's a fair question. You need to understand and believe that I only recently found out about her father and the size of her wealth myself. George, I want and need to learn all I can about running an organization made up of several businesses. Who better to learn from than you?"

George leaned back and crossed his arms, "Will I continue to have your complete loyalty? Will you stay with me after I teach you the details that make my system work?"

Charlie looked George dead in the eye and said, "Absolutely. Susan said she would love to come to the ranch and live here with me. I would imagine she has a beautiful home in Kansas City. But she moved to the little town of Elmore City, Oklahoma, when she married Jasper."

George shook his head, "Charlie, you couldn't make that up. Go be with Susan, get things settled, and bring her back here. We all will want to welcome her to the 101 family."

Charlie continued to look George in the eye and said, "George, I understand that you won't be paying me while I'm gone."

George smiled big and responded, "Why would I do that? I figure Walter has at least one high-powered lawyer, and of course, everyone knows he owns several large banks. Your education starts as soon as you get there. I figure I'll benefit from this trip too. Plus, how could it possibly hurt me and the 101 to add a Kramer to the family."

They both enjoyed a good laugh, but they knew George was right. They finished breakfast and headed to their offices.

Charlie called and got tickets for the ATSF railroad scheduled to leave out of Ponca City that afternoon. He would arrive in Kansas City before bedtime.

Charlie called Susan and couldn't wait for her voice as the phone rang once, then twice.

"Hello, this is Susan."

"How are you, Sweetheart?"

"Oh, Charlie, it's so good to hear your voice. I'm great, but this call makes it even better."

"I'll be there by sometime around 9 to 10 tonight. I have a ticket for the railroad that'll leave Ponca City this afternoon."

"Your boss is okay with this? I don't want you to get in trouble."

"I told him about you and our plans. He said to give you his best regards, and they look forward to meeting you. He's happy to let me come, and he said I should do whatever I need to so that you and I can marry. He wants most of my attention on his oil business, not worryin' about my sweetheart in another state."

"How nice, and he's a good businessman. I'll meet you at the station. Tell me again what time you're supposed to arrive?"

"The ticket office said at 9:00 pm local time. I can get a ride to your house."

"No, I want to meet you. I have a driver, and we'll be in a black Cadillac. I'll watch for you. I'm so excited; I can't wait to see you. It's pleasant out for this time of year, so I'll wear a bright yellow dress so you can easily see me if there is a crowd."

"I won't be able to miss that, I'm sure. I better git off this phone so that I can prepare for the trip. By the way, can we find a store where I can get a business suit? I sometimes need to dress differently in this new job, and I want to look all business there with you."

"We will, but not tomorrow. We both won't need any clothes tomorrow."

"I love how you think, my dear; I'll see you tonight."

He went into George's office and let him know when the train would leave Ponca City. George said, "I'll drive you into town to catch the train."

After lunch, they went to the depot and arrived as the train pulled into the station.

"Thanks again for the ride and for understanding about my need to be with Susan."

"That's okay," George said, holding out his hand. "You be safe and call me in the morning, so I know you're there and settled. Goodbye."

Charlie shook George's hand. "Goodbye, George." He then hurried to get on the train.

As the train pulled out of the station Charlie watched the prairie passing by the window. The sun was setting, and Charlie realized the sun was setting on one part of his life. He wondered what the dawn would bring.

Chapter Twenty-Seven
November 1918

It was a long six hours on the train for Charlie. He didn't try to sleep; he was too excited about the prospect of seeing Susan. The train was on time as it pulled into Kansas City's Union Station.

Charlie looked out the window on the depot side of the train, and there stood Susan. He could see her plainly in the bright lights of the station's platform. She stood there as promised in her yellow dress. *She's more beautiful than I remember and could ever have imagined*, he thought. He gathered his bags and rushed to the exit. As he stepped off the train car, he waved, "Susan, I'm over here."

She ran through the maze of passengers and threw her arms around his neck. A passionate kiss followed by a long hug.

"Charlie, it's been way too long. I so appreciated your letters and phone calls, but they weren't enough. They could never replace our talks on the creek bank. Do you understand what I mean?"

"I do, Sweetheart. It's been a long time for me too, you know?"

They walked arm and arm through Union Station past the Harvey House, and out front to the parked Cadillac.

The driver, Bernard, took Charlie's bags and followed the lovers to the car.

* * *

Charlie marveled at the homes as they headed to Susan's

house. "Is all of Kansas City like this? These homes are bigger than some hotels I've seen."

"No, of course not; we're in Ward Estates and the Country Club Plaza part of Kansas City. You know Father is a successful businessman, and he built a large house on Westover Road that we still own and live in. I've not lived in it long because I was away at Vassar College when he had it built."

In a few minutes, Bernard turned the Cadillac into a tree-lined driveway that went back about a quarter of a mile and rounded in front of a three-story mansion with four massive white pillars that framed a magnificent entrance.

With a devilish grin, Susan said, "Honey, we're home. I'm sorry it's dark, but you'll get a better look at the place tomorrow."

"Oh, I can see enough that I know that President Wilson doesn't live any better than this. How big is this place?"

"My father said it's about seven thousand square feet. It has four bedrooms and five baths. The most important thing is we have a big swimming pool."

"It's too bad that it's November as it would be fun to go swimming," Charlie said.

"But that's the beauty of it," Susan said slyly. "Father's doctor told him he needed to swim for exercise all year long, so he built what he calls his conservatory with plants, seating and a large indoor swimming pool. And he put in a heating system, so the water stays warm all year long."

Bernard took the Cadillac around to its garage. Susan and Charlie took his bags and went inside. Charlie thought he knew what to expect, after all, he'd seen the Miller's house down at the ranch, but he was surprised by what he saw. The entrance opened into a wide foyer with marble floors and ornate wooden side tables that held vases of what looked like fresh-cut flowers. Above the tables was a large mirror on the left, and a large painting of a man sitting on a horse on the right. Past the foyer, the marble floors continued. Directly ahead was a wide staircase that swept up to the second floor. To the left, Charlie saw a door leading into a parlor and a hallway leading to the back of the house. To the right was a set of double doors that led into a large dining room. Susan tugged him along and headed up the stairs to a guest bedroom. She said, "I wanted you with me in my room, but Father would never approve."

Charlie gave a low whistle. "This is bigger than the whole house my family lived in out in New Mexico." There was a large four-poster bed along one wall. The floor was dark wood with thick rugs laid atop it. A plush armchair sat in a corner and a dresser with a mirror over it was along another wall, as well as two doors.

"I understand, Sweetheart. I hope this doesn't make you feel uncomfortable. Are you okay?"

"Uncomfortable? Nah. It's still smaller than the house I am living in down at the ranch. I'm no longer the greenhorn that came out of New Mexico. I grew up poor, but I don't plan to live poor."

"I don't think that will be a problem. I have what Jasper left and what Father has shared with me. Once we marry that will be yours too, and we can grow our fortune from there." She gave a tug on his arm and pulled him close and kissed him, running her hand through his hair. She broke the embrace and walked toward the door. "Hey, let's get to the pool. It's private, and the staff is already in their quarters."

They went back downstairs, and Susan led Charlie to the back of the house and through another bedroom.

"Whose room is this?" Charlie asked.

Susan started to take off her yellow dress. "Mine silly." The rest of her clothes slid off to the floor. She went out a set of French doors across the patio and into the conservatory.

Charlie wasn't far behind, "Susan, what about your father? What if he sees us?"

"His office and bedroom are on the other side of the house. We'll be fine." She jumped into the pool and Charlie followed. The water was warmer than Charlie expected.

"This heating system is great," Charlie said after swimming the length of the pool. He stopped in the shallow end and stood up, water cascading off his muscles. He took in the building that housed the pool. The walls and ceiling were glass panes set within white painted metal frames. Rock pillars rose from the pool deck to support the ceiling, and a dozen varieties of plants grew from large pots. "This is amazin', Susan. It's bigger than most houses."

"Father always wants only the best." She swam toward Charlie, rubbing her hand against Charlie's leg. "There's a nice patio outside too, and if the weather stays warm we can enjoy it. Otherwise, we have the seating area around the pool."

Charlie turned and saw several deck chairs under some large potted palms. "We sure will." He eased back into the water up to his neck. "This water is nice and warm."

Susan dipped her head under then came back up and shook the water from her hair and smiled, "It's about to get warmer." She threw her arms around Charlie and gave him another kiss. They twirled in the water, able to do things they'd not had room to do in the creek down in Elmore City. Their hands traced familiar paths across their bodies as they got reacquainted with each other after so long apart. After too short a time they both gasped and then held each other, slowly drifting in the pool. Finally, Susan said, "Do you want something to drink?'

Charlie smiled, "That sounds good; got any beer?"

"I'll check the icebox in the barroom." She swam to the edge and climbed out of the pool, water dripped from her large breasts, and off her shapely legs as she walked across the patio. She went inside through another set of French doors. Charlie's eyes followed her every step. He drifted over and climbed out of the pool.

Susan returned through the same doors with a Heim's beer in each hand. "Here you go, big guy." They tapped the bottles together and each took a drink. "Let's sit a while and talk about our future."

"Good idea, Sweetheart." Susan grabbed a towel and wrapped it around her body as she sat in the wooden deck chair. Charlie decided to let the warm air of the pool room dry him off and he sat down next to Susan. They were comfortable in the setting and with each other.

Susan said, "You've been very excited about the opportunity George Miller has given you in your last few calls. Has he rekindled the interest in the business world I saw in Elmore City?

Tell me your new goals and take your time. We've all night." She turned in the deck chair and let the towel slide down.

Charlie reached over and stroked her arm. "Do you want to know about my business dreams, my family dreams, or both?"

"All of it, I want you to describe what you want as a perfect life."

"It would start with you as my wife. I adored you before I knew you had all this." He looked around and pointed to the house and grounds of the mansion.

Susan said, "My future happiness does not exist without you in it, Charlie, so we agree there. Now, what do you want to do with your time and talents?"

"I've always seen myself doin' somethin' around a ranch, and it's still a main interest of mine. But since I have been out on my own, I've learned about the general merchandise business, and over the past few months, I've seen how the oil and gas business is growin'. I don't want to do one business. I want to become successful in several. Just like George Miller is doing, and from what you've told me, your father. I don't know your father yet, but I admire what he's done."

"I love my father, and I respect him. He can be so kind and generous but also ruthless. You never want to lie to him, and you never want to cheat him. He'll destroy you. There's a story about how he lost a deal fair and square to someone he didn't care for at all. He went to the man's office and shook his hand because he respected him. He didn't like him, but he respected him. I know you can be kind. Can you be ruthless?"

"I believe I can. I've been pushed more than once in the past by someone or somethin', so I know I can handle tough situations. Even though I've dealt with bullies, rustlers, and bad men, I'm sure I've never faced some of the situations your father has. I want to believe I would do what your father has done, especially with the man who beat him fair and square." He took a drink of his beer.

"I believe you, and I know we both have some growing to do. We have time on our side, and it seems we share common dreams."

"I want to be respectful and respected. I can learn a lot from George Miller over the next few years about how he manages the businesses within the 101 industries, and I can also learn from your father as I get to know him better, can't I?" With those things workin' for us, we'll create our empire. Do you agree with me?"

Susan reached over and squeezed Charlie's hand, "I do. I'm excited by all this. I'll admit I was drawn to you at first by as pure a sexual lust as there could ever be. But Charlie, what captured me was our time on the creek bank when I got to know your mind, and the way you put ideas together intrigued me. Now I'm surer than ever; we'll be successful as business partners as well as loving and devoted life partners. I want to get married."

"We'll git married, and I want it soon. But, right now, we need to get some sleep. Over breakfast, we can create a list of tasks we must do over the next few weeks."

"Good idea, Honey. But there's one flaw in your plan, Charlie."

"What?"

"I'm not going to give you any time to sleep." She reached her hand over, letting it trace down the toned muscles of his chest and stomach until it rested where she wanted it. Charlie pulled her close, tossing the towel aside as they began their second time on dry land this time.

Chapter Twenty-Eight
November 1918

Charlie opened his eyes to find Susan perched on the edge of the bed. After their time at the pool, they'd managed to make it upstairs to Charlie's room. They'd been truthful to her father as they hadn't slept together, though Charlie had eventually drifted off after their fourth time.

Susan wore a white light-weight terry cloth robe that was not currently tied at the front, as she smiled and held a hot cup of coffee for him. He yawned and said, "Mornin' beautiful, how long have ya been up?'

"Long enough to get this coffee for you."

He took the coffee and said, "Thanks, you're an angel."

Susan let him take a couple of drinks and then set the cup and saucer on the nightstand. She pulled him up and said, "I think it's time we took a shower." She led him over to one of the doors and opened it. She dropped her robe and asked, "Are you ready?"

After their shower, they went to the breakfast room. The floor-to-ceiling windows allowed a panoramic view of the conservatory, tennis courts, and backyard.

As he took his seat, Charlie said, "This is beautiful. What a way to start your day."

Susan said, "I do love this room. This view is serene."

Charlie nodded, "I want this for us in Oklahoma someday."

"Honey, we'll make it happen; it's just a matter of when."

The cook, a woman about forty, medium height and a little chubby, walked into the room with a coffee carafe. She poured their coffee and asked, "What can I make you for breakfast?"

"Beverly, this is Charlie Kelly. Charlie, this is Beverly, and you go first."

"It's nice to meet you, Beverly. I'll have three eggs, bacon, fried taters, and do ya have biscuits?"

"I can make biscuits."

"No, that's alright, I can do with toast. But how about biscuits and bacon gravy some mornin'? I'd love to see how you make 'em. I'm known for my biscuits out at the 101 Ranch in Oklahoma. Maybe we can share recipes."

"Yes, sir, it'll be my pleasure. Miss Susan, what'll you have?"

"I'll have my usual poached egg and toast."

Beverly frowned, "Mr. Kelly, she picks at her food like a bird. I can't get her to eat."

He returned her frown with a smile and shrug, "Whattaya do?"

After Beverly left, Charlie turned to Susan, "We need to decide what we get to first. I know we said we'd take the day off and swim and make love. It's Saturday, and that makes sense, but we need to work on something, don't we? What do you have in mind?"

"We need to talk to my father and his legal advisor at the Kramer Group. He's my uncle as well as the corporate attorney. I know it's Saturday, but he'll be in his office today."

"That's a good idea. Who are ya talkin' about?"

"He's Curt Schlegell, and he's been with my father longer than I've been alive. Uncle Curt is my late mother's brother."

In walked a dapper older man already dressed in his three-piece blue pinstriped suit.

This must be Walter Kramer. He stood a good six feet tall, like Susan, and had salt and pepper hair and a thick mustache.

Charlie and Susan stood, and she moved over next to Charlie and put her arm around his waist, "Father, this is my Charlie." She looked up at Charlie, smiled, and said, "Sweetheart, this is my father, Walter Kramer."

Charlie offered his right hand, "It's an honor, sir."

Walter coughed and then cleared his throat, "Susan has

talked about you constantly for months. It interested me to hear you had transitioned to the oil business out on the 101 Ranch. I've known the Millers for many years. We need to continue our short talk on the telephone while you're here." He looked directly at Susan, "Harmon Goodenough will join us for dinner tonight. Please look your best." He returned his attention to Charlie, "You have a good day, young man."

Susan said, "Father, I have plans for Charlie and me this evening."

"Change them; I must leave immediately for my office. I'll be home by 6:00 pm, and Harm should arrive at 7:00."

Walter pivoted and walked out of the room.

Charlie smiled, "I believe he just sent us a strong message."

"There's no doubt that was his intent. We'll win him over; it's only a matter of time. I know I said we'd take today off, but I talked to my uncle yesterday, and he sorta expects us to come to his office today. I want you to meet him."

"I assume his office is near your father's?"

"They're next door to each other. That's okay; I'll not let father ruin my plans. Let's finish our breakfast and get dressed. I'm sure Uncle Curt will have some appointments set up for us to meet the Group leadership. You need to see the world that my father has built."

"That's good; he'll already have a meeting set up for you? And your father trusts this guy?"

Susan smiled and said, "He should; as I said, he's family. Uncle Curt has created every legal document for Father and reviewed every contract. Father refuses to sign any document before Uncle Curt had given his okay."

"Well, that's great, and you feel we need to go see him today?"

"Yes, I do. It appears we can't let a day go by that you aren't more comfortable with all aspects of my life here and Father doesn't become more comfortable with you. You know that I'm a wealthy widow, and up until now, that's been enough of a potential barrier for you to overcome. Now you need to see the whole picture."

"Susan, are you tryin' to scare me off?"

"My goodness, no, but you must be as prepared as I am to start to live in this world. Because Sweetheart, someday it could become ours."

"Fine, I'm ready to do whatever you think comes next, but now, I need to call George and let him know I've arrived safely and give him some idea about when I might be returnin'. We also need to get me to that clothin' store you mentioned."

Susan said, "I know, I own a department store, but—"

"Wait, you own a department store too?"

"Yes, but we'll go downtown to Wolff Brother's Tailor Shop for suits, ties, and shirts. Next door is Escott and Young's, where we'll get your shoes and socks. Does that sound okay?"

Charlie laughed, "If you're happy, I'm happy. But, if you own a department store here in Kansas City, why don't we go there?

Susan said, "Wolff Brothers carry the finest men's clothing in Kansas City, and I want you to wear only the best."

"Okay, as I said, I'm happy if you're happy. I need to use the phone."

"Use the one in the parlor. It'll be quiet in there."

Charlie went into the parlor and was in awe at the size of the room. He walked back to the doorway into the kitchen area and said, "This house keeps surprisin' me with how many rooms it has, and the parlor is another room that's bigger than the house in New Mexico."

Susan smiled and said, "I'll give you a tour of the house later today. You need to see this place as our home in Kansas City."

Charlie nodded and returned to the parlor and picked up the phone.

"Operator, please connect me person-to-person to George Miller at OK-101."

CHarlie waited a minute then the operator said, "This call is for George Miller."

"Speaking, hello, is this Charlie?"

"It's me. I'm doin' fine here in the lap of luxury in Kansas City."

"So, Susan has a nice place there, huh?"

"I was kiddin' her last night that the President doesn't live this good."

"What's it like there? How long do you think you'll need to stay?"

"We haven't talked everything through yet. But I'm happy to learn that Susan has a plan for us to win over her father, and we'll get married here. We'll meet with her uncle, who is the company attorney, in a few hours, and he is supposed to have meetings arranged for us to meet with the company leaders."

"Does that mean it may be days and not weeks?"

"I'm not sure, but maybe. I promise you we'll not waste time. I know I need to git back there as soon as I can."

"Okay, Charlie, I've someone here in the office. I'll let you go. Give me a call every few days and let me know how things are."

"Will do, George, goodbye."

* * *

After they finished breakfast, Susan's driver pulled the Cadillac around to the front door, and they were on their way.

Charlie craned his neck as he looked at the buildings in downtown Kansas City. "Susan, this place is so big. These buildin's are taller than any I've ever seen. Are we goin' inside one?"

"In the next block, we'll go into the Wolff Brothers and Escott and Young's stores. After we finish there, the tallest building in the city is the next block. It's fifteen stories tall, and our offices are on the top floor. That's where we'll meet with Uncle Curt."

"How did your father get that office?"

Susan's face showed a little frustration as she said, "Charlie... Sweetheart, he owns it. Someday I'll... or I mean, we'll own the place. It's the Kansas City Commerce Bank Building."

"Oh?" This place is bigger than I ever imagined.

"Has any of this sunk in, honey?"

He blushed as his eyes grew big and his jaw dropped. "It did, right then."

"Good. Let's get you some new clothes."

* * *

Charlie was in and out of suits, ties, shoes, and hats as men with tape measures draped over their shoulders fawned over him for the first time in his life.

Three hours later, Charlie stood in front of a mirror and admired how he looked as he wore a new three-piece gray suit, a white button-down shirt with a red tie, and a pair of black winged-tip loafers. Charlie said, "This is the first time I've ever worn a tie. I'll git used to this, but it does feel strange."

Susan said, "Welcome to the world of business conference rooms and making deals over dinner at the country club, Sweetheart." She ordered four more complete outfits to be made and sent to the house.

Susan said, "Let's go visit Uncle Curt. He expected us an hour ago."

"Do you think I look good in this suit? I've never had one before."

"You look great and completely natural in it. The main thing that sets you apart from most men in suits is your beautiful Oklahoma ranch hand tan. And that's a good thing. Now focus, we're headed into what will become our world. This is the biggest bank, any way you measure it, in Missouri or Kansas."

They walked through the lobby to a funny-looking wall. The wall opened up. Charlie jumped back, "What in the hell happened?"

Susan giggled, "Charlie, this is an elevator. We'll step inside, and it will take us up to our offices."

"You're teasin' me. This is a joke?"

"No, Honey." She looked at the operator and said, "Morning, Bill, take us to our offices. Step inside, Charlie."

They rode the elevator to the top floor. When the door opened, they entered a lobby dominated by an impressive reception desk. A large sign that read The Kramer Group was on the wall behind the desk. At the reception desk, a middle-aged lady with a pleasant face said, "Good morning, Miss Kramer. Oh, I'm sorry, Mrs. Blackaby."

"Kay, that's fine; I'll always be Miss Kramer to you, won't I? So, Father, has you here on Saturday?"

"You sure will. I remember when you were born. Your daddy was so proud. He rushed into the office with his arms full of boxes of Havana cigars. And yes, I'm here today, but only for another hour or so."

Laughing, Susan said, "Well, okay, and this is my fiancé, Charles Kelly. Uncle Curt expects us. Nice seeing you, Kay."

Charlie smiled, nodded, and gave a hesitant wave, "My pleasure, ma'am."

A few steps down the hallway, Charlie leaned over, "So it's official then, we're engaged?"

"So far as I'm concerned, we are." She looked up into his eyes and gave him her wickedest smile, "You did say you wanted me for your wife, didn't you?"

Charlie smiled back, "I sure did, I absolutely did."

They continued down the hallway to a back-corner office, and Susan rapped on the door jamb. A distinguished, gray-haired gentleman looked up. His eyes twinkled, and he smiled as warmth filled his face.

"Susan, come in, I haven't seen you in weeks. Where have you been? Give me a hug. And who is this?"

"Uncle Curt, this is Charles Kelly. Do you remember I told you about a dear friend who helped me through the loss of Jasper? This is that wonderful man. And you need to know, he's now my fiancé."

He offered his right hand, "Charles, Curtis Schlegell. Call me Curt, and if you've stolen the heart of this one, you must be a very substantial young man."

Charlie grasped Curt's hand and added his left. In as warm a voice as he could muster, he said, "It's my honor, sir. And please call me Charlie. Susan thinks the world of ya. I look forward to gittin' to know ya."

Susan said, "Can you update me on where we are with the meetings I requested?"

"Of course; have a seat," He gestured to the table in his office.

Curt said, "I know you said you wanted to meet with the four corporate presidents as soon as possible."

Susan nodded. "Tomorrow if possible."

"Tomorrow is Sunday," Curt reminded her. "I thought you and I could use either today or tomorrow to prepare and then have the meeting Monday. I know you wanted this to happen as soon as possible, and the four corporate presidents are in town. It could be one meeting here in the conference room or we could go to each business location.

Susan started to object but Curt held up a hand. "It's too early for you to be pulling stunts and making demands. They all agree that they want to meet you, they understand that Walter wants you to take over the business, but they aren't ready to be giving up their day of rest."

Susan nodded and Curt continued, "If you want, they have agreed to meet you here in my conference room on Monday, the eleventh, at ten."

Charlie could see that Susan was willing to accept the change, but she also looked like she'd just drunk some sour lemonade. He put a hand on her arm, "That gives you and me a chance to see the town."

Susan smiled and patted his hand. To Curt, she said, "Charlie will be my husband soon if all goes according to my plan, so I want him in the meeting with us on Monday. I want Charlie to feel that he can contribute to the discussion. After our marriage, I want him to have a formal role within the company as a future leader. "

Curt nodded, "No offense to Charlie, but I understood this meeting was to allow you to begin to expand your role because we've all seen your father's health deteriorating." He gave Susan a fatherly look. "Susan, he's still healthy enough to come to work every day, but he's been less energetic. You know he's been going home early on many days." Susan nodded. Charlie could see the sadness in her eyes.

"You've described this as a way to introduce Charlie to the company leadership," Curt said, "as a future leader. I'm not sure that's wise."

"Why?" Susan asked with a pout. "Charlie is going to become a part of the Kramer Group, an important part."

"I know that, but your engagement to Charlie hasn't been announced yet, and frankly, you haven't even mentioned it to your father yet, I assume."

216

The way that Susan's neck flushed was enough to tell Uncle Curt that he'd hit the mark. He chuckled. "Susan, darling, I don't care if you've not told your father yet, even though I know you've made your feelings clear in the past few months. Personally, I think Charlie here will make a great husband. Better than some other fellas."

Charlie realized Curt was talking about the man at the bank who'd been making advances on his girl. He'd never met the rascal, but he already didn't like him.

Curt pointed at Charlie. "Susan, if you go into your first meeting with the presidents, when you are trying to get them to know you better, and you shove this young fella in their faces as the next vice president of the Kramer Group, why they'll all revolt. They respect your father, and for that reason, they are willing to meet with you. They need time to get used to a woman as their boss, but they will come around. But parading Charlie out as a leader now is not the wisest of moves."

Susan pondered this, nodding her head slowly and biting her lip. Charlie suddenly realized how beautiful she looked as she worked through the issue. "You may be right, Uncle Curt," she finally said. "The presidents will have their minions along the wall of the conference room. That's where Charlie needs to sit this time." She looked at Charlie, "I guess you stay quiet and listen closely unless spoken to. The discussion should give you a good chance to learn a lot about the Kramer Group."

"Well, darlin'," Charlie said. "I don't know if I need to be there at all. I can always meet these men later."

"Let's discuss that over dinner," Susan said.

Curt smiled and said, "Whatever you decide they'll expect you to have your secretary there as well, one of the perks of the job. They'll accept him in that role."

"That might work but I don't want these men thinkin' that I may be gunnin' for their jobs. If I go with you to this meetin' and then a few months from now I'm introduced as your husband, they're gonna remember that."

"Well said," Curt nodded.

Susan looked determined, "I may still want Charlie there. I'll let you know before Monday." She looked back to Curt. "I have a general overview of each company from the information you gave me, and I'll learn more on Monday. Have they scheduled a tour for me of a location representative of their company? I want to see what they'll describe to me."

Curt said, "I don't think they've planned for a tour. Again, I can see you are chomping at the bit, but I caution you to go slow. You'll have plenty of time to get to know each of the different companies that make up the Kramer Group."

Susan said, "I'll consider that, Uncle Curt, but I may spring the request on them as a surprise, just to see how they react."

Seeing the humor in her last-minute request, Charlie said, "Curt, maybe it's good I don't work for her."

Curt grinned, "Charlie, she'll keep everyone on their toes, the way her father does."

Susan nodded, "I guess we're ready then. We'll see you Monday morning."

Curt smiled and said, "Now take Charlie to get some Kansas City bar-b-que. I love Pete's, and it's close by."

Charlie said, "I love bar-b-que, but I don't think juicy ribs and a three-piece suit go together. Maybe another time."

Curt chuckled, "I didn't think of that, and you're right. Pete's is so good, though."

Back in the car headed home, Charlie said, "Are you goin' to listen to your uncle's advice?"

"Possibly." She gave him a playful smile and took his hand in hers. "He made a lot of sense, but these men will need to get used to me running the company, not my father. I plan on making my mark in the business. Though maybe the first day isn't the time to upset the apple cart."

Susan placed her hand on Charlie's leg and lightly squeezed, "Well, I guess you get to meet Mr. Goodenough tonight."

"Who's he? Your father mentioned him this morning. Is he one of your father's friends?"

Susan laughed. "In a manner of speaking. He's the fellow at the bank that's been interested in me."

I'll be glad to finally meet this guy, Charlie thought. "Why didn't ya say this was the guy who's been chasin' ya this morning?"

"I didn't want you distracted by thinking about him all day." She gave his leg another squeeze. "Please be patient with Father, he only wants me to be happy. Harmon is someone he knows as a successful and valued member of the Kramer business family. He thinks that Harmon will be a good, safe, match for me. Respectable."

Charlie nodded but didn't want to say anything for fear of upsetting Susan.

"Even if you weren't already part of my life Sweetheart, I wouldn't be interested in him. He doesn't understand me and thinks I shouldn't be involved in any of the bank's business. I don't like him. We can get through this tonight and move forward."

"Yes, we can. I'm curious about him only because your father has supported him gettin' to know you." Charlie looked Susan in the eye, put his hands on the lapels of his suit jacket, and smiled, "Don't worry, I can be respectable too."

Susan laughed and kissed him.

Chapter Twenty-Nine
November 1918

Charlie, Susan, and Walter were seated in the parlor when Kathryn entered the room and announced, "Mr. Harmon Goodenough." She turned, stepped to her left, and raised her right hand indicating the gentleman standing in the doorway.

Walter stood, "Come in Harmon. It's good of you could join us."

Goodenough was a few inches short of six feet tall and couldn't have weighed more than 160 pounds. He was dressed in a nice blue suit, like the one Charlie had on, with shiny black shoes. He sported a handlebar mustache and appeared to be about thirty years old. He handed a coat and hat to Kathryn without a second glance or a thank you.

Walter walked across the room and shook Harmon's hand. He turned and gestured to Susan and Charlie who both stood up. Susan said, "Harmon this is Charles Kelly. He's my fian—"

Charlie interrupted her, "Friend from Oklahoma," he took a step forward and held out his hand. Harmon gave it a shake and Charlie was conscious both of how soft Harmon's hand was, and how rough his own hand felt. He was careful not to squeeze too hard, like some of the ranch hands liked to do to test a man's metal. Charlie didn't think Susan would mind but figured it wouldn't look good to her father. "It's a pleasure to make your acquaintance. I understand you work in banking for the Kramer Group."

Harmon said, "That's correct. My you're a big fella. What do you do for a living if you don't mind me asking?"

Charlie said, "I'm with the Miller's 101 Ranch working directly for George Miller in the oil business."

Charlie thought he saw Harmon's eyebrows twitch up at that. Before they all could take their seats again, Beverly spoke from the doorway to the dining room, "Dinner is ready, please come seat yourself and I'll serve the meal."

Walter headed toward the door, "Yes, let's all find our place at the table."

As they entered the dining room Walter pointed to the large table sitting under an electric chandelier. The table was big enough to sit twelve people, easily, but had been set for four. Walter took his place at the head of the table and gestured. "Susan, you sit on my right, and Harm, why don't you sit next to Susan. And Charlie you can sit across from her on my left."

Charlie smiled, "Of course, I'll be happy to."

The meal consisted of prime rib, baked potato, and vegetable medley accompanied by Cabernet wine. The conversation was pleasant but stilted, with Charlie and Harmon constantly eyeing each other and then Susan. Susan managed to keep the conversation light, talking about non-business and non-ranch things, always staying ahead of either her father or Harmon in directing the conversation.

As everyone appeared to be finished with their meal, Walter said, "Let's return to the parlor for a glass of my new favorite after-dinner drink. Harvey's Bristol Cream Sherry."

Susan said, "That sounds wonderful, Father." Walter stood and headed back to the parlor. As the others stood up from the table, she looked at Charlie and said, "Are you ready for something sweet?"

He looked over at Goodenough and then back to Susan, "As sweet as one of your kisses?"

Susan giggled, "Of course not, Sweetheart."

Goodenough's face reddened as he looked away, adjusted his tie, and cleared his throat. He walked briskly into the parlor and Charlie managed to not laugh.

Walter sat in a big armchair near the fireplace, which had a fire blazing, while Harmon sat on one of the couches. He'd left room for Susan to sit and gave her an imploring look, but she directed Charlie to the opposite couch and sat down as close to Charlie as she could without sitting in his lap. Beverly poured each of them their first glass of sherry and departed as Walter lifted his glass. "Everyone raise your glass and let's toast a pleasant dinner."

Goodenough gathered himself and added, "And to our continued success at Kramer."

Charlie said, "Absolutely."

Goodenough turned to Charlie, "You said earlier you worked at a ranch. Are you a cowboy?" He sneered and did his best to make "cowboy" sound like an insult.

Charlie nodded, "Proud to be one. But over this past year, George Miller asked me to work directly for him to assist in overseeing the eighteen different businesses that make up the operation with an emphasis on the 101 Oil Company. We recently brought in a gusher out north of Cushing, Oklahoma that should add as much as a million dollars a year to the 101 Ranch bottom line."

Walter leaned in, clearly interested, and said, "Charlie, I didn't know you were working across more than one business for George. What have you learned so far?"

Charlie's shoulders reared back, his chest out and chin came up as he said, "I've learned how the various businesses can work together to complement each other when you provide the right guidance. I know the cattle business well. I'm knowledgeable on most anything involving agriculture. I worked for Susan and Jasper in their mercantile, so I have a solid background there, but it's the oil business that has my interest right now."

Goodenough rolled his eyes, cocked his head, and sneered, "Sounds like you either can't hold a job or you haven't found something you can master."

Susan's nostrils flared as she glared at Goodenough. Charlie saw this and immediately said, "I suppose you could think that." Stay cool, he's trying to bait you. "But, you know, I'm glad the owners of those one hundred and ten thousand acres of prime

Oklahoma ranch land and a large growing oil business don't agree with that assessment. With such a large operation, involving many separate business interests," Charlie looked over at Walter, "it's important to have broad knowledge about how all the businesses interact, instead of mastering only one."

Susan leaned back in her chair and smiled.

Walter coughed and then said, "Harm, I think he may have a point there. I wouldn't have been as successful with the Kramer Group if I'd only had a narrow focus on just one part of the business."

"Yes, sir," Harmon said, chastised. "But ranching and oil are different from banking and everything else we do. Didn't I hear that the Miller 101 Wild West Show lost a lot of money?"

Charlie wasn't sure how to respond to that but didn't have to as Walter asked, "You seem agitated, Harm. Are you okay?"

Goodenough leaned back, swallowed hard, and said, "I'm alright, I guess it's time for me to go." He set his sherry down and stood up. "Susan, I'll see you at the office."

Susan said, "You're leaving so soon? Why you haven't finished your sherry. Have a safe drive home."

Charlie and Walter stood as their guest headed to the front door. It took a moment for Kathryn to be summoned and for Harmon to put on his hat and coat. He turned as if to say something else to Susan and Charlie plastered a big smile on his face and waved. Harmon shook his head and walked out the door.

Charlie looked at Susan and smiled broadly, "Was it something we said?"

Walter turned back into the parlor and grinned, "Okay, maybe you won that round, Charlie."

Susan said, "Father, Harmon Goodenough can be an arrogant asshole. I've never liked him."

Walter said, "Watch your mouth daughter." He coughed and then continued, "I can see he felt threatened tonight and he didn't handle it well. He's solid at the office, but that alone doesn't make him right for you."

Charlie and Susan quietly nodded and smiled.

Chapter Thirty
November 1918

Walter smiled and said, "You kids enjoy your evening. I'll be in my office for a bit and then to bed." He turned and headed to the hallway that led to his wing of the house.

They said their goodnights and Susan and Charlie sat on the couch and finished the sherry.

"I can see why you don't like Mr. Goodenough," Charlie said. "He sure don't live up to his name where you're concerned."

Susan giggled. "He's from a well-to-do family and he went to school back east. If he just stuck to banking and minding his own business, he wouldn't be so insufferable. But he's always trying to please father so he can get closer to me."

"Well, I think we managed to put a damper on that tonight."

Later Charlie and Susan walked out to the conservatory. Charlie with a bottle of Cabernet and each with a full wine glass. It wasn't long before they were naked on their lounge chairs and had enjoyed their wine.

With a twinkle in her eye, Susan said, "I think we need to get back in the pool and unwind from the day."

Charlie said, "I agree. But first, let me say, you handled yourself well in Uncle Curt's office today. What I mean is, you agreed to a compromise on the meeting structure that will be better for your transition as you replace your father someday. I agree with Curt, you need to establish that role within the company before you bring me into a position that might threaten these men and their futures."

Susan said, "Yes, and I got what I wanted. Father wants me strong and happy. I know he wants me to take over for him when he retires. Now can we get in the pool?" She stood up and pulled Charlie into her naked embrace. Charlie kissed her and let his hands caress her body and gently squeeze her breasts. They made it into the water but didn't get much swimming done.

* * *

Early on Monday morning Charlie and Susan were sitting at the table in the breakfast room talking about the meeting scheduled for that morning. Despite her confidence, Susan was a bit nervous, and Charlie was doing his best to tell her that she'd do fine. The business presidents wouldn't know what hit them.

Kathryn walked in and said, "Mr. Kramer would like you to come to his bedroom. He wants to talk with you."

Susan looked at Charlie as she bit her lip, "Both of us?"

Kathryn said, "Yes, he wanted both of you."

As they entered his bedroom Walter was sitting in a large, four-poster bed, several pillows propped behind him for support. He was dressed and had a cup of coffee in one hand. The remains of a simple breakfast sat on a tray on the large bed. He held up the morning paper. Large print at the top read, "GREAT WAR ENDS". Walter said, "I doubt either of you have seen this yet."

Susan shook her head, and Charlie said, "No, sir, but this is wonderful news."

Walter nodded, "It is, for the U.S. and the Allies, but Susan, dear," he turned to look at his daughter. "I just received a telephone call from Curt. He said that the board presidents want to postpone your meeting. They are letting their people off to celebrate the victory, and they want to celebrate too."

Charlie thought Susan might be angry, or at least sad at this change in plans, but she smiled and said, "I understand. After so long of the war, we all need to celebrate a little."

Walter nodded. "I knew you'd understand. Curt got them to move the meeting until Wednesday. I'm going to head to work in a bit. You know me, I can't take a day off."

They left Walter's room and returned to the breakfast room.

"Are you really not upset?" Charlie asked.

Susan leaned her head on his shoulder. "Maybe a little. But everyone in the country has been praying for this day to come. And waiting two more days won't matter."

"Do you want to go out and see how everyone is celebrating?"

"No," she smiled at him. "I'd rather stay here and celebrate with you. Just the two of us."

* * *

On Tuesday morning, after breakfast, Charlie went into the parlor to give George another call. After the operator connected them, and they said their greetings, Charlie asked, "How is everything at the ranch?"

"Well, most of the boys were up late celebrating our win over the Kaiser, and not a few of them are having to work with hangovers this morning."

Charlie chuckled. "No rest on a ranch."

George agreed, then said, "That goes for you too, Charlie. I need my best man back here."

"I was hoping to get another week if I could. Things are going well here, but Susan's father hasn't given his blessing yet, and there's this other fella still thinking he can worm his way into her father's good graces."

"I can sympathize with that," George said, "but I'm afraid in this case business needs to take precedent over romance. E.W. Marland had to leave for Pennsylvania today; there was a death in the family, and he needs to be there to sort things out."

"I'm sorry to hear that," Charlie said.

"Normally, this wouldn't' be a big concern, but this time it put me in a bind. There's a court hearing next week in Pawhuska that requires someone from the 101 Oil Company to be present. Marland was going to do that."

Charlie nodded as he held the receiver to his ear. "But with him gone, there ain't no one else but me."

"Normally I'd be happy to give you more time, Charlie," George said. "But I need you here. I'll try and make it up to you in the future."

"I appreciate that, but it's not needed. You hired me to do a job, and I need to be there to do it. Could I ask that you let me return on Sunday? That way I have a few more days with Susan to convince her father I'm the man for her. She has an important meeting with the different company presidents tomorrow and she wants me to be there."

"I think that's doable. I still want you to give me whatever insight you can into the Kramer Group and attending a board meeting is just the thing. I can give you 'til the weekend, but I need you here ready to work on Monday."

Charlie promised he'd be there Sunday night and they ended the call. Charlie went back into the breakfast room. Susan was drinking her coffee and scanning the morning paper.

"George needs me back at the ranch," Charlie said as he sat back down.

"Oh, no! So soon?"

"Yep." Charlie ate the biscuits and gravy that Beverly had made for him. He told Susan everything that George had said about Marland and the court hearing next week. "George has agreed I can stay the rest of the week, but I'll need to head back on Sunday morning."

Susan reached her hand over and placed it over Charlie's. "Then we'll need to make the most of the time we have this week. There's still a lot to do."

"With the meeting tomorrow and convincing your father we should marry."

Susan lifted her coffee and held it before her. She gave Charlie a knowing smile. "Well, sure, but I was thinking of other, more intimate things." Under the table, Charlie felt her foot rub up and down his leg.

* * *

Charlie and Susan hadn't had time for a swim after breakfast, but Susan had insisted that they take a shower before they went to the bank. They'd done that and spent more time "drying each other off" that they needed a second shower to clean up. Finally, after making love three times that morning they got dressed and went out for lunch at the bar-b-que place Uncle Curt had recommended. Charlie had to admit the food was good, though not as good as when they held a bar-b-que on the ranch.

As they walked into the Kramer offices after lunch, Kay stood at her desk and said, "Ms. Kramer!" She waved to them urgently. As they approached the desk, Charlie could see that she had been crying.

"Oh... darling. Mr. Kramer was taken to his doctor's office. He coughed up blood at a luncheon at Mission Hills Country Club."

Susan grabbed Charlie's shoulder in a tight, panicked grip, and said, "Oh my goodness. Is he still there? Charlie, we gotta go."

"Wait," Kay said. "His doctor saw him and sent him home with orders to rest over the next couple of days."

"Call the garage and tell them what happened, and we are coming down now," Susan told Kay. She nodded and spoke into a speaking tube while Charlie and Susan went back to the elevator. The ride down seemed to last forever, and Susan tapped her foot impatiently the entire time.

"I'm sure your father is all right," Charlie said as they reached the ground floor.

Susan was walking before Bill had fully opened the doors. Charlie had to chase after her. "He probably is, but I want to hear it from him, and his doctor."

They had to wait a couple of minutes before Bernard pulled the Cadillac up to the front door of the Kramer Group. But he accelerated away as soon as the door was shut and it wasn't long before Susan ran up the steps and into the foyer at home, with Charlie on her heels. She hollered, "Father, where are you?"

Kathryn, the maid, hurried into the room, "Susan, he's in his bedroom. The doctor just left. I don't think he's asleep."

Susan turned to Charlie, "Come with me."

Susan walked briskly toward Walter's room. Walter Kramer sat in his bed. He still wore his slacks but had a dressing gown on over his clothes. He held a copy of the morning paper in one hand, and he raised his right hand toward Susan as he said, "Susan, I'm alright."

"No, Father, you're not," Susan said as she marched across

the room and sat on the bed Charlie walked to the foot of the bed but didn't want to get in Susan's way. "You've not been alright for a while now. What did your doctor say?"

"He's still not sure what my problem is, but it's worse. I have times when I can't get my breath, and I start to cough and wheeze. Today was the worst attack I've had. I feel better now, but it's exhausting when I go through that."

Charlie said, "Sir, how can we help you?"

"I don't need any help. I'm fine. The doctor wants me to rest."

Susan gave her father a stern glare. "Are you going to listen to your doctor this time and rest here at home?"

"I can rest at work. I just won't see anybody or take any calls."

Susan shook her head emphatically. "No, father. Not this time. You need real rest. You know you'll get dragged into something if you go into the office."

Charlie stepped up and put a hand on her shoulder. "I would be happy to stay here with you, sir. That way you won't feel lonely."

"But you'll miss the meeting tomorrow," Susan said.

Charlie shrugged. "I know but being here to help your father is more important."

"Then I'll call and have Uncle Curt cancel the meeting."

Charlie and Walter both said, "No," at the same time.

Walter patted Susan's hand. "No, dear. This is exactly the time you need to be there. You need to show my business partners that you will be running the show going forward."

"And you can tell me what happened when you get home. It will be as good as if I was there." He kissed her on the top of her head.

"Charlie, I'm glad you're here for Susan. Son, it's time I admitted that it's obvious to me what Susan has seen in you all along. I haven't been able to have the discussions with you I wanted, but we'll be able to talk some over the next few days, I'm sure."

Susan leaned over and kissed her father's cheek. She said, "I wanted you two to get to know each other better, but I didn't expect it to happen like this."

"Well, something I learned on the ranch was to always make the best out of any situation. I'd be happy to talk about what the

101 Oil Company has been doing."

Walter said, "Splendid idea. Charlie, we can talk oil. I'm interested in getting into that business. And you can also fill me in on what's happened out on that glorious ranch too."

Charlie smiled, "I'd love that."

Susan stood up and said, "Right now, you need some rest, so we'll leave you alone for a while."

Chapter Thirty-One
November 1918

On Wednesday morning Charlie came down to breakfast alone. Susan was in talking with her father to go over the meeting agenda and discuss what topics she needed to press the others on, and which she could leave alone. Charlie tried to enjoy his bacon, eggs, toast, and coffee, but it felt different without Susan there, which seemed odd to Charlie since she was in her father's bedroom. He wondered if he'd feel this way after they go married and Susan had to be away to deal with something for the Kramer Group. He still believed that it was his responsibility to provide for Susan, that had been how he'd been raised, but he was starting to see how Susan didn't need him for that reason, not in simple terms of money or providing a home. He realized that his relationship with Susan was more about the other things he could provide her: love, attention, support, and maybe that was enough, but he hoped they'd be able to make a strong business partnership as well.

Susan finally came into the breakfast room a little before nine. She wore a stunning dress that highlighted her natural beauty while also projecting power. To Charlie, she looked both lovely and formidable at the same time.

"Wow, you look gorgeous," he said.

Susan gave him a quick kiss. "Thank you. Bernard's pulling the car around now. I want to get to the office in time to go over any last-minute details with Uncle Curt."

Charlie got up and walked with her to the front door. "I'd love to be there with you," he said as he helped her into a long fur coat.

"I do too, but I think it is good that you'll be able to spend some time with father. He's close to agreeing to our engagement, and this is your chance to win him over."

Charlie nodded then kissed Susan. "Go impress the hell out of them."

"I will."

She walked out of the door and got into the Cadillac. Charlie watched her from the door, ignoring the cold until he couldn't see the car anymore.

* * *

About midday, Charlie was seated in the breakfast room as he enjoyed both a sandwich made with left-over prime rib and the view across the patio and yard when Walter walked into the room. Charlie said, "Good, you're up and around."

Walter said, "Yes, I'm feeling much better. Beverly, is there some more of that beef I see in Charlie's sandwich?"

Beverly said, "There sure is, I'll make you a sandwich too. How does sweet tea sound for your drink?"

"Perfect."

Walter sat across from Charlie, enjoying his sandwich, tilted his head, raised his eyebrows, and said, "Now, Charlie, I want to hear more about your oil business experiences. How's E. W. Marland and George Miller doing?"

Charlie leaned in and said, "They're fine and happy we brought in that gusher."

"And you say that one well will bring in a million a year?"

"Yep, Hank is confident it's that good a well."

"Who's Hank?"

"Hank Thomas. He works for Marland drillin' for the oil."

Walter wiped his mouth and put his napkin aside, "Susan mentioned there was gunplay, and you contacted Pinkerton and got them involved. Tell me more."

Charlie gave a complete rundown of what happened and made sure he included details on what he learned about the oil business from Hank.

Walter's eyes sparkled and said, "That's impressive, Charlie. I see why Susan says you're a keeper. We'll talk more later. I've got to make a phone call to Los Angeles, and then maybe I'll listen to Susan and my doctor and take a nap. Enjoy your afternoon."

Walter stopped short of the hallway, turned, and walked a few steps back to Charlie, "I know the 101 Ranch is a big place and now I know there are eighteen businesses involved there. Has Susan indicated the size of Kramer to you?"

"No sir, she hasn't."

"Charlie, I'm beginning to see you as a strong contender to become my son-in-law. You need to understand The Kramer Group is worth about half a billion dollars. That's why I'm careful, young man."

Charlie sat in his chair trying to understand what Walter just told him.

Walter smiled, turned, and walked down the hall.

* * *

Curt and Susan arrived home from their day of meetings and walked into the parlor as Beverly finished preparations for dinner. Charlie greeted Susan with a kiss, and whispered in her ear, "I missed you."

She said, "I need to change into something more comfortable; come with me."

Curt said, "I'll go find your father."

Charlie followed Susan to her room and enjoyed the view as she changed into a cream-colored silk blouse with nothing under it and beige pants.

When they arrived in the kitchen area Walter and Curt were waiting in the dining room. Walter said, "How was your day, Susan? Charlie and I had a nice one. He told me more about what he's been doing in the oil business."

Susan said, "It was a full and busy day; Uncle Curt and I will give you two a full report later. I'm hungry and it looks like Beverly has something that smells wonderful ready for us."

After they finished their meal and each had a glass of Cabernet in front of them Walter lifted his glass and said, "Fill Charlie and me in on your day." He coughed and then smiled, "We promise not to interrupt you, too much."

Susan looked at the notes she had brought with her, "Yesterday afternoon I called Curt and told him I wanted to meet each of the men at their offices, not at the Kramer building."

Walter turned to look at Curt and raised his eyebrows but didn't say anything.

"We started at the Kansas and Missouri Southern Railroad. Owen gave me a tour of the office, and he started to give me the information about the finances and revenues, but I steered the discussion to the deal between KMS and Rock Island."

"What did he say?" Walter asked.

"Owen said they're interested. The agreement centers on their need to have access to our maintenance roundhouse and to store idle cars here in Kansas City. They don't have the financial reserves to build the facilities they require. We want to have better access to tracks owned by them headed southwest through Oklahoma, Texas, and into New Mexico."

Walter leaned forward, "I assume Owen is looking at the increased passenger traffic we see coming over the next decade."

Susan nodded, "Yes, he feels if we get access to their tracks, we'll be ready for it."

Walter smiled, "Did you ask Owen about the capacity in our roundhouse? Do we have the types and quantities of train cars ready to support gaining access to the southwest routes from Rock Island?"

"Yes, of course, I asked him that, Father," Susan said. "We can provide what they require for maintenance and storage. We have the cars we'll need for the next twenty-four months, and we can acquire more rolling stock. We could include that in our deal with Rock Island. I don't have a firm dollar amount they want or need to borrow."

Walter leaned back, "Good, really good work, Susan. I know Rock Island wants to expand west to Denver, did that come up?"

"It did, and to do that, they need strong financial support."

Charlie said, "George would want to know how much they want to borrow from us."

Susan grinned at Charlie, "From us, huh? I like that. We don't have a figure yet."

Curt said, "I asked Owen if the Rock Island folks are prepared to sign a long-term lease for roundhouse space. And, if they'd consider selling us equipment as part of any financial deal? We could help them generate capital through that process as well."

Walter said, "Those are good questions. Susan, I assume you told Owen he's authorized to negotiate with Rock Island for each of these items discussed?"

"I did. I also said I want to complete the deal in two weeks. We had to leave at that point, but I will follow up with Owen next week."

Susan took a sip of wine and said, "Then, it was on to the Hartsfield's Department Store to meet with Anson Peabody. I began the conversation with, 'Anson, if you don't have any issues that you need me to hear, I have a lot of interest in your plans to expand into Oklahoma, and Texas.'"

"How did Anson take it when you took him off script?" Walter asked with a smile.

Susan laughed. "It took him a minute or two to get his bearings." She smiled at Charlie, and he could picture Susan enjoying making Mr. Peabody squirm.

"Anson confirmed that he wants to expand into Oklahoma and Texas, but not as Hartsfield's. He wants to target small cities, maybe county seats not as an upscale department store but more as a smaller dry goods store."

"Chester R. Abrams is running a store like that, isn't he?" Walter asked.

"He is," Susan said. "Jasper met Abrams and J.C. Penney years ago at a merchants meeting here in KC. They told Jasper that they had a vision to target smaller towns with their stores. I think we should contact Chester and see if he's open to a joint venture with us."

Charlie interjected, "Jasper mentioned him to me. He said Abrams wanted to own stores focused on smaller towns. He does sound perfect for what Anson described."

Walter said, "What happened?"

Susan said, "When Anson heard me mention Abrams, he struggled to control his excitement. He loved that I appreciated the idea and that I could provide a key person to make it happen."

Walter said, "That sounds about right. Anson has always had good ideas about expansion. I can visualize his excitement."

"I told Anson that I will make the contact with Abrams and see if he's willing to meet me here to discuss everything."

"That's an excellent idea," Walter said, finishing his wine.

Susan nodded, "From there we traveled to Strawberry Hill and met with Rice Coburn. Like the others, he tried to give me the basic financial overview, but I interrupted him and told him I wanted to go into detail about Pendleton and the impact they have had on Strawberry Hill here in Kansas City."

Walter said, "Did he give you the background you need?"

"He shared that fifteen concrete companies were profitable here in the Kansas City area a year ago. Some couldn't take on the biggest jobs, but all found their niche. Then Pendleton Concrete started intimidation and underbidding to eliminate the competition. Pendleton started with the smaller companies, and now only one competitor is left."

Charlie said, "Who's that?"

Uncle Curt said, "Missouri Concrete. They're owned by Jim Townsley. They own a large quarry and a concrete plant over in Independence."

"Yes, and Missouri's owner has been around a long time, and Rice said you won't intimidate the owner. But, without new work, he can't last forever," Susan added.

Walter said, "Do we have any ideas to correct this?"

Susan said, "I told Rice that we should meet with Townsley about acquiring Missouri Concrete."

"You did?" Walter asked.

"Yes," Susan said with a confident smile. "The Kramer Group could offer Jim the position of President of the company and have him run it. Under The Kramer Group's umbrella, we would protect him from Pendleton's financial threats. Rice thought that was a good idea, but he was concerned about Pendleton's use of physical intimidation and violence."

"What sort of violence?" Charlie asked.

Curt said, "The word is that Pendleton has connections with gangsters back east. Pendleton has used men with guns to threaten other concrete manufacturers. I got a call yesterday from another contractor, and he told me there were six people in the hospital after a run-in with some of Pendleton's henchmen."

Charlie looked at Walter and said, "This sounds like the rustlers I dealt with in Oklahoma a while back. Their crimes didn't end until they were put in jail."

Susan said, "Father do you have a problem with my meeting with Mr. Townsley?"

Walter said, "Go do it. That's our best option."

Charlie said, "If Strawberry Hill and Missouri Concrete are under the Kramer Group they could crush Pendleton."

"That's the idea," Susan said.

"But Pendleton is likely to resort to violence when you announce any sort of deal. There could be trouble," Charlie said.

Curt said, "I told Rice I was having dinner with the Missouri Attorney General tomorrow night at a fundraiser. I'll discuss this with him. The AG will make sure there won't be any trouble."

Susan said, "Okay, we have a plan, we'll call Jim Townsley tomorrow, and see if he'll come under the Kramer Group umbrella. We wrapped up the day with a visit to Gordon Brayton at the Kansas City Bank of Commerce. I spend so much time at the bank already that Gordon and I just discussed the Texas acquisition. He wants to acquire Texas State Commerce Bank. They're about our current size. The Texas oil industry has exploded, and I agree with Gordon now is the right time for us to move in."

Walter said, "Where are their current branches located?"

Susan said, "They're in the northern and western parts of Texas. The larger cities are Dallas, Ft. Worth, Childress, Lubbock, Midland, Odessa, and Waco."

Charlie said, "Does that mean that the cities of Austin, San Antonio, Houston, and all along the gulf coast aren't served by this bank?"

Susan said, "We asked that and yes, but Gordon believes based on his investigations, that there's a bank system that serves those locations that Kramer can acquire."

Walter said, "Has Gordon made any overtures to the Texas State Commerce folks?"

Susan nodded, "Gordon said he talked with their President at a conference in Oklahoma City back in June. Over drinks, he learned that they're open to an acquisition. They need to position themselves to grow along with the oil boom. His research tells us they are short the cash reserves needed."

Walter pointed a finger at Susan and Curt. "I want you to pursue this. I recommended that Gordon take the lead and I'll get involved, if required when we finalize negotiations."

"You mean I'll get involved," Susan said with a laugh.

Walter joined her. "Yes, you'll get involved. But don't put me out to pasture just yet."

"Where else would you go," Curt asked. "The stud barn?"

They all laughed at that.

Chapter Thirty-Two
November 1918

The next morning Susan went into the Kramer offices, and as planned, Charlie stayed at the house.

Charlie sat at the table with his coffee cup when Walter walked into the breakfast room, "Good morning, son. I assume Susan has gone to work?"

"Yep, she left about fifteen minutes ago. Did ya git your breakfast?"

"I did. Beverly brought mine to the bedroom. I could have come out here." He smiled, "But I let her spoil me a little. Speak of the devil." He looked over to the doorway and smiled, "Beverly, can you bring me a cup of coffee? I want to chat with Charlie for a while."

She nodded as he took a seat across from Charlie.

Charlie said, "Are ya feelin' better this mornin'?"

"I am, but I still get short on breath too easy. You told me a little about the 101 Oil Company yesterday. I'd like to know some more details about what you've experienced, Charlie."

"I've only been workin' in that area of the 101 operations for a few months. But I've learned a lot from Mr. Miller and Mr. Marland in that time."

"I got that impression yesterday," Walter said. "But you mentioned a fellow named Hank that I got the feeling that you were quite impressed with as well. I'd like to know more about him."

"Yes, Hank Thomas. He's maybe thirty-five years old and has been around the oil business all his life. He worked with everyone who's been successful in the Oklahoma oil fields. Even Marland says he's never seen anyone who could find oil the way Hank does."

"And you worked with this guy?"

"Yep, he's the person who I was with at the Yale well site out north of Cushing when we brought in the gusher. Hank said all along that we would strike oil and that he thought it would be a good well, and it sure was."

They talked for another hour. Walter asked for more details about the drilling operation. Then he said, "Charlie tell me more about that bad situation with this Willard you mentioned earlier."

"That was the part of the oil field experience where I could use my background to help out. I had never been shot at, but I had dealt with bad guys who were willin' to hurt ya and even kill ya if they had to. In New Mexico and Oklahoma, I'd been in situations where I needed to personally address men who were up to no good. The situation required me to take charge and I did so. Things worked out for the best."

"That's impressive. It shows me you have good instincts in critical situations. And more than that, you act on those instincts. Some men can see what should be addressed, but few have the nerve to act." Walter turned to look out the windows, clearly in thought. After a couple of minutes, he turned back and looked Charlie in the eyes. "What are your long-range plans for your oil field experiences? Have you thought about that yet?"

"I have a dream," Charlie paused and looked at the table, then up to Walter. "I shared it with Hank, and I've not mentioned this in any detail to Susan, but I guess you ought to know. I want to own an oil company. I want to create Kelly Oil Company, and Hank is willin' to become part of it. He'll run the exploration, drilling, and production part of the Kelly Oil Company. Marland is the money side of the 101 Oil Company, and he certainly knows the oil business. But it's Hank that finds and produces the oil. He's willin' to come with me when I find the financial backing for Kelly Oil. I told him we could be partners, where he would run the operation, and I would be his Marland, and he loved the idea."

Walter leaned back in his chair and took a sip of coffee,

smiled, and said, "That's a solid plan, Charlie. Align yourself with an expert and grow a business together. We need to talk some more, but what would you say to the Kramer Group backing your venture with Hank?"

"My first thought is that it would be a dream come true. Hank said we would need at least one hundred thousand to get a solid oil company started."

Walter leaned forward, elbows on the table, and smiled, "Let's explore the idea some, but my doctor advised me several years ago to swim as often as I could to improve my arthritis. So, I'm going to go for a swim right now." He coughed and cleared his throat.

Charlie said, "Are ya alright?"

"I'll be okay."

Walter went and changed into his swimming outfit, and they then went out to the conservatory. Charlie said, "The pool sure is nice. Susan loves to swim and I'm finding it to be something I enjoy as well. I like how the walls and a lot of the roof are mostly glass. It makes you feel like you're outside."

"That was what I wanted. I'm going to take a dip, and Beverly is fixing us an afternoon snack; are you hungry?"

"I'll be ready for something when you're done."

Charlie watched Walter get into the pool but then looked up at the ceiling and watched clouds drift by as he thought about everything that had happened in the past two days. *Five hundred million dollars!* This number had been running through Charlie's mind like a wild stallion ever since Walter had mentioned it yesterday. He'd known that Susan was rich, and her father was an important businessman, but the size of The Kramer Group hadn't settled in until Walter's talk yesterday and then hearing about Susan's meetings.

I know that Susan and I are meant to be together, and I told Susan I was willing to grow into the role she wants for me, but I didn't know I was gonna have to grow that big.

Charlie continued to watch the sky as he let that reality sink in. After a minute he realized, *Susan is the woman I want to spend my days with, and together we can meet any challenge.*

"Char... Cha..." *cough* "Char..." *cough*.

Charlie looked down and saw Walter go under the water in the pool. Charlie ran and dove in. He pulled Walter to the surface and got him out of the pool and onto the concrete apron.

Charlie screamed, "Beverly! Kathryn!"

Charlie rolled Walter to his side and began pounding on his back to get Walter to cough and breathe.

Kathryn came to the French doors. She cried out, "Mr. Kramer! What's wrong?"

"Call the hospital, fire department, or police," Charlie said. "We need help here immediately."

Kathryn hurried off and Charlie continue to pound his back. Walter began to cough up water, and then a little blood came out of his mouth and nostrils. He said, "I... couldn't get my breath there for a while. Charlie..." cough, "you saved my life."

Charlie said, "We'll have some help here in a few minutes. You take it easy."

Orderlies from the hospital arrived and took Walter for observation, despite his protestations that he was feeling better. Charlie drove one of the other cars Walter owned to the hospital. Charlie called the bank and spoke to the operator. "This is Charlie Kelly; I need to speak with Susan Kramer."

The operator made a connection, and Charlie heard the voice of Walter's receptionist.

"Ms. Blackaby isn't available right now."

"Kay, it's Charlie Kelly. Walter is in St. Joseph's Hospital on Linwood Boulevard. He almost drowned in the swimming pool at the house. I got him out in time, and I need you to get word to Susan and Uncle Curt."

Kay said, "Charlie, I see them coming off the elevator. Hold on... Susan, it's Mr. Kelly."

"Hello Sweetheart, we just got back here from a meeting."

"Susan you and your uncle need to come to St. Joseph's Hospital. Your father almost drowned in the pool earlier. He going to be okay, but he may need to stay here. I haven't heard anything."

"Oh my God! We'll be there as soon as we can."

Susan and Curt arrived in less than twenty minutes and were ushered to the room where Walter was resting. Charlie was seated next to Walter's bed and stood as Susan and Curt entered. Susan said, "Oh Charlie, how is he?"

Walter roused up, coughed, and said, "I'll be alright thanks to my new hero, Charlie."

Curt said, "What happened, Walter?"

"I was feeling pretty good, so I decided to swim a few laps this afternoon. On my third lap, I started coughing and couldn't get my breath. I tried to scream, and the coughing got worse."

Charlie said, "I heard him and saw his head go underwater. I jumped into the pool and was able to pull him out. I hollered and Kathryn heard me and called the hospital."

Walter reached over and squeezed Charlie's hand and said, "You did what it took to save me. I was drowning." He looked at Susan, "My sweet daughter, you sure know how to pick a winner. From what I can remember he was as calm and as level-headed as they come."

With tears flowing Susan said, "Father, I love you, and I am so glad Charlie stayed home with you today."

Walter grinned, "Me too."

A distinguished bespeckled man of medium build in a white smock entered the room. Charlie said, "This is Doctor Franklin, and he's been caring for your father, Susan."

He looked at Susan. "You must be the daughter."

Susan wiped tears from her cheeks, "I am. Will he be alright?"

Franklin said, "Yes, all indications are that he will make a full recovery. But he does have a persistent cough that put him in jeopardy as he was swimming. I can't be sure what is causing the cough but keeping him here in the hospital will not be necessary, so I've signed his release. You may take him home."

He looked directly at Walter, "Mr. Kramer, please take it easy for a few days and if the cough gets worse see your family doctor or come back here and see me."

Walter and Susan loaded into the Cadillac and Charlie and Curt took the other car and they returned to Westover Road.

As they entered the foyer at home Walter said, "Charlie we

didn't get our afternoon snack and now it's past dinner time. Are you as hungry as I am?"

Charlie laughed, "I sure am, how are ya doin'? Ya act like you're okay."

Walter continued walking toward the kitchen and said, "I'm tired, but I want to eat and hear about my daughter's day."

Susan's mouth went slack, as she slowly shook her head, "Well I never. Okay Father, let's get you and your hero fed. And maybe we can talk about business later."

Chapter Thirty-Three
November 1918

The Cadillac pulled up in front of Union Station. Bernard got out and went to the trunk while Charlie and Susan waited in the car. Susan put her arm on Charlie's and said, "I wish you didn't have to leave so soon."

Charlie nodded. "I made a promise to George, and I'll keep it, but I sure wish you were comin' with me."

She rubbed his shoulder. "I will soon, Sweetheart. And now that Father has agreed that you can be my fiancé, it will happen."

Charlie smiled. "I guess saving your father's life did the trick. Maybe I should have started with that?"

Susan swatted his arm, but then also laughed. "Charlie, how horrible. But I'm glad you were there in the end. Father would have come around eventually but you being there helped him see you as the bright, quick-thinking, decisive man I have always seen in you."

"I wish we didn't have to keep it a secret," Charlie said.

Susan tilted her head, "Me too, but Father wants to make a proper announcement at the Kramer Group Christmas party next month. In his eyes, this is as much a business arrangement as it is for love, and Father needs to lay the groundwork for it. Besides, our wedding will be a big social event and such events must have the right amount of pomp and ceremony."

"You know I have to let George know, otherwise he may not let me visit for the party."

"Only if you swear him to secrecy," she smiled. "He knows a

lot of the same people and Father will be upset if he's not the one making the announcement."

"George is a good man, he won't blab."

There was a polite knock on the car window and Bernard opened the door. Charlie unfolded his frame from the car and turned to help Susan out. She gave him a fierce hug and kissed him. "Call me when you get in."

Charlie grabbed his bag, another new gift from Susan to fit all his new clothes, and said, "It may be late, I don't want to wake you."

"I won't be able to sleep until I know you've arrived."

Charlie nodded and took a step toward the station, Susan grabbed his arm, as if her touch could keep him with her. Charlie hesitated until just the tips of their fingers were touching. Charlie smiled at Susan, "You're making this harder than it needs to be." Off in the distance, a train whistle punctuated his words. He stepped back into her arms and gave her a long kiss, finally breaking their embrace.

He tipped his hat and said, "That's gonna have to last you a while, don't waste it." He then turned and headed into the station.

* * *

Three weeks later Charlie found himself standing on the platform at the Ponca City train station bundled up against a cold west wind. Next to him, George stamped his feet to ward off the cold.

"I'm impressed with how you handled that issue over in Pawhuska."

"I'm sorry it took me this long to resolve everything," Charlie said.

"No need to apologize. You were handicapped with Marland being gone at first, but even when he returned it still took the both of you a week to get it all settled out. He told me you had everything in hand, and he'd wished he'd stayed another week in Pittsburgh."

Charlie accepted the compliment, and said, "That's good to know, but I was mighty happy to see him walk into the courthouse."

"Don't be too modest, Charlie, you represented us well and I'm thankful for you stepping up as you did."

A whistle sounded and both men turned to look down the tracks to see the train pulling into the station, the west wind blowing the coal smoke across the plains.

Charlie turned to George, "Thanks again for lettin' me return to Kansas City to attend this shindig Susan's father is throwin'."

"My pleasure. I'll be glad when I can finally tell everyone this secret you made me keep. And how else am I going to know when the wedding will be. May wants to know so we can be there."

"I'll try and put in a good word, but Susan's been telling me how her father has taken over the guest list. At times she's wondered if he's plannin' a wedding or a meetin' of the board of directors."

George laughed, the sound carrying over the hiss of steam from the locomotive as it pulled to a stop. Charlie and George walked toward the first passenger car. They said their goodbyes and in less than ten minutes Charlie was headed north.

* * *

Susan returned home to find Charlie and Walter sitting in the breakfast room laughing at a Mutt and Jeff cartoon, "Okay, what's so funny?"

Walter said, "Bud Fisher sure writes some hilarious things in his cartoons. How was your day?"

"Busy, and mostly because we have our company Christmas party tomorrow night. Harmon Goodenough was a complete pest. He insisted you had planned for him to accompany me to the party and that we would announce our engagement. Father, I've never been on a date with him. It took all of my willpower to not tell him that I was already engaged to Charlie."

Walter started to speak and coughed. He recovered and said, "That is my fault. I know I put you both under a lot of pressure to keep everything quiet. When Harm asked me the other day about the party, I couldn't say anything, and he must have taken my silence on the subject as an acknowledgment that I wanted you to go with him to the party." He looked at Charlie. "I guess I made things more complicated than they needed to be."

"I'm not worried. I'm sure we'll be able to handle this in a respectful way at the party."

"Well, he'll know how it is as soon as father announces our engagement," Susan said.

"I assure you before the night is out, everyone at that party will know who your future husband will be," Walter said.

* * *

The Kramer Group Christmas party was held at the Mission Hills Country Club on December 14th. Light snow was falling outside, but inside it was warm as hundreds of guests filled the space. Charlie felt a little overwhelmed as he'd met so many different people that evening. Currently, he held a glass of punch in one hand while Susan clung to his other arm. Another of Walter's friends walked up to the couple and Susan said, "Charlie, this is J. C. Nichols."

Charlie shifted the punch so he could shake hands. Nichols said, "Pleasure to meet you, young man."

"Mr. Nichols is on the Mission Hills board and has known Father for many years."

"This is a wonderful club, sir," Charlie said. Nichols thanked him and the drift of friends and acquaintances continued to churn in the room.

Charlie whispered to Susan, "When's your father goin' to make the announcement? I feel like I'm trying to dance through a field filled with cow patties."

Susan coughed at the image and patted her chest. "Soon, Sweetheart. Father wants to make it the last thing in the evening."

Charlie suppressed a sigh as another worker from the Kramer Group came up to say hello. Charlie kept scanning the crowd looking for Harmon Goodenough, but he still hadn't seen the man. He was wondering if Harmon had decided to skip the party.

Charlie felt a tug on his arm as Susan led him through the crowd. Susan deftly moved through the crowd and soon Charlie found himself in front of a tall, older gentleman wearing an expensive suit and holding a cup of punch. "Charlie, this is Anson Peabody."

Charlie gave a polite greeting to the head of Hartsfield Department stores, then Susan said a few words, and before Charlie knew it, she tugged him through the crowd again. Charlie was soon introduced to Owen McGill, the head of the Kansas Missouri and Southern railroad. Another polite greeting and soon Susan pulled Charlie away.

"Darlin', you're moving through this crowd like a wrangler on his prized cutting horse, but why are you in a hurry?"

Susan said over her shoulder, "I saw Harmon arrive and I wanted us to seem too busy to talk. Besides, I needed to introduce you to all the company presidents."

Charlie craned his neck but couldn't see Goodenough in the crowd. "But Sweetheart, at this rate they'll hardly remember me."

Susan looked up at Charlie and winked but didn't slow her pace. In the next ten minutes, she'd introduced Charlie to Rice Coburn and Gordon Brayton. As Susan pulled Charlie away from a bewildered Gordon, Charlie said, "Maybe we can stop and get a refill. I'm sure you're parched after all those introductions."

Susan smiled and they walked toward the serving table where a large crystal punchbowl was tended to by a club waiter. Walter was there also refilling his drink.

Charlie and Susan approached Walter as he said, "Dear, I see you've been making the rounds with Charlie. Maybe take a break so he can catch his breath."

They refilled their cups and turned to watch the crowd. "I've enjoyed meeting everyone, sir," Charlie said. "This is a wonderful party."

Before Walter could respond, a voice slurred, "Why have you been avoiding me all night, Susan?"

They all turned to see Harmon Goodenough standing at the end of the serving table.

His eyes on Susan, Goodenough said, "I think it's time for me to get you away from this rube." He reached for Susan's arm.

Susan pulled her arm away and took a step toward Charlie, "I don't think so. You're out of your mind, Harmon."

In a voice loud enough for everyone nearby to hear, Goodenough said, "Surely, you're not saving yourself for this hayseed here. That would be an embarrassment to your father."

"Harm," Walter said, "Don't make a spectacle of yourself."

Harm ignored Walter and took a step toward Charlie. "Susan deserves better than a two-bit cowboy."

Charlie struggled to control his anger as he said quietly, "I think you need to leave mister."

Goodenough again ignored the warning and placed his hand on Charlie's chest and shoved him. Charlie staggered back, more from surprise than any actual harm. Susan slapped Goodenough across his face, the sound resounding like a gunshot across the room. Conversation stopped and everyone in the room turned their attention to the foursome.

Walter stepped between them, "Goodenough! You need to leave." His voice rose so everyone could hear him. "My daughter is escorted tonight by her fiancé Charles Kelly. They will be married with my profound blessing. You," he pointed a stern finger at Harmon, "need to protect your employment with the Kramer Group. You need to leave the premises immediately."

Goodenough staggered back a step and gathered himself, taking in the entire assemblage of Kramer Group leadership and others staring at him. His face paled and he ran a hand through his hair. He looked back to Walter and sputtered out a couple of incoherent syllables then closed his mouth. With his head down, Harmon Goodenough walked directly to the stairs and out the front door of the clubhouse.

Susan hugged her father, "Thank you so much; that was wonderful."

Charlie said, looking at the crowd still fixated on him and Susan, "I guess the cat's out of the bag now."

A cheer rose from the guests and several of them pushed forward to congratulate Susan and Charlie.

When the well-wishers dwindled Walter said, "Well now, I guess you two need to set a date, don't you?"

Susan said, "Only one date will do for the wedding event of the year." Walter and Charlie looked at her and she smiled, "Why,

Valentine's Day, of course. I want this to be something that Kansas City will talk about for years to come."

Walter laughed, "Don't make me sell a company to afford the wedding, okay? Charlie and I have plans that require startup money."

Susan looked at Charlie, "What have I missed?"

Chapter Thirty-Four
December 1918

A few days after the party Charlie and Susan quietly ate their evening meal in the breakfast nook, both looking out at the patio and conservatory. Charlie pointed out the windows and said wistfully, "Those have been our favorite places, haven't they?"

Susan sighed, "It's been heaven. Can we take them with us?"

Charlie looked directly at Susan and winked, "The 101 Ranch is huge. It's on the Salt Fork of the Arkansas River and there are some beautiful spots there—big trees, clear water, seclusion. We'll make one of them our special place."

"What's this I hear about the 101 Ranch?" said Walter as he walked into the room.

Susan grinned, "We love to find places we can go and enjoy a romantic evening. I know we'll find our place at the 101. Anywhere with Charlie is my heaven. I told him it'll be the way we had it on the bank of Rock Creek."

As he leaned forward, eyes bright with excitement, Charlie said, "And I said yes, it will."

Walter took his seat at the table, "You kids are sure fun for this old man. It's wonderful to see you so much in love. My health concerns me and how much I'm dependent on you, Susan. Right now, I need you here, not in Oklahoma."

Charlie nodded, "We understand, sir. We're here to support you."

"Charlie, I appreciate that, but you need to get back to the

101 soon. I didn't mean to go behind your back, but I called and talked to George Miller. He's a fine man and has allowed you to come here, but I asked enough questions that I know he needs you there."

Susan said, "Maybe you better go back there for a while, Honey. I'm going to be gone some too. Gordon has asked me to accompany him on a business trip."

Charlie said, "But, what about our wedding?"

Walter said, "I'm okay if you two want to go to the courthouse, but I would love to give you a beautiful ceremony with all the trimmings."

As she finished the last of her meal, Susan said, "And you will, Father. We announced it would be on Valentine's Day, and Valentine's Day it will be. That gives us almost forty-five days to put it all together. Charlie, you can go back to the 101 and get caught up, and Father, you should feel better by then, and I'll be better prepared to do my job for Kramer at that point too."

"That works for me," said Walter.

Susan said, "Charlie, I'd love to go spend a week or two with you at the 101 before the wedding, but I need to go back east and meet with the president of the New England Bank of Commerce. While I'm back there I'll have dinner with a couple of my classmates from Vassar. I'm hoping they'll be able to be part of our wedding."

Walter said, "I'm glad you're going to Boston with Gordon. I know Andrew is looking at some potential projects overseas and those banks may be available to pick up sometime within the next year or so."

"Who's Andrew?" Charlie said.

Susan said, "Andrew Mellon, and among other things he owns the New England Bank of Commerce."

Charlie smiled, "Okay, then I'll head to the 101 tomorrow. Susan, you'll be leaving in a day or two anyway, right?"

"Yes, day after tomorrow."

Walter said, "Charlie, don't forget about my proposal on Kelly Oil."

Susan said, "What are you two up to?"

Charlie reached over and took her hand, "We may do some business sometime soon. I need to talk with Hank when I get back there."

With a big smile on his face, Walter said, "I can't imagine a better way to get into the oil business."

With that settled, Charlie stood and said, "I think it's time Susan and I take our wine to the conservatory. I want to thank Beverly for that fine meal."

Walter said, "You guys spend as much quality time together as you can before Charlie leaves for Oklahoma."

"Thanks, Father; we will, and I love you."

Walter stood and smiled, "I love you both." He looked over and nodded at Charlie, then headed toward his end of the house.

As Charlie placed his wine glass on the side table next to his chair, he looked at Susan as she unbuttoned her blouse. "Whatcha doin'?"

Mocking him, she said, "Is this all new for you? You've not seen me do this before?"

He grinned and shook his head, "Well, I guess that was a stupid question. I'm happy to help ya if needed."

"Oh, I'm already about done here. You better get busy yourself."

They were skinny dipping in the pool in no time. It would be Charlie and Susan's last night together at Westover Road for a while, and they filled it with fun, foreplay, and hours of passion.

* * *

The following morning Charlie called George and told him he would be arriving that evening. He and Susan got him packed and to the train station to catch the afternoon train. Susan hugged him before he boarded, "I miss you already, but George needs you and you need to be there for him and the 101. I love you."

Charlie kissed her, "I love ya, too. I'll be back soon."

Charlie arrived in Ponca City after dinner and was met at the train depot by George and May Miller.

As Charlie stepped down from the passenger car, George said, "It's good to have you back. I hope you're ready to travel because

Marland needs you to join Hank in Payne County tomorrow."

Charlie said, "Is there a truck available for me? If so, I'll leave right after breakfast."

May said, "George, how rude, I swear, you're all business. Charlie, welcome home. We missed you."

Charlie grinned, "Thanks, May. I can't wait for you to meet Susan."

They piled in the Miller's Buick, and when they arrived at the ranch, Charlie called Susan to let her know he was safely at the 101.

"Good, you must be tired."

"I'm a little tired but mostly excited to get caught up here and return to Kansas City so we can be married."

"Charlie, we need to let your family know about the wedding and help them arrange to come if at all possible."

Charlie was silent for a moment, long enough that Susan said, "Charlie?"

"You're right," Charlie finally said. "I hadn't thought of that. I can write Mom."

"No," Susan said, "This is too important. You need to go down to Maud and talk to them in person."

"You're right, I should go down to Maud and visit them."

"I think that would be best. In fact, you should spend Christmas with them since I'll be back East."

"Your right and I'll talk to George. Tomorrow is Friday. Maybe I can go down this weekend."

"Let me know what you decide, Sweetheart. I'll let you go so you can get some sleep."

It wasn't long before he was in bed and was fast asleep.

* * *

The next day, Charlie met George for breakfast at the ranch café. He finished off his second cup of coffee as George arrived and took a seat across the table.

The waiter poured George's coffee and refilled Charlie's as George said, "Last night we didn't talk about what you'll face down at the well-site, but we need to before you head down there.

Hank and his crew have started the third well on the Yale lease. Well number two came in two weeks ago, and it now produces a few hundred barrels a day. Marland is thrilled with that area, and he and Hank expect this third well to produce as much oil as the others or more."

Charlie leaned in, "There's a but coming; am I right?"

"You are. A few oil companies have hit gas and oil on the 101 ranchlands, and now Marland wants to have Hank focus his exploration efforts around ranch headquarters. He needs you to go down and oversee the work in Payne County to allow Hank to come up here with a crew."

"I can do that. Has Hank already come up and scouted out where he'll be drillin'?"

"Yes, he and Marland spent some time here after Well number two came in and before Hank went down to start number three. They've targeted the Bar L area and maybe later down around Morrison."

"Should I expect any issues in Payne County?"

"Hopefully, all you do is work the logistics support to pick up the oil at the first two wells and whatever the crew needs at number three. I'm concerned about drilling here on ranchland. There are at least three other companies already here, and we're losing land that supports our beef business."

"Would I be more valuable here as a negotiator between companies, Boss, and the cattle themselves?"

"Maybe, but let's try Marland's plan first."

Charlie took his last bite of eggs and bacon, "Okay, George, I'm packed and ready to head out. First, I'll be marryin' Susan on Valentine's Day."

"Congratulations. You'll never forget an anniversary that way."

Charlie chuckled. "I need to let my family know and arrange for them to be in Kansas City. I need to go down to Maud if that's okay with you?"

"I was hoping you'd be able to get started down in Payne before Christmas," George said, and Charlie wondered if he'd made one too many requests of his boss. George took a sip of his coffee, then set the cup down. "You've not mentioned your family much. Have you visited them since you started here at the 101?"

Charlie felt like George had been listening in on his and Susan's phone call last night. He shook his head, "No, sir. I've been focused on being a top hand here at the ranch."

"I appreciate that, but a man's family has to be important too. That's something you need to remember as you start your own family." George stood up and finished the last of his coffee. "Take some time over Christmas to visit your folks. I'm sure they'll be happy to see you. You can start in Payne County afterward."

"Thanks, George. I'll give ya a call from the Cushing Hotel after the holiday."

* * *

Charlie left the ranch the next morning. It was cold and the sun hadn't yet risen as he drove south. The morning turned into a fine, sunny day as he drove, and Charlie enjoyed driving along and seeing all the oil wells sprouting up across the prairie. Around lunchtime, he arrived in Maud and it wasn't long before he'd found his folk's house on the west edge of town. It was a large single story with mature trees in the front and back yards and sat on a few fenced acres with some outbuildings and a corral behind the house. He sat in the truck for a minute staring at the house. Finally, he got out and walked up to the house, and knocked on the front door.

A shapely blonde opened the door and screamed, "Charlie! It's you, oh my gosh." She jumped into his arms and hugged his neck.

Charlie said, "Annie?" He took a step back to look at his sister. "My, you've grown, and my oh my, you're a beautiful young woman."

The doorway was immediately filled with Charlie's family. Dan and Jess stood on either side of the door. Jess didn't look very different from what Charlie remembered, but Dan had grown at least three inches and his skinny arms had become lean and muscled. Walking up and putting her hand on Jess's shoulder was his mother. Charlie thought he could see more wrinkles on her face, but she gave Charlie a huge smile. The last to arrive was Charlie's father. Joe walked up and stood between Jess and Dan. Charlie felt his stomach flutter a bit as the last time he'd seen him, Joe had been running from the marshal and had only given Charlie his grudging approval for him to leave out on his own. Joe stood still for a moment, looking at Charlie on the porch, then smiled and said, "Hey, everyone git back and let him in the house. Charlie, it's mighty good to see ya, son."

The others stepped aside as Charlie walked into the front room. "It's good to see ya too, Dad. I've come to spend Christmas with y'all, if y'all have me, and I have some news that I needed to share in person."

Ellie said, "Don't be silly, of course, you are welcome here for Christmas. But your other news sounds scary. I hope all is well with you?"

"I'm sorry, I didn't mean to scare ya. Dan and Jess give me a hug, fellas."

After all the greetings, they went into the large kitchen and gathered around the table. Ellie started a pot of coffee, and everyone wanted to know what Charlie had been up to.

Charlie said, "It's been too long since we've been together, and for that, I'm to blame. I've been workin' hard to create a good future for myself, but I coulda come here before now."

Joe said, "That's fine that ya said that, son, but the road goes both ways up to the 101, and we've not traveled it either. Now, what's on your mind?"

"I'm gittin' married—"

Annie squealed her excitement and Dan and Jess both started asking him questions at the same time. Finally, Ellie shushed them all, "Hush up so he can tell us."

"Well, I'm marrying the wonderful lady I met in Elmore City back in '17 and we want to be together from now on. I love her with all my heart and she me. The ceremony will be in Kansas City on Valentine's Day. We would love to have ya there with us."

Annie said, "Charlie, that's so exciting. Kansas City, why there?"

"That's Susan's home. She grew up there. My fiancé is Susan

Kramer Blackaby. Her father is a businessman there in Kansas City."

Joe leaned back in his chair and said, "Son, I'm proud of ya, finding someone to spend your days with, but I don't see how we can afford the trip. I've got the service station; Jess works at the store, and Dan's up at a ranch. Plus, the cost of railroad tickets and a place to stay. We're doin' well, but I'll admit we're just startin' to get ahead after our move from New Mexico."

Charlie grinned, "Folks, Susan and I figured that could be the case. This is sudden and doesn't give ya any time to plan. All the costs will be covered for you. It's that important to me, Susan, and her father that we'll pay for everything. You'll have rooms at Susan's family home. It's a big house with lots of bedrooms. All we ask is for you to make arrangements to have enough time off to make the trip."

Jess said, "It sounds like her family must be well off if they're able to afford all of this."

Charlie smiled and said, "They are. And they want to do this. It means a lot to me."

Dan said, "I'm sure I can arrange to be off for a week or so. That should be enough time, right?"

Ellie said, "We all can, Charlie. We'll come; I don't want to miss this."

Joe grinned, "Mom's right. We'll be there. Make the arrangements, son, and we'll be there."

Charlie said, "Then that's settled. Dad, can we take a walk out back?"

"Sure, son."

Ellie said, "Don't take long. Lunch will be ready soon."

Charlie and Joe rose, and they went out the back door and walked out under a big blackjack oak, its limbs bare under the winter sky.

Charlie clasped his right hand to his chest, closed his eyes, and sighed, "Dad, I'm so happy to see you and everyone doin' as well as y'all are." He opened his eyes and looked directly into his dad's, "Especially you, Dad; you've come a long way, and so have I. We needed to have our space and a fresh start. I'm sorry it took that, but I'm also glad we did it." He offered his hand to his dad and said, "Are we good?"

Joe wiped a tear from his cheek and said, "We're better than that. I'm so sorry to have put you through all that, but you're a strong man, and maybe a little of that strength comes from the times you covered my tracks. I love ya, Charlie." Joe stepped up and hugged Charlie.

"I love ya too, Dad," Charlie said, returning the embrace. "I can't wait for ya to meet Susan and her father."

Over the next few days, Charlie spent plenty of time getting reacquainted with everything his family had been doing. Jess showed him the general store where he worked as the assistant manager, Joe showed him the service station, and Charlie was impressed to see that he had been teaching himself to fix cars. He and Dan took a long ride on the day before Christmas out to the ranch where Dan worked as a hand. Dan's boss was impressed that Charlie had worked at the 101 and they spent most of the day talking about ranching while Dan showed Charlie the horses he'd been training. On Christmas Day Annie convinced Charlie to help her make the family meal, insisting that he show her Grandma McDaniel's recipe for biscuits.

The morning after Christmas Charlie got his bags together. Dan had already gone to the ranch to work, and Jess was getting ready to go open the store. Joe, Ellie, and Annie saw Charlie off. "I'm glad Susan convinced me to come visit you," Charlie said as he hugged his folks goodbye.

"We are too," his mother said. "I feel like I know her so well now that you've told us about her. We can't wait to meet her in person."

"I'll get all the details worked out with Susan for ya to head up to Kansas City."

His folks waved goodbye as Charlie started the truck and headed out of Maud.

Chapter Thirty-Five
January 1919

Three weeks later, Charlie had sent his family the information needed and had everything smoothed out in Payne County. The third well had come in without a hitch and was already producing a hundred barrels a day.

The phone rang in his hotel room as Charlie was almost out the door for breakfast. "Hello, this is Charles Kelly."

"Charlie, George, I'm glad I caught you before you left the hotel. How are things down there?"

"No problems here. Well, number three looks great. It's producing better than we had initially hoped. Oil transport is running smooth, and the new road to the third well will be finished in a day or two so the oil will get out easier. I know you didn't call for this update, so whattaya need?"

"Marland had to go to Pittsburgh for an emergency, and the situation here has become heated between Hank and some of these other companies. Hank has barely started his setup to drill. I think you're needed up here more than where you are."

"I can be there today. Let me go to the well-site and let the leadman know what's happenin', and I'll be there this afternoon."

"Sounds good. Come find me when you arrive."

* * *

Charlie drove into the 101 Ranch main gate that afternoon and parked in front of the White House. He went directly to George's office, his secretary already gone for the day, but when

Charlie opened the door George was also out. He'd have to wait to find out what was going on.

Charlie walked next door to his office and called Susan.

"Hello?" Her voice sounded like sweet honey to Charlie's ears after so long, though there was a question in her tone.

"Susan, this is Charlie. Are ya okay?"

"Yes, I was just on the phone with Father, and I thought he had called me back. How are you, Sweetheart?"

"I'm great. I'm back at the 101. George needs me to handle some issues that would have normally been up to Marland. E. W. is back east on some personal business."

"Nothing dangerous about the issues I hope, since Marland would have been involved, right?"

"I don't think so. All George has told me is that there's some conflict here between some oil companies. I'm learning that when oil is involved, so is a lot of money, and that tends to make folks defensive. I'll know more after I can talk with Hank. How's your father?"

"About the same. He comes into the office for half days. I'm pretty much in charge of the Group. I say that but we have strong leaders in every company, and that makes my job easier."

"When you're involved in decisions that involve the amount of money that comes through Kramer, it's not easy. The final decisions are startin' to fall to you the way it sounds."

"Yes, more and more; my father has asked me to make those decisions. He wants the men leading the companies to see me in that role. Right now, the only tough issue involves the construction company and Pendleton. Enough said. George has asked you to become Marland, and that tells me he trusts your judgment."

"I hope so. There's a lot of money and resources at stake here too. This is a good experience for me, and I'm happy he's givin' me the chance to prove myself. You're sure things are okay?"

"Yes, Sweetheart. I don't want you to worry."

"Alright, I sure miss you. We're less than a month away from our wedding now. I can't wait."

"Yes, and the plans have come together. Mission Hills Country Club will be a beautiful location for our ceremony. Father requested Mr. Nichols help us as he did with the Christmas party. Sweetheart, I have Gordon Brayton at my office door. I need to let you go. I love you."

"I love ya, too. We'll talk soon. Say hello to Gordon for me. Goodbye."

* * *

The next morning Charlie got up early to visit Tony. The horse almost turned his back on Charlie, until he brought out a sugar cube he'd swiped from dinner last night. Tony eventually forgave Charlie for being gone so much. With a promise that they'd go for a ride as soon, Charlie walked toward the café when he spotted Hank come in the gate in a company truck, "Hey buddy, good to see ya."

Hank waved, "It sure is, Charlie. Where ya goin'?"

"To the café for breakfast and hopin' to see ya there."

"I'll put this truck in the lot and be there in a few minutes."

Hank joined Charlie, and after they ordered their food, Charlie leaned back, smiled, and said, "Okay, what's goin' on here that has George so worried?"

"A month or two ago, there were maybe four oil companies wantin' to drill out on the Bar L part of the ranch. It's now down to just the Foster and the MG Oil Companies, but they're gettin' hostile."

"What do ya mean by hostile? Are they shootin' at each other as we had down in Payne County?"

"Not yet, but it could git that bad soon. MG Oil Company claims Foster Oil is drillin' on land they have leased. No one seems to have any paperwork that proves who's right."

"That doesn't make sense to me. That's 101 property and part of the Ponca territory the Millers acquired years ago. Marland should have somethin' official to show who has the rights to drill out there."

"I agree, Charlie, but George didn't find it in Marland's records, and Foster has a well started, and MG Oil is mad as hell sayin' they have the rights, not Foster."

"Sounds like I have my work cut out for me," Charlie said as they dug into their breakfast. A few minutes later George walked in for his morning coffee.

After saying good morning all around, Charlie asked, "George, have you discussed this Foster and MG Oil conflict with Marland?"

"Yes, and what has happened is both companies have rights to drill on Bar L property, and those leases share a boundary. It appears that Foster has drilled on land that MG Oil thinks is on their side of that boundary. What concerns me is that I can't find the survey information Marland said was completed and is in his files."

Charlie put his coffee cup down, "Oh, that's great. A document that could settle this does exist, and we can't find it. Do we know who did the survey and if they kept a copy?"

Hank said, "That's the question of the moment, Charlie."

George said, "I don't have that answer. Marland, of course, would know. I'll reach out to him today. You planned to go out to the Bar L today, right Charlie?"

"Yep, I'll start there and try to put all this to bed as soon as possible. There's a solution that will satisfy everyone."

Hank finished his last bite and said, "I'll go git my truck, and we can ride out there together."

Charlie said, "Okay, and George, please find out what ya can from Marland. I'd call him, but the way it sounds, I better git out to that drillin' site this mornin'."

"I agree with you. I'll have something for you when you get back here this evening."

* * *

In the truck on the way to the Bar L, Charlie said, "Hank, Marland told me about the interest in the Bar L for oil, but there must be other locations, what do ya know?"

"I like the area down around Morrison myself. Why?"

"I'm thinkin' maybe we offer an alternate location to MG Oil as a way to settle this. We'll see what happens today."

When they arrived at the drillin' site, they found a derrick erected with a large Foster Oil Company sign on it. TO Charlie's eye they looked to be ready to drill. Several Foster men stood near the derrick eying another group of men nearby that stood next to a couple of trucks that had MG Oil written on the doors. Hank drove over to the MG group and stopped.

Charlie got out of the truck and walked over to the group. "I'm Charles Kelly, of the 101 Oil Company. Who's in charge of your crew here?"

A man in a gray business suit, about forty years old, stepped forward. "I'm Mitchell Gilliland; I own MG Oil."

Charlie offered his hand, "Pleased to meet ya. I understand we may have a situation here."

Gilliland shook Charlie's hand. "That's one way to describe it." There were nods and agreements from the other men around him. "That oil derrick is on land that I have leased through your company. I've tried to get with E. W. Marland for days, and he has not responded. I'm more than upset at this point and I expect you to solve this problem today."

"That's exactly why I'm here. And I'm happy you're here. Do you happen to know where the owner of Foster Oil is?"

Gilliland pointed at a man who stood near a tent located about fifty yards from where they were. He wore coveralls and was taller than Gilliland and appeared to carry considerably more weight. He also looked about forty years old.

Charlie said, "Thanks. I'd appreciate it if you'd stand here while I introduce myself to that gentleman. I'll be back shortly."

Gilliland crossed his arms. "I'll be here."

As Charlie and Hank walked toward the Foster Oil owner, Charlie said, "I noticed at least one of Gilliland's men had a holster on his belt with a revolver in it. I sure don't need for there to be any reason for that to be used."

Hank said, "Hopefully not. There's no Pinkertons here to get in front of any bullets that start flying."

As Charlie neared the tent, he said, "Hello, I'm Charles Kelly, I represent the 101 Oil Company. I want to talk with ya."

A couple of men stepped out of the tent. One had a holstered pistol, and the other took a step toward Charlie and offered his hand, "I'm Leon Fordice. I own Foster Oil. Are you here to clear the riff-raff off my drill site?"

"I'm here because there's a dispute over who has the rights to this piece of land. I'm aware both you and Mr. Gilliland have lease agreements to explore for minerals on Bar L land. What seems under dispute is exactly where your leases exist. I want to recommend a solution, but I need at least a day or two to investigate this issue. Can I git ya to hold off on any further work until we can meet at my office at the White House the day after tomorrow?"

Fordice said, "I'm not sure why I should stop. I'm within my rights here."

"Mister, ya may be right, but there is a gentleman over there who disagrees. I'm willin' to spend my time to git to the bottom of this or at least create options that should satisfy everyone. I need a day or so to work on this. That's all I'm askin'. I don't see a need to involve a judge and certainly not firearms," Charlie nodded to the other man. "I hope ya see it that way too."

"Sitting here without drilling is costing me money."

Charlie said nothing and looked Fordice in the eyes.

Fordice hesitated for a moment, glancing over Charlie's shoulder toward where the MG men waited, and said, "Fine. I'll shut down until we meet as long as Gilliland stays off here too. I don't want to come back to find he's raised his own derrick."

"I'll make sure that Gilliland and his men abide by those terms."

Fordice nodded, but his lips were set in a thin line. "I'll be at your office the day after tomorrow. But, at that point, we need to walk away with an agreement."

Charlie offered his hand, "That's my desire too."

They shook, and Charlie headed back toward Gilliland. As he arrived everyone there could hear the drilling equipment shutting down.

Charlie said, "Mr. Fordice has agreed not to start any drilling until we can get this resolved."

"Start drilling?" Gilliland exclaimed. "Why ain't he tearing his derrick down?"

"Because we still need to resolve the issue of exactly whose lease it is on this part of the Miller ranch," Charlie said, being sure to stress exactly on whose land they all stood.

266

Gilliland's face grew red, and Charlie gave him the same glare he'd just given Fordice. When he was sure he had the man's attention Charlie said, "I need ya to come to the White House day after tomorrow. We will discuss a way to resolve this dispute. Until then I need you and your men to stay off this location."

Gilliland looked like he'd chewed on a lemon. He spat on the ground and said, "I'll be there. You can assure me we'll have a resolution?"

"This issue will be resolved. I'll see ya then."

They shook hands, Charlie and Hank got in Hank's truck, and they headed back to headquarters.

Hank said, "Okay, what's your plan, big guy?"

"I'm still workin' on it. But I think we'll have a solution. Can we drive down to Morrison?"

* * *

Charlie, Hank, and George had breakfast together the day they would meet with the Foster and MG oil companies. George said, "I need to host the meeting, so when they arrive, bring them to my office, and we'll use my conference table."

Charlie said, "Fine, but I want to lead the conversation if you don't mind, George."

"Of course. I don't mean to say your word isn't good enough, but these men have known Marland and me for some time now. I want no doubt in anyone's mind that if an agreement happens that the 101 Oil Company agrees to it as well. That could mean something beyond what's put on paper."

Charlie said, "I'm okay with that. I only want to guide the discussion to the resolution I believe we'll have at the end."

The trio finished their meals and were back in the White House when Fordice and Gilliland arrived. Charlie met them, "Good mornin'. Mr. Miller has requested we use his office, so please follow me."

George stood as they entered his office, "Welcome to the White House. Please find a seat at the table over here." He pointed to the conference table and walked over and stood at his place at the head. Charlie and Hank sat to his right side, and the other men were seated opposite them on George's left.

George said, "Before we start, can I get anyone a coffee or something to drink?"

When no one responded, Charlie said, "Then Mr. Miller, I guess we can start."

"Yes, Mr. Kelly, please take over."

"Gentleman, I've spent the last thirty-six hours completing a review of what I could find on your leases. Mr. Marland departed abruptly for Pittsburgh because of a family issue, and he mistakenly took the 101 copies of your leases in his briefcase with him. That's unfortunate but not critical to the solution of this dispute."

Gilliland said, "Why would you say that? I contend that the current drill site is on land my company has leased."

Charlie smiled, "I have a question for you. Have you been down in the Morrison area?"

Gilliland sat up straight, "Uh, yes, I have. Why?"

Charlie stood and walked across to a map of Oklahoma that took up considerable space on one wall. Charlie tapped the map at a spot south of Ponca City. "The 101 owns or has the rights to considerable property down there." He looked at Hank, "Mr. Thomas believes the land there is as likely to have oil and gas discovered as anything you believe you have leased at the Bar L property. While I admit that it is unfortunate that we cannot resolve the issue of the current lease right now, I propose, in the interest of allowing both operations to continue without waiting for Marland to return, that we void M.G. Oil's current lease at the Bar L and replace it with a lease down at Morrison on an equal-sized piece of property we agree on. Mr. Fordice has already invested time and money in the Bar L drill site and can resume operation immediately if you, Mr. Gilliland, agree to this option."

Gilliland joined Charlie across the room and looked at the map. He rubbed his chin, "I know that some oilmen have said that Morrison has potential."

"Including you," called Fordice from the table. "Or did you forget our conversation over at that coffee shop in Drumright?"

Gilliland grimaced and admitted that with a nod. To George, he said, "What assurances will you give me if I move my opera-

268

tion down there?"

Charlie said, "The same as you got with the lease on the Bar L. If you hit oil, then good, but if you don't, then that's your own problem."

George said, "Mitchell, this is a good compromise. If you want to stick with the Bar L lease, then we have to wait for E.W. to return so we can clear this up. I won't be having any disputes on who drills where on my land. Charlie's come up with a good compromise that's fair and allows everyone to get to work right away."

Gilliland returned to the table and sat down. He turned to Fordice. "Leon, you willing to give me another day so I can have my geologist pick a good spot down in Morrison?"

All eyes turned to Fordice. "I'd be a fool to disagree with that request, but I think you owe me a steak dinner at least."

Gilliland nodded, "As long as it comes from one of George's cattle."

They all laughed and the tension that had been present as an undercurrent in the room eased. Gilliland turned to Charlie. "You are mighty good at creatin' options that work. My time and money will be better spent there than arguing over the Bar L."

Fordice laughed, "Mitchell, why didn't we think of this ourselves when we could see what was starting between us?"

Gilliland grinned, "I guess because we're hardheaded, Leon."

George stood, "Then I believe we're done here. All we need to do is locate the Morrison property to replace the Bar L for MG Oil and do the paperwork, agreed?"

Everyone in the room said, "Agreed."

* * *

After the oil men left, George said, "Damn it, Charlie, that was good work. Marland couldn't have done better."

Hank said, "Why didn't ya wanna let me and George know what ya had planned?"

Charlie leaned back in his chair and said, "I wanted to use my idea, and if it went well, I wanted to own that satisfaction. If it didn't go well, the blame should be mine alone."

George said, "Charlie, I'd want you to take whatever time you need to work with Gilliland and Hank to give him what he needs. Together you and he should be able to find the right property and get it all documented in a few weeks, shouldn't you?"

"I better. It's less than a month before my wedding date. I have a beautiful lady in Kansas City who expects me to show up on time."

Chapter Thirty-Six
February 1919

Charlie sat in the ranch café sipping his coffee when George arrived and joined him.

"Good mornin', George. We need to talk…"

George interrupted, "I know, Charlie. It's February 9th and you're still here on the 101. We need to get you to Kansas City."

Charlie chuckled, "Yep, I was talkin' with Susan last night. Things are about ready, except the groom is not in Kansas City."

"Look, you've done all I've asked of you and more. Let's get you a ticket for the next train heading to Kansas City."

Charlie said, "That sounds good. Gilliland has signed all the documents, and Marland will sign them when he gets back here. I guess you'll sign as well, right."

"Yes, but we can wait for Marland to return. I'll see to it Gilliland gets what he needs."

Charlie said, "I'll call Susan and let her know I'll arrive this evening. We want you and May to come to the wedding if you can. I can't believe I haven't mentioned that before. Susan was goin' to send you a formal invitation, and I told her there was no need I would invite you personally."

George laughed, "She sent us an invitation anyway. May and I will be there. That's okay, Charlie. I did have you focused on other issues for the last few weeks."

They finished breakfast and headed to the White House.

In his office Charlie called Susan, "Hello, Sweetheart; I'll arrive at Union Station this evening."

"Oh, wonderful. I can't wait to see you. I'll wear that yellow dress again so that you can find me easily."

"Perfect. Is there anything new since last night?"

"Your folks arrive tomorrow, and we have a lot of folks who'll arrive today, especially from back east. I'll fill you in when you get here. I'm so glad those problems worked out for you there."

"Me too, and by the way, I'm glad you sent the formal invitation to the Millers. I didn't bring it up until this morning."

Susan said, "You've been busy, and the invitations should come from us as a couple anyway, so I included them. I love you."

"Love ya too. See ya tonight."

* * *

Charlie stepped onto the arrival platform at the Kansas City Union Station in the chilly evening air. A beautiful woman in a bright yellow dress immediately embraced him.

"Welcome home, Charlie." She kissed him, and they walked into the station and out the front doors to where Bernard waited.

Susan said, "I had considered the Harvey House here for our evening meal, but Father wanted to meet with us tonight. So, we need to hurry home. It's past his bedtime already."

"Sure, Sweetheart; how's he doin' today?"

"Today was a good day. He came to the office, and several guests got here for the wedding and came to the office to see him."

"Really, who?"

"How about I let father share that with you, okay?"

He warmly squeezed her hand, "You're full of surprises, and I do enjoy a mystery, so sure."

They arrived at the Westover home and went into the breakfast room and found Walter.

Walter stood, and with a big smile on his face, he opened his arms, "Charlie, my son, welcome home."

Charlie hugged Walter, "It's good to be back. You look well."

"I'm not, but thanks for your kindness. Let's sit. I need to discuss some things with you both." He gestured to the breakfast table on which was set out roast beef sandwiches, rolls, and coffee. "I know I was interrupting Susan's dinner plans with you, so I had

Beverly set out some food."

"This is fine," Charlie said as they took their seats.

Walter smiled, "I thought you might enjoy them. Now let's have a very serious chat about you two and your future. I've made some plans, and I hope they'll put a smile on your faces. If not, I apologize now."

Charlie said, "I'm sure we'll be happy, right, Susan?"

"That depends; what have you done?"

Walter reached over and patted her hands, "Let me share it with you before you get in a tizzy."

"Okay, I'll be quiet," she said, but she crossed her arms and made as if to pout.

He leaned forward and looked at a pad of notes he had in front of him. "First, I've been extremely pleased, Susan, with your performance over this past year or so and especially since my health has forced me into half days and no travel."

Susan said, "Good, I'm glad—"

Walter gestured for her to stay quiet, "Let me continue, I've finalized what we discussed previously, Susan; you're now the Chief Executive Officer. I'll remain the Chairman, but you'll run the company. I've arranged to have the quarterly meetings held here with you in charge. I know you have plans to go to Oklahoma with Charlie, and that's fine; you'll get weekly updates from me, or Curt and the company presidents will continue to operate as they have been. This will begin immediately, although, from a practical standpoint, it will start when you end your honeymoon."

"We haven't even discussed a honeymoon," Charlie admitted.

Walter nodded, "I thought so. I've arranged for you to honeymoon at our cottage on Jekyll Island if you allow it. It's wintertime, and I figured a place with warmer weather would be nice. You can get away from everything Kramer and 101 and that might be just what you two need."

Charlie said, "Jekyll Island? I'm not aware of that place."

Susan said, "It's off the coast of Georgia. We own a place there. It's beautiful, and Father has been a member there for many years."

Walter said, "I have several friends who established the Jekyll

Island Club and asked me to join as part of the founders group."

Charlie said, "It sounds pretty nice and exclusive. Would I know or have heard of any of these people?"

Susan laughed and patted his hand, "Father might not give you the full answer. Yes, Charlie, the membership is limited and includes names such as Rockefeller, Morgan, Vanderbilt, Macy, Goodyear, Crane... do I need to go on?"

"Holy Shit! I'm sorry, sir, but geez..."

Walter laughed so hard he almost fell out of his chair, "Charlie, you better get used to those names. Most of them will be at your wedding. Several arrived today and visited me at my office."

Susan said, "Father, a week or so at Jekyll Island sounds perfect."

Walter smiled, "Good. I've arranged that and the staff there will support you for however long you choose to stay. And speaking of arrangements, the Kansas City Club has worked out great for our guests. J.P. called me, and the accommodations are great."

Charlie said, "Is that J. P. Morgan?"

"Yes, son, he and his wife, along with others, are here to welcome you and Susan as future members of the business world."

Susan said, "Charlie, you'll find your place with these folks just as you did at the 101 Ranch. There's nothing more influential in the ranching world than the 101, and you mastered that. You've already proven yourself to Father, and it's only a matter of his friends and business associates getting to know you for you to prove yourself to them."

Charlie leaned in and grinned, "I'm excited to meet everyone and continue to learn more about Kramer and the world you have built, sir."

Walter grinned back at Charlie, "That's great, but I have one request."

Charlie swallowed, "A request?"

"Yes, would you be okay with calling me Father, not Sir?"

Charlie's arms went up toward the ceiling in a vee shape as he said, "Yes, oh yes. I'd be so thrilled to call ya Father."

Susan wiped a tear from her cheek as she said, "Father, you've made me so happy."

"Walter stood and said, "Well, I'm a little tired. Excited but tired. I think it's time for me to go to bed. You enjoy the rest of your evening."

Charlie and Susan stood and went over and hugged Walter.

Susan said, "Goodnight, Father."

Charlie said, "Git some rest, Father."

Walter smiled, "Goodnight."

Chapter Thirty-Seven
February 1919

The Kelly family arrived in Kansas City on Monday, February 10th. Charlie and Susan were at Union Station to meet them and stood on the platform as the train slowed to a stop. Charlie spotted Dan as he exited the train and hollered, "Brother, over here."

Dan waved and turned back and motioned to Annie and the rest to follow him.

As the family assembled, Charlie said, "Everyone, this is the love of my life, Susan." He pointed as he said, "Sweetheart, this is my father, Joe, my mom, Ellie, and my brothers Jess and Dan. And finally, this beautiful young woman is my sister Annie."

Susan said, "It's my honor to meet you. Charlie is the love of my life, too. Let's get out of here so we can sit comfortably and talk. My father, Walter Kramer, hired a transportation company to meet all our wedding visitors to take them to their lodging, so motor cars wait to take you to our Westover home. Charlie and I rode here in our family Cadillac and will follow you there."

They loaded the luggage and passengers into the motor cars and headed home.

* * *

Charlie and Susan followed the cars that carried the Kellys up the long drive. They got out quickly and went directly to the front porch as the Kellys climbed out of their vehicles. Dan said, "What's the name of this hotel?"

Charlie laughed, "This is the Kramer house. Susan's home."

Dan gave a low whistle as he took in the large white columns. "You coulda fooled me."

Susan quickly added, "It will be our Kansas City home by the end of the week, Honey."

"I guess that's right. Anyway, welcome, family."

As they entered the front foyer, Ellie said, "Good Lord, Joe, would ya look at the size of these rooms."

Joe said, "Yes, Mother, it's all big, and it must cost a fortune to heat and cool this place. I don't see how Charlie will afford this on a cowboy's pay."

Charlie looked at Susan and they both smiled.

With Beverly's help, Kathryn led everyone to their rooms to unpack and then brought them back to the dining room where Walter, Susan, and Charlie waited.

After everyone was there, introduced, and each had something to drink, Walter stood and said, "Joe, Ellie, and children, welcome to Kansas City and our home. I want to immediately share my gratitude for giving us and the world, Charlie. He is the finest young man I've ever met. I'm thrilled he has come into Susan's life and look forward to having him in the rest of my life. Also, the fact that your children have finished high school, speaks volumes about your determination to have them become some of our country's future leaders. I have tremendous respect for you, Joe, and Ellie, and I look forward to our visit this week to get well acquainted."

Joe nodded, then stood, "Thank you, Walter. This house, this home is beautiful, and I look forward to gettin' to know you this week too." Joe laughed, "Charlie had shared a few things, but I now see he left a great deal out about how successful you must be as a businessman."

Walter returned the laugh, "I understand you own a business too. You and Charlie both make some money in gas and oil. You're ahead of me there, and I hope to learn from you."

Charlie and Susan took Dan, Jess, and Annie out onto the patio. The day was bright but the air chilly, though nobody seemed to mind.

Charlie turned to Susan, "I'll let ya start."

Susan said, "Annie, I would love it and consider it an honor if you'd be a bridesmaid. I have a lifelong friend who will be my Maid-of-Honor, and I want you to stand with me too."

Annie's eyes widened, she took in a gulp of air, and her hand went to her mouth as she stood still for a moment or two.

Charlie said, "Sister, are ya okay?"

With tears down her cheeks, she said, "Are you sure, Susan?"

"Yes, Annie. I'm sure."

"Yes, oh my goodness, yes. I would love it."

Charlie said, "Good. That's settled. Dan and Jess, I want you guys there with me. I'll not say who's the Best-Man and who's the Groomsman, you can figure that out, but I want ya both there,"

Jess said, "Dan, you be his Best-Man. I'll be happy to stand up for you, Charlie."

Susan said, "It'll be a beautiful ceremony, and you three have made it more special by being part of it."

They went back inside and shared the news with the parents. Walter stood and offered a toast to the bride and groom.

* * *

The next few days went by fast as Charlie and Susan were surrounded by their visitors. On Thursday morning they were sitting in the breakfast area with Annie when Susan's maid of honor, Emma Brayton, the daughter of Gordon Brayton, came to the house. "I'm finally here, Susan," Emma said. "I'm sorry, but I've been in St. Louis on a visit to meet my future in-laws." Emma was a year younger than Susan and was engaged to a young attorney who worked for Kramer. Emma and Susan had been friends from childhood and were roommates at Vassar when Emma joined her there in Susan's second year.

Charlie grinned as he shook his head and said, "Susan, do ya believe that?"

Susan chuckled as she stood and walked toward Emma, "It does sound like she made it up, doesn't it?" She hugged Emma, turned to the table, and said, "I want you to meet Annie, Charlie's sister. She'll stand beside you at the wedding as my bridesmaid."

Emma said, "Good morning, Annie. My, you're as pretty as Susan told me you were."

Jess and Dan joined them later. They discussed the last-minute details of the wedding ceremony before Jess and Dan went to jump in the pool. They spent the rest of the day lounging and relaxing in the conservatory, Susan and Charlie sitting next to each other holding hands and enjoying everyone's company.

Chapter Thirty-Eight
The Wedding

Charlie, Dan, and Jess were driven by Bernard from Westover to the Club House at the Mission Hills Country Club at noon on February 14, 1919. As the Cadillac stopped in front of the entrance, Jess asked, "Are all the houses and buildings in Kansas City as big as what we saw on our way here?"

Charlie said, "Hold on, let's get out of the car first."

Dan said, "Yeah, where are we? This is another big and fancy place."

As they walked into the clubhouse, "No, not every house in Kansas City is big and fancy, but most are in this part of the city. Susan's dad is one of the original members of this place, and he helped fund it. Walter Kramer is one of the wealthiest men in this country. Not the city, not the state, but the country." Charlie stopped and looked around. He could see part of the ballroom from the lobby; he marveled at the elegance, "Would ya look at that?"

Dan said, "What is this place, Charlie?"

"It's the Mission Hills Country Club. That's the ballroom. As I said, Susan's father helped build this. Businessmen come here to play golf and tennis, socialize, and sometimes do business. It's a place where the members and their families can come and enjoy themselves. This is a private club for people who desire to enjoy a life filled with only the best."

They walked into the ballroom, where Jess pointed up at the chandeliers, "Would you look at those fancy lights. I've never seen the like."

Charlie said, "I came here a while back with Susan for a Christmas party. I was shocked my first time here too, Jess. I tried not to show it, but this place is special."

Dan's eyes widened and he swept out his right arm to take in the entire room, "Every table has eight chairs around it and a fancy cloth on it that seems to glow from gold to silver as the light hits it."

Jess stepped closer to a table, "Yes, and in the center of every table, there's a huge silver vase with flowers, and there are large feathers in the middle of the flowers. Charlie, this had to cost a fortune. Is this where everyone will come after your ceremony?"

Charlie smiled, "Yep, and we better go downstairs to the men's locker room and get dressed." He turned and led them to the stairs. "I'll show you the place where the ceremony happens after we dress."

* * *

Although the weather was beautiful for February in Kansas City, the ceremony was inside. A gazebo altar had been created with a gauze-like fabric over the frame and elegant posts were used to drape the fabric across the room. A variety of white flowers were placed strategically to create a garden effect.

As Susan's Father escorted her to the altar, Charlie stroked the back of his neck and sighed. He turned to Dan and whispered, "She's so beautiful, and she's all mine, brother."

Dan said, "You're a lucky man."

Susan's dress glimmered in the soft light of the room. The front of the dress's bodice created a deep vee that showed off her cleavage, and the bodice was backless to her waist. The train was a magnificent twenty feet long. Susan was a picture of happiness and elegance as she arrived on her father's arm.

Bishop Thomas Lillis of Saint Joseph's Catholic Church conducted the ceremony which went by in a blur for Charlie. He remembered saying "I do" at the right moment and putting the wedding ring on Susan's finger, but little else stuck in his mind. Soon enough Bishop Lillis ended the ceremony with the traditional words, "Now Charlie, you may kiss the bride."

He did, and the crowd roared its approval.

Bishop Lillis said, "Charlie and Susan wish for you to join them immediately in the ballroom for refreshments and dancing. Mr. Kramer has arranged to have a popular new orchestra play for you. The Paul Whiteman Orchestra will provide music for your enjoyment."

The list of attendees read like a Who's Who of society and government. From Missouri Governor Fred Gardner and many others from elected offices to the Morgans, Vanderbilts, and others from the business world, the ballroom was a mass of influential people all there to celebrate and welcome the young couple of the hour into their world.

Within the first hour of the celebration, Susan and Walter had introduced the business world's and society's biggest names to Charlie. They then took Charlie around to meet the Kramer Group company presidents. Each leader was gracious and shared some form of genuine welcome message to Charlie. Rice Coburn, the Strawberry Hill president said, "I promise to do a better job protecting your wife in the future. No more gunshots, I promise."

Charlie looked at Susan, then Walter, and back to Susan, "What's he talkin' about, Susan?"

Susan said, "Don't get upset. While I was out on a construction site there were shots fired. I can fill you in later, but everything is settled now. Enjoy today, please."

Rice said, "Mrs. Kelly, I'm so sorry, I thought..."

Walter said, "Rice, it's fine, go on and get yourself another cocktail."

"Okay, but you need to fill me in soon," Charlie said.

Walter excused himself and Charlie and Susan continued to visit with the attendees.

Later Charlie walked over to where Walter sat and leaned down, "Father, how are you?"

Walter said, "If you mean physically, I'm tired and ready to find my bed. But, otherwise, I'm delighted and so proud of you and Susan. Thanks, son, for asking."

"I'm concerned you'll overdo it today."

"I probably am, but this is the happiest I've been in a long time. I wouldn't miss this for the world. Help me get to that podium, will you?"

Charlie held out his arm and led Walter across to the podium set up at the front of the ballroom. Walter gestured to Susan, and she soon joined them. The couple stepped back as Walter said, "Can I have your attention for a moment." He paused and then said, "I know we've had the customary toasts from the Best-man and so forth, but I need you to raise your glasses once more before we continue the dancing. As the Father-of-the-Bride, I want you all to know that I couldn't be happier and prouder to welcome Charles Kelly into my family. He and Susan are as perfect a match as I've ever witnessed. You younger folks will get to see them become true leaders across this country." He turned to the couple and raised his glass, "To you, Charlie, and the rest of the Kelly family, welcome. I love you, young man, and thanks for making my Susan so happy."

Charlie placed his arm around Susan's waist, listening to the applause from the guests. Then he kissed her.

Author's Notes

Some of the events, people, and places described within these pages are based on fact, while most are pure fiction and hopefully make for a good story. I must thank Joe Glazer, historian and member of the Board of Directors of the 101 Ranch Old Timers Association, for his time, the tour of the 101 Ranch site, and his encouragement.

About the Author

E. Joe Brown has published three memoirs and his writing has been included in the Baseball Hall of Fame. He's a member of SouthWest Writers, the International Western Music Association and president of New Mexico Westerners. He's served as a New Mexico State Music Commissioner and on the International Western Music Association Board of Directors where he's influenced the culture of New Mexico and the Southwest through music, poetry, literature, and education. He is a proud retiree of the USAF. Joe lives in Rio Rancho, New Mexico with his wife.